Safe Harbour

Safe Harbour

Luanne Rice

PIATKUS

Copyright © Luanne Rice 2002

First published in Great Britain in 2002 by
Judy Piatkus (Publishers) Ltd of
5 Windmill Street, London W1T 2JA
email: info@piatkus.co.uk

First published in the United States in 2002 by Bantam Books,
a division of Random House, Inc.

The moral right of the author has been asserted

A catalogue record for this book is available from the British Library

ISBN 0 7499 0609 X

Printed and bound in Great Britain by
Mackays of Chatham Ltd, Chatham, Kent

For Nita Taublib

ACKNOWLEDGMENTS

Thanks and love to my aunts, uncles, and cousins in Hartford, Providence, and the four corners of the world, for showing me how lucky I am to come from a big family and revealing to me what it means to always be there for each other.

Thank you to Amelia Onorato, my sage and wonderful niece, always and forever.

Eternal gratitude to my teacher Laurette Laramie. As time goes on, I appreciate more and more the things you taught me.

With affection and gratitude to Susan Corcoran and Christian Waters, for inspiring me with their story of the fountain at Lincoln Center.

With appreciation to Lind Bayreuther for technical assistance, knot school, and helping us pull the boat out.

Many happy returns of the day to Jeff Woods. May you always remember the softest of breezes, the coolest of summer swims, and the friendships that were born in that magical land between the train trestle and the high tide line.

And finally, thank you to my childhood friends from Point O' Woods. The years may pass, but I know that wherever you are, the beach is in your hearts as it is in mine.

PROLOGUE

THE WIND BLEW HARD, WHIPPING NEWPORT HARBOUR into whitecaps. Dana Underhill peered beneath the brim of her cap, assessing the situation. This was the last day of sailing lessons. All the kids were supposed to race against each other, she and Lily would hand out trophies, and the summer would be over. "Come on, Dana," the kids called, impatient to start.

"It's getting rough," she said, watching to see whether the har-bourmaster would hoist small-craft warnings.

"Please, Dana? Come on, you taught us right! What good are sailing lessons if we can't handle a little chop?"

"Yeah, Dana. Please?"

"You know we can do it!"

"What do you think?" Dana asked, glancing across the Boston Whaler. Her younger sister Lily's blond hair formed a wild, kinetic halo in the wind. Even at eighteen and twenty, they were insepara-ble. Sailing was their passion; teaching racing to wealthy young Newporters was just their summer job to pay for the art school they attended together.

"Summer's not officially over till we hand out these trophies," Lily said as the boat rocked.

The small fleet of Blue Jays jostled against the floating docks at the Ida Lewis Yacht Club. The sails were already rigged, the two-person crews installed beneath the exuberantly swinging booms. The sound was deafening: halyards clanking, sails thwacking, lines slapping. The young sailors were a study in grace under tension. Many summered on Bellevue Avenue or Ocean Drive, attended the finest prep schools, seemed—with zeal foreign to Dana—to consider competition a way of life.

"We sailed to the Vineyard last weekend in much worse," Polly Tisdale called.

"My father said if I don't come home with a trophy, don't come home," Hunter Whitcomb said. "Race or die!"

"Yikes," Dana said.

"Do fathers really say that?" Lily whispered.

"Not ours," Dana said. The sisters had learned to sail at Hubbard's Point, Connecticut, a sweet and comfortable family beach that was a far cry from yachting life in Newport.

Dana paused, crouched at the helm of the Boston Whaler, admitting to herself once again that she and Lily were the wrong instructors for this job, when her eyes fell upon Sam Trevor.

"Our boat's going to win," he said, his glasses crooked and his grin braces-bright as he stared with open adoration at Dana. The youngest kid in class, Sam had the jib, with Jack Devlin manning the tiller.

"You think so?" Dana smiled.

"Dream on, four-eyes," Ralph Cutler sneered. Barbie Jenckes, his crewmate, let out a haughty laugh. "You're not even supposed to be sailing here. You don't belong to the yacht club. You're just a little wharf rat . . ."

"Enough," Dana said dangerously. Barbie was almost right. Sam's family didn't have money. He went to public school. His mother worked at the local lobster company. Dana and Lily had spotted him hanging around the docks early in the summer, challenging them to a bowline-tying contest, and Dana had been unable to resist him.

The small and eager third-grader had had the air of a friendly beagle. Sweet and clumsy, with glasses perpetually slipping off his freckled nose, he had tied the worst bowline Dana had ever seen. She had picked up on his loneliness—the facts that his mother worked, his brother was in college, and he was essentially alone for the summer. He missed his brother the way Dana would miss Lily, so she had found a place for him.

"Let me show 'em," Sam said to Dana, his eyes shining.

"This is the real thing," she said, holding his gaze. "High wind, a field of fast boats."

"Walk home, Sam," Hunter Whitcomb warned. "The rest of you too. This race is between Ralph and me."

"Speak for yourself, Hunt," Laney Draper piped up. "Though I do agree that Sam should be disqualified. He didn't even pay for lessons!"

"Dana gave me a scholarship," Sam said, a shadow of anxiety dulling his grin.

"Ralph's father raced here when he was young, and so did mine," Hunter said. "Our mothers too. How about yours, Sam?"

"Sons of fishmongers don't quite get it," Ralph said.

"That's mean," Lily said.

Dana watched the sons of Newport's two richest men eye each other across their bows as Sam jumped to his feet. Nearly capsizing the fourteen-foot Blue Jay, he grabbed hold of the mast to steady himself.

"She might clean fish," Sam yelled, his face red and glasses slipping, "but she'd be ten times prouder of me than anyone could ever be of you. She'd be crazy with pride. She'd be gigantic-huge-gargantuan with pride, you rotten snobs. Let us sail, Dana. I'm gonna show them. . . ."

"Let him," Lily breathed.

Dana held his gaze, wishing he would sit down. Small and scrappy, his speech had brought tears to his own eyes. He slashed them away, not wanting the other kids to see.

Dana's heart swelled for him. She wanted to go hug him, but she knew that would only make things worse. The crews were laughing at him, and Jack Devlin—his own skipper—looked as if he wanted to jump ship from embarrassment. The wind hadn't dropped, but it hadn't increased either. Lily's eyes sparkled with emotion, leaving Dana no doubt over what she should do.

"Okay," Dana said, staring directly at Sam. "We're going to race." The entire class began to cheer, getting straight to work on their sails and lines, preparing to leave the dock.

"That's my sister," Lily said proudly.

"That's my friend," Sam replied, beaming.

"You ready?"

"You bet I am! I'm not going to let anyone down, Dana—my mom or you. She's going to have my trophy on the fish case," he said, his cheeks scarlet as he tried to hold back hiccups.

"Just be careful," Dana called to everyone in the fleet, but especially to Sam, watching the boom nearly clip his head as he ducked beside Jack. Some of the kids waved, but most, including Sam, were already focused on the race.

WHILE JACK HELD the tiller, Sam worked the jib sheets. He was glad he had his back to Jack, because he didn't quite have control of his face. His cheeks and chin were still twitching from trying not to cry. Not just because of the things Hunter and Ralph had said about his parents, but because for a minute he had worried that Dana might listen to them and not let him race.

He should have known better.

Dana was his friend. They were special to each other. Sam didn't know how he knew, but he did. She had a sister, he had a brother. From the very first minute they talked to each other, they had started being friends. It was weird; he was only eight, in third grade, and she was a beautiful grown-up.

Unfortunately, their friendship had started with a lie. He had tricked her into letting him join the class. After watching sailing school for one week, he made his move.

It was July. Early one morning, before the students arrived, he started crabbing on the yacht club dock. His heart was pounding as he heard her footsteps coming down the weathered boards. His mother was always working, Joe was on some ship a million miles away, and Sam was bored and hurt in a way he couldn't put into words. Sailing looked so cool and free, something that would take him far from the darkness of his own home.

"What are you using?" Dana had asked.

"For bait? A fish head," Sam had said, remembering how he'd scavenged the bluefish head from his mother's pail, how she had yelled for him to stay out of the garbage.

"Do you eat the crabs you catch?"

"No, I watch them," he'd said. "I'm gonna be an oceanographer when I grow up. Just like my brother."

"What do you see when you watch crabs?" she had asked, crouching down.

He had shown her: the way they scuttle sideways, hiding in the shadows of his bucket, the way they use their claws to tear the bluefish flesh, their bottle-green color designed to camouflage them underwater, the fact they were cleaning machines eating anything that drifted to the bottom of Newport Harbour.

"And I thought they were just crabs!" When she smiled, her whole face changed. It was bright as the sun, Sam thought. Brighter than any summer day.

"What's your name?" she had asked.

"Sam Trevor. What's yours?"

"Dana Underhill."

She had paint around her fingernails and streaked on her sailing shorts. The colors were pale green and cobalt blue. When she saw him staring at her hands, she said, "Oops. Didn't use enough turpentine."

"What were you painting?"

"A picture of the harbour."

"Are you an artist?"

"Trying to be."

"Wow. I thought you were just the sailing teacher." Flustered, he talked faster. "I don't mean *just*. I mean I think it's cool you're the sailing teacher. You don't know how much I wish I knew how to sail."

"Well, that makes us even. I thought you were just crabbing, and you're a future oceanographer."

That's when he hit her with the zinger: "I wish you could teach me how to sail."

"You do, do you?" she asked, beaming.

He nodded. Then, because the desire to learn was much stronger than he'd known, he said, "More than anything."

"I'd be very happy to teach you to sail," said Dana Underhill, and from that incredible moment on, Sam was a member of her class.

"Hey, Sam," Jack called now above the rising wind.

"Yeah?" Sam asked, perched on the gunwale, trying to hang out over the rough gray water, to balance his weight as the small boat heeled over. They were on a starboard tack, beating out to the starting line. Dana was driving the crash boat, and her sister Lily had just sounded the one-minute horn.

"Don't screw up," Jack warned.

"I won't," Sam promised.

"When I say 'ready about,' concentrate on the jib, okay? Don't be watching the weather, being Mr. Junior Scientist."

"Don't worry about me," Sam said, straightening his glasses and giving Jack a big smile. Jack's family had just moved to the area, so he didn't have any old friends to sail with. He almost always got stuck with Sam, and Sam didn't want to let him down.

Mainly, he wanted to do well for Dana. He glanced over at the crash boat, saw her see him and wave. He felt a shiver go down his spine, knowing she was looking out for him. After this race, summer would be over and she would go back to art school in Providence. At least she and Lily got to be together. Sam's brother was far away, on his quest to become an oceanographer.

"Hey, Sam," Jack yelled. "Eyes on the fleet, okay?"

"You got it, skipper!"

The centerboard hummed with their increasing boat speed. Sam felt the vibrations through his legs and spine. Lily sounded the thirty-second horn, and Sam hit the stopwatch. The boats began to maneuver closer to the starting line. Dana steered the Boston Whaler out of the way. She gestured to Sam, silently suggesting a tactic, and Sam passed it on to Jack.

"Veer that way." Sam pointed.

"We'll hit," Jack said, staring at the pack of boats.

"No, we have space," Sam said, estimating wind direction, current, and speed. "We'll be first across the starting line."

"Starboard," Jack shouted, sliding under Hunter's bow.

"Screw you," Hunter bellowed as he lost his wind.

"That one's for the fishmonger," Sam yelled, locking eyes with Hunter.

"You little shit," Hunter said, throwing the tiller across, coming about with a loud clatter and roar as the sails luffed, then caught the wind.

"Ten seconds," Sam called to Jack as they glided perfectly toward the start. "Nine, eight . . ."

"Ready about," Jack said. Trying to stay ahead of Hunter, he had misjudged the wind. Sam had an oceanographer's instinct for conditions, and he knew that Jack was making a mistake. But Jack was captain and Sam was crew, so he had to go along. He grabbed the jib sheet and tore it from the cleat. Doing so, he dropped the stopwatch, and his terminal klutziness kicked in. He bobbled the line. The wind ripped it from his hand and his arm went out to grab it. Like a lost kite string or an escaping balloon, the nylon line was just out of reach.

"Oh, God," he exclaimed. They were two seconds from the start, Hunter was passing, and Dana was watching. Without thinking, Sam lurched forward to clutch the white line.

"What the hell . . ." Jack shouted. Two, one: Lily sounded the starting blast.

"Sam, sit down!" Dana cried out, and it was the last thing in the world Sam Trevor heard before the boom came swinging across the beam with all the force of a freight train, cracking him in the skull and knocking him overboard.

"DANA, HE'S BLEEDING," Lily screamed as they sped across the waves.

"Don't take your eyes off him," Dana called, losing sight of

Sam's inert body. Trying to prove himself cool, he had defied the rules and failed to put on a life jacket. His jeans were dark blue, the same color as the water, his jacket a faded shade of greenish-gray.

"Hurry," Lily cried.

Mere seconds had passed, and already he had disappeared under the surface. One hand on the wheel, Dana pulled off her boat shoes. She unzipped her jacket and realized Lily was doing the same. They had learned everything about the water together. They had taken lifesaving back at Hubbard's Point, practicing rescues on each other.

The sisters brushed fingers for luck and strength. Their eyes met for just a second, and then they dived in. The water closed over their heads. Dana's lungs were full of air, and she saw bubbles escaping from her sister's mouth. They felt as if they owned the sea. It was their domain, and they swam straight for Sam as he drifted down toward the bottom.

They reached him at the same time. Blood gushed from a cut behind his ear, tinting the murk reddish. Dana slid one arm around his chest, and Lily came under from the other side. Their legs moved in synchronicity. Enveloping the boy, they were in their element, gently bringing him to the surface.

Their heads bobbed up, and together they supported Sam. He lay cradled in their arms, and the sisters looked down into his face. Dana felt the force of the sea coming through her legs. Treading water, her feet brushed Lily's. Their legs might have been fish tails, so easily did the girls stay afloat. Bending her lips to Sam's, Dana breathed into his mouth.

Suddenly, Sam coughed and spit out water.

"He's back to life," Lily said.

"What happened?" he asked, choking. As he struggled to free himself, they held him tightly in their arms.

"Well, let's get you into the boat, and I'll tell you," Dana said.

They were floating together, face-to-face, and his eyes sprang wide open as he stared at Dana. His glasses were long gone, and it took a second to bring her into focus. "It's you. . . ."

Lily laughed. "Did you think she was a mermaid?"

"She saved your life, that's all," Jack Devlin said from above.

"You did?" Sam asked with unmistakable delight, gazing at Dana with horror-movie drips of blood running down the side of his face.

Dana just smiled, supporting him in the water.

"I'll never forget this, Dana," he said, holding her hand.

"Lily too," Jack said. "They both saved you."

"I mean it." He brushed the blood out of his eyes. "Never. As long as I live. You two sisters never have to worry—I'll protect you forever."

Dana and Lily smiled. The wind had died, and the sun broke from behind a dark cloud, spreading strange butterscotch light across Newport Harbour. The spires of St. Mary's and Trinity churches gleamed on the hill, and the hulls of several hundred boats glistened on their moorings. Dana's eyes met Sam's and held.

"Do you think I'm kidding?" he asked.

"Come on," Lily said, trying not to laugh. "Let's get you into the boat now."

"Just because I'm young," he said, "doesn't mean I can't do it. Just wait, you'll see."

"You're my hero," Dana said, her smile growing larger, "and if I ever need help, I'll know who to call. But listen to Lily and let us get you into the boat. You can save us some other time, okay?"

"Okay," Sam said, allowing himself to be lifted from the water, sounding for all the world as if he had just made a promise.

CHAPTER 1

Twenty-one years later

THEY WERE SISTERS AND THEIR MOTHER AND AUNT WERE
sisters. Quinn and Allie Grayson sat on the wall by the road, waiting for Aunt Dana to arrive from the airport. She lived in France.
She was an artist. She was different from every single person they
knew. Every time a car drove down their dead-end street, they craned
their necks and Quinn felt a funny flip in her stomach. She wondered whether Allie felt it too, but she didn't want to ask.

"It's not her," Allie said when the Tilsons—the new neighbors—
drove past in their green station wagon for the third time in an
hour.

"Three times. Back, forth, and back again. What do you think
they're doing?"

"Buying every plant the garden center has. Their yard is a
showplace."

Quinn gave her a fishy look. "Showplace" was just the kind of
thing Allie would say. She had picked it up from hanging around
their grandmother, who was inside the house, way too much.

A different neighbor, Mrs. McCray, rolled down the window
of her blue car and smiled. Mrs. McCray had owned her house

forever, had known their mother and aunt since they were younger than Quinn and Allie were now. She was old with white-blue hair, and her rocks had the best tidal pools with the most crabs and starfish.

"Is Dana here yet?" she asked, smiling.

"Not yet. Any minute now," Allie said, but Quinn just stared straight ahead.

"It's marvelous—very, very exciting. To think of her coming all the way from Europe for an art opening! Some artists work all their lives without becoming known. We are all so proud of her. She and your mother got their start painting on my rocks, you know. I still have the pictures they gave me."

"Aunt Dana's the best there is," Allie said.

"Yes, she is. But she'd better not forget where she got her start. Tell her I'll see her at the Black Hall Gallery tomorrow night. We all will!"

"Lucky us," Quinn said under her breath as Mrs. McCray drove away.

Allie didn't reply. She resettled herself on the stone wall. Looking more carefully, Quinn saw that Allie was posing. She had arranged herself to best advantage, legs tucked beneath her bottom, the spring sunlight striking her bright yellow hair.

"You want her to paint you, don't you?" Quinn asked.

"I don't care," Allie said.

"No, you do. I can tell."

Allie wheeled around. "You might have changed your clothes," she said, eyeing Quinn's torn jeans and faded sweatshirt. At the sight of her sister's hair—which Quinn had twisted into sixty-three skinny braids, all looking like a bunch of boinged-out springs—she shuddered. "You want to drive her straight away."

"I couldn't care less what she does," Quinn said. "Whether she stays or goes, who cares?"

"Oh, my God," Allie said, peering down the road. Shade from the tall oaks and pines dappled the tar, making the approaching car look dark and mysterious. It was an airport sedan, dark blue with dents, the kind Aunt Dana always took when she visited. Up the hill, a door slammed shut. Without turning around, Quinn knew their grandmother had stepped outside to see. The car door opened, and a small woman got out. She was about the same size as Quinn and Allie's mother, with silvery brown hair and bright blue eyes, wearing jeans and a windbreaker, looking more as if she'd stepped off a sailboat than out of a city car.

"She looks like Mommy," Allie said breathlessly, as if she'd forgotten, as if they hadn't just seen her a year earlier.

Quinn couldn't speak. Allie was right. Aunt Dana had always looked like their mother. She was the same size, and she had the same curious, friendly, about-to-laugh expression in her eyes. In spite of that, Quinn scowled and couldn't quite imagine what made her say the words that came out of her mouth: "She does not."

"You two have grown so much in a year, I barely recognize you," Aunt Dana said.

"How long are you staying?" Allie asked, running straight into the street and their aunt's arms.

"Just about a week," Aunt Dana said, smiling across Allie's head at Quinn. "Aquinnah Jane. Is it really you?"

Quinn's feet started to move. They jumped off the wall and took three steps toward her aunt. But suddenly they turned and ran—fast, faster, down Cresthill Road, toward the rocks in front of Mrs. McCray's house, to the hidden tidal pool where no one—especially Aunt Dana—would ever find her.

SAM TREVOR STOOD before his lecture class at Yale, loading the tape into the cassette player. All eyes were upon him. Fifty-five students, future oceanographers all of them, were about to hear the tape of whale sounds his brother and Caroline had recorded in Greece.

"I believe you will hear irrefutable proof that cetaceans talk to one another in a language just waiting to be translated," he said. "The work of Malachy Condon makes a fine beginning, but we shall go further. If I can just get this in . . ."

A girl in the back of the room giggled. Sam's glasses slipped, but he caught them with one hand and slid the tape in with the other. Pushing the play button, he gazed across the sea of faces.

"We only have two more classes before finals. I thought you were lecturing today," a dark-haired girl said.

"I was," Sam said. "But I decided to let the whales speak for themselves. My exam will cover what you hear today and, more important, how you interpret it." Then, leaving the tape playing and students groaning, he walked out the classroom door and down the hallway of Crawford Hall toward the faculty parking lot.

Sam was a responsible guy. He never shirked his teaching duties, and he hoped he wasn't doing that now. But he had a feeling in his chest, pressing harder by the minute, impelling him out to his van.

Scanning the shoreline arts page in search of a movie last weekend, he had seen her name: Dana Underhill.

"An opening reception of this artist's work will be held on Thursday, June 17, from 6 to 8 P.M. at the Black Hall Gallery. Ms. Underhill, who resides in Honfleur, France, will attend."

Sam had never planned to see her again. He had gone to college, then graduate school, and there had been girlfriends along the way. Then he took the Yale job and started to think of her again. It was subtle, nothing much more than a map reference that he had always associated with her. She and her sister, Lily, came from Hubbard's Point in Black Hall, just thirty miles east of New Haven.

She had taught him to sail. He could head up the Sound, come around the Point, show her that he remembered everything she had taught him.

But she no longer lived in Connecticut. Her career had taken her away. He knew, because a year and a half ago, right after starting at Yale, he had run into Lily at the Long Wharf Theater. She was there with her husband, and Sam was there with his date, Claudia Barton. The memory came hard and fast, hitting Sam like a hurricane: Dana's sister, Lily. His other lifesaver.

"And Dana?" Sam had asked after Lily had filled him in on her own life.

"She's so far away, Sam," Lily had said. "I wouldn't be able to stand it if I didn't know she's following her dream."

"Her dream?" Sam had asked. His hands shaking, he had jammed them into the pockets of his jacket so his date wouldn't see.

"To paint every sea there is," Lily had said. "She's lived on so many coastlines, always finding little cottages with a view of the water. Remember the last time I saw you, what was it—eight, nine years ago?"

"Ten," Sam had said quietly.

"That's right—the year we had Quinn. Anyway, remember I told you Dana was renting that house on Martha's Vineyard?"

Sam had nodded, not quite able to reply, afraid Lily could read his mind.

"Gay Head," Lily's husband said to her as if Sam weren't even there.

Lily had squeezed her husband, but she had smiled at Sam. "That was the beginning, Dana's search for the perfect seascape. Someday I know she'll have enough, she'll get famous, and she'll come back home."

Sam recognized the sadness in Lily's eyes. He knew how she felt; he had a brother like Dana—Joe was a treasure-hunting ocean-ographer, and he constantly traveled the world. Sam missed him like crazy, and he could see Lily felt the same way about Dana.

"She will," Sam had said to make Lily feel better. "Of course she'll come home. I might have been young, but I remember how close you were. She wouldn't want to leave you for too long."

"I hope you're right," Lily had laughed. "She has two nieces who miss her almost as much as I do. We visit every summer, but mainly they know her through her postcards."

"I know that story," Sam had said. He had one in his back pocket, a postcard sent by Joe and his wife, Caroline, from Greece.

"Are you an old friend of Lily and Dana's?" her husband had asked.

"Oh, Mark," Lily had said, taking his hand. "I'm so sorry. It's just, seeing Sam really brought me back. If there's one person I know would commiserate with me about missing Dana, it's Sam. They meant a lot to each other that summer—sailing lessons in Newport, right, Sam?"

Aware of Claudia's growing interest, Sam nodded. Now Lily was going through her handbag, pulling out an envelope, handing Sam a picture.

It was of Dana. Claudia leaned over to see, and Sam reached past her for the photo.

She was so beautiful, even more so than he had remembered. Her eyes were the color of sky. Her body was slight, dressed in paint-stained chinos and a linen shirt. He could see the paint around her fingernails, no rings on her hands.

"Is she married? Does she have kids?"

"No and no. She and I taught Sam sailing," Lily said to Claudia with a hint of apology in her voice.

"I wouldn't be here if it wasn't for them," Sam said.

"Team Underhill," Mark said, smiling as he hugged his wife.

"Man overboard," Lily explained, leaning into Mark's embrace. "It could happen to anyone."

"Teaching kids to sail, saving their lives, all in a day's work," Mark said.

"He *is* a very good sailor," Claudia concurred. They had raced at Block Island during the summer. When Sam looked up now to smile at her, she had backed away from the picture. Claudia was resident in psychiatry at Yale–New Haven; Sam had been drawn to her perception and insight. He could see that she was using those gifts, seeing straight past the picture and Lily, wanting to know more about Dana.

"Where is she now?" Sam asked, staring at the picture.

"That was taken in France," Lily said. She went on, talking quickly now as the houselights blinked and people began to file back into the theater.

"France?"

"Yep," Lily had said over her shoulder, letting herself be pulled back inside by her husband. "That's where she lives now, in Honfleur, on the coast of Normandy. She says it reminds her of Black Hall . . . I tell her that means she should come back home."

And now she had, Sam thought, driving his Volkswagen van onto I-95. Dana was in Black Hall for an art opening. The article had said she still lived in Honfleur, which meant she was just home for a visit, maybe only for the art show. He wondered what she would think to learn that he had become an oceanographer after all. Sam hadn't seen her in almost twelve years but he was going to see her tonight. He was just looking up an old friend.

Or at least that was what he told himself.

A DAY AFTER her return home, the Black Hall Gallery was packed with neighbors, strangers, art lovers, friends of Dana's and Lily's. Dana couldn't believe this day had come. She had learned to paint in Black Hall, but this was her first exhibition here. She felt both excited and nervous as everyone walked past her paintings. From habit, she wished Jonathan were with her.

Her canvases were huge, great washes of blue and green, always of the sea, often with a hint of sunset or moonrise along the horizon. Some showed the evening star or a crescent moon. Each painting had a secret hidden in the waves, and Dana stood still, knowing no one would notice. Lily was the only one who ever did.

Her niece, Allie, wouldn't let go of her hand. Her other niece, Quinn, was nowhere to be seen.

"Mommy really did it," Allie said.

"She did, she absolutely did," Dana said. "She wanted me to have a show in Black Hall, and she wouldn't quit till the gallery owner said 'uncle.' "

"It wasn't that hard," Allie giggled.

"This is a very prestigious gallery," Dana's mother, Martha, whispered. "They only exhibit artists who are really top-notch. See the Renwicks over there?"

Dana glanced across the wide, airy space. Clustered around the gallery owner were Augusta Renwick and two of her daughters, Clea and Skye. Although Dana knew them only by sight, she felt honored to have them there. Augusta was the widow of Hugh Renwick, one of Black Hall's best-known artists of recent times.

"I can't believe they're here for little old me," Dana said.

"Well, they are, sweetheart," her mother said. "Along with everyone else in town."

Having had one-person shows of her work in New York, Deauville, and Montreal, why did she feel ten times more nervous here at home? This show was a thrill, and Dana owed it all to her sister. Two years ago, Lily had started badgering her for slides and submitting them to the Black Hall and other local galleries. The owner had admired her use of color and light, and he had liked the idea of a local artist, now living abroad, coming home. With scheduling the only real issue, this June had been the first possible date for both parties.

"What do you see in there?" Dana asked Allie, staring at a moonlit sea.

"Dark water," Allie said. "With silver on top."

"Nothing else?" Dana asked, wanting her to see what her mother always saw.

Allie shrugged and shook her head. "Why do you always paint the sea?"

"Because I love it so much."

"The water looks different in every painting. Black, dark gray in that one, turquoise blue in that one . . . but when we were little, you used to say it was all one sea, the same salt water, right?"

"The same water in different places," Dana said, squeezing her hand. "Every coastline has its own character." It had almost stopped mattering where she lived as long as she could see the sea from at least one window in her house.

Now, looking for Quinn, she spotted her standing by the hors d'oeuvres table. Forced to wear a flower print dress, Quinn had accented the ensemble with hiking boots on her feet and a heavy chain around her neck. Her strangely braided hair made her resemble a wiry shrub or a drawing by Dr. Seuss.

"How do you spell 'psycho'?" Allie asked.

"P-s-y-c-h-o," Dana said. "Why?"

"Because that's what Quinn looks like with her hair like that."

"Will you ask her to please come stand with me? I flew all the way from France to see you guys, and she hasn't said two words," Dana said.

"You came for the art show," Allie corrected.

"That's not the main reason, and you know—" Dana began.

Suddenly, Allie pulled her hand away and walked over to her sister. Dana watched as Quinn seemed to listen, then strode out through the open door with Allie following. By the time Dana got outside, her mother following behind her, the two sisters had disappeared.

Dana breathed steadily. She was jet-lagged. Just yesterday she had been standing on the hill, gazing toward the English Channel at the exact spot where Eugène Boudin had painted with Claude Monet, inventing Impressionism in the process. She had packed her clothes, walked through the studio she had shared with Jonathan. Now Dana was in Black Hall, surrounded by friends and neighbors examining her own work. She hoped no one noticed she couldn't quite look at it herself.

"Are you going to tell me your plans?" her mother asked now that they were alone.

"You know them, Mom. I plan to stay for the week, then go back to France."

"Dana," her mother said, placing her hand on Dana's arm. "I told you on the phone, and I'll say it again. I don't want you to go. You belong here. Just look around—can't you feel the support? You can't tell me you get that in Honfleur, as beautiful as it might be. And you know you're going to need it."

"Mom, don't," Dana said. "Where did the girls go?"

"Running wild, as usual. Allie's fine, but Quinn is a terrible influence. Last Sunday I caught her smoking a cigarette. Twelve years old, and there she was, puffing away!"

"I'll talk to her."

"Oh, a lot of good that will do. What makes you think she'll listen? She hasn't listened to one word anyone's said in months."

"She will," Dana said. "We're special."

Her mother snorted. "So special you can't even stay."

"Mom . . ." Dana began.

Her mother's face looked so old. It was tired and lined, and there was an unfamiliar hardness behind her formerly soft blue eyes. When Dana reached for her hand, it felt cool and dry, and she didn't squeeze back. They were mother and daughter, but it was as if their connection had been broken.

When Martha Underhill slid her hand away to walk back into the gallery and rejoin the party, Dana closed her eyes. She thought of her cottage on the English Channel, of its whitewashed stone walls. What did it mean to her, after all? It was just real estate with a beautiful view to paint out the window. She and Jonathan had tried—fumbling all the way—to love each other there. Her assistant, Monique, had kept it spotlessly clean. Remembering that, she shivered.

She thought of sailboats rocking in the harbour at Deauville; to supplement the income from her not-frequent-enough sales, she sometimes gave sailing lessons there. Then she thought of Lily.

She wanted her sister.

Of all the people in all the world, Dana wanted her sister to walk through the door. They'd bag this party in a second. She wanted to grab her sister's hand, run down to the water, and find a boat. Lily's girls could come with them, and together they could all sail away. Her heart was absolutely ready to be poured out. She craved a gripe session with the girls: a chance to bash Jon and trash Monique. A gentle breeze, a broad reach, and her sister were exactly what Dana needed.

Instead, she just walked down the gallery steps, past the boxwood hedge. As she breathed in the clear summer air, her attention was drawn to a blue van. The driver climbed out, and Dana slowed down, then stopped in her tracks. He was tall and strong-looking, rearranging the bouquet of flowers he had brought. She was mesmerized by the sight of such a big man fiddling with daisies. Her heart kicked over, but when he lifted his eyes and looked straight at her, it flipped back. He was quite young, certainly no older than thirty. Suddenly Augusta Renwick exclaimed with delight, and the young man turned to her, and it didn't matter anymore.

Dana headed down the blue stone walk, away from the crowd, in search of her nieces.

"SHE SAID YOU haven't said two words to her," Allie pleaded.

"I have two words for her," Quinn said. " 'Fuck you.' "

"That is so rude and crummy."

"Pick one," Quinn said. "Rude or crummy. You're so dramatic."

"I'm not the one with Brillo head."

"No, you're the one with empty head, you stupid baby."

Allie's eyes welled with tears. Two big ones plopped off the lids, down her pink cheeks. Quinn tried not to look, but it was hard. They had walked out the gallery's front door and sneaked in the back, and now they were sitting under the food table, hidden from sight by a long tablecloth. Face-to-face, she couldn't exactly pretend she didn't see her sister crying.

"Stop that," she said.

"Stop what?" Allie asked, sniffling hard. She knew Quinn hated it when she cried, so she was trying to make herself stop.

Just to change the subject, Quinn brought the cigarette butt out from behind her ear. She had found it on the gallery steps, not even half smoked. Filching matches from the owner's desk had been a snap. Now she struck one, lit the butt, and took a drag.

"Don't do that," Allie begged.

"Why not?" Quinn asked, blowing out a puff. Smoke filled the small space, leaking out under the cloth's hem.

"You could die. Smoking kills—don't you listen in school?"

"Everyone dies," Quinn said. "So who cares?"

"I do," Allie said, and now she really couldn't control herself. The tears got bigger and started falling faster. To Quinn they looked clear and solid, tiny jellyfish rolling down her sister's face.

"Allie," Quinn said, holding the cigarette in her cupped hand the way she had seen it done in movies. "You know why she's here, don't you?"

"The art show."

"Bull. That's not why."

"She says it's all the same sea, the same salt water . . ." Allie cried.

"But the houses are different, the people are different. We'd have to learn French, Al. Besides all that, I hate her."

"How can you hate her? She's Mommy's sister," Allie wept.

"That's why," Quinn whispered, staring at the lit part of the cigarette as if it were the beacon of a lighthouse. "That's the exact reason why."

Suddenly feeling unbearably claustrophobic, Quinn pinched the cigarette out and stuck it behind her ear. Then she threw back the tablecloth and scrambled through a forest of legs, Allie right behind her. People laughed and gasped, but Quinn didn't care. She just wanted to get away.

BLACK HALL was exactly as Dana Underhill had remembered it: peaceful, elegant, suffused with clear yellow light that seemed to bounce off salt marshes and tidal creeks, to paint the shipbuilders' mansions and church steeples, to trickle down the Connecticut River into Long Island Sound. Just as Honfleur was the birthplace of French Impressionism, Black Hall was where the movement had first started in America, and as an artist, Dana could understand why.

"Hey," the voice called.

When she turned around, she saw the young man coming after her, still holding his flowers. She saw that she'd been right, that he was just about twenty-eight or twenty-nine.

"Where are you going?" he asked when he'd caught up.

"I'm looking for someone," she said.

He laughed. "They must be back there, at your opening. Everyone came to see you."

She didn't stop walking. The June air was fresh and cool. It blew through the trees, made Dana pull her shawl a little tighter. She wore a white silk sheath and black cashmere wrap. Her earrings and necklace were silver lilies, to remind her of her sister. She wore them whenever she felt a little nervous or thought she might be afraid. Lately she had worn them to soothe her broken heart.

"Is it kids?"

"Excuse me?"

"Are you looking for two girls—your nieces, Lily's kids?"

"How do you know?" she asked, stopping short as her heart began to pound.

"I saw them go by. They look just like you and Lily," he said.

"You know Lily?"

"Knew her," the young man corrected Dana, and again she felt the kick in her heart. "You don't know who I am, do you? I thought you recognized me back there, when I first got here, but you don't, do you?"

She flushed, not wanting him to know she'd been thinking he was cute. "Tell me . . ." Dana began, her mouth dry, "how you know Lily."

"You both taught me how to sail," he said, handing her the flowers. "A long time ago. Back in Newport."

She blinked, staring from the bouquet into his eyes. They were smiling, anticipatory.

Dana spun back. The summer before her senior year at the Rhode Island School of Design, she and Lily had worked at the Ida Lewis Yacht Club. Dana had hoped to follow in the footsteps of Hugh Renwick and paint on the Newport wharves; even back then, to support her art, she had taught sailing to kids. Was this one of them, all grown up?

"Don't you remember me?" he asked, his voice deep yet soft.

Dana peered more intently into the young man's eyes and felt something move inside her chest. She saw herself and Lily treading water, holding an unconscious boy between them in their arms. The harbour was summer-warm; she could almost feel her sister's feet brushing her legs underwater.

"Sam . . ." The name came out of nowhere, out of the past.

"You remember me," he said, grinning widely.

"We never forgot you. Lily told me she'd seen you somewhere— at the theater, wasn't it?"

"A little over a year ago," he said, nodding. "Those are her girls?"

"Yes." Then, trying to smile, "How did you know?"

"Well, they have the Underhill eyes. And she told me you don't have any children of your own."

"No, just nieces. That's enough," Dana said. But her eyes failed to smile. "What brings you here? Are you an artist?"

"Far from it." He laughed. "I'm a scientist. An oceanographer to be exact. Remember the crabs?"

"I do," she said, beginning to smile as she pictured him on the dock. "I do."

Grinning, Sam gazed down at her. He was quite tall; Dana had to tilt her head back to look into his face. He was full of good humor— every part of him seemed to be smiling. The sun was setting behind the Congregational Church's white spire, and the scratched lenses in his glasses reflected the declining golden light.

"I'm a marine biologist," he said. "My brother gives me grief—he's an oceanographer too, but the geologist-geophysicist variety. Joe says studying whales is for nerds, that sediment's where it's at."

"I remember you talking about your brother," Dana said. She could see him now, that little boy playing on the docks, catching crabs and throwing them back, missing the older brother who had gone to sea. Her heart caught, missing her sister, and her eyes filled with tears.

"He married a girl from Black Hall," Sam said, his gaze growing serious as he noticed the change in her expression.

"Oh," she said, carefully wiping her eyes.

"I teach in New Haven now. Yale," he said with a shrug, as if he'd just gotten caught bragging. "Joe and Caroline got married two years ago and they travel a lot, but whenever they come back to Firefly Beach, I'll get to see them. It's great." Laughing, he focused on her eyes. "What am I telling you for? You know, right?"

"I know?" she asked, figuring he was referring to his brother: "Caroline" had to be Caroline Renwick, daughter of the art legend, Hugh Renwick of Firefly Beach.

"How great it is to come home and see your sister."

"Oh, yes."

"You guys were really close. It was like a package deal—show up and get taught by not one but two Underhill sisters. Is she here tonight?"

Dana didn't reply. Thoughts of Hugh Renwick evaporated. Now she was remembering the package deal: Dana and Lily in the crash boat, coaching the fleet, feeling the summer breeze on their skin, picking out harbour scenes they wanted to paint.

"You came home to see her and her kids?" Sam persisted.

"I came home to see her kids."

His face was made for looking quizzical. Tilting his head, he pushed his glasses up. His eyes crinkled slightly. Dana smelled the wildflowers he had brought her and thought of beach grass filled with rosa rugosa, cornflowers, Queen Anne's lace, and daylilies. She could see Sam didn't know what to say next, so she said it for him.

"Her daughters. They're my charges," Dana said, and the word sounded so formal, it made her laugh. *My sweethearts, my darling nieces, my sister's beautiful girls,* would have sounded more natural. "My charges," she said again.

"But I don't get it . . ." he began.

"She left instructions in her will," Dana said. "That if anything ever happened to her and Mark, I should take care of them."

"In her will," Sam said slowly.

"I should come home from wherever I was, it said, to look after them. Well, I was in France. Trying to paint and living my life. I did come home for the funerals, of course. But then, my mother seemed to have everything under control, taking care of the girls . . ."

"What happened, Dana?"

"They drowned. Lily and Mark," Dana said. Her chest caved in when she said the words: It always did. But she breathed deeply and gazed at the beautiful sky, and somehow she kept herself from crying. That part was getting easier. What she felt inside was one thing, but what she showed to the world was becoming simpler to control.

"Oh, Lily," Sam said.

Turning from the sky to Sam Trevor, Dana was surprised to see tears in his eyes. It was as if the feelings in her own heart had somehow shown up on this near-stranger's face.

"I'm so sorry," he said.

"Thank you," Dana said, gazing back at the sky, at the sharp white steeple piercing the golden-blue twilight. Down the street, people had come out of the gallery to see where she had gone. She heard their voices far off, a million miles away. She felt as if she were in a trance. "She died ten months ago."

"And you've come home to raise her daughters?"

Dana shook her head. "No, to take them back to France with me."

"Oh," Sam said.

The crowd had spotted her. Dana heard her name being called. The voices were louder, calling her back. A cake was about to be cut. A toast had to be made. This was her homecoming, however temporary. She was a Black Hall artist, and her sister had made sure the world was going to know it.

The evening star had come out. It glowed in the west, a tiny hole in the sky's amber fabric. Dana looked for Lily everywhere: in a field of flowers, in a cup of tea, in the sky. Blinking, Dana stared at that bright star and made a wish. Closing her eyes, she thought of her sister. She could see Lily's eyes, her yellow hair, her bright smile. Reaching out, she could almost touch her. . . .

Sam didn't move. He didn't speak, and he didn't try to steady her, even though she felt herself sway. She was under her sister's spell, standing in the center of town, trying to touch the evening star. Lily seemed so close. She was right there, right there. With her eyes closed, Dana could feel Lily as if she had never left.

But when she opened her eyes, she was alone with Sam. The gallery owner and her mother were calling her name. Still holding the bouquet of wildflowers, Dana turned around, and together she and the young boy of long ago walked slowly past the white church toward the art gallery and its waiting crowd.

CHAPTER 2

HUBBARD'S POINT HAD BARELY CHANGED IN DANA Underhill's forty-one years of life. Located in the southern section of Black Hall, the land jutted into Long Island Sound and formed a rocky point. This was a summer place for working people: It lacked the panache and grandeur of certain beach areas to the east. The yards were tiny, the cottages nearly on top of one another. The original builders—grandparents and great-grandparents of the current owners—had been policemen, firemen, grocers, salesmen, telephone linemen, and teachers.

What it lacked in tone, the Point more than made up in natural beauty and human warmth. Everyone knew everyone else. They called hello as they walked or drove by; they kept an eye on each other's kids. Children Dana had grown up with had kids of their own. Gardens bloomed in bright profusion, and window boxes exploded with color. Honeysuckle scented the air, and dark pines blanketed yards with soft needles. Rabbits lived on the hillsides, and squirrels nested in the trees.

The houses on the Point's east side were built on rocks, great slabs of granite and quartz tufted with grass, sloping down into rock coves and tidal pools. The houses facing west overlooked the beach and swale—a white crescent strand curving along the Sound, backed by a gold-green marsh.

The Underhills' house, perched on the highest part of the Point, overlooked both beach and rocks. A shingled cottage built by Martha's parents in 1938, it had survived that year's famous hurricane and many storms to follow. Weathered gray, it blended austerely into the ledge, nestled among red cedars and wind-stunted oaks, brightened only by Lily's overgrown rose and perennial gardens.

"Pretty weedy, huh?" Allie asked, monitoring Dana's expression.

"Oh, it's not too bad," Dana said, sipping her coffee. Sunday morning after the art show, they sat on stone steps, shaded by a sassafras tree. The people next door were cooking breakfast, and the smell of bacon filled the air. Across the street, the McCrays' house—home of Old Annabelle and her daughters, the Underhill sisters' best friends the McCray sisters—was just coming alive, voices drifting out the open windows.

"I think it is." Allie looked worried. "Those rambler roses are choking everything. You can't even see Mom's herb garden. She planted lavender, rosemary, sage, and thyme that were supposed to come back every year. But I don't see a bit of it."

Putting down her cup, Dana began to clear out some of the dead leaves and trailing briars. She uncovered a shrub of sage, soft and green; digging deeper, she found a thatch of silver thyme sprigged with tiny triangular leaves. Pricking her finger on a thorn, she licked a drop of blood. Through the house's open windows, she heard the TV blaring, tuned to a morning show. Instead of coming out with Dana and Allie, Quinn had stayed inside to watch.

"Does Quinn watch a lot of TV with Grandma?" Dana asked.

"Not always," Allie said, crouching beside Dana and pulling out weeds. "But sometimes."

"She doesn't want to talk to me, does she?"

Allie shook her head.

Dana chewed her lip. Quinn had always been strong-willed,

stubborn about things that mattered to her, but she had never stayed mad at Dana for this long before. Weeding the garden, Dana felt the dirt with her fingers. It was stony, filled with bits of granite, pure Hubbard's Point. The soil here was different than it was anywhere else in the world, and touching it gave Dana a lump in her throat.

Dana's relationship with Hubbard's Point, especially now, was far from simple. For one thing, the place had nothing to do with plots of land. She loved it as much as a person, and her feelings about it were just as complicated. She came back to herself here. It was the only place on earth where she couldn't hide from her deepest truths. And every inch of it reminded her of Lily. She felt her sister's loss more here than anywhere else, and everything else paled in comparison.

"Your mother would not want Quinn to be avoiding me."

"Quinn knows that."

"Is this because I stayed away all year? I came for the funeral, then left again?" If she had to, Dana was prepared to explain herself.

"Well, she didn't like it, but that's not why."

"Then why won't she speak to me?"

"Well," Allie said, her face serene. "That's because you want to take us back to France. And she doesn't want to go."

EVERYONE THOUGHT QUINN was watching *Meet the Press* with Grandma, even Grandma. Lying on the sofa, covered with an afghan, Quinn had simply rolled off and stuffed pillows under the covers while Grandma stared at the screen. Then she had sidled upstairs, out her bedroom window, and down the oak tree growing right by the house.

Secrecy was paramount. Tucked into the waistband of her shorts she had a pen. Once she hit the ground, she held the pen between her teeth, exactly the way a pirate would hold a dagger. Then she ran down the narrow stone path to the beach stairs.

Onto the footbridge, across the creek, along the soft sand, Quinn ran for her life. She bit the pen, dashing like a wild Pequot. Eastern woodland Indians had roamed this land hundreds of years ago. They had hunted and fished, roasting their catches in the natural fireplace beneath the stone boulder in Mrs. Fitzgerald's yard.

Quinn knew plenty about Indians. For one thing, her real name was Aquinnah, which was Wampanoag for "high ground." Her parents had named her that because they had met and fallen in love at a place of high ground. Quinn intended to become an anthropologist when she grew up. She was going to go to Connecticut College, just a few miles away, to study Pequots, Mohegans, Nehantics, and Wampanoags.

One place she wasn't going to go was France. Running swiftly down the beach, she passed several families setting up camp by the high-tide line. Beach chairs, blankets, buckets, crabbing nets, umbrellas: memories of another life. Nearly banging into some happy father standing ankle-deep with his little kid, Quinn swore out loud.

"Hey, watch your language!" the father scolded.

"Sorry," she called, more from habit than because she meant it. People like him didn't understand. They didn't know that togetherness didn't always last forever, that even the happiest families could be destroyed in a second.

Picking up the pace, she ran past the beached sailboats by the seawall, past the crabbing rocks, and up the crooked hillside path, into the forest trail that led to Little Beach. This was a nature preserve, the perfect place for imagining woodland Indians. Trees encroached on the narrow path, which bent around boulders and fallen logs.

Looking both ways, Quinn stopped. The coast clear, she shouldered through thick underbrush until she reached a downed oak. Squirming beneath its broken branches, she lay on her back. Fingertips extended—farther, farther—she wriggled her hand into a hollow and withdrew a plastic-wrapped package.

Now that she had her treasure, she tucked it into her waistband and bit harder on her pen. Running through the woods, she cast furtive glances from side to side. Breaking out of the woods, the path streamed onto a white sand beach. Quinn blinked hard, getting used to the brightness.

Little Beach was deserted. She used to come here with her mother to search for sea glass and skip flat stones. Just around the bend was Tomahawk Point, where rich people lived, and then Firefly Beach, where that great artist's family still lived. Ol' Hugh Renwick might be more famous, but Aunt Dana was better. Holding her precious package, Quinn darted behind a big pink-gray boulder speckled with mica, glittering like black stars in the morning sun.

Her heart pounding, she held the Ziploc bag to her chest. It felt damp, from spring nights in the fallen log, and she hoped no moisture had gotten inside. The log would be a great place to hide cigarettes or beer, but this was contraband of a different sort. Unwrapping the plastic, she pulled out a blue notebook and began to read from an entry written nine months earlier, in October.

> *Grandma's no different from Mom. After all that "you can trust me" crap, she did the exact same thing Mom did: read my diary. What does it do, run in the family? She read the parts about missing Mom and Dad, about wishing I'd been in the boat with them. I figured something was up when she started talking about the shrink again. I am counting the days till Aunt Dana gets here. Then Grandma can go back to her old-folks condo, and we can live with someone who doesn't feel the need to monitor our every move. Aunt Dana is cool. She is very cool. In fact, she is snow-ice, North-Pole, and deep-sea cool. I wish she'd come here soon. I don't get why she has to live over there, so far away, when I want her here.*

Then she turned to a page written in January, several months later, reading every word carefully.

> *This is bad. This is very bad. First of all, I'm pissed out of my gourd that I have to walk a freaking (say "fucking," Quinn, not "freaking,") okay, fucking, mile through the woods to write in my freaking diary. Just so Grandma won't go rooting through my undies to find it and freak out when she reads what I'm about to write. Here goes. Aunt Dana is losing*

it. I mean, really losing it. She'd better not wait till summer to come live with us. She'd better get over here right now. For one thing, I'm so sick of Grandma complaining about how cold the house is, how tired she gets walking down to the street to get the paper, how much easier it is at the old-age condo, where people bring everything to her door and keep the heat cranked up to ninety-five degrees. Aunt Dana keeps saying she's going to come, and then she doesn't. She says she's getting ready for her art show, that she has one or two or fucking three more paintings to finish, that she wouldn't want to disappoint Mom. I don't get it. I thought she loved me. Allie has Grandma, but I'm supposed to have Aunt Dana!

Our parents wanted her to have us. We're supposed to be living with her, not Grandma. I know Mom went to the Black Hall Gallery to arrange the art show, but Mom's not here now. I am! And I helped with the art show too. I went with Mom when she brought the slides.

Maybe when Aunt Dana comes here for the show and moves into our house, everything will be fine. We'll go back to how it used to be. Mom won't be here, but having Aunt Dana will help. I keep remembering how she looked at the funeral. Just like a Kabuki warrior: scowl, hiss, grunt. Very, very horrible. She walked straight . . .

Not wanting to relive the scene of horror, Quinn licked the tip of her felt pen and turned to a clean page. She began to write, and the words flowed from the point. Small waves hit the shore, splashing spray into her face. Ignoring it, Quinn got lost in the world of emotion, pouring it all onto the page in the beauty of that early summer morning.

I hate the world. I hate the world, I hate the world, I loathe and execrate the world. She's the biggest jerk ever to live. That's right, I said "she." Which "she" you might ask? Well, take your pick. Grandma, Allie, Aunt Dana, and Mom. They pester, whine, connive, and die, in that order. Grandma pesters me to act normal, Allie whines and cries

*about what's going to happen next, Aunt Dana thinks she's
going to get me and Allie to move to France with her, and
Mom read my diary and got shocked by the kind of person I
am and then died. How did I ever get born into a family like
this? I'm not going to France. I mean it, I don't care what they
do to me, I am not moving to France. I can't believe I'll never
see Mom again. She read shit she wasn't meant to read, and
went ballistic. She hated me, and the big joke is, I don't even
blame her.*

*Today I swore in front of some perfect father and kid, and
he yelled at me. Better me than his kid though. Yell at your
kid and the next wave just might tear you apart. Here today,
gone tomorrow. I used to love to sail. Mom said I could be in
the Olympics. Now I hate it.*

I AM NOT MOVING TO FRANCE.

When she finished writing, she felt a little better. The sun felt
hot on her face, and the receding tide made the rocks and sand smell
like seaweed. Everything was salty: the sea, the kelp, the sargassum
weed, her wet cheeks. Licking her lips, she carefully wrapped her diary
in plastic. On the horizon, small sailboats danced on the waves.
White sails, blue sky. Quinn reached into her pocket. She took out
the gift and, as always, left it on the rock nearest the tide line.

It was time to hide her diary and return home.

THE GIRLS WERE nowhere to be found. Dana felt restless from
jet lag and seeing her family again, so she wandered down to the
garage at the foot of the hill, by the road. Lifting the heavy door,
she stepped inside. It smelled damp and musty, and English ivy had
broken through some slats and concrete to climb the inside walls.

The old sailboat rested on a rusty trailer, off to the side. It was a
Blue Jay, paint peeling from its wooden hull. Taking up space, it
had been filled to overflowing with rakes, shovels, bags of lime,
empty cartons, the Christmas tree stand, a clam basket, fishing rods,
and a bag of empty bottles. The varnished mast had blackened in
spots, and the sail bag was speckled with mildew.

Dana and Lily had learned to sail in this boat. Running her hand along the sides, Dana remembered how they had pestered their father, begging him to let them have it. He had given his permission, told them they would have to earn the money to buy it themselves. When she got to the stern, Dana had to take a deep breath before looking at the transom. There it was, the name:

MERMAID

Even knowing it was there, her heart beat faster. Her fingers traced the letters. She and Lily had painstakingly made the stencil, and Lily had brushed on the white paint. They had painted one mermaid with round breasts and two tails because that was how they sometimes felt: as if they shared a body, as if they had two tails to propel them through life.

"Here you are," Dana's mother said, leaning on her cane and peering into the dark garage. "Oh, it's so damp and cold in here."

"Hi, Mom."

"I thought we should talk before the girls came back. When do you plan to leave?"

"I told you, Mom. On Thursday. Did you find their passports?"

"They're in Lily and Mark's safety deposit box."

Dana nodded. She should have remembered. Lily had gotten each girl a passport upon birth—Quinn on the Vineyard, Allie here in Connecticut—knowing that with Dana's hunger to live abroad, there would be many trips to see their aunt. As executor of Lily's will, Dana had received the list of the box's contents.

"You know my opinion," her mother said as if she had no feeling whatsoever, as if she were numb from the neck up.

"Yes. You want me to move in here so you can move back to your condo. But I can't do that, Mom. My studio's in Honfleur. I have two commissions right now, and they're both in progress. The girls will love France. They're so smart, they'll pick up the language right away."

"Why are you making this so hard?"

"Hard?" Dana asked.

Her mother stared straight through her. "Pretending that this has anything to do with logistics. You moving here, them moving there . . . sweetheart, this is your home."

"I know," Dana said. Out of the corner of her eye the boat loomed large. Lily's half of the mermaid seemed to be smiling wider. The sight of it caused Dana's heart to squeeze tighter. Every sight, every smell, reminded her of Lily. Why couldn't all love be like what they had had: open, honest, true, real, forever? She thought of Jonathan's deceptions, and her stomach hurt. Being at Hubbard's Point without Lily, even for four days, was nearly unbearable.

"Mom, why is the boat in here?"

"Excuse me?"

"The girls should have been using it." Dana examined the flaking paint, the barnacled bottom.

Martha shook her head. "No, I don't think that's a good idea. I don't believe they want to either."

"But why not?"

"They don't like to go out on the water anymore," her mother said, conjuring that other boat, the one Mark had built, going down in the Sound that moonlit July night.

"It's sad to see it just sitting here," Dana said, running her hand along the rail to block the image out. "Did Lily use it a lot?"

"Well, she used to. Quite a bit. Taught the girls on it, was absolutely proud of how Quinn took to sailing . . ."

"A chip off the old block," Dana said, picturing Lily sailing at Quinn's age.

"But she didn't that last year," her mother said. "Mark had bought the big sailboat, and Lily spent a lot of time out with him. Aside from that, the house needed quite a bit of upkeep, and she took care of that."

"Upkeep . . ."

"After I broke my hip," Martha Underhill said, leaning against the wall and carefully watching Dana's face, "taking care of the house and yard got to be too much. Even going up and down stairs took effort. That's when I decided to give this house to Lily, Mark, and the girls."

"And they loved living here."

"Yes, they did. I always worried that you'd feel resentful, that you might think I was playing favorites."

"I didn't think that," Dana said, but with a tug of her heart, she realized that in fact, in some deep-down way, maybe she had.

"You've made a life for yourself. Painting, traveling . . . You were our free spirit. Lily and I kept wishing you'd move back home, but we got used to your way. Once a year, sometimes twice, you'd come to stay. Even less often once you fell in love with Jonathan. I got it through my head that you wouldn't want the house as much as Lily would."

Dana nodded. The garage was chilly and dark, and she hugged herself thinking of where falling in love with Jonathan had gotten her.

"Was I right?"

"Yes, Mom." Dana smiled.

"I know you love the girls," Martha said, her voice dropping an octave. "That's why Lily made you their guardian."

Dana nodded, wanting to reach for her mother.

"They've been through so much. My God, Dana. To uproot them from their home at a time like this? How can you think of doing it? You learned how to paint right here—at Hubbard's Point. I don't see why you can't do it here now."

"You think it's about painting?" Dana asked, feeling the blood drain from her face.

"Painting or Jonathan."

"It's not Jonathan," Dana said, her body stiff. "That's all over."

"Well, painting, then," Martha said, looking around, without even a comment about the breakup—that's what she expected from Dana. Her relationships had never lasted long, and her family had stopped expecting them to. They knew painting came before any human being—even them. "Your canvases are huge. They'd barely fit through our door. But we could make it work. Build a studio, or even this garage—we could call Paul Nichols to put in a skylight!"

Dana couldn't breathe. Hadn't her mother noticed the way she'd walked around the Black Hall Gallery, unable to even look at her own paintings? They mocked her, that's what it was. Everyone thought they were recent work, done during the last year, but they weren't. Dana had dragged them out of storage because they were all she had. She wouldn't say it out loud to anyone, but she couldn't paint. She hadn't been able to since Lily had died.

"It's not the space," Dana said instead.

"Well, your model, then. How you use her, I don't know. I haven't seen a human figure in your paintings since you used to paint Lily. But Lily told me you'd hired an Asian girl. . . ."

"My assistant, Monique," Dana said in a daze. "She's Vietnamese. Her family had moved to France after the war . . . Paris first, and then they opened a restaurant in Lyons."

The girl was so beautiful, had been through a great deal, and lost family members in the fighting and its aftermath. Dana's figure work was her least strong suit. When she decided to paint mermaids, she asked her assistant to be her model. Monique, with her small frame and lithe figure, her firm muscles and graceful legs, had seemed perfect. Besides, Dana had a soft spot for people away from their families, and she had wanted to help by giving her more work.

"Yes, Monique. Lily was glad you had company in your studio. She said that was supposed to be her role, but since you and she lived so far apart, Monique would have to do."

"Lily wrote to her," Dana remembered. Monique had opened the letter and read it quietly. Unsentimental, she hadn't understood Lily's motivation. When she threw the blue stationery into the studio wastebasket, Dana had retrieved and read it:

> *You are with my sister every day, and I envy you. Dana says you're beautiful, that you will make a great mermaid. Do you have any idea what that means? Mermaids are so special to us—they're like guardian angels. For Dana to choose you to be her mermaid is very significant. She says you are far from home, far from your family. I'm sure that makes her feel closer to you. She's far from us, and we miss her so much.*

By then Dana had already figured out that Monique's relationship with her family was very different from hers. Monique's distance from them was emotional as well as geographical. She wasn't particularly interested in getting close to Dana either, and Lily's letter had meant nothing to her.

"Having a model was just an experiment. It didn't work out," Dana said.

Her mother's face fell. Talking about the size of canvases and the height of doors and models and new skylights must have made her feel hopeful, as if they were making a plan. Dana understood. She almost felt that way herself.

"Oh, sweetheart," her mother said, sounding tired, and for a second their eyes locked.

"Aunt Dana," Allie called from up the hill. "Someone's on the phone for you—Sam Trevor."

"Who's that?" Martha asked.

"Someone I used to know," Dana said. Touching the Blue Jay, her fingertips tingled. She took another look at the sailboat's stern, at the mermaid with two tails. Sometimes she thought she needed a second tail just to keep her on a straight course, that without Lily she was lost. Not looking at her mother, aware of the sorrow and vigilance in her eyes, Dana walked out of the garage and began to run up the hill.

IT TOOK DANA so long to get to the phone, Sam didn't think she was coming. He stood in the kitchen of Firefly Hill, aware of Augusta Renwick rocking on the porch, just out of earshot. Since Joe had married Caroline, the Renwicks had let Sam know that this was his home too, that he could come here anytime he wanted. He had felt sort of guilty, being too busy at Yale to drive the twenty-five miles to Black Hall very often, but he had taken this opportunity—with Dana in town—to drop in on his brother's mother-in-law.

"To what do I owe the pleasure of this visit?" Augusta had asked, holding his hand as she'd led him onto the porch. At her age—late seventies, eighty? Sam couldn't tell—she was by any measure still a true beauty. With long white hair falling over her black velvet opera cape, she looked stunning and dramatic. Sam could imagine the great artist Hugh Renwick falling in love with her, buying her the famous black pearls she wore now and always.

"To see you, of course, Augusta," he'd said, kissing the back of her hand.

"Oh, dear child," she'd said, laughing elegantly. "That's just delightful of you to say, but we both know it's total bullshit."

"Excuse me?" Sam had asked, reddening.

"Listen, I was at the gallery, remember? I saw the flowers you brought, and both Clea and Skye said you looked positively enthralled to be talking to Dana Underhill."

"Actually, Augusta, I definitely came to see you. I was in the neighborhood, and I wanted to visit my—" Sam had begun, but she'd cut him off.

"Don't even bother with that, Sam. I'm old, and I'm family. You don't need to pussyfoot around with me. Go call her—the phone's right in there."

And so he had. The little girl—Dana's younger niece, he supposed—had taken the message, run out to call her aunt, then returned to breathe into the receiver. Her breathing sounded husky, as if she had a cold or an allergy, or as if she had been crying, and to amuse them both, Sam whistled "Anchors Aweigh" while they waited.

"You whistle good," she said.

"Yeah?" Sam asked.

"Uh-huh. My dad whistled like that."

"Did he whistle 'Anchors Aweigh'?"

"I don't think so."

"Hmm," Sam said. "I don't blame him. It's not my favorite song or anything, but it's pretty easy to whistle. If you grew up in Newport, Rhode Island, like I did, you'd hear a bunch of Navy guys whistling 'Anchors Aweigh' when they were walking down Thames Street, and you'd be whistling it too. Go ahead—give it a try."

"I don't know the song."

"It goes like this." He whistled a few bars.

The kid did her best. Her whistle was terrible.

"My aunt's a great artist."

"That she is."

"Did you go to her show?"

"I did."

"My mom planned it."

"She did an incredible job," Sam said, taking a deep breath.

"Well," the little girl said. "Here she is."

The cord clattered, and Sam heard the muffled sound of a palm being held against a mouthpiece. Certain words filtered through in a child's voice: "whistle," "Navy," and "great artist." Then Dana cleared her throat and came on.

"Hello?"

Sam's heart was racing, and it took a second for his voice to work.

"Hey, Dana," he said. "It's Sam."

"Hi, Sam."

"Well, I'm in the area, visiting Augusta Renwick, and I thought I'd give you a call."

"Really? Thanks, Sam. How are you?"

"I'm fine," Sam said, staring out the kitchen window at the cliff overlooking Long Island Sound. He knew Dana was just a few miles down the coast, and he wondered whether she was hearing the same waves. "I've been wondering how you are."

"Well . . ." she began, stopping as if the answer was too hard or complicated to get out.

"The thing is," he said, "I thought maybe you need to talk."

She waited for him to go on. Her breathing sounded surprisingly like her niece's: soft, unguarded, strangely emotional.

"And I was wondering," Sam continued, "whether you'd like to have dinner with me before you go back to France."

"Dinner?" she asked, as if she'd never heard the word before.

"The thing is, I'm in Black Hall right now. At Firefly Hill, like I said. I'll probably spend the night, and I thought maybe I could pick you up and take you to dinner. The Renwick Inn, maybe . . ."

She paused then, the silence stretching out. He wouldn't rush her. She was going through a lot, maybe more than she knew. Sam knew how close those sisters were; he knew from his own feelings for Joe.

"Oh, Sam," she said finally, something unrecognizable in her voice—tears? A grin? Grief? "I don't think so."

"No?"

"I wish I could. It's sweet of you to ask. But there's so much to do, and we leave for Honfleur on Thursday."

"I know," he said. "I was hoping to see you before then. To say good-bye."

She paused again, as if she was thinking that over.

"You meant a lot to me," he said, his voice thick. "You and Lily. Don't think I don't know what this must be like for you."

She said something too muffled for him to hear.

"What?" he asked.

"I don't think anyone knows that," she said, quietly hanging up the phone.

AUGUSTA RENWICK ROCKED in her chair, gazing across the Sound. There, just east, was the spot where Joe had excavated the old wreck. She could practically see the research vessel *Meteor,* and she wished it would sail back with Joe and her daughter Caroline aboard. But they were off in Turkey, treasure-hunting in the Bosporus, and she was extravagantly happy to have Sam there instead.

His voice drifted through the open door, friendly and low. What a fine man Sam was, so very kind. Augusta thought of how much he had grown up these last two years—taking the teaching post at Yale, coming into his own from the obviously daunting shadow of his older brother.

When Augusta heard the click of Sam hanging up the phone, she bit her lip. Her fingers went to her black pearls, working each one as if it held a nugget of wisdom. "Mind your own business," one pearl said. "Let him find his own way," said another. "Don't meddle," said the third. In her old age, Augusta was learning a lot about being a mother.

But rationalizing that Sam wasn't biologically one of her children, she had just the opening necessary. Watching the waves break along the sands of Firefly Beach, she cleared her throat and straightened her spine.

"What did she say?" Augusta demanded as he came out the door.

"Well, she can't have dinner tonight."

"Tell me why. She has to have dinner tonight—as an artist, she needs her strength, and as a woman taking care of children, she needs it even more."

"I guess she has other plans," Sam laughed, wind blowing his hair across his face. Augusta wished he would take those glasses off. They made him look too smart, and she knew Dana Underhill would be a sitting duck if only she could see the heart and soul in Sam's golden-green eyes.

"You are far too good-natured," Augusta said, shaking her head. "Don't be too understanding, young man."

"What was I supposed to do, Augusta? Tell her I'm coming no matter what she said?"

"That's what Hugh would have done," she said, thinking of her husband. "And your brother, Joe."

At that, Sam fell silent. He sat in the chair beside Augusta, and together they rocked companionably. She could see the tightness in his face, and her heart broke a little in her chest. Sam wasn't like Hugh or Joe. He was just as strong, but he had a much more gentle way. Augusta didn't want to see him lose it; neither did she want to see him miss his chance.

"You like her, don't you?" Augusta asked.

"I do," he said. When he glanced over, the boyishness was gone from his eyes. His face was weatherbeaten—sun- and windburned, with lines of sadness around his mouth. "You see through me. I came to visit you, but I want to see her too. I've never gotten her out of my mind."

"Just like Joe," Augusta said, marveling as she reached across the space between their chairs and held Sam's hand. "The way he never forgot Caroline. Long love must run in your family."

"I'm thinking it does."

Augusta watched him, the way he was looking east, toward Hubbard's Point. Although she didn't know the Underhills well, she had seen them around town over the years. Their daughters had gone to school together, and Augusta thought she remembered seeing Dana and Lily at some of the Firefly Beach bonfires. Now her gaze drifted east as well, and she thought of how many of her children—biological or not—had found love on this strand of shore.

"Sam?" she asked, still holding his hand.

"Yes?"

"Go for a walk," she said softly. She thought of how many times she and Hugh had walked along that beach, how many times they had kissed with the waves licking their feet.

"Where?" he asked, slowly turning his head so she could see the fire in his green eyes.

"You know, dear," Augusta said, rocking again, looking over the Sound as she thought about Hugh. "You know where."

"She said she doesn't want to have dinner tonight."

"I know." Augusta knew all about Lily Grayson's death last summer, and she could only imagine what her sister—and mother—must be suffering. But Augusta had encountered sudden death herself, and she knew that isolation must sooner or later be broken. "If she needs time and space, you should let her have it. But listen to me, Sam: not too much time, and not too much space."

"What are you saying?"

"Take that walk. See where it brings you, and see whom you see."

"You mean walk to Hubbard's Point?"

Augusta nodded. "Whether you actually talk to her tonight is beside the point. Gestures matter, Sam. Leave your footsteps in the sand, and you just might set something into motion."

"That sounds far too wise to ignore."

"I'm thrilled you see it that way," Augusta said, smiling. "Would you make sure you repeat your impression to my daughters? I'd like them to know a Yale professor considers me wise."

Laughing, Sam kissed her forehead and took the long flight of stone steps down to the beach.

THE GIRLS WERE QUIET. They were lying on separate sofas on opposite sides of the living room while a sea breeze blew through the open windows and twilight left silver and rust-red tracks on the Sound's surface. Dana sat in a chair, sketch pad on her lap, looking at the beach.

A few people were having a late swim. The ice cream man was parked in the sandy lot, waiting for the after-dinner strollers. A lobster boat plied the buoy-dotted bay, pulling pots. Dana breathed slowly, remembering her and Lily's lobster business. They had borrowed their father's dory, taken out a fifteen-pot recreational license, and become lobsterwomen for the summer.

The memory made her smile, and then, because it was so happy, made her skin tingle. Everything brought back thoughts of Lily. When she looked at the ice cream truck, she remembered Lily's favorite flavor: toasted almond. When she saw the lobster boat, she could see her sister grinning, holding a lobster in either hand, heard her laughingly call them messengers from the mermaids.

There, at the end of the beach, she saw a figure coming down the path from Little Beach. Dark and shadowy from the distance, she imagined it might be Lily herself. Coming home to see her, to get her, to take her back to the sea. But the person wasn't Lily at all; it was Sam.

Without taking her eyes off him, Dana reached for the binoculars. The eyepieces pressed to her face, she swept the beach. There he was; the glasses wavered as she got him in sight. He came down the steep trail between the scrub oaks and salt pines. His footing sure, he ambled from the path onto the sand.

She saw that he was wearing jeans and a T-shirt, looking more casual than he had at the gallery. His arms were tan and strong, and she wondered what an oceanographer could possibly have to lift to give him such muscles. Observing him at this distance, knowing he couldn't see her, her heart sped up.

Sam Trevor was a very handsome man. His hair glinted in the

late-day light, as gold as the grass that grew in the marsh. He walked slowly, looking over the water. What was he thinking? she wondered. Had he walked all the way from Firefly Beach?

The idea seemed dangerous and passionate. Although the walk wasn't very long—no more than two or three miles—it was fairly arduous. Dana could picture the rocky promontories he had crossed, the tidal bight—rushing from the swale into the Sound—that he must have jumped.

What was he doing now? Standing still, he turned away from the water to look up the hill. He was staring straight at her house. Ducking slightly in the chair, Dana pushed herself back from the window.

His arms were out, as if he wanted to give her something. Her heart pounding, she tried to imagine what it was. She felt so upset by being there, so broken by Lily's death, she knew she should accept any gift sent her way. Still watching Sam with the glasses, she saw him bend down, pick up a stick.

"What's out there?" Quinn called from across the room.

"Nothing," Dana said, staring at Sam.

"Mom was always keeping track of things with the binos. Birds, fish . . . what is it, an osprey hunting?"

"Probably," Dana said, her throat raw. Lily had sat in this chair, pressed these same field glasses to her eyes. Thinking of the birds Lily had watched, the ospreys she had seen diving for their catches, Dana's eyes filled with tears.

With no ospreys around at the moment, she decided to keep watching Sam. He walked back and forth, making footprints on her beach. Then, using the stick, he seemed to be drawing in the sand. The tide was coming in, and the waves washed over the silvery, hard-packed flats. Straining her eyes, Dana saw that Sam wasn't drawing at all. He had written one letter:

D

Dana's chest ached. It hurt from the inside out, as if her heart had bruised itself beating against her ribs. That old, familiar letter glistened in the sunset light, one straight line with another veering out—curving away, as if in departure, then veering back, as if it had decided to come back home.

D.

So many words began with the letter D. Distance. Death. Deauville. Decision. Determined. Destination: France. And then, of course, there was Dana.

"That osprey catch anything yet?" Quinn asked after another minute.

"Not yet," Dana answered, her voice barely a whisper. Sam had started walking back the way he had come, toward the path to Little Beach and the other beaches beyond. She stared at his broad back, wondered whether, if she ran fast, she could catch up to him. And if she did, what she would say.

Instead, because it was not only easier but the only thing she could think to do, she turned her binoculars on that single letter in the wet and shiny sand, flecks of mica glistening like black stars, and watched it until the waves took it away.

CHAPTER 3

MARTHA UNDERHILL HAD LOVED HER LIFE FOR A LONG time. Born and raised a Connecticut Yankee, she had relatively simple tastes. She drove a Ford. Her favorite meal was clam chowder, baked haddock, and French fries. Although her heart was still in Hubbard's Point, she now lived in Marshlands Condos, eight miles away: This house was too big for her now. She had been married to one man—Jim Underhill, her daughters' father, the love of her life—for thirty-two years, until his death from a stroke.

Jim had been her childhood sweetheart. They had gone all through New Hampton schools together. When he threw her coat up into a tree one snowy January morning in third grade, her grandmother had told her that meant he liked her. He gave her his arrowhead collection and his father's World War I medals. Her mother made her give them back, but already her fate—and their love—were sealed.

Married at twenty-two, they wanted kids right away. They tried and tried, but she couldn't conceive. Her heart hurt once a month when she'd see that rusty red stain, when she'd hear about

Jim's sisters getting pregnant, when she'd see her old school friends pushing baby carriages.

Jim went to war. He was a navigator-bombardier in the 8th Air Force, and he was a great hero. Everyone, especially Martha, was so proud of him. He flew missions over Normandy, Cologne, and Dresden. The losses were terrible, and she spent the whole war with her stomach in a knot. Once he was shot down over occupied France, and he'd parachuted into a tree. Hanging there, dangling from the branches, he had held his breath while a battalion of German soldiers stopped beneath him for a rest.

Martha didn't hear the story for months, during which time she had assumed he was dead. Those were the darkest days of her life. Lying in bed, the curtains closed, she would press her chest, trying to keep her heart from breaking out. She had thought she was a widow, and the word itself was terrible, but the worst part was imagining a whole life without Jim, without the babies she had not stopped hoping they would have.

Then, one miraculous day, the phone rang, and the sorrow ended: Jim's voice came over the wire, direct from a hospital in London. "I'm safe, darling. I'm alive, I love you, and I'm coming home."

Come home he did. They got started right away, back on their plan to have children, and when six months had passed without success, something shifted in Martha. What difference did it make anyway? They had each other. No one had ever loved a man the way she loved Jim, and she felt absolutely cherished as his wife. His roofing business was booming, and without children, Martha spent time beachcombing, collecting shells and driftwood.

Sometimes she made things. It seemed like more than a hobby, but she felt pretentious calling it art. Jim encouraged her, and after a while she began to show her work in local craft fairs. When they inherited Martha's family place at Hubbard's Point, she began selling her beach sculptures through the women's club, at their annual clambake and Fourth of July celebrations. Her friends paid good money for her pieces: driftwood draped with old net decorated with sea glass, periwinkles, razor clams, and dried seaweed. Although her sculptures had a certain sameness, they sold as quickly as she could make them. To her amazement, she became known around the beach as "the artist."

"My work is my baby," she used to say when asked if she minded not having children. It never ceased to amaze her how forward some people could be, but that response seemed to do the trick. She had even started believing it herself—most of the time, anyway. Certain sights—a happy family on the boardwalk, for example, or a mother teaching her children to swim—could stop her in her tracks. She'd get a headache, or a feeling of exhaustion would overtake her, and she'd have to go up to the cottage and lie down until the pain passed.

And then it happened: After fifteen years of marriage, when they were thirty-seven years old, Martha and Jim Underhill conceived a child. One early spring day, she experienced morning sickness for the first time. The nausea was overwhelming. She subsisted on saltines and ginger ale, delivered like clockwork by Jim. If anything, he was more traumatized than she. Since the rubber cement she used to glue her work made her even sicker, she stopped making sculptures.

Nine months later, her true purpose in life was revealed: to be Dana's mother. How happy Martha felt, how content and awed and fulfilled. She put sculpting on the back burner. Once in a while she'd start something, but she found she'd rather be with Dana. All she wanted to do was be a mother, love her baby, have another.

She had Lily exactly two years and two months after Dana was born.

Now, rocking on the porch, Martha stared out at Long Island Sound and thought back to that time. Those first few years, she hardly sculpted at all. Sometimes it bothered her, the way she poured all her love and creativity into her family, and she'd begin a new piece.

It was always so hard to finish. The girls would want to play, or Martha would have errands to do, or she and Jim would finally get a little time to themselves. When the girls proved to have artistic talent, Martha nurtured it with all she had. She was a mother of daughters, and when some clod at the post office asked whether she wished one of them was a boy, she'd look him straight in the eye, smile, and say, "Oh, no."

If only she had had them younger, she thought now, rocking and gazing across the half-moon bay at Little Beach. Perhaps if she weren't so ancient, she wouldn't find everything so impossible to bear. Now the most consistent joy in her life was her shar-pei, Maggie.

Martha Underhill was seventy-eight years old. When she looked in the mirror, she hardly recognized her own face. She had lines and wrinkles, her chin line was no longer sharp, her eyes had lost their sparkle. Those eyes frightened her: They looked shell-shocked, as if she had been through the worst life has to offer.

Which, of course, she had.

Looking back over her life, she could think of five terrible, horrible times. Those weeks when she'd known Jim was missing in action, presumed dead; her mother's death; her father's; the shocking loss of Jim; and oh . . . she could hardly stand to think of it even now.

Losing Lily.

Lily Rose Underhill Grayson. Martha's second baby, her simpler daughter, the light of everyone's life. Lily had made her family smile just to see her. Dana had loved her from the first minute; Martha and Jim had been prepared for sibling rivalry, but it had never materialized. Dana and Lily were water girls, always on the beach together, inspiring each other to swim farther, sail faster. Martha believed it was because of Lily that Dana had turned to painting water—cross-sections of the ocean, because she and her sister were of the sea. They had loved it, and it had taken Lily away.

Rocking softly with Maggie at her side, Martha closed her eyes tight. Clouds scudded across the June sky. Down on the beach Dana and Allie walked the tide line; Quinn was nowhere to be seen. Knuckles to her mouth, Martha tried to keep from crying out. The pain wasn't in her hand, wasn't even in her hip: so deep inside, she couldn't begin to say where it was.

Lily, her easy child, was gone. Her ashes, along with Mark's, rested in an urn on the mantel. Turning her head, Martha looked at it now. The container was brass and square. It was solid, utilitarian, with nothing decorative about it, meant to hold the ashes just long enough to dispose of them. Quinn, however, refused to entertain such a possibility.

The little girls, Martha's granddaughters, seemed so precarious, as if they had parachuted into an enemy tree of their own. If Martha's arthritis weren't so severe, she could continue to live with them. She could hold them together, let them stay in their home.

Dana was determined to take them away. What would she do with two small girls to think about? Martha knew she thought she was acting in their best interest, that moving them away would be less painful in the end. Dana would show them France, she would take them on weekends to Paris and Rome and Dublin. It would be a life beyond their wildest dreams.

At that, staring down the gentle hillside at the small white beach, Martha dropped her hands into her lap. Maggie jumped up to lick her fingers. Didn't Dana know that the best dreams weren't always wildest? That Connecticut could be just as beautiful as Europe, that a shingled cottage could be twice as magical as any stone house? That love didn't have to be wild or dangerous or with a man who didn't love her enough back?

And that children needed their grandmother at least as much as she needed them?

"WHAT'S FRANCE LIKE?" Allie asked, collecting shells.

"Like a painting," Dana said. "Beauty everywhere you look."

"But it's beautiful here," Allie said.

"Yes, it is. But don't you want to see somewhere different?"

"I guess so. Not Quinn though."

"She'll love it once we get there," Dana said. "You can have the same rooms as when you visited—you liked those, didn't you? You liked being able to see the English Channel, and Quinn couldn't believe the house was almost four hundred years old. I'll fix up a section in the barn so you can have your own studios."

"Studios?"

"For art," Dana said. "You're both wonderful painters."

"Quinn doesn't paint anymore. She says she hates it. She hates everything."

"Don't worry about her," Dana said softly. Hearing the strain in Allie's voice, she put her arm around her shoulders. She remembered times she'd been worried about Lily: when she had the measles, for example, and after she got a D in algebra two quarters in a row. "We'll take care of her."

"I want her to be okay," Allie said. "But sometimes I don't think she is."

"Where is she now?"

"Little Beach, probably. That's where she goes."

Dana nodded. She had gone there, too, when she'd wanted to hide from her family and friends. The beach was quiet just then, hardly any people to be seen. It was only June, and some school systems, unlike Black Hall, were still in session. Some families came down for weekends, others wouldn't return to Hubbard's Point until full summer. The Underhills had winterized their cottage and lived there year-round.

Dana had a pack of childhood friends, most of them with kids of their own. Marnie McCray—now Marnie Campbell—especially. One of the girls across the street, she had two daughters, and she would know what to do. But Marnie and her girls hadn't yet arrived for summer at the Point, so Dana decided to follow her own instinct; telling Allie to go up to the house, Dana went off in search of Quinn.

QUINN HEARD HER coming through the path. Huddled behind the big rock, writing in her diary, Quinn heard twigs breaking and leaves rustling, and she knew: It was Aunt Dana.

They had always had a magical bond. Long-lasting, as long as Quinn had been alive, they had been connected in ways they couldn't explain. Quinn loved her mother and father: no mistake about that. But the first face she remembered, the first eyes she'd ever seen peering into hers, were Aunt Dana's.

There was an explanation, of course. The minute her mother went into labor, she'd put out a search party for her sister, painting at Squibnocket Point; Aunt Dana had hopped into the first car and driven down-island to the hospital in time to be Quinn's first official visitor.

As the years went by, Aunt Dana had spoiled her like crazy. She had bought her all sorts of wild presents—French clothes and white boots and toys no other kid had and a pink bike and a tiger kitten. The minute she'd walk into the house, Quinn would vault off the closest surface into her arms, and not be put down for the rest of her aunt's stay.

There had been times—sleepy, content times—looking into her aunt's face, when Quinn had called her Mommy. The mistake would last for just a second; Quinn would know it was from the warm bottle and the soft blanket and the smell of her aunt's paint and the old, familiar look in her clear blue eyes.

Dana had taught her how to sail. Her mother too, of course, but especially Aunt Dana. Quinn had admired her aunt's instinctive ability to find the wind, and she'd wanted it for herself. She had latched on to her mental toughness, her sense of direction, her spirit of competition.

"Quinn!" her aunt called now. "I know you're here."

Flattening herself against the big rock, Quinn tried to blend into the shadows and sand. Waves splashed her feet. Holding her plastic-wrapped diary under one arm, she furiously dug a deep hole just above the tide line.

"Quinn . . ."

Stepping out from behind the rock, Quinn came face-to-face with Aunt Dana. Just seeing her made Quinn's chest tighten and stomach clench. Quinn looked down at her own feet, counting ten toes over and over. She had a tidal wave in her heart, and if she wasn't careful, it was going to drag her into the sea, all the way past everywhere else to Japan.

"I thought you might be here," Aunt Dana said steadily.

"Why?"

"Because it's where I used to come."

"It's where everyone comes," Quinn said, making her voice cold.

Aunt Dana looked around. She raised her eyebrows, making

her eyes wide. One thing about her, she had a deadpan sense of humor and liked to make her nieces laugh, and Quinn knew what she was going to say an instant before she spoke. "I don't see anyone else here," she said.

"That's because it's only June, and not everyone's at the Point for the summer yet."

"So we have it all to ourselves."

"For three more days."

"We're not leaving forever, Quinn. We'll come back a lot—as often as you want."

"How about every day? That's how often I want."

Aunt Dana took a step forward, and Quinn sat on the hidden-diary spot, just like a hen hatching eggs. "You know this is hard for all of us," Aunt Dana said. "I've never been a mother. I don't know what to do, I'm just trying to do my best."

"You're still not."

"Not what?"

"A mother."

Aunt Dana looked stung. She blinked, as if she couldn't believe what Quinn had just said. Her blue eyes looked fairly wild, and her silver-brown hair blew across her face in the sea breeze. Brushing it away, she composed herself.

"Your parents made me your guardian, you know?"

Quinn didn't reply or blink.

"When I first found out, after I got over the shock and the nightmare—well, you know, I thought, oh, I'll move back to Hubbard's Point. I'll pack up my studio and live there."

Quinn tilted her head, interested.

"It's my home, after all. I know every inch of this place. I learned how to paint here. My nieces won't have to get used to somewhere new. I'll be closer to my mother. It's the best thing for everyone."

"So what happened?" Quinn asked, her voice quivering. The high tide was getting even higher. Just a few more inches, and the next wave would reach the spot where she'd buried her diary.

"Lily and I loved this spot," Aunt Dana said, looking around. To Quinn's dismay, her aunt's eyes filled with tears. "We loved the beach so much. Everywhere I look, I see stories. God, I hope no one ever builds here. Over there"—Aunt Dana glanced up at the soft white sand leading into the woods—"the story of our family picnics—how some Sundays Mom would fill up a basket with sandwiches and lemonade, and we'd all come over here to eat and swim. And over there, where Lily and I used to go spearfishing for blackfish. And back there, in the woods, how we used to go looking for the slave grave. And how we used to catch blue shells in the creek. And how we'd sail past on our Blue Jay."

"Those are good memories," Quinn said.

"They were good when she was here," Dana said, her eyes hard. "But with her gone, I can hardly stand them. I'm afraid I'll go crazy if everyplace I look reminds me of her."

Quinn felt her veins and arteries tighten so much, there wasn't a bit of blood running through her body. She knew exactly what Aunt Dana meant. But for her, the fear was quite opposite: She was afraid if she left Hubbard's Point, those memories would slip away and she'd never get them back again.

"Quinn?"

"You sound like Mom."

"How?"

"The way you're talking about change—hoping no one ever builds here. She hated when things she loved changed, disappeared. That's how she was about places. She was protector of the land—like here at Hubbard's Point, at the Vineyard."

"Do you think that's bad?"

"Sometimes. You can't keep everything the way it used to be. You just can't."

"I know, Quinn. But you can feel upset when it changes."

Quinn clenched her fists, hoping Aunt Dana didn't notice. She thought of the big fights that erupted that last month, knowing they had had to do with change.

Not speaking, she watched her aunt climb on top of the big rock. Aunt Dana opened her arms to catch the wind blowing in off the Sound. She stood there with her arms out for such a long time, the waves did come up a few more inches. Digging down, Quinn retrieved her diary. Hastily shoving it into her waistband, she glanced up to see if Aunt Dana had noticed.

Her aunt was oblivious. Quinn might not even have been there. Aunt Dana was hugging the wind, almost dancing with it, moving around and around the top of the rock. She seemed to be gazing out to sea, down the beach, into the wooded path—seeing scenes and stories of her life with Quinn's mother, invisible to Quinn or anyone else.

The strange thing was, Quinn was seeing scenes of her own. This spot on earth belonged to her and her family. It was theirs, and there could never be another place like it. Quinn saw the rocks where she and her father had gathered mussels, the patch of poison ivy where Allie had gotten such a bad case, the reeds their mother painted every season, across the cove the Point where their house was located. And at her feet, on the rock nearest the water, was the secret gift she always brought and always left.

"I'm not going to France," Quinn said, palms pressing against the diary.

"I'm not staying here," Aunt Dana said, staring over the water like the figurehead on a ship.

CHAPTER 4

DURING THE LAST DAYS, SAM TREVOR HAD PRESIDED over study sessions and final exams and attended an end-of-term faculty party. He e-mailed Joe, and various colleagues in Nova Scotia and Woods Hole, finalizing plans for the summer. One night he went to the movies with Jenny Soames. But in the back of his mind, the whole time, was the uneasy feeling of something left undone. He could practically hear Augusta telling him what to do.

So on Thursday, the day Dana and the girls were scheduled to leave for France, Sam found himself driving out to Hubbard's Point. The sky was blue and clear. With the windows open, fresh air circulated through the van. July was days away, real summer right around the corner. School was out for another year, and Sam should have been feeling lighthearted.

Instead, his insides flipped, as if he were in the middle of final exams himself. Traffic on I-95 was heavy. He had Augusta's voice in his head, telling him to pass everyone on the right. He inched across the Saltonstall Bridge, wondering what time Dana's flight left. His heart was a mako banging into the shark cage, trying to get inside. What if he missed her?

Well, what if he did?

He had to ask himself the question. Here he was, a college professor, barging into someone else's life. He understood the student-teacher connection, how students came and went over the years. He was just another kid from her past. He'd never even met her nieces. But driving along, he pictured Lily's face at the theater that night, and he knew he had to see Dana again. She had told him he didn't understand what it was like for her, but he thought he did.

Sam really thought he did understand.

"EVERYONE READY?" DANA asked, checking her watch for the third time in five minutes.

"Where's Kimba?" Allie asked in a panic. "I can't find him anywhere."

"Stay calm," Martha said. "We'll find him."

"What a baby," Quinn growled. "Still dragging that scrap of feline around."

"He's not a scrap!" Allie trembled.

"Sure he is. His stuffing's been lost for years, and you've practically rubbed the fur right off him. Gray, Allie! He's all gray, not bright orange the way he's supposed to be."

"Shut up!" Allie screamed, flying at Quinn. "Don't say that about Kimba! Mommy gave him to me. How dare you, how dare you?"

"Get her off me," Quinn howled. "She's messing my hair. Get her the hell off my hair!"

"Girls," Martha breathed, trying to push them apart as Dana got her arms around Quinn's waist and yanked from behind. The girl's brown hair, twisted into sixty-three kinks, each held in place by a covered elastic band and clenched in a death grip by Allie's fists, smelled like sweat and salt water. Dana wondered when her niece had last washed her hair, but she realized that now wasn't the time to ask.

"Ow," Quinn screamed, tears flying from her eyes. "Get her off me!"

"Take it back about Kimba," Allie wept, holding tighter. "Take it back, say he's not a feline scrap."

"You want her to let go or not?" Dana whispered into Quinn's ear as she and her mother tried to pry them apart.

"He's not a goddamn feline scrap," Quinn screeched, and Allie instantly let go, collapsing to the floor in a sobbing puddle of misery.

"I have to find him," Allie cried. "I can't leave without him."

"Of course you can't," Martha said, drawing herself up and offering Allie her hand. "Come on. Let's search the house. You probably left him under the covers when you got up this morning."

"I already looked there," Allie said, letting her grandmother pull her up. Dana and Quinn watched them climb the stairs.

The living room was bright with sunlight. It beamed down the Point, striking the rocks, bouncing off the water. Many years before, when her parents had winterized the cottage, the old sash windows in front had been replaced by modern sliders. A broader view and fantastic light compensated for the loss in charm. Still holding Quinn from behind, Dana was moved by the scene.

"That's what you have to look forward to if you take us to France," Quinn said, pulling away and brushing herself off. Several elastics had come off in the melee, and she set to fixing her braids.

"What's that?" Dana asked.

"Allie turning into a hysterical mental case ten times a day."

"Hmm. I didn't think she was out of line."

"Excuse me?"

"I seem to remember an Ariel doll," Dana said, handing her an elastic that had shot onto the sofa. "She was your Kimba. You wouldn't put her down, couldn't go to sleep without her."

Quinn slid her a slit-eyed gaze. She seemed about to speak, but instead she clamped her jaw tighter and kept working on her hair.

"That was your favorite movie. *The Little Mermaid*—you'd watch it all day if we let you. Then one day your mom and I went to the New London Mall, and what do you think we saw in the card shop window?"

"Cards," Quinn replied in her best sarcastic tone.

"Ariel," Dana said steadily.

Concentrating on repairing her braids, Quinn flinched. Dana saw it but made no move to embrace her or encourage a response. She knew her niece was on the edge: of leaving childhood, of leaving the country, of leaving home. Wishing Lily would inspire her with the right message, Dana held her breath and waited for it to come.

Whatever the wise words might have been, they were too late. Before Dana could say anything more, Quinn let out a fiery exhalation and ran two stairs at a time into her room. As Dana stared at the mantelpiece, her gaze traveled unfocused over photos, shells, the broken Atmos clock, one of her mother's old driftwood sculptures. Something was missing, but she couldn't make out what it was.

She was too busy thinking about the last moments with Quinn, wishing she had said something better, something wiser. Checking her watch, she walked into the kitchen to wait for the car and wonder why her decision to leave suddenly felt so wrong.

QUINN FLOPPED ON her bed, on her stomach, pointing the remote at her TV. Would she have her own TV in France? Dubious. Seething from what had just happened downstairs, she clicked the button and started the movie.

So Aunt Dana thought *The Little Mermaid* was her favorite movie? Well, think again. Pressing rewind to the best part, she let the tape begin to play.

Silence. A long corridor. First a shot of a man's big feet. The sound of his breathing. Shadows moving in clear Sunday-morning light. A woman's whisper: "Get ready. Here she comes!"

Quinn's heart began to pound. The suspense was killing her, as it always did. The man reached for the woman's hand—there! You could see their fingers clasp right on the screen, which meant he was holding the video camera with one hand. "Come on, honey," the woman said, out loud now, pleasure and excitement audible in her voice. "Quinny! In here!"

Six more seconds: six, five, four, three, two, one—and then, bursting on the scene, the star of the movie. Aquinnah Jane Grayson! Baby extraordinaire. No teeth, no hair, the meanest crawl you ever did see. Arms scrabbling and feet kicking out back, she makes her way down the corridor. Grinning at her parents, she's the baby who ate Hubbard's Point.

"Da, da, da, da," the baby gurgled.

"She knows my name," the man said proudly.

"Oh, she does," the woman said, scooping the baby up into her arms. Now the camera was on both of them, Sunday-morning light pouring over the mother's yellow hair and the baby's hairless head, over the newspapers scattered across the bare wood floor, over Long Island Sound sparkling out the window.

"Da-da-da," the baby laughed, reaching for her father's face, bumping the video camera and making it shake.

"Say 'Mommy,' " her father said, with so much love in his voice. "Come on, sweet baby. Say 'Mommy' so your mother won't feel left out."

"I don't feel left out." Her mother smiled, her eyes filled with love. Quinn paused the video. She stared at the grainy screen, memorizing every feature on each face.

"Mommy," she whispered now, just in case.

Down the hall, in real, nonmovie time, came the sound of her sister crying. Grandma was trying to comfort her, saying that when she found Kimba, she'd send him by overnight mail to France. "I can't leave without him," Allie was screaming. "I can't, I can't."

Quinn tried to breathe. She started up the movie again, but its magic, for the time being, was lost. This could be the last time for many months she would ever see her favorite movie again. Katy Horton, her best friend, had told her that American videos didn't work in France. She said that it was a matter of money, like most things in the world. The French wanted you to buy their videos, so their VCRs were incompatible.

With Allie wailing, Quinn felt as if her insides might melt. Her sister's cries went straight to her stomach. It was all she could do to hold herself back, from running down the hall to make everything better, but this was for Allie's own good. Rolling off her bed, she practically fell onto her suitcase. Unzipping one corner, she reached her hand inside and felt around.

She pulled them both out at the same time.

Her Ariel doll with her bikini shell-top and mermaid's tail, with her auburn hair twisted—not unlike Quinn's own—into as many braids as she could make, and Kimba—or what was left of him—Allie's beloved scrap of feline, of baby lion. Lying on her side, she buried her face in the two toys, letting the smell of her and Allie's childhood fill her nose.

As Aunt Dana came upstairs to join the search, Quinn smelled herbs and salt, fall leaves and apple cider, watercolors and wooden boats, her mother and her father. Aunt Dana sounded worried: The car wasn't there yet.

"Have you called to check on it?" Grandma asked.

"I'll do that now," Aunt Dana said.

"I can't leave without him," Allie cried.

See, Quinn knew that. Allie was nothing if not loyal. They each had their bottom lines, objects of love they couldn't leave behind. Allie's was Kimba, but Quinn's was a good deal more complicated than that. She wouldn't want to go away without Ariel, but if forced, she could survive. Other things, maybe not.

For the greater good, Quinn held on to Kimba. Aunt Dana couldn't be so heartless that she'd make Allie leave without him. Quinn was banking on her aunt's heart, but if that failed, she'd fall back on her sister's piercing screams. No sane person would attempt to fly to France with those sounds in her ears.

Just then the door flew open, and Allie ran in. As if she were a bloodhound and her nose had the scent, she threw herself onto Quinn's body. Snatching Kimba from her sister's grip, Allie held him up in triumph.

"I knew it!" she yelled. "I knew it was you!"

"Quinn, I'm very disappointed in you," Grandma said from the doorway.

"You jerk," Quinn whispered to Allie. "It was going to be perfect. Now we have to go!"

"Huh?" Allie asked, cuddling Kimba in pure rapture.

"Well, we have a problem," Aunt Dana said, frowning as she joined Grandma in the doorway. "The car service messed up. They have my order, it's right on the books, and they confirmed it when I called last night, but somehow the dispatcher forgot to send the car out today."

"Yes!" Quinn said, pumping her arm.

"Mom, can you drive us?" Aunt Dana asked.

"Honey, those New York airports make me crazy," Grandma said. "All that traffic."

Checking her watch, Aunt Dana frowned. Quinn didn't want to see her upset, but suddenly she felt a lifting from within, as if the sun were rising and rainbows were pouring down. It was going to be okay, they weren't going to leave after all, her parents had heard her prayers. Aunt Dana was saying something about local cabs, super-saver nonrefundable tickets, not enough time, and Quinn felt herself starting to smile.

When Allie, looking out the window, said the bad-magic words: "He's here."

"Who?" everyone asked at once.

"The driver, I guess. Someone I don't recognize, coming up the hill. We must be going after all," Allie said, as Quinn felt the happiness fizzle out of her.

THE MINUTE DANA came to the door, Sam saw the tension in her body and uncertainty in her eyes. The two children stood behind her, looking worried and angry, with an older woman a few steps behind them. The house was small and plain, its gardens overgrown. But the site had one of the best views Sam had ever seen, anywhere in the world.

"I had to come," he said, staring through the screen door at Dana.

She stood in a cluttered kitchen. Sam had the impression of books and shells and paintings on the wall and copper pans hanging from an overhead rack—it was busy, real, filled with life. Dana didn't reply, and suddenly Sam thought: She doesn't want to leave.

"I wanted to say good-bye."

"We're not *going* anywhere," the elder of the two kids said.

"It's been a rough day," Dana said, her eyes welling up. "No one wants to do what we're doing."

"The taxi didn't come," the same girl said. "That's not our fault."

"No one wants to?" Sam asked, catching Dana's words.

She shook her head. "But it's not as easy as all that. I bought the tickets. They were expensive. And aside from the fact we might not want to go, there's the other fact that we can't stay here. At least I can't—"

"Are you driving us?" the younger girl asked, smiling in a pure, lighthearted way that made Sam think exactly of Lily.

"Shut up, idiot," the angry, braided girl exclaimed.

Sam wished they wouldn't go. He hadn't seen Dana in a long time, but he was very glad to be seeing her just then. There were things he'd like to tell her, others that he wanted to learn about her life. Old friends were rare enough, and when Sam reencountered one like Dana, he was in no great hurry to let her go.

"To the airport?" the little sister asked, still with that smile.

"You can't ask him to drive us," the older sister said, incredulous at the very suggestion.

Sam certainly hadn't planned this, but the idea wasn't bad at all. If they had to go, at least he'd have a little extra time with Dana. "I'd be happy to," he said. "If that's what your aunt wants, I will."

"Sam, you don't have to—"

"I know," he said, nodding as the idea took hold and he heard Augusta's voice in his head, egging him on. "But I'd like to—I really would. I mean, how else will you get to the airport?"

"Good point," Dana said, starting to smile.

"Let him," the younger girl said.

"You're a jerk," the older one hissed at her sister.

"Okay, Sam. We'll take you up on it," Dana said. "Come on, everyone—get your bags."

Sam pitched in, lifting suitcases and canvas bags. He noticed how the older child grabbed her suitcase and refused to let him near, but he let that pass. He was too busy congratulating himself for driving out here today, too busy feeling thankful to Augusta for pushing him along.

THEY WERE RIGHT ON TIME. Sam knew his way to JFK, and he explained that he had made the trip before to pick up and see off Joe and Caroline. The blue van bounced over the potholes; it was a camper, with Sam's tent and other equipment stowed in back. Quinn seemed intrigued, but she had too much invested in being angry to ask any questions.

Dana sat in the front seat, wondering whether she was doing the right thing. While Sam asked the girls questions about the beach and tidal pools and whether they'd ever thought of being oceanographers, Dana tried to keep her heart from beating out of her chest.

Gazing out the window, she watched Connecticut slide by. She loved this state. Her sister had lived here for most of her life, and Dana had returned as often as she could. The low hills, the dark green thickets of mountain laurel, the stone bridges over the Merritt Parkway: She could honestly say it was the landscape of her heart.

Yet she had always felt the pull to travel away. California, Canada, Greece, Italy, France: new and different oceans, coastlines, houses. Lily had always teased her, told her she was just afraid.

"Afraid of what?" Dana would ask.

"Afraid of settling down," Lily had said. "You're afraid your life will look like mine."

In a way, her sister had been right. Hearing her niece's silence in the backseat, Dana's heart ached. Being their aunt had always seemed so easy. Lavish them with gifts and attention, then send them back to their parents. As much as she loved her family, her place at Hubbard's Point, she had always enjoyed the freedom to leave.

Painting was her gift. The ability to see beauty and meaning in life, allow it to flow through her and onto the canvas. With it came certain responsibilities; where other women put their husbands and children first, Dana did the same with her art. She had no husband, no kids. *When you have a gift,* she remembered telling her own protégé, *you have to sacrifice a lot of what you once might have wanted very much.* Jonathan.

"What's Honfleur like?" Sam asked now.

"It's wonderful," Dana said as much for her nieces' sake as for his. "It's an ancient port, with tall, narrow houses on three sides of the harbour. Sidewalk cafés where you can eat crepes and drink apple cider, hillsides filled with orchards. The light there is incredible, the best any artist could hope for."

"We're not artists," Quinn reminded her.

"What are you?" Sam asked, looking into the rearview mirror.

"Excuse me?"

"If you're not an artist, what are you?"

"How am I supposed to know?" she replied. "I'm only twelve."

Sam laughed. "With hair like that, you know who you are."

"What about my hair?" Irate, she leaned forward.

"Nothing. I like it. But you can't tell me it's not there for a reason. Like, when I was a kid, I didn't mind wearing glasses."

"Glasses? What do they have to do with anything?"

"Well, I wanted to be a scientist. Hate to say it, but I thought glasses made me look the part. Half the time now I want to trade them in for contacts, and I sometimes do, but that's another story."

Glancing over, Dana looked at Sam. He drove easily, as if he liked doing it. His hands were very big, the size she'd expect for someone as tall as he—he must be six foot three, she figured. He wore the same style of glasses she remembered from when she first met him—round wire-rims. Behind them, his eyes were hazel. Looking over, he caught her watching him and smiled.

"He did look like a scientist when he was a kid," Dana said.

"You knew him when he was a *kid*?" Quinn asked, disbelief in her voice.

"Younger than you," Sam said.

"My age?" Allie asked.

"Eight," Sam said. "I knew them both. Dana and your mother."

Silence filled the van and grew. Dana heard the pounding of both girls' hearts, and although she might have bet otherwise, it was Quinn who spoke first.

"You knew our mother."

"Yes, I did."

"How?"

"She taught me sailing," Sam said. "She and your aunt."

"You sail?" Allie asked.

"Yeah," Sam said, sliding a glance over at Dana.

"You do?" she asked.

Sam nodded. "From that summer on, I've never stopped. Last year I bought a Cape Dory, and I live onboard. When you come back from France for a visit, I'll take you all out."

"I don't sail anymore," Quinn said loudly. "I used to, but now I don't."

"Me neither," Allie said.

"Oh," Sam said. Dana saw him redden slightly, and she knew he was thinking of Lily. She could see he felt sorry to have brought it up, and it made her realize what a very nice young man he had become.

"I'd like to go out on your boat," Dana said.

"You would?" Sam asked, turning to her quickly, a wide grin transforming his face.

"Yes. I'd like to check on your progress. Make sure you remember everything Lily and I taught you."

"You two were tough," Sam said. "We all thought you were so nice, but one sloppy jibe and you'd have us doing drills all afternoon."

"I'm still tough." Dana smiled. "Just ask my students in France. It's not all painting over there, you know. I still teach sailing, and when someone jibes when I say tack, forget it. I'm a brute." But she thought: It's no painting over there. It had been so long since she had picked up a brush.

How does an artist know why her painting has stopped working?

Is it preferable to analyze, pull the whole thing apart bit by bit, lay the elements out to better understand them? Or should she put on blinders, refuse to look at anything at all, curl up and wait for inspiration to return? Glancing back, she wondered whether her painting would come back with the girls there, whether she was wrong to hope they might become her muses.

"Well, you and Lily taught us to sail right," Sam said. "That's all I can say."

"They taught us right too," Quinn said.

Allie laughed, and Dana relaxed. The ride was getting easier. The girls' fear and anger weren't so palpable. Maybe she was doing the right thing after all. And then Quinn kicked the back of Dana's seat so hard, she felt it in her spine.

Sam jammed on the brakes, but Dana gestured for him to just keep driving. Although Quinn didn't speak, Dana knew what she was thinking: If Lily was such a good sailing teacher, why hadn't she been a better sailor herself? How had she drowned that clear July night with her own husband in their own boat?

The rest of the ride to JFK felt uneasy, and Dana wanted it over with. Once they got on the plane, she told herself, she'd be able to handle things better. The kids would be distracted by the flight, by the movie. She had chosen three seats right over the wing, for stability. Dana would sit in the middle, and both girls could rest their heads on her shoulders. . . .

When they got to the airport, Sam drove into short-term parking. Dana would have expected him to drop them off at the door, but she felt strangely grateful to have his company a little longer. He carried their luggage, except for Quinn's. She wouldn't let him, or anyone, touch her bag.

At the check-in counter, Quinn refused to put it on the scale.

"It's a carry-on," she insisted.

"The plane will be crowded," Dana explained. "Why not just check it here, so we can go duty free shopping without lugging it around?"

"I want to lug it," Quinn said, her eyes wild. "Daddy used to take it on business trips, and he said it was *carry-on*. If it was good enough for him to carry on, it's good enough for me! Easy on and easy off, he always said. It's regulation size! It has wheels and a handle! So if I want to lug it—"

"It is regulation size," Sam said steadily, as if Quinn had just stated the most reasonable request possible. "Looks like carry-on to me . . ."

"Fine," Dana said quickly. "No problem."

She sighed, shuddering with the force of her niece's emotion. She hadn't realized that the worn black suitcase was sacred, that Mark had used it on his frequent trips. She watched Sam bend over, admiring the case's construction. Quinn pointed out the wheels, and she let Sam test the retractable handle.

"Excellent luggage," he said.

"Very," Quinn said, her lower lip quivering as it had when she was a baby, when she'd be overtired or frustrated, when she felt close to crying. Dana wanted to hug her, to look her in the eye and remind her that they had traveled together before. But it seemed the child couldn't raise her gaze. She stared at the old suitcase, at the place where her father had gripped the handle, as if she could bring his hand into focus.

Hesitating, filled with doubt, Dana heard their flight called over the loudspeaker.

"Well," Sam said, "that's you."

"Ohhh," Allie said, looking into Sam's eyes as if he could save them. "I would sail with you, maybe," she said. "If we didn't have to go."

"Maybe someday," he said.

"It's time," Dana said.

Sam walked beside her, straight toward the security gate. She liked the feeling she had with him by her side, and that surprised her.

"Have a good flight," he said, looking at her with such warmth in his hazel eyes that she suddenly felt everything just might be okay.

"We will," she said. "Thank you so much for driving us. I appreciate it more than you can know."

He nodded. They hesitated for a minute, and then Sam reached forward to hug her. It lasted only a second, but she gripped his arms and felt some of his strength flow into her. Standing back from Sam, she flashed a reassuring smile at her stony-faced nieces.

"Come on, you two," she said. "We're off to France."

"Try not to get too excited," Quinn muttered.

Aware of Sam watching them, Dana shepherded the girls forward. They waited in line, behind other travelers to France and elsewhere. When the time came, the people slid their belongings onto the conveyor belt. As the X ray picked up every image, Dana and her nieces walked through the metal detector. She was one step closer to France, her studio.

With one last wave to Sam, she became aware of the inspectors opening Quinn's bag. At first, assuming the action was routine, she wasn't concerned. But then she saw Sam step forward, alarm on his face.

"Is there a problem?" Dana asked, walking over.

Quinn went pure white, rushing forward to throw herself onto her father's suitcase. "Leave that alone," she gasped, ripping the officer's hands off the bag. "Don't touch that, goddammit."

"Move away from the table," he ordered.

"Give it to me!" Quinn pleaded.

"What's in there?" one man asked.

"They think it's an explosive," someone in line exclaimed, and the buzz of voices grew sharp and loud.

"Would you care to explain this?" asked a female guard, slim and Asian, who bore a shocking resemblance to Monique.

"Get your fucking hands off it," Quinn yelled.

Dana's hands went to her mouth. As the inspectors frowned and began to examine more carefully the large metal box they had taken from Quinn's bag, Dana walked forward and slid her arms around her niece.

"Sweetheart, Quinny," Dana said, her voice shaking. "It's okay. Don't worry."

"Mommy and Daddy," Quinn gasped.

"Grandma will kill you when she finds out you took it," Allie said.

"We weren't ready," Quinn said as if hypnotized. "We weren't ready to scatter their ashes. How could I just leave them there?"

"Quinn," Dana said softly.

"Ashes?" the customs official frowned. "You mean remains? That's what's in here?"

"Would you please give that to me?" Dana asked, still holding Quinn and facing the woman.

"Lady, you'd better check with France," said someone else in line. "You can't just go bringing someone's ashes over in carry-on luggage!"

"Yes, you can," a woman shared. "I know someone who scattered her husband over the Tuileries. . . ."

"Please, Aunt Dana!" Quinn said, her eyes swimming. "Get it. . . ."

When the Monique-like officer handed the brass container to Dana, she put it straight into Quinn's hands and watched the girl hug it to her chest, head down to hide the tears streaming down her face.

"Move along," the official ordered. "You're cleared to go."

Grabbing her handbag and the girls, Dana heard a loud voice.

"Dana, over here."

It was Sam. He was standing just across the barrier, his eyes wide open, and his hands held out like someone waiting to catch a pass. Her heart steadied slightly, just seeing him still there.

"Aunt Dana," Allie said. "We're going the wrong way."

Quinn just sobbed, holding the brass container.

Dana couldn't quite speak. Looking from one niece to the other, she bent down to see into Quinn's eyes. "Are you okay?" she tried to ask, but Quinn wouldn't look at her.

"Quinn?"

They kept walking against the grain of travelers heading for France.

"We're going to miss the plane," Allie said, sounding anxious.

"I think that's what your aunt has in mind," Sam said quietly as they came around the security gate, and Allie said "oh" as Dana just leaned into Quinn.

Taking Quinn into her arms, making sure not to jostle the brass box, Dana held her only sister's elder daughter and knew her days as a free-wheeling artist were over, that she was in for the ride of her life.

CHAPTER 5

SAM DROVE DANA AND THE GIRLS BACK THE WAY THEY had come. Although the sky was still light, dark shadows fell across the highway. The flight they had just missed would have left at seven p.m. Planes flew overhead on their way to Europe, their vapor trails catching the orange light of sunset. Looking up, Sam wondered which of those flights his passengers should have been on.

"What made you change your mind?" he asked Dana.

She took so long to respond, he thought maybe she hadn't heard. But then she turned fully around to check on the girls. Both were fast asleep, as if even so short a journey had completely exhausted them. They slumped toward each other, Allie's smooth blond head resting on Quinn's tangled brown one.

"Quinn," Dana whispered, staring at her for a few seconds.

Sam waited. He knew exactly what she meant, but he wanted to hear Dana say more, to understand what she was really thinking.

"The look in her eyes when they took everything out of her bag," Dana said quietly, picturing it.

"Not a simple kid," Sam said lightly.

"Not at all," Dana said, a snort escaping somewhere between laughter and tears. "She never has been. Give her six choices, and guaranteed Quinn will pick the hardest way."

"You could have gone, you know."

"What do you mean?"

"You could have passed through. Once the guards knew what they were dealing with, that it wasn't drugs or a bomb, they would have let you go."

"I know," Dana said. "They cleared us."

"So why didn't you let her take the ashes with her, stick to your plan?"

Dana stared out the van window. It was past dusk, and deer were edging out of the woods along the Merritt Parkway. Their eyes glowed in the passing headlights, and they grazed without much apparent fear on the tall grass.

"Because now I know. She needs to be here," Dana said.

"Here?"

Dana nodded. Glancing across the seat, Sam saw that her eyes were wide and alert. Her russet hair, glinting with silver, was stylishly cut. She wore black pants and a jacket, and he thought she looked exactly like an artist bound for Europe.

"In her parents' home," Dana said. "As much as my mother tried to tell me, I had to see for myself. I can't take her away from there right now."

Sam cleared his throat. He had to ask—not to be cruel, but to understand. "Why did you think you could?"

"Because Lily took care of them," Dana whispered.

"Lily—"

"She took care of the girls, and I take care of myself. That's what I'm used to. I didn't think I could stand being at Hubbard's Point, in Lily's house, so I decided not to put myself through it. I thought I could get them to adjust to my way. Kids are so much more flexible, I thought. Until I saw Quinn's face . . ."

Sam nodded. On his own at an early age, he had learned how to carry his own weight, rely on himself for most things. He took what came his way—from Joe and the rest of the world—with gratitude and real joy and not much clue how to work others into the equation. Now, looking over at Dana, he saw her grappling with the same stuff.

They crossed onto I-95 and drove in silence most of the way. Sam turned on the radio. When he was alone, he liked to sing out loud. Now he saw Dana's lips barely moving, and he realized she was used to doing the same thing. She seemed comforted by the music, so he let her listen in peace.

Just past the Connecticut River, he turned onto the shore road, and they drove over the Ibis River, through the Black Hall marshes, and under the train trestle into Hubbard's Point. The small guard's shack—unmanned until the summer people arrived—stood on the side of the road, and Sam saw her nod toward the locked door, as if in silent greeting.

Instead of going home to France, she was coming home to Hubbard's Point. Sam drove up the winding road past empty cottages and groves of oak and pine. As if sensing how near they were to their own beds, Quinn and Allie began to stir. Something made Sam clear his throat and look across the front seat, until he was sure Dana was paying attention.

"You're a good aunt, Dana Underhill," he said in a voice too low for the girls to hear.

"I'm not sure about that," she said, and he noticed her staring at her fingernails with intensity, as if she hated them for not being rimmed with paint. Could artists work just anywhere? She probably did her best painting in France, couldn't wait to get back to it.

"You might not be," he said, "but I am."

Her mother had been loading up her car, preparing to return to the condo, and she looked up as the headlights came down the street. Sam parked at the foot of the hill. In a sleepy voice, Allie said, "Grandma." Quinn said, "Home." Dana said nothing, but she was staring at Sam as if he held the secrets to the universe.

"I'm sure," he said again, more firmly than before. Dana took his words in. Then, nodding, she took a deep breath and opened the van door.

DANA AND HER MOTHER stayed up late drinking tea while the girls played in the yard. Their nap in the car had refreshed them completely, and now they wanted only to run in circles and use their flashlights to draw pictures in the sky. Maggie lay in the cool grass at her mistress's feet, watching the action.

"I realized the minute you drove away," Martha said, "that the box was gone."

"The *minute* we drove away?" Dana asked, trying to picture it.

"Okay, so I wanted to have a word with Lily. I walked over to the mantel, as I've done a hundred times since I've been alone with the girls, to tell her they were in safe hands, flying away with you, and guess what I found. Or didn't find."

"I know," Dana said, sipping tea. "Quinn had it in her luggage."

"Her father's magical, wonderful, mysterious travel bag," her mother said with what sounded like resentment, or at least resignation. Maggie, as if sensing Martha's distress, let out a low growl.

"Do you blame her for using Mark's bag?"

"I'm just saying, if only she knew what Lily thought of her father's trips, she wouldn't be so madly in love with his suitcase."

Dana poured more tea. This was one of those classic moments when she wished Lily were there. It was vintage their-mother. Martha would make a mysterious, slightly—but only slightly— disparaging comment about someone in the family who wasn't there to defend himself, and then, if pressed, would refuse to say more. Just to test her, Dana smiled.

"What did Lily think of Mark's trips?"

"Mmm," her mother said, shrugging. "It doesn't matter now, does it? The point is, you are here. The girls are here. The stars are all out. Summer is going to be fantastic."

"Fantastic!" Allie called, swooping in close enough to pick up her grandmother's word. "Fantastic, fantastic!"

"Summer, summer, summer," Quinn cried, arms out like a gull in flight.

"I like Sam," Allie sang, running in wide circles.

"Sam, Sam, Oceanographer Man," Quinn chimed in.

"Yes," Martha sighed. "What a nice young man for driving you down, but especially for driving you back. I am so unutterably glad you decided to miss that flight."

Dana nodded, watching her barefoot nieces play with mad abandon in the same yard she and Lily had run through many years before. A rabbit—one of the family of rabbits that had lived on Hubbard's Point since before Dana could remember—scampered into Rumer Larkin's yard. Dana watched Maggie taking it all in through deep brown eyes. Velvety brown eyes, so like those of someone Dana knew well.

A vision of Monique flashed across her mind: Part of it felt terrible that a dog's gaze should remind her of that young woman of whom she had once been so fond, whom she had once used as her mermaid model. She thought of Sam, of what he had said about her being a good aunt, and hearing her nieces sing and picturing Monique, she said, "Yes, I think maybe I'm glad we decided to miss it too."

EARLY MORNINGS AT Hubbard's Point were chilly. Dana needed a sweater just to fill the bird feeder and water the herb garden. She walked around the yard, listening to the Point come alive. A school of bait fish had swum into the beach below, and terns and seagulls were working loudly. Allie ate her Cheerios on the top step, humming to herself as she threw cereal to a squirrel. Quinn had left without a word, as she had the four mornings since their thwarted departure, to watch the sunrise from Little Beach.

Dana directed the spray from the hose at the rosemary and thyme plants, stopping to pull weeds. The ashes were back on the mantel. Her mother was back at the condo. Allie hung on to Kimba. Quinn spent nearly every daylight moment outside. Dana thought about her paintings-in-progress, wondering when she would ever get back to France. She and the girls were going through the motions of living together, carrying on as usual, when there was no "usual."

This childhood home of Dana's was most definitely her sister's house. Lily's sheets and towels filled the linen closet. Her pots and pans lined the cabinets. Under the bathroom sink were her pink rubber gloves. Her taste in reading tended toward poetry, mysteries, and self-help. Perhaps that last, more than anything else, had surprised Dana: With her good life, what help had Lily needed?

Lily, unlike Dana, had chosen the path of their childhood. Family life, normal routines, a husband and kids. Art was a selfish profession: Dana had wanted to stay available to her muse as much as possible.

She would go out with men she met, enjoy their company, sometimes long to get closer. Once, with Philip Walker, she had almost gotten it right. They had gone out for eight months, six years ago. He was a lawyer, intrigued by her work. At first, she had been in love with the novelty of a conventional life.

But then she'd be seized by inspiration, stay up all night trying to mix the exact right shade of blue, have to sleep all day and miss the events, whatever they were: the picnic, the sail, dinner with a client, the drive to meet his parents. Philip didn't understand, and she wouldn't have expected him to. No man understood her.

Until Jonathan.

She had avoided artists for so long. Men artists had lives like her own—too focused on their own work to share life with another painter. But Jon Hull had seemed different. At the beginning of their time together, he had made her believe nothing could come between them. He had watched her work and told her she was the most brilliant artist there was. He had told Dana she was his artistic hero.

Not to mention the most beautiful woman in France. He didn't care about women his own age. He never looked twice at French girls. Watching Dana paint in her studio, the blinds slanted to get the right light, Monique lying on the daybed—he'd barely even glanced at the younger woman with her taut brown body curved, posing like a sea nymph. He had seemed—for those months Dana had found herself falling in love with him—to have eyes only for her.

But that seemed like years ago, Dana thought now. The Vietnamese woman was no longer her friend, Jonathan no longer her lover. Trust had been shattered. Dana could hardly stand to look at beautiful young Asian women. She would see men Jon's age and feel shame wash over her, asking herself how she could have been so stupid as to think it could have ever worked.

Watering the herb garden, she wondered whether Lily's shelves contained any self-help book on older women whose boyfriends had gone from fantasizing about their artist's models to sleeping with them. She wondered whether there was any self-help for a woman who had come to hate all twenty-five-year-old women with honey-colored skin and tightly toned bodies.

When the sun had risen high over the bay and the two Brothers north and south—rock islands inhabited only by seagulls—Quinn came home. Moving furtively through the yard, as if she didn't want Dana to notice her, she slipped into the house.

Following Quinn inside, Dana found her looking through the kitchen cupboards. Bright morning sun splashed across the highly polished fir floor. Dana couldn't help remembering the linoleum that had been there when she was young, admiring Lily and Mark for pulling up the old tiles to discover the natural wood beneath.

Growing up on Martha's Vineyard, Mark had been a carpenter. He had apprenticed with a builder, become one himself. Lily had loved his work—no one had ever been so turned on, watching a man swing a hammer, wield a level. But when he had become a developer, she started getting nervous. Lily loved nature. She adored woods and fields. Why build new houses over beautiful land, she wondered, when there were already so many wonderful old ones?

"Would you like me to make you breakfast?" Dana asked, remembering how she had encouraged Lily to be diplomatic there, to ask herself whether—as the wife of a builder—she was being supportive by suggesting that everyone live in old houses.

"That's okay," Quinn said.

"I used to like it when my mother made me pancakes or waffles."

"We have hot breakfasts on weekends."

"I don't see the pancake police," Dana joked. "What do you say we break the rules and have some on Monday?"

"Usually I eat granola during the week," Quinn said. "Grandma buys it for me, but I guess she didn't last week. She thought we—"

"Were going to France," Dana finished, having a flash craving for a brioche and café crème.

Quinn blushed, reaching for the Cheerios. "That's okay," she said quickly. "I'll eat Allie's cereal. She won't mind."

Dana nodded, taking the half gallon of one percent milk out of the refrigerator. Quinn looked at it stoically, then poured it into her bowl. Allie had already told Dana they liked two percent, that anything less reminded them of blue water. Dana had started a grocery list and stuck it to the refrigerator, telling the girls to write down whatever they wanted her to buy.

So far, the only items were in Dana's handwriting. She missed her friends Isabel and Colette in France. She missed the way things used to be with Jonathan—the meals they would eat at cafés in Honfleur, at long farmhouse tables in their kitchens, on weekend trips to Paris. She missed Reblochon, chèvre, and Camembert. She hankered for *poulet fermier*. This list illustrated the bizarre change in her life: Popsicles, spaghetti, yogurt, fruit juice. She looked from the list to Quinn, quietly eating at the kitchen table. Pouring a cup of coffee, Dana sat beside her.

"Why don't you put granola on the list?"

Quinn shrugged. "I don't really need it."

"But if you want it, I'll get it."

"Cheerios are fine."

Dana sipped her coffee. Before leaving for the airport, Quinn had been acting like a holy terror. Since coming home, she was sweet and docile, as if afraid of making any waves, as if she thought one wrong move would make her aunt change her mind and load them onto the next plane.

"Why do you go out every morning?" Dana asked.

Quinn's left hand went to her head and surreptitiously began to pull her braids. "I don't know," she said.

"You leave so early. Before Allie or I are up."

"Do I wake you up? I'm sorry if I do."

"No, you don't. I'm just trying to find out more about you."

At that, the old familiar scowl came back to Quinn's face. "What's there to find out?" she asked. "It's not very interesting. I just like the sunrise."

"I like it too. It's one of my favorite times to paint," Dana said, then regretted it. She hadn't painted at sunrise in nearly a year.

"It's one of my favorite times to . . ."

"What?" Dana asked, leaning forward as if she could pull the words out of Quinn's mouth. She wanted to understand her niece. Quinn had a world of secrets locked inside; Dana could read it in the tightness of her jaw, the lines around her eyes.

"You're just like Mom," Quinn said, suddenly sounding sad.

"Is that bad?"

"You're an artist. Everyone says you're such a free spirit, so I thought you must be happier, happy enough that maybe you wouldn't have to oversee what I'm doing every second."

Pulling back, Dana didn't know what to say.

"I didn't mean that," Quinn said quickly. "Mom just, well, she was strict, that's all."

"What did you mean, that I'm happier? She wasn't happy?"

"No, she was. I don't know what I mean. Forget it—paint or something. Why don't you?"

"Why don't I paint?"

"Yes."

"I will," Dana said.

"You should," Quinn said, dropping her bowl into the sink, walking out of the kitchen. Dana watched her go. A thought flashed past, like the just-glimpsed tail of a comet. What had her mother meant the other day when she'd made that comment about Mark's business trips?

Had he cheated on Lily? Dana didn't want to believe that, and she didn't think so. But she knew from experience that it could happen. She knew that one minute a man could be telling the woman he loved his fantasies, and the next—when she was so overcome with grief over her sister to paint or love or even listen much—he could break her heart by making those fantasies come true.

But then it was time to enroll Allie in swimming lessons, so Dana went looking for towels and forgot all about Quinn and her mother's words, and the fact that she didn't even want to paint.

QUINN FELT BAD about clamming up on Aunt Dana. The thing was, she could spot a bonding moment a mile away. Getting close again was not in anyone's best interest. Ever since their last-minute reprieve at the airport, Quinn had been so wrapped up in feeling lucky and thankful, she'd done her best to stay out of trouble. She made her bed every morning. She refrained from teasing Allie. Her lungs were now a no-smoking zone. When the granola ran out, she switched to Cheerios without complaint.

But this morning, she'd nearly blown it. There they were, sitting in the kitchen the way Quinn and her mom used to, on the verge of a heart-to-heart talk. Aunt Dana had said sunrise was a favorite time to paint, and Quinn had nearly said, *it's my favorite time to write.*

Red flags, buzzers, and air horns!

How stupid could she be? Wouldn't it just be easier to hand Aunt Dana her diary, walk her to the easy chair, and invite her to sit down to read it? Quinn had to give herself credit. She had found a great hiding place. It was far from the house—a good fifteen-minute walk—and that was her safety factor.

Aunt Dana was more like Quinn's mother than she could have imagined. She loved seeing the girls be creative. Her eyes would grow soft at the mention of painting or writing. If Quinn had said she liked to write at sunrise, Aunt Dana would be begging to be allowed to read her stories.

Nice little tales, Aunt Dana would think. Full of children and bunnies and seashells and friendly porpoises. Or maybe, considering that Quinn was twelve now, Aunt Dana would expect boy-girl stories, how the pretty girl and the gentle boy went rowing out to South Brother for a picnic.

Guess again.

Quinn wandered through the house. Aunt Dana had taken Allie down to the beach to sign her up for swimming lessons, and Quinn looked through the binoculars to find them. There, all the way at the end of the beach, they were milling around with the few mothers and kids who had arrived for the summer so far. Never mind that Allie could swim to the raft by herself, that Quinn had taught her to do the sidestroke and dead-man's float. The family tradition—dating back to when their mom and Aunt Dana were young—was to take swimming lessons until you were ten, to make sure you could handle any emergency.

That's how Quinn knew the accident was a lie.

Her stomach dropped out, just thinking about it. Peering through the binoculars at her sister and aunt, she felt as if she were standing on a diving platform, that the platform had simply disappeared under her feet. Raising the glasses higher, she scanned the Sound, the water where her parents had died.

Today the sea was flat calm. Motorboats droned like bees in the distance. There was Long Island across the way. Her heart throbbing, she remembered her mother telling how she and Aunt Dana used to sail to Shelter Island. She remembered stories of how they and a pack of their friends had once swum all the way to Orient Point. Seven miles across the Sound!

So how had Quinn's mother—who had taken swimming lessons till she was ten, who had boldly swum all the way across Long Island Sound, who was the best sailor around—drowned within sight of their house? It was right out there, just past the bell buoy on the Wickland Shoals, Quinn thought. She stared at the spot, binoculars trembling in her hand.

Quinn knew how. Lowering the glasses, she stepped away from the window. The sight of all that water was making her sick. Now, alone and safe in her own house, she closed her eyes and let the feelings press in on her.

This was her house. These four walls held secrets that only her family knew. Aunt Dana had lived here once, Grandma's mother had built it with her husband, but the house belonged to Quinn, Allie, and their parents. Her father had replaced the roof, improved the kitchen. Every board, every nail, every rug, every bookshelf, had absorbed their secrets.

The secrets were in Quinn's heart and in her diary. She loved her family so much, she would guard them forever. Whispers and cries; she could almost hear them now, coming through the walls. Her diary had saved her from hearing them alone, and she had written down everything she heard, everything she knew.

Walking through all the rooms, she visited familiar things. The dictionary stand in the upstairs hall, her mother's watercolors of the four seasons, her father's tennis racket. Touching the handle, the place his fingers had gripped, filled Quinn with so much electricity, she had to sit down.

If only she had started writing her diary later. Her mother had read it. Quinn could almost hear her mother's voice now. That soft voice, trying to explain the things Quinn had written about. Quinn had listened, her face red-hot with embarrassment, with fury, feeling so mad and upset that she couldn't even hear the words. Quinn hadn't forgiven, and she bet her mother hadn't either.

Two days later, her parents were dead.

Her mother, who could swim across the Sound, who could swim underwater through the rock pools across the street with just one breath, who had taught Quinn to sail the way a butterfly flies, and her father, whose shoulders were so broad and his swimming stroke so sure, who could swim to the raft with both Allie and Quinn on his back, had drowned.

Quinn didn't know the exact details; she couldn't quite let herself picture or imagine, not even when writing in her diary, exactly how they had done it. But she believed that her parents had died on purpose.

Died underneath the sea.

Sunlight shimmered on the surface of the bay, and light bounced up the hill into the house. Water was everywhere. Quinn turned her back on the windows, but the sea's reflection danced in mirrors and picture frames, surrounding her. Who could find the answers? Who could know the truth?

Mermaids swim out there, her mother used to tell her when she was little. They have hair like seaweed and tails like fishes, and they live in the deepest part of the Sound. They play with lobsters and juggle clams, and they open oysters for pearls to bring home to their mothers.

On full-moon nights they spread their nets across the sea, catching silver bait-fish to wear in their hair, and on moonless nights they dry their nets on the dark rocks where young girls, if they aren't careful going home, could trip and be pulled into the waves.

Quinn shivered to think of being pulled into the sea. She thought of mermaids, and she thought of lobsters, and she knew the answers wouldn't come from them. And then she thought of oceanographers. They were scientists who studied the sea, studied the deep, could learn things no one else knew.

"Sam, Sam, Oceanographer Man," Quinn whispered into the empty house as she wondered when her aunt would see him again.

Her circuit of her home had brought her back to the upstairs hall, to her father's tennis racket leaning against the dark wood wall—exactly where he had left it the day he had died. Quinn had never let her grandmother move it or even touch it, but she moved it now. Grabbing her father's racket in both hands, she ran into her bedroom. Smashing her mattress, Quinn swung. Her pillow, her blanket, the lamp beside her bed: Quinn swung blindly, beating her room for the answers she did not have.

CHAPTER 6

SAM LAY ON THE MAKESHIFT BENCH, LIFTING WEIGHTS in the sun. Sweat ran down his body from heat and exertion as he decided to do another set. The boat rocked beneath him, and he thought about going sailing. Instead, he added twenty pounds on either side of the one seventy he already had on and kept lifting.

His muscles burned, and he knew that was good. As a scientist he knew that a person's memories were stored in the cells, deeper than the conscious mind could reach, and right now every inch of Sam's body was remembering something he wanted to forget. Working out was the best way he knew to do that.

Sam's boat was moored in Stony Creek, a section of Branford, Connecticut, close to New Haven and the Thimble Islands. That morning he had rowed half a mile in to the town dock, run eight miles, had coffee and a bagel, and rowed back out. Although he had abstracts to read and an article to write, he had brought his weights up on deck instead.

This was a routine of long standing. Sam had been a skinny kid with a strong older brother. Not only small for his age, he also came from a poor family—the worst sin possible in Newport. For his sixteenth birthday, Joe had given him a set of barbells and said: "You can't live in a mansion or join the yacht club, and you can't wake up tall, but you can kick their rich asses. Get busy."

The sun baked down, so Sam closed his eyes. His gray T-shirt was drenched as he pushed the limits. "Thirteen, fourteen, fifteen," he counted, feeling the fire in his pectorals and biceps. The set finished, he lowered the weights and let himself breathe. Joe, right about most things, had been wrong about one: When he was seventeen, Sam woke up tall. That year he went from five seven to six feet. The next year, by the time he started Dartmouth, he was six three. The barbells had started coming in handy, because Sam had a plan.

Waking up tall had gotten him thinking he had power. The kind of power that made all things possible, that made dreams come true. Sam knew a few things about himself. He was loyal, and he had the longest memory of anyone he knew. He was the elephant of Newport: When someone showed him an act of kindness, he never forgot.

He never forgot Dana Underhill.

She might never realize what she'd done for him that long-ago summer. She had invited him into her sailing class, taught him the skill he loved more than any other. When he found the water and sailing, he found his heart. Without knowing, she had pulled him from an abyss deeper than any ocean trench.

Some adults would never understand what childhood could be. The ones who had grown up happy and loved, who had never seen their parents hurt, who had most of what they needed: Those adults couldn't know.

For Sam, growing up as worried about food and rent as his mother was, angry that everyone else had more than him, childhood hadn't been easy. His school pictures were hard to look at— he could see the worry and pain in his face, the tension in his posture.

It took a hard-luck kid to know one, and Sam recognized his female counterpart in Quinn Grayson. The girl was in the right place though. She had no idea what she was dealing with, having an aunt like Dana.

Dana, he thought now, picking up the weights again.

He'd never forget what she'd done for him, but he wanted to forget what he'd done about her. He thought of his secret visit. The shame was still strong, surging along his nerves.

How could a person divide memory? Keep some, throw out the rest? Gritting his teeth, Sam lay on his back in the hot sun and began to lift. His biceps and triceps, his deltoids, felt the pain. He had grown tall, he had made himself strong, but certain things he couldn't change.

One thing he knew for sure: He wasn't going to abandon her now.

He had read the signs in Quinn's eyes, and he knew what Dana was in for. He knew, because he had been there himself. To pay Dana back for what she'd done for him, Sam was going to help her through this. He had the ongoing dolphin observations from Bimini to analyze, the meetings in Nova Scotia to cancel. He wasn't going anywhere. He just hoped he could keep himself divided.

Then his phone rang down in the cabin, and he swore he knew before the answering machine picked up. He heard the voice, hesitation mixed with bravado. Spellbound, Sam listened to the invitation. It was as if he'd willed it himself. He held the weights, suspended over his chest, listening. He'd have to shuffle things around to make the timing work, but he would.

This was the call he'd been waiting for.

QUINN HAD BROKEN the lamp beside her bed.

Dana found it when she went upstairs with the basket to collect everyone's dirty clothes to take to the Laundromat—sitting on granite, their house lacked a decent septic tank and the capacity to run a washing machine.

She was overwhelmed with trying to mother her orphaned nieces, trying to learn everything there was about running a house—something she'd never had any desire to do—and feeling generally burdened by the time she reached Quinn's room. There, shoved into a corner of her closet, was the lamp. Kneeling down, Dana gathered the pieces together.

The lamp's base had been a ceramic shell: a channeled whelk. Lily had made it in eighth grade—sculpted it from clay, traced the whorls, formed the opening. She had fired it in the junior-high kiln, painted and glazed it pale pink. Their father had wired it, turned it into a lamp. For years it had sat on an old oak dry sink downstairs, but Quinn must have appropriated it for her bedroom.

Now it lay in pieces.

Why had she hidden it? Dana wondered. Did she think she'd be in trouble? Should she be in trouble? Asking herself these questions, Dana thought about how badly suited she was for full-time, on-the-job aunthood. She didn't know the first thing about child psychology or parenting techniques. What was she supposed to say to a kid who had broken her mother's eighth-grade masterpiece and hidden the pieces in the closet?

This might be just one real-life moment too many, Dana thought.

She was worn out from Allie's swimming lessons. Not from watching her niece, who was poetry in motion, intrepid about putting her face in the water. But from three days—so far—of standing around with the other kids' mothers, talking about window boxes and mixed doubles and the women's club.

She had scoured the group, looking for old friends, but she hadn't recognized a soul. Instead, she had stood there, longing for the France of beauty and solitude, of melodic language and artistic history, feeling the absence of her close friends, Isabel and Colette. And in spite of herself, she missed Jonathan.

From swimming lessons they had walked around the boat basin to tennis lessons. More standing around, some of the same mothers. Dana wasn't used to this. Everyone was friendly; although no one mentioned Lily, Dana could feel their sympathy and curiosity. But Dana felt herself edging away so she wouldn't have to talk.

She was used to the isolation of painting in her studio—except for Monique, posing, and Jonathan, painting at his easel—and she felt nervous, trying to think of the next thing to say. Isabel always left Dana alone until she was ready to call her, when she had finished working; Colette sometimes dropped by, but she'd wait in the garden for Dana to emerge from her studio.

On the other hand, picturing Allie swinging that racket with all her might, biting the tip of her pink tongue with total concentration, made Dana smile with pride. Allie was a force-ten child, throwing herself into everything she did, just like a tiny hurricane, just like her big sister. They both had the potential to be world-class sailors.

A tennis racket lay on the floor under Quinn's bed. Leaning it against the wall, Dana felt pleasantly surprised and happy. She hadn't thought Quinn was very interested in sports these days. She had given up sailing, for which she was a natural. Maybe they could have a game of Canadian doubles, Dana on one side of the net and her nieces on the other, just as her mother had done with Dana and Lily.

The laundry basket full, Dana paused in the upstairs hall. A small square, each of the house's four bedrooms led off it. An old church lectern holding the family's big Webster's dictionary stood against one wall, the linen closet cut into the one adjoining. Directly opposite were four paintings by Lily.

Leaning closer to examine them, Dana could see they were of the four seasons. Watercolors of Hubbard's Point in winter, spring, summer, and fall. The paintings were small, unfinished-looking, more like studies than works in themselves. No larger than four by six inches, they were framed in driftwood.

There wasn't a house in sight. Dana had to smile. Her sister had painted the Point before any houses were built on it. That was Lily: She loved nature so much. She was a total preservationist: She wanted the places she loved to stay the same, and she wanted the people she loved to stay the same too.

Dana remembered the urge to paint, and she tried to feel it. Her work wasn't little watercolors but huge, soaring canvases. Four by six feet, big enough to contain all the emotions she was feeling on any given day. Deep sea, blue water. She could see her studio, remembered when the muses used to come for her. They spoke French, and they told her to pick up her brushes and paint the water across the sea.

For a while, she had even seen Monique as her muse. She had met the small Vietnamese woman through an artist friend in town.

New to Normandy, she had come to be near artists. Twenty-five, working at odd jobs, she was trying to earn enough money to enroll in art school. Dana, with a soft spot for people on their own and far from home, had hired her as an assistant first, a model later.

What did an artist known for vast seascapes need with a model? Well, Dana's strong suit had never been the human figure. Life-drawing classes had been her nemesis at RISD. She could paint the sea in her sleep. Water was her medium, and sometimes it felt to Dana that she had entered it herself, was painting it from the bottom of the ocean.

But Dana wanted to perfect her figure work too. She needed to draw from real life. Monique had been willing. She would undress as she walked into the studio, flinging herself onto the sofa or plastering her body against the wall. She could hold a backbend for half an hour, other poses even longer.

Her dark chocolate eyes were steady and knowing, as if she were older than her years, had seen sights Dana could only imagine. But she was sweet as well; she would bring Dana flowers she'd picked on the way. She brewed tea for them to drink. Once she had brought Dana pictures of friends she'd made in Paris—two smiling, vibrant girls with blond hair.

"One Swedish, the other American," Monique had said. "Far from home, like me."

"Vietnam . . ."

"No," she had laughed. "My parents immigrated long time ago. They have a restaurant there."

"Are they still in Paris?"

"No, Lyons. But both places—Paris and Lyons—are over for me. I'm here now."

"Do you miss your family in Lyons?"

Monique had cringed then. "Don't talk about that, Dana. Home is far away, and I am here. Life is not good back there, so I think about the future, not the past. Always the future. What will make me happy, you know?"

"Mmm," Dana had said, sketching faster to catch the troubling spirit pouring off the young woman's body. Dana felt protective toward her, the way she sometimes felt about Lily, as if Monique were a younger sister. At the same time, it was tense and exciting, and in some way Dana knew Monique had just dared to express the things Dana only touched on—Monique was a freer spirit than Dana ever wanted to be. Watching her bend her nude body, writhing like a mermaid in a deep bay, Dana fought a sudden uneasiness.

Jonathan would walk into the studio to watch. He and Dana had been living together for six months by the time Monique came along. Their commitment was new, but Jon had convinced her it was unbreakable. Dana—new to that kind of love—had allowed herself to trust him.

Of course he would stare at the model: He was an artist too. He would sketch Monique as she posed on the bed, his crayon smudging the tilt of her breasts and the rise of her buttocks, the smooth length of her honey-brown legs.

"She's nothing compared to you," Jon would whisper into Dana's ear as she painted the younger woman's body draped in seaweed, swimming through the sea.

"Are you sure?" Dana would ask, and his kisses would reassure her.

"He loves you so much," Monique said one day when she was getting dressed. "I hope I have a boyfriend who loves me like that someday."

"You will. You're very beautiful, Monique."

"Really?"

"Yes. Don't you know that?"

Monique shrugged, smiling shyly. But Dana had had the feeling that she did know exactly how lovely she was, that for her, compliments were just another sort of payment, almost as important as the francs she received for posing.

After Lily's death, when Dana had stopped painting, there had been no need for Monique to come around anymore. She had asked Dana if she could clean her house, sweep up her studio, run errands in town—anything to earn a little more money. Honfleur wasn't Paris—there weren't as many jobs. But until she decided to move on, she needed to support herself.

Dana had told her she could stay in the studio. In return, she would do the housework. In retrospect, Dana saw how dumb she had been. She had turned herself into a fool.

In grief, her painting had dried up. In many other ways, so had she. Unable to paint or think, she had wanted only to sleep and be held. After so many years of being alone, unwilling to settle down with anyone—even Philip—she had found herself wanting only to be wrapped in Jonathan's arms. As if he were a safety net, as if he could hold her and never let her drop, keep her from feeling Lily's death, she had wanted to feel his body against hers. Painting—all forms of art—seemed gone forever.

"I've lost it, Lily," she whispered now, saying the words out loud for the first time in the old house, leaning against the linen closet. "I can't do it anymore."

Not in this place anyway. Not where the memory of Lily was so strong. Perhaps she could in France. When she went back there, settled back into her studio with Jon gone and Monique banished, maybe Dana would discover that the block had been dissolved, that she'd feel like painting again.

Summer, she thought, staring at Lily's paintings. One season. That's how long she would give this new life. She could make it through one season here at the Point: swimming lessons, the other mothers, broken lamps, trips to the Laundromat. No sailing at all.

Once the girls were used to her, she could start again, easing them with her to France, to her studio. Painting had always been her lifeline, getting her through everything. Breakups, disappointments, her father's death . . . she had never expected it to fail her when she needed it most.

Just then, the telephone rang. She started to answer, then changed her mind. It was probably one of the mothers asking Dana if she wanted to join the women's club. Or if she could take turns driving the kids to miniature golf, for ice cream, for pony rides. She knew she wasn't up to dealing with any of that, so she let the answering machine pick up.

"Hi, everyone, it's Sam. Guess our machines are talking to each other. It was good to get your message and sure, I'd love to come.

To answer your question, I eat everything, and I can get there by seven. Hope that's not too late, but I have to analyze some dolphin data and fire it off to Bimini. See you tonight, and thanks a lot for inviting me."

Dana listened. When he had hung up, she played the message back again. Sam Trevor was coming for dinner. He ate everything. He'd be there by seven.

And Dana hadn't invited him. Staring at Lily's paintings of the four seasons, she zeroed in on summer and mentally counted the days till its end. Stalking through the house, planning to confront the girls, she found a note on the refrigerator in Quinn's handwriting: We're crabbing on the rocks.

The rocks were just across the street, through her neighbor's yard. The more she thought about someone mysteriously inviting Sam without first asking permission, the madder she got. But then she pictured Sam: smiling, friendly, kind enough to drive them to the airport and back. Dana knew she could use a friend, and a part of her wanted to see him. But when she opened the kitchen door to run over and find the girls, she saw Marnie McCray Campbell coming up the hill.

Dana had known Marnie since birth. Three years younger than Dana, one year younger than Lily, Marnie had been their lifelong friend. Her grandparents had built her cottage, and her mother and Dana's mother had been close friends growing up. Then they had daughters—Marnie had two sisters, each of whom had daughters themselves. Two doors down were their close friends the Larkin sisters—Rumer and Elizabeth.

"It's a colony of sisters," Dana's grandmother had said long ago, watching so many little girls play in her yard.

All Dana knew now was that she'd never been happier to see anyone in her life. She walked through the kitchen door and held out her arms. Marnie ran straight into them, and for a few seconds it was like holding a younger sister.

"I can't believe you're here," Marnie said.

"I can't believe *you're* here," Dana said into her hair. She shivered, feeling all the years melt together. She was six years old all over again. Lily was just inside, Marnie's sisters, Lizzie and Charlotte, were waiting down the hill. Their fathers were fishing, their mothers were waiting to take them to the beach.

"No, you can't?" Marnie asked in a tender voice.

Dana shook her head, pulling herself together.

"No, of course not. Because I usually spend summers on the Riviera," Marnie cracked.

Dana laughed. Marnie, like Lily, was very funny. They had never failed to make their older sisters laugh.

"Well, I know that," Dana said.

"We got down late last night," Marnie said. "I looked up the hill and didn't see lights on, or I would've stopped by then. I'm so happy you're here."

"We were supposed to be in France," Dana said, watching Marnie's face to see whether their mothers had talked and passed the news on to her.

Marnie nodded. "I heard. The mother figures were very concerned. You know, the language barrier, the girls being so far away, you know the whole story . . ."

"Yes, I do."

"I told them you know what you're doing. Lily wouldn't have entrusted her daughters to you if you didn't."

"Lily," Dana said. At the first mention of her sister's name from this old friend, she welled up and so did Marnie.

"I miss her so much," Marnie said.

"Me too. I keep thinking she'll come home."

"I looked down at the rocks just now and saw Quinn and Allie crabbing, and for two seconds I thought, where's Lily? If the girls are there, she can't be far away."

"But I'm here instead."

"Consolation prize," Marnie said, hugging Dana again.

"Thanks."

"How are you holding up?"

"I thought that missing Lily would be the hardest part, and mostly it is. But the girls are giving me a run for my money. Especially Quinn."

"I love her Bob Marley look."

"Her hair." Dana smiled. "I was just on my way over to your rocks to grill the daylights out of her. Seems she and/or her sister, but I'm betting it's Quinn, called to invite someone for dinner tonight without my permission. And he's coming!"

"Who is he?"

Dana shook her head. "Someone she hardly knows. The fact is, Quinn barely speaks to me, but she picks up the phone . . . she must have rifled through my bag to get his number."

"But who is he?"

Looking her square in the eye, Dana tried to see what Marnie was getting at. "He's an ex–sailing student of mine and Lily's. He's an oceanographer at Yale now, and through a bizarre set of circumstances, he drove me and the girls down to the airport and back last Thursday."

"Ah," Marnie said, as if that explained everything.

"What?"

"A connection to their mother."

"She has me. I'm Lily's sister."

"Too close," Marnie said.

The oak leaves rustled overhead as a warm sea breeze blew up the hill. Dana sat down right where she stood, on the top step of the long stone stairway. Way back in 1938 her grandfather had set three pennies in the mortar, and the copper had thinned and turned green. Dana stared at them as if she could make the dates and Lincoln's worn face come into focus. Marnie hadn't told her anything she hadn't known, but suddenly everything seemed clearer.

"What happened here?" Dana whispered. "In this house?"

Marnie didn't reply, but she sat down beside her.

"Something's wrong. Was Lily unhappy?"

Marnie didn't reply. She stared at the pennies herself, frowning and uncomfortable.

"Quinn said something the other day about me being happier than Lily."

"Maybe she thinks that because you're so glamorous. You live in France, you paint all the time. . . ."

"Glamorous." Dana shook her head. "Turpentine instead of perfume. If she only knew. But back to Lily."

"I don't know much more than you do, Dana. Lily seemed happy. She was a wonderful mother, she and Mark seemed to love each other. I'd see them at the beach or on the rocks. He bought that big boat. . . ."

"Why didn't she launch *Mermaid*?"

"I think because they spent so much time on *Sundance*. The girls already knew how to sail small boats—they were great at it. Lily said Quinn had the potential to sail in the Olympics. She thought it would be good for them to spend some time on the water in a bigger boat. Besides, I think sailing helped her forget that stuff in his job. Really, that's the only thing I can think of."

Dana looked up in surprise. "What stuff?"

Marnie opened her mouth, then caught herself. She wasn't a gossip, and Dana knew it. Had Mark had financial problems? Was that what her mother had hinted about, what Quinn perceived as her mother's unhappiness?

"Nothing, Dana. Lily said something to me once in passing, and I'm just a big, stupid blabbermouth."

"What was it—the eternal conflict?"

Marnie looked puzzled.

"Between Mark being a developer and Lily being a dyed-in-the-wool preservationist."

Laughing, Marnie nodded. "I know. Lily wanted to save every habitat there was—not just for endangered species but for every bird, mouse, moose, moth, minnow, pigeon, seagull. She really did have to look the other way when Mark got going on some of his projects."

"Mark was very conscientious," Dana said. "He paid attention, for Lily. So, was that the problem?"

"I suppose it was. In a way—he was doing a project she wasn't crazy about. I don't think it caused that much tension, but it did upset her a little. Anyway, Lily knew how excited Mark was about the new boat, and she wanted him to be happy."

Dana found herself absently weeding the garden by the stairs. Thoughts whirled through her head about the boat, money, real estate development, Lily's happiness and Mark's happiness, whether Lily thought it was the same thing, whether it actually was. What did Dana know about marriage? She pushed down a thought of Jon. But the suppressed emotions made her chest hurt, so she pulled more weeds and changed the subject.

"She loved our little boat," Dana said.

"I know. I remember the summer you two earned the money to buy it. You were the biggest entrepreneurs this beach has ever seen."

Smiling, Dana recalled their paper route, their lobstering business, their hot dog stand. Those were old, old memories, and it made her laugh to remember them. Feeling much better, she stood up with a handful of weeds. "I guess I'd better go cancel dinner with the oceanographer. At least I don't feel so much like clobbering Quinn."

"You're going to cancel?"

"You don't think I should?"

"Well, I was just thinking. If whoever invited him felt strong enough to call, maybe it's important."

Dana paused, peering at her friend's face. Summers in the sun had left a few small lines. Sunlight came through the leaves, turning Marnie's long hair glossy-black. They had stood in this exact spot, as their mothers had before them, over the course of many years. "How do you know so much?"

"Trial and error. Figuring out that kids are smart too, that sometimes they know what they need better than I do."

"Okay."

"And sometimes they don't. Like when Cameron asked for a horse tattoo because she likes horses. But I think inviting an oceanographer for dinner might fall into the first category. Maybe Quinn wants him here for a reason, and you won't know it till he comes."

"We're assuming it's Quinn who called him."

Marnie raised her eyebrows. Then, "I'm going home to check on the young crabbers."

"Will you tell them I'm going grocery shopping and I'd like them to come? They'd better learn that if they invite someone for dinner, they have to cook for him."

"Dana, are you really staying for good?"

"To the end of the summer anyway. The girls' school plans are still in place in France."

Marnie nodded supportively. "Okay, if that's what you think. You're the boss, not the two old mothers."

"I'm sure Martha and Annabelle would love hearing you call them that."

Marnie clasped Dana's hand. "Your mother started it. She called Lily and me the two young mothers. When Lily turned thirty-seven, she thought it was too much of a stretch, but your mother said no, hang on to the position as long as she could, until Quinn and Allie have girls of their own."

"As long as she could . . ." Dana said, feeling a shiver go down her back.

"Dana, thank God they have you."

"Thanks for saying that, Marnie."

The two old friends hugged, and then Marnie crossed the street to send Quinn and Allie home.

CHAPTER 7

STANDING AT THE STOVE, DANA THOUGHT ABOUT HOW much Lily had enjoyed cooking. Dana had sent her copper pans from Paris—the ones she was using now—and she had always noticed how much love Lily seemed to pour into the meals she made. She would take her time, measuring ingredients with care, running out to the garden for fresh herbs. Dana could see Lily now, crouched by the small stone wall, picking sprigs of rosemary and thyme.

Inspired by her sister's memory, Dana walked outside. A west wind blew up from the beach. Kneeling by Lily's herb garden, Dana ran her fingers through the leaves. She knew that cooking had been one of Lily's art forms, just as gardening and raising her children had. Dana had been too busy working, trying to paint the perfect undersea scene, to really understand.

"What are you making for dinner tonight?" Allie asked, coming out the kitchen door.

"Bluefish," Dana replied.

Allie looked worried as Quinn came out to stand beside her. Cooking for her nieces so far, Dana had taken the easy way out:

wanting to bribe them a little, she had bought their favorite pizzas and frozen dinners. That way they got their choices, and no one was faced with comparing Dana's cooking to Lily's. Today, shopping for supper, she had gone to the fish store and picked out something she knew would be easy to grill.

"Is there something wrong with bluefish?" Dana asked.

"Don't make Aunt Dana feel bad about getting bluefish," Quinn said, jabbing her sister. "If the guy's an oceanographer, he'll probably love it. Lots of people do. It's their favorite meal."

"But it's not yours?" Dana asked, looking into Allie's eyes. Her younger niece shook her head.

"When Mom made bluefish for Daddy," Allie said in a small voice, "she'd make macaroni and cheese for me."

"That can be arranged," Dana said.

"For me too," Quinn said, "but I'll have fish tonight. To help you out, Aunt Dana."

"Thank you," Dana said, staring down at the garden. The spicy scents of sage and thyme rose around her and the girls; Lily's presence was so strong, Dana felt that if she turned around, her sister would be standing right there.

"What are you doing?" Quinn asked. "Sitting in the herb garden?"

"Well, I was thinking of your mother. What she would pick to go with the bluefish."

"Some of this," Quinn said, breaking off a piece of rosemary. Then, pulling out a handful of thyme, she handed the whole bunch to Dana. "And some of this. When she cooked with her herbs, she said she was cooking with love."

Dana closed her eyes and smelled the herb bouquet. Tendrils of thyme fell from her hand, tickling her bare knee. Her senses were so alive right now, she felt prickles on the back of her neck. Was that what she was doing? Cooking with love? She wasn't sure she had ever really done that before.

"What time's he coming?" Allie asked.

"Seven," Quinn said a little defiantly, as if she thought Dana might be mad. Dana brushed her lips against the tangle of soft stems and leaves, then pulled both nieces into a hug. They didn't resist, and Dana didn't let go. She thought of Sam, due to arrive at seven, and she wondered what it meant that tonight she was cooking with love, and her old friend Sam Trevor was coming for dinner.

THE AMAZING THING was, Quinn wasn't being lectured. Aunt Dana, probably the world's worst cook, was peacefully making dinner for someone she hadn't even invited. Hovering in the kitchen, Quinn wondered what her aunt thought about the situation. Maybe she assumed Sam had invited himself over. Or perhaps she thought she had asked him herself and just forgotten.

That was probably it.

The strange thing was, Quinn wasn't even sure why she had called him. After she had gone mad with her father's tennis racket, beating her poor mattress and pillow and accidentally—tragically— breaking her mother's shell lamp, she had walked like a zombie into Aunt Dana's room and gone through her bag. She had been formulating a plan already, it was true, but when she found Sam's number, her fingers did the dialing as if they weren't even attached to her body. Her voice had left the message.

Had she expected him to actually call back?

The answer had to be no, because when Aunt Dana announced to her and Allie that he was coming, Quinn nearly had a heart attack. She had felt the redness starting in her chest, zooming into her face like lava in Mount Vesuvius. Watching Aunt Dana pick herbs she had no idea how to use had made Quinn want to sink into the earth.

Guilt city.

Aunt Dana was trying so hard to be nice and fair, like a wonderful Mary Poppins–style aunt making up for almost taking them to France. She hadn't even yelled at Quinn. In fact, besides shooting her looks of concern, Aunt Dana seemed positively calm about the whole thing. Quinn almost felt like sitting on the floor and letting the whole truth pour out. If it wasn't so scary, confession would be a great relief.

Worst-case scenario, it could really piss her aunt off, and then . . . who knew what she might do?

One thing really bothering Quinn was this question: If Aunt Dana was really settling in, why hadn't she started painting? Why hadn't she sent to France for her special paints and supplies? And why wasn't she launching the boat? Quinn almost hoped Aunt Dana would, so she herself would be forced to sail again.

But she was too close to being in trouble to ask. To make up for what she had done, Quinn threw herself into helping.

She ripped up lettuce for a salad and showed Aunt Dana how to make her mother's dressing. She ran down to the garage and unearthed her father's special bag of apple wood charcoal, cut from a tree on the Vineyard—that oily bluefish needed all the help it could get. She helped Aunt Dana arrange the herbs on the fish.

"Are we eating outside?" Quinn asked, hoping.

"It's windy," Allie said. "The bluefish will cool off too fast and taste even worse."

"Good thinking," Aunt Dana said. "How about the dining room?"

Quinn could almost feel Allie wishing she could take her words back. When Aunt Dana asked Quinn to set the dining room table, she really had no choice. Having called Sam, she had brought it on herself.

This was the hard part.

The family never ate there anymore. Grandma had let them eat on trays in the living room, and Aunt Dana seemed to like eating in the kitchen.

The dining room table reminded Quinn of her parents. It was made of oak. They never covered it with a tablecloth. The grain was dark and swirly, with pictures that told a story. Each person got a place mat with a different ship. Quinn's was *White Star*, Allie's was *Eliza Nicholson*, Mommy's had been *Istamboul*, and Dad's had been *James Baines*. Putting out the place mats, Quinn found her hands shaking.

She couldn't give her parents' place mats to anyone else. But there weren't any more in the cupboard. Quinn solved the problem by sliding all the mats under the lowest bookshelf. The table looked bare, but she hoped Aunt Dana wouldn't notice.

To make up for it, she put out the crystal candlesticks and a centerpiece of periwinkles and scallop shells and channeled whelk-egg cases. This was an important night. The conversation had to be led to the sea. What better way than by mollusks and bivalves?

"That looks beautiful," Aunt Dana said, coming in to check.

"Thank you."

"I like the way you arranged the shells."

Nodding, Quinn walked around the table. She placed her hands on each Hitchcock chair to make sure her aunt understood where everyone had to sit. "Allie and I are here and here," she said, touching two chairs facing each other. Then, hoping she wouldn't get any grief, she slid the two armchairs, usually opposite each other at the table's ends, to flank the side chairs. "You sit in this one, and he sits over there."

"The table's cramped this way," Aunt Dana said. "We need chairs at the heads."

Quinn froze. Her braids were like shock absorbers, and they felt the impact of all the emotions she was trying to keep inside. She had to stay calm, but she wanted to punch her fist through the wall. She felt as if her braids were electric, glowing like wire coils.

"No," she said with a softness she did not feel.

"Quinn, I lived here a long time before you were born. There's always a chair at each end of the table. Grandpa sat in one and Grandma in the other."

Quinn shook her head. Allie had come out of the kitchen to stand close behind her. Quinn felt her small body giving off the same heat Quinn felt inside, and she heard Allie breathing through her nose like the monster that ate Denver.

"No one sits there," Quinn said.

Aunt Dana smiled. She looked really pretty, and her eyes seemed as if they wanted to laugh. They wanted this to be one of those funny times—Quinn knew her position in the family. She was the stubborn kid. She had wacky ideas—her mother called them "original"—that didn't always make sense at first. Aunt Dana started to move one of the chairs, and Quinn clapped her fingers down on her aunt's hand with a force that left no doubt as to her degree of seriousness.

"No, Aunt Dana," Quinn said.

"Quinn, I know these were your parents' chairs, that those were their places."

Sorrow washed through Quinn. If her aunt understood that, why was she making it so hard? Staring at the seats, Quinn thought: They sat there every night.

"Are," Quinn whispered. "Not were."

"Okay. Are."

Staring through narrowed eyes, Quinn refused to look away from the seats.

"But there's not room for four people at this table unless we put the chairs where they belong. See? We'll all be scrunched up, banging each other with our elbows."

"Bluefish flying everywhere," Allie said.

"Shut up, Al."

"I don't want to be banged by *elbows,*" Allie said.

"You're a jerk. You'd better hang tight to Kimba, because I know a nice window he might fall out of."

"Look," Aunt Dana said, prying them apart as the pressure in Quinn's chest made her think she might explode. "We know the real story, don't we?"

"What real story?"

"That those are your parents' places. No matter who sits in the chairs, they're just borrowing the space."

"Borrowing?"

"Yes. Someone can sit in your mother's chair, in your mother's place, but we'll all know the truth."

"That it's really Mom's."

"Right."

For some reason, the next question was so hard to ask, Quinn almost couldn't get the words out. "Are you going to be the one to sit there? In Mom's seat?"

"I could." But then, at Quinn's expression, Aunt Dana smiled. "But I don't have to. Sam could sit there. I could sit in your father's."

Quinn nodded. "Borrowing their places."

"Temporarily."

"Like Daddy's buildings," Allie said. "Where people pay rent and don't stay forever."

"Butt rent," Quinn said.

"To sit in those chairs," Allie continued.

"Exactly," Dana said.

Quinn almost smiled. The sensation came hard and fast, on top of wanting to cry, so she blocked them both by giving Aunt Dana the hardest frown she could muster. "If you're really staying, where are your paints?"

"They're coming."

"Really?"

Her aunt nodded. She didn't look very happy about it, and for a minute Quinn wondered whether she was lying. Until last summer, she'd thought she had the most honest family in the world, but once a person was lied to by her parents, she just never knew anymore.

"Can you paint without Monique around?" Quinn asked.

Aunt Dana's head jerked around. "How do you know about Monique?"

"Mommy told us about her, how she was your studio helper. She wrote her a letter, but Monique never wrote back. She kept waiting."

"Well, Monique wasn't really the writing-back type."

"How come?" Allie asked.

"Well, you've heard your mother call me a free spirit, right?"

"Yeah," Quinn said.

Aunt Dana was quiet, as if she were thinking something very serious. It took the last of her smile away and made her look sad. "I wanted Monique to be like a little sister. She was far from home, and she wanted to be an artist. The thing is, many people have that desire. . . ."

"But not the talent," Quinn said, cutting to the point.

Aunt Dana nearly smiled, but not quite. "I don't know about that. Anyway, some people try to live like artists. They can't always paint the way they want to, but they're drawn to an artistic way of life."

"They're wanna-bes," Quinn said. "I know what that is. They wear black and smoke a lot."

"Like you," Allie said.

"Shut up, Al."

"I never thought of Monique as a wanna-be," Aunt Dana said, her eyes deep and her mouth soft. "I thought of her as someone with promise. She hung around the studio—modeling was part of it, but she also helped me build canvases and clean up my paints. She was shy about showing me her sketches. She'd come to Honfleur for the same reason I did—because Impressionism had started there. Many artists made their way to that town. Monique was making a pilgrimage . . ." Aunt Dana swallowed, and was it Quinn's imagination, or was Aunt Dana trying to talk herself into something?

"What color clothes did she wear?" Quinn asked.

Aunt Dana smiled now. "She did wear black, and she did smoke. Those were trappings your mother and I never bothered with."

"You didn't have to," Quinn said. "You were too busy painting—the real thing."

"Thanks," Aunt Dana said, looking really touched, as if she appreciated what Quinn was saying.

"Is that how you knew she was a free spirit—like you?" Allie asked.

"Well, I'm like a stick-in-the-mud compared to Monique. She's really free." Aunt Dana frowned, thinking. "Rules, conventions, etiquette—they don't apply to her at all."

"So that's why she didn't write back to Mommy?" Allie asked.

"That wasn't nice," Quinn said. "She might be free, but she's not nice."

Aunt Dana didn't reply; she still had that far-off hurt in her eyes, as if she had seen and felt something she didn't want to talk about.

"So she's not your studio helper anymore?"

"No, she's not," Aunt Dana said quietly.

"You're an artist, but I never see you doing art," Allie said, voicing similar worry.

"Then I'll make us place cards—to keep us all in the right seats. Do they count?"

Quinn shrugged, but Allie said happily yes. It was six o'clock.

There was an hour before Sam arrived. Quinn had knots in her chest, and she knew she had to write in her diary. She could just about make it to Little Beach and back in time. Edging through the door, Quinn was almost free. But then Aunt Dana looked up.

"The ship place mats that used to be here," she said. "We haven't used them since I came, but I know they must be around somewhere. If you come across them, Quinn, will you put them back on the shelf?"

"Sure," Quinn said, turning red again. "If I find them."

WHEN SAM KNOCKED on the kitchen door, he couldn't help noticing—as he had on his last visit here—the great view. Over the garden and stone terrace, he looked past the beach and marsh to Long Island Sound. Still admiring the vista, he smiled when Dana answered the door.

"Hello," she said.

"Hi," he said, handing her the wine he'd brought. "Thanks for inviting me."

"You're welcome. It's good to see you."

Standing aside to let him in, Dana kissed his cheek. As he bent down, Sam lightly touched her waist. She looked beautiful tonight, tanner than she had been a week earlier, sea light reflecting in her blue eyes. Slim in beige slacks and a white shirt with the sleeves rolled up, she looked just like she had on the docks in Newport.

"Hope you like bluefish," Allie said cheerfully, "because that's what we're having."

"Let him get in the door," Dana said. "Before you chase him away."

"As a matter of fact, I love bluefish."

"You're just being polite," Dana said. "I'm told it's the worst thing I could have bought. Unfortunately, I was told too late."

"No, I'm not. I'm dead serious. It's one of the coolest fish around."

"Why?" Quinn asked.

"When it's time to eat, I'll show you," Sam said, following everyone into the living room.

While Dana opened the bottle and poured two glasses of wine, Sam looked around the room. Quinn wanted him to try out the telescope pointed toward Orient Point, and Allie showed him the stone fireplace her grandfather had built in the midst of a hurricane.

"Leave him alone, Al," Quinn said. "He wants to look through the telescope. Right, Sam? See what's out there?"

"The Sound," he said.

"Oceanographers can look at the sea and really see it, can't they?" Quinn asked. "Even when the water's cloudy, or there's seaweed on the bottom, they can see things other people can't."

"We try." Sam laughed.

"Like what?" Quinn asked.

"Well, that's the Wickland Shoals out there," he said, adjusting the eyepiece. "That's where my brother Joe excavated the *Cambria*. You girls must know about her, right?"

"The old shipwreck," Quinn said.

"Your brother was involved in that?" Dana asked, handing him the glass.

"Yes. About two years ago. Heard about the gold, brought most of it up, saved the wreck. It's how he got together with Caroline, his wife."

"Lily told me about it," Dana said. "We used to read about the *Cambria* in school, walk down Firefly Beach to look for pieces of gold."

"Your brother saved the wreck?" Quinn asked, and when Sam looked over, her eyes were very bright.

Sam was about to answer her, when he caught Dana's expression. It was one of surprise, as if she hadn't expected Quinn's enthusiastic reaction, and then Sam thought about how Lily and her husband had drowned in their sailboat somewhere in Long Island Sound, that Quinn might not want to hear about such things.

"He did," Sam said. "My brother's a treasure hunter."

"Are you one too?" Allie asked.

"No, I'm just a marine biologist. Joe calls me a fish man. I go out on research vessels and study whatever swims."

"And to think we once pulled you out of Newport Harbour."

Dana smiled, sipping her wine as she sat between the girls on the sofa.

"Saved my life," Sam said, looking over at her. The words were so simple, but she didn't know what they meant to him. Both girls giggled, thinking he had to be exaggerating.

They all talked for a while longer, and then Dana began to fix dinner. Sam offered to light the grill. At twenty-nine, he had the bachelor life down to a science, and he often grilled fish off the stern of his Cape Dory. Both girls accompanied him outside, listening intently as he gave them a quick lesson on the bluefish's sensory capabilities, pointing out the dark line down their sides that acted as a sort of sonar.

"Sonar, like submarines?" Quinn asked.

"Just like that."

"We learned about that in school," she said. "How some creatures send out sound waves that bounce off things and echo back with a picture."

"That's a good way to describe it," Sam said, aware of Dana moving around in the kitchen. She had acted happy to see him at first, but now she seemed distracted, as if her mind were elsewhere. He had the idea she was glad to have him talking to the girls, giving her a few minutes alone.

"Can you find something underwater?" Quinn asked.

"Depends," he said, listening for Dana, checking the fish.

"Because I—" Quinn began, but just then the door opened. Stepping out, Dana held up a big wooden fork and spoon.

"Would you like to toss the salad for me?" she asked Quinn. "Since you did such an incredible job making it?"

"I'm asking Sam something," the girl replied.

"It's okay," Sam said. "We can talk later." Wanting only to be helpful, he realized instantly he'd made a mistake. Quinn's face clouded, then crumpled. She looked about to cry, but she didn't stick around long enough for anyone to be sure. Turning on her heel, she ran down a path between the houses and disappeared.

"Want me to go after her?" Sam asked.

Dana looked distressed, but she slowly shook her head. "It's okay," she said. "She'll be back."

"Did I say something wrong?"

"No. Not at all."

"She has to be alone for a little while," Allie said, looking up at Sam as if she wanted to reassure him. "She always does."

"Well, let's the rest of us eat," Dana said. "I'll keep a plate warm for Quinn."

"If you don't like bluefish, I'll let you have some of my macaroni and cheese," Allie said. Sam felt touched. He followed Dana and Allie into the dining room and sat in the seat at one end of the table.

He knew it was his because Dana had painted a small place card with his name on it, a tiny watercolor of two girls pulling a young boy out of Newport Harbour, a fleet of Blue Jays racing in the background.

SAM WAS GOOD COMPANY. Dana sat in Mark's place at the table, watching him in Lily's. He ate everything on his plate and then asked for seconds. Dana figured he was being polite, but it made her feel good anyway; she wondered what he'd think if he knew his place card was the first thing she had painted in months. Quinn's empty seat was glaringly obvious. Dana kept glancing at it, wishing she would return.

Allie talked twice as much as usual. Sam asked many questions, as if his favorite dinner companions were orphaned girls and silent, worried aunts. Occasionally, Dana would stand up, drift into the living room, and look for Quinn through the binoculars. She knew she was being a terrible host, but Sam seemed to be holding his own. He asked Allie about her summer so far and listened without interrupting once to her talk about swimming lessons.

"How did you learn to swim?" Allie asked.

"My brother Joe had a boat," he said. "He was ten when I was born, and he used to row me around Newport, out past Castle Hill. He claims he threw me overboard when I was a baby, and I swam after him all the way back to the dock."

That caught Dana's ear. "Really?" she asked, smiling at the

picture in her mind, Sam swimming through the harbour after his big brother.

Sam grinned from the other end of the table. "That's what he says. It must be true—I don't ever remember not swimming."

"Sounds like something Quinn would do to me," Allie said. "We used to sail together, all the time . . . she taught me. Is it okay if I go upstairs, Aunt Dana?"

"Sure," Dana said. Watching Allie go, Dana stopped smiling. She knew Allie was going to put a light on for Quinn, a beacon that would shine all the way to Little Beach. Her mouth felt tight, and her chest ached. She saw Sam watching her, and he leaned forward.

"You're worried about Quinn," he said.

Dana sat very still. She cleared her throat to be very sure her voice would work the way she wanted it to. The evening was almost over. Sam would be leaving soon, and things would get back to normal—or their version of normal—then. "I know where she is, and I know she'll come back—she always does. . . ."

The look in Sam's eyes stopped her. "Let me go find her," he said.

He sounded so quiet and sure. Dana tried to shrug, to show him that this wasn't very serious, but she couldn't. She was frozen in her seat. Somehow he knew what she was feeling inside—she could tell by the way he didn't blink or look away, by the way he wouldn't believe the fakeness of her smile.

"Dana?" he asked.

He meant well, but she wouldn't let him. She had opened herself up once before, and she couldn't do it again. If he was just an old friend, if she didn't feel as if he were looking inside her right now, it might be different.

"She'll come home," Dana said quietly.

"You're taking such good care of them," he said.

At that, Dana's eyes filled. She looked down at her plate so Sam wouldn't see.

"You are," he continued. "Lily would be so proud of you. She'd feel so good to know her daughters are in such good hands."

"I want to believe that," Dana said.

"Let yourself, Dana. None of this—any of it—is your fault."

"Fault?" she asked, wondering about his choice of words.

"Quinn running off, even Lily dying. None of it."

She stared at the candle, wondering what he knew about such things. He was only twenty-nine, Jonathan's age. Life hadn't shown him enough to give him such wisdom. But his voice was low and kind, as if he knew she was having a hard time, and he wanted to help her through it.

"We put herbs on the fish," she heard herself say.

"They were good too. Are they from the garden by the kitchen door?"

"Lily's herb garden," Dana said.

"She planted them herself?"

Dana nodded, thinking of how the herbs came back year after year with this temperate coastal environment.

"It's like she played a part of the night, of making dinner," Sam said. Dana gazed at him down the table. The sun had started setting, and the sky was filled with dark rose light. It poured through the windows behind him, cascading over his arms like molten gold. She thought of Lily being part of the dinner, and she closed her eyes.

" 'Cooking with love,' " Dana whispered. "That's what Quinn said her mother would say when she cooked with herbs."

"Sounds like Lily."

Sam was very genuine. Dana had no choice but to trust the kindness she heard in his voice. She didn't have to open her heart, forget what she'd been through with someone very close to his age, but if she wanted, she could take him up on his offer to find Quinn.

"I'm worried about my niece," she said now.

"I know."

"I don't want to leave Allie here alone—"

"Let me go. Just tell me where. . . ."

Dana nodded, making up her mind. "Do you know how to get to Little Beach? It's just across the main beach, up the path and into the woods. . . ."

"I know the way," he said, his eyes lighting with something between humor and embarrassment. Dana wondered what he was thinking, but then he went on. "It's the path I take when I walk over from visiting Augusta at Firefly Beach."

"Oh," Dana said, reddening herself as she remembered the *D* in the silver twilight sand. Looking up, she and Sam started to smile. It was as if he knew she had seen but neither one knew how to mention it.

Her gaze fell upon a sprig of herbs on the platter, and Quinn's words came back to her: cooking with love. What did that mean, after all? Here she was, the head of her broken little family. One child was upstairs, the other had done her nightly running away. Sam had offered to find her, and all Dana could think to do was to let him.

"She'll be over there, sitting by the rock at the Point," Dana said now.

"Okay. Be back soon," he said, pushing his chair away from the table and walking out the door. Watching him go, in spite of the steady breeze coming through the windows her face still felt hot.

But that *D* in the sand had nothing to do with it.

CHAPTER 8

IT WAS NEARLY DARK. QUINN SWORE AT HERSELF FOR
not bringing a flashlight. She had matches in her pocket, so she
made a small fire from dry driftwood twigs and pages ripped from
the back of her journal. Mosquitoes flew right through the smoke
to bite her neck. She ignored them. Huddled by the big rock, she
wrote as fast as her hand would go.

> He's up at the house right now, and I'm at Little Beach.
> Why, you might ask? Why would I mastermind a dinner with
> the scientist, then leave before the bluefish even hits the table?
> Because I'm an idiot, that's why. An idiot savant, but an
> idiot all the same. What good is the savant part if it follows
> the idiot part?
> Things get under my skin. That's the whole goddamn
> problem. If my skin was a circus tent and you could lift it up
> and walk inside, you'd find elephants and tigers and trapeze
> artists and clowns and a ringmaster. Three rings' worth of
> stuff going on under my skin.

Like what?

Well, like the dinner table. Aunt Dana did her best to work it out, but it wasn't good enough. Just looking at it set for four made me want to upend it and send the dishes flying. All I can think of was the last dinner, with all of us there, everything happy and normal. Six hours later? Split in half—

And no matter what Aunt Dana said, I didn't want her and Sam sitting in Mom and Dad's places. But the straw that broke the camel's back was when I was working my way up to asking Sam my big question—laying the groundwork— and Aunt Dana interrupted to get me to toss the salad. Why did I have to get so mad? I try to control it, but the things under my skin have a mind of their own.

Other things under my skin: Mom, Dad, the way they used to be so happy and the way they started fighting, Aunt Dana not painting, her planning to drag us back to France with her, the

Quinn stopped writing. Her fire crackled, the wood shifting. That's all it was. She put her pen to paper for one more second, then heard it again: someone coming through the path. Jamming her diary into the plastic bag, she peered around the rock. It was Sam.

"Nice night for a walk," he called across the beach.

"If you like mosquitoes," she said.

"They hate me," he said. "I never get bitten."

"Lucky you."

"You missed a good dinner."

"She'll give me some later."

"I don't know about that," Sam said, coming to sit on the rock beside Quinn. He had a very serious look on his face.

"What do you mean?"

"You're trying pretty hard to tick her off. One of these days you might succeed."

He had Quinn's attention. Frowning, she peered at him over her fire. "Go on," she said.

"I know the deal, Quinn. Your life sucks."

"What do you know about it?"

"So did mine when I was your age."

"Yeah? Like how?"

"Never mind. I'll tell you someday. The details aren't that important. It's what I did to get out of it that mattered."

Quinn let out a long exhale. This figured.

"What's that?" he asked.

"I get it," she said. "You're trying to relate to me. Just letting me know you know what I'm going through. All grown-ups think that. Well, guess what? You *don't*."

The sun had disappeared into the woods, but the sky was filled with sunset. Every cloud was gold, and red light poured onto the water's calm surface. Fish—probably bluefish—broke the surface beyond the breakwater, and gulls began to gather from all over.

"You're right," Sam said after at least a minute of watching the birds. "I probably don't."

"What?" Wheeling around to see his face, Quinn tried to keep track. How could she fight someone who wouldn't stay steady? One minute he was relating, like all those other adults, and now he was backing down.

"I don't know shit about your life."

"Good. We've got that straight." Shaking her head, Quinn reached into her pocket and pulled out two half-smoked cigarettes. She had found them on the boardwalk earlier, and she offered one to Sam—anyone who would swear to a kid would probably smoke.

"You want cancer?" he asked. "Good way to get it."

That gave Quinn pause, but pride required her to re-pocket one, then stick the other butt in her mouth and light it straight from the fire.

"Tell me one thing, Ms. Grayson."

"What?" she asked, strangely thrilled to be called Ms. Grayson.

"If you're going to pull a big dramatic exit and then act rude to me when I come to find you, why'd you bother asking me to dinner in the first place?"

Halfway through a smoke ring, Quinn choked on his question.

"I just, I don't know, I thought . . ." Quinn began.

"Don't beat around the bush. I don't have time for that."

Quinn dropped the cigarette into the wet sand and stared out at the Sound. Past the feeding fish and diving birds, past the bell buoy and green can, past the line of waves breaking on the Wickland Shoals, past the places she'd loved to sail. All warmth had drained out of the sky, leaving fields of black. Stars broke through, but they stayed high, not yet fiery enough to reflect in the sea.

"What's out there?" he asked.

"The magic land," she said. "The Hunting Ground."

"Land?" he asked. "There's nothing from here to Long Island."

"Underwater. The land underwater."

"The sea bottom?"

Quinn nodded.

"What can I help you with?" he asked, and something about his voice reminded Quinn of her father offering to help her with her math homework. She turned away so he wouldn't see the memory in her eyes.

"Quinn?"

"Answers," she said.

"To what questions?"

In that moment, Quinn stared from the fire to the sea and gathered every bit of strength the elements had to offer. Energy flooded her body, surrounding her heart, and when she spoke, her voice was very steady. "I'd like to hire you."

"Hire me?" He almost laughed, but didn't. "For what?"

"I want to know what's down there."

"You want a topographical map? Like the kind oceanographers use?"

Quinn nodded. She thought of sonar bouncing off the bottom, hitting seamounts, guyots, trenches, or whatever the Long Island Sound equivalent might be. She imagined sound waves finding schools of bluefish, whales, and mermaids. She pictured them locating the wreck of her parents' boat.

"I could help you with that," he said.

"It has to be before we leave," she said.

"Leave?"

"Aunt Dana doesn't plan on staying. She says she's not, but I can tell—she's taking us back to France."

"How do you know?"

Was it her imagination, or did Sam look surprised, even upset?

"Because she's not painting. And she's not sailing. Her and Mom's old boat is just sitting in the garage. If Aunt Dana were really staying, she'd have launched it by now. When we visit her in France, she's always sailing. She's just killing time here until it's time to go."

"I hear you're a good sailor."

"Used to be. Now I hate it."

Sam sat quietly, taking that in. His elbows rested on his knees, and his bare feet were sunk deep in wet sand. The incoming tide splashed his—and Quinn's—ankles, but he hardly seemed to notice.

"You think she's really going back, huh?" he asked.

"Yeah, I do."

"Well, let's see what we can do about that."

"Can I hire you?"

"Sure."

"How much?"

"Let me think about it," he said.

"Okay, on two conditions."

"What's that?"

"One, don't tell my aunt about our deal."

"Fine. What's the other?"

"Don't tell anyone but me what you find."

"What do you *want* me to find?"

"I'm not ready to tell you."

"Fair enough. But why's it such a secret?"

"That's for me to know. If it's not a deal, just tell me."

"It's a deal, Quinn."

"And you'll let me know how much?"

"Yeah. I will." They shook hands.

He stood then, and even though they hadn't really settled the details like when, where, and how much, Quinn stood, too, and covered the fire with sand. When he turned his back, she quickly buried her diary. Glancing to make sure he wasn't looking, she left the gift on the rock. Then she ran ahead, to lead him through the dark path on the way back to the main beach.

Overhead, stars and fireflies lit the trees. Quinn didn't think it was pretty or anything. She was just noticing. Bats swooped down to circle their heads, and neither she nor Sam even flinched. That was a good sign. He didn't scare easily.

Something about the walk made Quinn feel different. Not good, not even quite hopeful, but different. As if life in the not too distant future might change slightly.

If you'd asked her last year, Quinn would have thought change was the dumbest idea she'd ever heard. Why change what was almost perfect? She had lived in a house full of love. Sailing had been her joy and her dream. Her parents had their secrets, but back then she hadn't known they had the power to destroy. No, Quinn had been ignorant in her dumb, innocent bliss.

Now change sounded okay. Not a big upset or transformation, like moving to France, but a small one, like knowing the truth. She was going to hire Sam, and someday soon she would know enough to change a little.

DANA WAS WAITING by the door when they got home. Quinn ran past, as if nothing had happened. She grabbed her plate from the oven and took it to eat upstairs, in front of her own TV. When Sam came in, Dana gave him a grateful look.

"You found her. Thank you."

"You're welcome."

The coffee was on, so Dana fixed a tray with cups, milk, and sugar and carried it into the living room. Allie was up in her room too. With the windows open, the sound of waves breaking on the beach came up the hill; it should have been restful and lulling, but Dana felt churned up inside.

She set the tray on a glass table. The seating area was cozy: one sofa flanked by two armchairs. The table was covered with books, magazines, votive candles in low crystal holders, a blue china bowl filled with moonstones, and four flat stones delicately painted with flowers by Lily.

"Are you sure you don't have kids of your own?" she asked, sitting at one end of the sofa as he took the adjacent chair.

120 · *Luanne Rice*

"Yes," he laughed. "Why?"

"Because you're so good with them. I'm sorry for not remembering—do you have younger brothers and sisters?"

"No, I'm the youngest. It's just me and Joe."

"Then how do you do it? Tell me fast, because I have a lot to learn."

"I hang out with Clea and her family sometimes. She's my sister-in-law's sister, and she has a boy and girl about Quinn's age."

"Clea and Caroline Renwick," Dana said. "And their sister, Skye. They ran in a different crowd than Lily and me. When there was a party at Firefly Beach, we'd hear the music carrying across the water and sneak out and run down the beach to see."

"What did you see?"

"It was like another world," Dana said, staring out the window as she remembered. "We felt like two Cinderellas peeking into the ball. People drinking champagne, dancing under the stars, swimming at night . . ."

"Another world for me too," Sam said. "When Joe married Caroline, they invited me inside. I wasn't sure I belonged at first. Took me a while to figure out they meant it."

Dana heard the insecurity in his voice. It lasted only a moment, and then it was gone. But hearing it made her remember how he had looked as a little boy.

She could see him in his faded shorts, ripped and mended T-shirt, and dirty sneakers, next to the other kids in their yacht club clothes and new Top-Siders. She remembered his cowlick and the frown line between his eyebrows. Looking at him now, tall, slender but muscular, relaxed and leaning on the sofa's arm, she felt something jump inside.

"The outside looking in," Dana said.

"That's it. I never knew you and Lily ever felt that way."

She nodded. "I think it's what made me like you so much in the first place."

He didn't reply, and she wasn't sure, but even sitting in the dark he seemed to be turning red. "You ever feel it now?" he asked.

"Maybe," she said quietly, gazing out the window again. "I

think a lot of artists do. We don't quite fit in, and somehow that feeds our creativity. We have to create other worlds to feel right."

"Your worlds are underwater," he said. "Your paintings, I mean. All that blue . . . so many different shades. You wouldn't know unless you spent a lot of time on boats."

Right now, staring at the night sea, Dana was seeing blue. So dark it was almost black, the water was flecked with starlight and just the hint of a rising moon.

"Underwater worlds," Sam continued. "The water column: the sea bottom, groves of seaweed, marine life, always the mermaid."

"The what?" Dana asked, her voice trembling.

"The mermaid."

No one spoke. The only sounds were the waves breaking and a far-off boat engine. "How do you know?"

"Well, I see it," he said, looking directly into her eyes.

Again, she felt that strange jump inside. He watched her steadily, his gaze open and knowing, and Dana had to look away.

"No one else does," Dana said. Then, correcting herself, "Except one person."

"Lily?"

Dana nodded. "I painted mermaids for her. I always did. But I camouflaged them so no one else could see. I hired a model so I could get it right. But even she didn't know what I was doing. . . ." She laughed softly, remembering Monique's profound lack of interest, the way she would just lie there, her mind a million miles away. That was good, Dana thought now. It kept her out of Lily's and my world.

"Where'd you find a mermaid model?"

"She was human. One hundred percent human," Dana said quietly.

"Well, you fooled me. The mermaids you paint look like they belong in textbooks of pelagic species. How do you do it, blend them into the scene?"

"I worked their tails into the kelp, I turned their scales into a school of fish. No one else sees them."

"Not even the girls?"

Dana shook her head.

"I guess I see them because I was once rescued by them. That's how it felt that day in Newport. When I came to with my head bleeding, being kept afloat by you and Lily."

"Oh, Lily would have loved that. You thought we were mermaids." Dana smiled, not telling him that she loved it too.

"Have you painted any of the Sound?"

"Not since I've been back," she said, her chest tightening. "Home is tricky. I don't find it easy to paint here."

"No?"

"I always live far away," she said. "I'm not exactly sure why, but it seems to feed my painting. Where I live is always beautiful but always unfamiliar. Lily used to say I thrive on being off-balance."

"Quinn feels off-balance now," Sam said.

Dana glanced over, waiting for him to go on. Suddenly, the darkness seemed too much, so she leaned over and lit the candles on the table. His eyes glowed, and his skin looked quite tan. In this light, she could see the muscles in his arms. They looked very strong and well-developed, as if he spent as much time working out as in his lab. She stared at the way his upper arms strained against the short sleeves of his white polo shirt, and she found herself feeling incredibly attracted to him.

"She does?" Dana asked, blushing as she looked away.

"Well, she doesn't sail anymore."

"I noticed."

"And she wants you to paint."

"I know. She said that before you came."

"Are you going to?"

"I'll start soon." Was it a lie or a promise? A breeze came through the open window, and Dana watched the candle flame flicker. It looked almost as unsettled as she felt. She loved talking to him, hearing the insights he had into her niece.

"Well, it's getting late," he said, setting his coffee cup down on the table. "What time do you want me back here?"

"Back here?"

"In the morning. Actually, I can't make it tomorrow. I have to analyze some data coming in from Bimini, turn it around, and send it to Lunenburg. Friday I have some meetings at Yale. But how about Saturday?"

"Sam," Dana began, wondering what she was missing. "What are you talking about?"

He stood up, stacking his and Dana's cups on the tray.

"To get the boat ready," he said. "So we can launch it."

"The boat . . ."

"The one in the garage. Quinn told me about it. She might not want to, but you're going sailing, Dana."

"I am?"

"Yeah, you are," Sam said, and the way he said it made her start to smile back, sent a shiver down the length of her spine that had nothing to do with the breeze coming through the open window.

CHAPTER 9

"I NEED SOME MONEY," QUINN SAID MATTER-OF-FACTLY.

"For what?" her aunt asked.

"Things," Quinn said. Then, taking a deep breath because she knew she had to be patient, and because Aunt Dana wasn't up on kids and finances, she made sure to speak kindly. "You're not supposed to ask."

"Why not?"

"You're supposed to trust me."

Aunt Dana was sitting outside on the stone terrace, reading her mail, waiting for Grandma to come over for tea. The white market umbrella was up and the pots of geraniums and petunias were in full bloom. Aunt Dana wore a big straw hat and dark glasses, and she looked as if trust for Quinn was the furthest thing from her mind. Staring silently, she let the letter drop to her lap.

"I know," Quinn said. "You're thinking I constantly run off and mouth off. 'Why should I trust you?' is what you're about to say, right?"

"No. I was about to say 'How much money do you need?' "

Quinn could barely smile. This was too easy, and now she felt guilty for the move—Aunt Dana was a sitting duck. She was trying so hard, wanting her nieces to accept her. She'd probably give Quinn anything she asked for. Calculating fast, Quinn figured she could get Sam to do the work for fifty clams.

"Fifty dollars," she said.

"Hot dog stand," Aunt Dana said.

"Excuse me?"

"You'll have to earn it. You could get a paper route, but I'm sure the Point's already covered. If you have a hot dog stand and charge a dollar fifty each, you'll have to sell only thirty or so hot dogs. Not counting sodas. I'll front you the startup costs."

"Mom never made me work," Quinn said, outraged. "She gave me an allowance."

"How much of an allowance?"

"Five bucks a week."

Opening her bag, Aunt Dana pulled out a five-dollar bill and handed it to her. "Here. Now you have to earn only forty-five."

"Who's that letter from?" Quinn asked, changing the subject and making it sound like an accusation.

"Jonathan Hull."

"Who's *that*?" Quinn asked, staring at the onionskin envelope postmarked Honfleur, France.

"My old boyfriend," Aunt Dana said, going back to reading her letter and leaving Quinn with her mouth wide open and the five-dollar bill flapping in the summer wind. Aunt Dana had had many boyfriends over the years, but Quinn had no idea that one of them was still in the picture—she could say "old boyfriend," but if he was in the past, what was the letter all about? Quinn thought of Rumer Larkin, the lady who lived a few doors down. She was about Aunt Dana's age, but she was already one of— what were they called?—"Les Dames de la Roche." The old ladies of the Point who never married, didn't need men. Her mother had seen a unicorn once. Rumer helped hurt animals, and Quinn had heard her talking to them. They were weird, but in a cool way. If only Quinn could get Aunt Dana to be a Dame de la Roche—and forget about that Jonathan Hull guy back in France.

Recovering eventually, she walked through the sliding door into the house.

The brass box was back on the mantel. Quinn went to stand before it. This was the little altar she visited every day, the exact reason she didn't want her parents' ashes being scattered anywhere. They were right here, where Quinn needed them.

"She has a boyfriend," she said out loud. "In France. No wonder I feel her wanting to go back there. And she's making me work to earn the money to hire Sam. It'll be worth it: I'll find out everything that happened to you. Whatever it was, I'll know. And I'll take care of your debt. . . ."

Quietly, she listened. If her parents could talk to her, if she could hear their voices, she believed she knew what they would say: *We love you, we love you, we love you so much.*

But if they loved her so much, why had they died?

SATURDAY MORNING Dana got up early. Knowing Sam would be there by nine, she went down to the garage to clear things out from around the boat. The sky was hazy with locusts humming in the trees, letting her know the day was going to be hot. The girls had ridden their bikes to the post office and then were going to the store to buy supplies for their hot dog stand. Dressed in work clothes, drinking a second cup of coffee, Dana felt more excited than she had expected.

The old boat looked tired. Its trailer was rusty, one tire flat. The paint was peeling, and the bottom was coated with very old, dried algae. She assembled scrapers, wire brushes, paper masks, and a new can of antifouling bottom paint.

A bushel of kindling and a paper bag of soda cans stood behind the trailer. Dana cleared them away, then moved several rakes and garden tools. She righted a tipped-over flowerpot and moved Mark's fishing rods to the back wall. Several lures were lightly hooked to a wooden beam. Working them free, she reached for his tackle box to stow them inside.

The plastic box was padlocked.

That surprised her. No one locked a tackle box. What could possibly be inside—rusty hooks, worn leaders, lead sinkers? Dana jiggled the small brass lock, moving the hasp. Maybe Mark hadn't wanted the girls to hurt themselves on fishhooks. Or perhaps he had found a new place to hide valuable documents, like the deed to the house.

Dana worked the lock a little harder. She tugged hard, examined the padlock. This was interesting. Her curiosity building, she held the box before her eyes as if it were a Christmas present. She shook it. Still, the lock didn't give. Bemused and knowing she'd get to it later, Dana set the box down and stuck the lures back where she'd found them.

Soon afterward, Sam pulled up out front. He wore his painting clothes: an old T-shirt and shorts stained with that distinctive chalky, royal blue paint used on boat bottoms.

"Looks like you've done this before," she said.

"I paint my boat every year," he said. "It's a ritual of spring."

Dana offered him coffee, but he said he'd stopped for some on the way. They got right to work. They wore white masks even for scraping off the accumulated barnacles and algae. The bottom paint was the most toxic stuff there was and would prevent future growth. Glancing over at him, around the edges of his mask, Dana noticed that he had sleep wrinkles on one side of his face.

"Did you sleep well last night?" she asked.

When Sam looked over, she couldn't miss the delight in his eyes peering over the mask. It sparked a shock of emotion in her, and she smiled at him. "Yes, thanks for asking. Did you?"

"I did," she said. "Something about that old house just lulls me to sleep. It's like being in a rocking cradle."

"Because it's your childhood home?"

"I guess so," she said, vigorously scraping. "All those happy memories."

"Tell me one."

Dana kept working, but her mind spun back. There were so many. Some blended together, but others were as clear and distinct as a full moon in the sky. "Let's see. The day Lily and I bought this boat. Our father drove us over to Old Mystic; we paid for it with money we'd earned ourselves, and when we got it home, we went sailing right away. It was incredible—a beautiful breezy July day."

"How long ago was that?"

"A long, long time ago," she said through her mask. "When Lily and I were younger than Quinn and Allie are now."

They worked for a while in silence, and then they met at the back of the boat. There, on the transom, was the mermaid with two tails. "Your symbol," Sam said. "You were painting mermaids even then."

"I guess I was. We both were—Lily painted half of her."

"We'll leave her alone," Sam said protectively. "Work around her."

Dana's gaze slid toward him. She thought of the way things came together and dissolved. Lily's life was right here, in this garage. Her heart hurt so much, working on this old boat, and she knew that Sam knew. She put down her scraper, feeling the tenderness he had for her and Lily's history.

"Are you okay?" he asked.

"I'm not sure," she said, staring at the paint scraper. How could she answer that? The clear-cut answer was no, she wasn't. Lily was everywhere—or, to be more accurate, memories of Lily. She had loved her sister so much. This little boat was where their two passions—sailing and painting—had come together.

"Does it make you want to paint again?"

"I hadn't been thinking that," she said.

"Maybe it would help," he said.

"Help how?"

"Ground you. Give you something to focus on besides missing her."

The earth shifted. Dana could swear it really did; that a small earthquake occurred right there in the old garage. Holding herself steady, she knelt beside the Blue Jay and concentrated on the transom. It had been Sam's words: missing Lily. Those were huge words, and they took in more than he, or even Dana, could imagine.

This was the hardest part for Dana—seeing the section she and Lily had painted together. Was it possible these old brushstrokes were all that was left? Dana thought of all the painting she had done over the years, all the mermaids she had hidden there. As Lily had said in her letter to Monique, they were supposed to be their guardian angels, saviors from the deep. . . .

Watching Dana from the corner of his eye, Sam had started to work again. Scraping harder, he had paint chips flying everywhere. Blue flecks covered his hands and forearms. His shoulders strained his gray T-shirt—black with sweat—and his muscles glistened.

"You'd think it would be simpler," she said, making herself smile. "Here you are, doing a good deed, and I'm a basket case."

"Really? I don't think that."

"You're just being polite, saying that."

"No, Dana. Really—if you're not ready to launch the boat, we don't have to. We can stop right now."

"I'm tempted. But thinking about me and Lily buying her, sailing her, makes me think about the girls—Quinn and Allie. What they're missing with her in the garage."

"So we'll keep at it?" Sam asked.

"Yes," she said, attacking the job with new vigor. They were across the boat from each other, and she glanced over now and then. His eyes were bright, curious, as if even scraping paint made him happy. Dana knew she had been that way once. It was the part of her Jonathan had been drawn to: awake, alive, open to the world.

Now she had armor on. It couldn't be seen, and it wasn't material, but she couldn't for the life of her begin to take it off. Being with Sam, feeling his concern, made her want to soften her heart. She wanted to go back to how she had been when this boat was new—in love with the sea and sky, hardly able to wait a minute to go sailing across the waves. Now she felt so guarded, so hurt by what life had given her, she hardly wanted to step outside. Her sister had died, and her boyfriend—the man she had loved because he had seemed to want her for who she really was, love her because she could paint as if she lived under the sea—had been too impatient to wait and see what might come next.

The sanding complete, they started to paint. Down the road, Winnie Hubbard rehearsed, singing scales. People strolling down Cresthill Road slowed to check things out. Some called hello, others just passed by. Rumer Larkin drove past in the barn truck, hay bales piled in the bed. Marnie, getting into the car with her daughters and armloads of library books, backed out of her driveway and called hi through the open window as she pulled away.

"Friendly place," he said.

"Everyone knows everyone," she said, brushing with thick, even strokes.

"Newport used to be like that. Do you remember?"

"I was there for only two summers, but yes—I do. It was a really fun place, and if you had a boat, you fit right in."

"I didn't have a boat," Sam said.

"Neither did I," Dana said. "I was just the sailing teacher. But we used to hang around Bannister's Wharf after work, meeting people from all over."

"I saw you there once," Sam said, glancing across the boat. "My mother worked on the next dock over. She had to stay late one night, and I was wandering around, waiting for her to finish. I saw you and Lily at the Black Pearl."

"Were we behaving ourselves?" she asked, picturing the lively outdoor nightspot.

He laughed. "You were the center of attention. Guys were swarming all over you. I remember hoping you wouldn't ask them to go sailing instead of me."

"Did you think I would?"

"I wasn't sure. I couldn't believe you'd asked me at all." Leaning over, he painted with fierce concentration. His glasses had slid down his nose, and he bumped them up with his shoulder. "I was a runt from the wrong side of town, and the other kids were all preppies waiting to happen. I never got over you letting me sail."

"You were a student just like the rest of them. I didn't care about pedigrees, and neither did Lily."

"I know. You were both great. But when I saw you with those

guys at the Black Pearl, I thought, forget it. She's going to kick you off the boat so fast . . ."

"Never. They never stood a chance," Dana said. She had dated her share of Newport sailors, but they weren't really her type. Even back then, as young as she was, she had been serious about her art, not just looking for fun on a hot summer night.

"Well, I'm glad. I would have fought to stay—I loved those lessons so much."

"There wasn't anything to fight. I couldn't resist you, Sam." She laughed, relaxing as she remembered how much fun they had had. It felt good to flirt a little. Since breaking up with Jonathan six months earlier, she had kept her guard up, but what was the harm in this kind of banter? When she glanced up from painting, she saw that Sam had stopped working.

His eyes were very intense over the edge of his mask, as if he were waiting for her to go on.

"What?" she asked.

"I was just a wharf rat," he said.

"But a cute one," she said, her eyes drawn to his shoulders again, not understanding why he suddenly seemed so serious.

"You know," he began, tugging the mask off his face, "there was a time I would have killed to hear you say that."

"When you were eight?" Taking off her mask too, she smiled. "Somehow I don't think you would have even noticed. All you cared about was learning how to sail—as fast as possible."

"Not when I was eight," Sam began. "When I was older, and you were living on the Vineyard . . ."

Dana's mouth dropped open. How would he have known that? She thought of Jonathan, telling her that he had seen her on the quai, watched her at the market. Sam's words brought back that memory of being seduced by Jon, and she suddenly felt off balance.

The girls came wheeling up to the garage on their bikes, air whistling behind them. Quinn's basket overflowed with hot dog rolls and yellow mustard. Allie's contained the paper plates and napkins.

"Aunt Dana, Mr. Porter at the store gave us a free bottle of ketchup for good luck because we bought so much stuff!" Allie announced.

"I think he did the same for me and your mother when we had our hot dog stand."

"You guys are having a hot dog stand?" Sam asked.

"Yes, tomorrow," Allie said. "We put up signs all over the beach. We're raising money for a good cause."

"Like what?"

"I don't know," Allie said. "It's Quinn's, and she won't tell me what it is. But she says it's good, so I'm helping."

Dana waited for Sam to ask Quinn and be told it was none of his business, but he didn't. Once again she admired his sense around the girls, and she wondered whether she'd overreacted before.

"I didn't know you were coming today," Quinn said, leaning on her handlebars and staring hard at Sam.

"Well, I thought it was about time your aunt got the boat in the water. So here I am."

"Hmmm," Quinn said, giving that statement due thought. Deciding she approved, she climbed off her bike.

"Think you'll want to go sailing again?"

Waiting for Quinn to reply, Dana's heart sped up. But Quinn just shook her head. "I don't think so. Don't hold your breath waiting, okay?"

"Deal," Sam said.

"Are you coming back?"

"When?" he asked.

"Tomorrow. For the hot dog stand."

"Sure," he said. "I'll try."

Nodding, Quinn unloaded the basket. She handed the mail to Dana, including a red-and-blue-bordered airmail envelope from Jonathan. Wordlessly, she carried her purchases up the hill. Allie stayed to watch the painting; waiting till it was done, she politely asked Dana to take her swimming.

Sam wiped his hands with turpentine. "I'd better be going," he said, handing her the can and rag.

"Thank you, Sam," she said.

"For leaving?" He grinned.

"No. For this—" She pointed at the boat. "It was a lot of work."

"Well, I didn't have plans today."

"Seriously," she said, their eyes locked. She wanted to know what he was thinking, what he was getting out of spending a beautiful summer morning painting an old boat with her. "Why did you come?"

He placed his hands on her shoulders and stared straight into her eyes. Slowly, a smile came to his face like the sun rising out of the eastern bay. "Because a sailor should have a boat to sail."

"A sailor?"

"You, Dana."

Dana swallowed, acknowledging what he'd said. Her heart began to beat faster, as if she'd just felt a fresh salt breeze in her hair, but she couldn't quite smile.

"Can I ask you something?" he said, taking a step forward. When she nodded, he went on. "What do you think I want? Why do you seem so suspicious of me?"

"Because I've learned the hard way," she said, holding Jonathan's letter, "that people aren't always what they seem to be at first."

"But sometimes they are," Sam said.

Dana couldn't dispute that. It was only after he drove away, when she stood by the garage admiring the freshly painted *Mermaid,* that she thought of how he had mentioned seeing her when she had lived on the Vineyard and wondered how that had come about.

She thought about how she and Lily had lived in Gay Head, how Lily had met Mark, her island man. A carpenter, he had come to their house to fix a broken porch rail. Lily had fallen in love with him, and six months later, he had proposed to her on Honeysuckle Hill, a small rise covered with flowers and vines, with long views from Gay Head to Menemsha, across the trees and ponds. "That's our sacred ground," Lily had proclaimed, and every year on the anniversary of his June sixth proposal, she and Mark returned there to camp out.

Quinn had been conceived and born on the island. All of

Mark's old friends had showered her with love. They had baby-sat. Lily had taken her for long hikes and bike rides all over the island. A lifelong Vineyarder, Mark had kept them on the island as long as he could. But the year-round economy off island was better, so Lily had tempted him home to Hubbard's Point. From there, he had started his real estate development company and become quite well off.

Sometimes old friends contacted him for jobs. Some were willing to leave the island, but most weren't. That was the thing: Mark wasn't allowed to build there. Because Lily had adored the place so much, revered the incredible natural beauty of the moors and beaches, Mark had agreed to never develop Vineyard land.

When winters got tough and men were out of work, some agreed to fly to New York or Hartford or Louisville or Dayton— wherever Mark Grayson was building his new tract. He liked to hire islanders but never at the expense of excellence. Proud of his buildings, he wanted only the best.

Thinking of those things, wondering about his last projects, Dana sat on the wall to read the letter from Jonathan. The sun shined down, causing her to squint. He wanted to know whether she wanted the things from her studio. Her paints and canvases were just sitting there, and he couldn't believe she didn't want them. All she had to do was ask, and he would ship them to the States.

She crumpled the letter and held it in her hand.

THE NEXT MORNING it started to rain, and the bad weather lasted for four days. Quinn panicked the first day, but by the second she was near despair. Wind had torn down the few signs that hadn't already been ruined by raindrops. The hot dogs, mustard, and ketchup would keep, but all that money for fresh rolls!

"They'll be stale," she said. "They'll have little green mold dots."

"No, they won't," Aunt Dana said, putting the plastic bags into the freezer.

"The buns are ruined," Quinn said. "Ruined!"

"I'm telling you, all will be well. When I was your age, the exact same thing happened. We had put up signs, everyone had promised to come, and then the rains came instead. Quinn, it was like a tropical deluge. My mother did the same thing I'm doing now: put things in the freezer to wait it out."

"What happened?" Quinn asked. "Did you get to have the stand?"

"We did."

Quinn cringed inwardly. She didn't want to show Aunt Dana how much it hurt to hear her say "we." She noticed it always, but on dark rainy days like this, thinking of the other half of Aunt Dana's "we" made Quinn's bones ache.

"You will too," Aunt Dana said. "You'll make plenty of money to buy whatever it is you're saving up for."

Quinn was silent, imagining the things Aunt Dana thought she wanted to buy. Normal twelve-year-old-girl stuff: CDs, short skirts, baggy pants, makeup, pierced earrings. The idea of such things seemed as far away to Quinn as the distant shores of Long Island, across the Sound.

Closing her eyes, Quinn felt in her heart the one thing she wanted to buy with the money. One answer, one little answer.

She thought of her aunt's pictures, the ones she had seen at the Black Hall Gallery: big squares of water, each painting like a photograph of one small section of the sea. She imagined bringing into focus that spot under the Sound where her parents had been lost, framed in her mind like one of Aunt Dana's pictures.

"There," Aunt Dana said, looking into the open freezer door, letting the frosty air billow into her face. "All packed away. Those hot dog rolls are safe from mold now, Quinn."

"What if Sam doesn't come back? What if it rains so long, he forgets about the hot dog stand?"

"Then we'll call and remind him."

"I want him to come."

"I know you do."

"Do you too?"

Aunt Dana looked surprised to be asked, instantly on guard. "Sure," she said carefully. "I like Sam."

Quinn nodded. She wasn't sure why, but she wasn't reassured. Aunt Dana didn't sound as if she meant it. Quinn had felt good, coming home to find Sam helping paint the boat. He balanced things out a little, a man in this house of women. Grandma certainly hadn't had any men around when she'd stayed with them, and Aunt Dana's boyfriend Jonathan—whoever he was—was far away in France. Besides, Sam was the only one who could help Quinn.

"Would you like a cup of tea?" Aunt Dana asked, putting her arm around Quinn's shoulders. "We can sit by the window and wait for the rain to pass."

"No, thank you." Quinn tried to smile. Longer to wait, she thought. One more day until she could earn the money to pay Sam. One more day she had to wait for her answer. The minute Aunt Dana left the room, she ran out into the rain to go to Little Beach and sit on her rock.

CHAPTER 10

HEARING A KNOCK ON THE DOOR, DANA CALLED OUT, "Come in!" She was sitting in the living room, midway through writing a letter, when Marnie walked in wearing a streaming yellow slicker. She stood off to the side, trying not to drip on the floor.

"It's okay," Dana said. "With all the wet bathing suits that have come through this house, I think we can handle a few raindrops."

Marnie laughed, shaking off like a wet dog, hanging her slicker on a hook by the stone hearth. "You're right. All those times we trekked in with sandy feet, leaving little wet patches on the cushions when we sat down . . ."

"I did the same at your house. Beach life . . ."

"We're so lucky to have these places," Marnie said, looking around the room at the salt-darkened wainscoting and old wicker furniture.

"And the grandparents who built them."

"And gorgeous young sailors scraping paint in sweaty T-shirts. Hello, Adonis!"

"Adonis?"

"That handsome and, incidentally, rather intriguing fellow I saw you painting with."

"Oh," Dana said, feeling herself blush. "That was just Sam."

" 'Just' Sam? He looked like more than enough to me."

"I've known him a long time. He's an old sailing student of mine and Lily's—dating way back."

"What's wrong with 'way back'? That makes getting to know each other so much easier."

Dana became silent. She agreed with Marnie. *Really* knowing someone was more important than she had ever, in her solitary life, imagined. But that took years. Young men didn't even know themselves. If that was true, how could they ever know someone else?

Sam seemed so deep, different than other people his age, as if he had already lived through a lot, understood the ways she and the girls felt. But that was probably just a trick of her mind. She couldn't afford to think like this. He'd get tired of their lives, their dramas and trauma. Who would want to hang around a single aunt and her two orphan nieces for very long? Not Jonathan, that was for sure. . . .

"Well, anyway," Marnie continued, "I like imagining you with Sam. He looked nice, and you were laughing, as if you were having fun. Fun is good, Dana."

"I know," Dana said, staring at a small dark spot across the cove.

"What good is being a world-traveling artist if you don't have a little fun in your life? I hope it's not Sam's age. Age is about the least significant thing going. Older, younger, who cares, if someone makes you smile? It doesn't matter."

"Age matters," Dana said, glancing down at the letter on her lap.

"What do you mean?"

"My last boyfriend was younger. It didn't work out."

"I'm sorry, Dana," Marnie said. She had picked up on the hurt; Dana couldn't hide it, even after six months.

"My boyfriend—my ex-boyfriend," she said, "was ten years younger. I told myself it didn't matter. We had so much in common that had nothing to do with age. He was a painter, and we shared a studio in Honfleur. We took trips, painted en plein air, set up our easels by the Bosporus, the Aegean. . . ."

"It sounds idyllic."

"It was for a while." Dana blinked, her gaze drawn to the mantel. She stared at the plain brass box, and her throat ached. "When Lily died, everything changed. I couldn't paint; some days I couldn't even get out of bed."

"We all felt that way," Marnie agreed.

"Jonathan couldn't understand," Dana said. "He tried at first— he has a sister he loves, and I think he imagined how he'd feel if anything happened to her. But he got tired of me."

"*Tired* of you?"

"Impatient, I guess. I couldn't paint; I didn't want to travel anymore. I couldn't see the point of it . . . I had a model, and I fired her."

"A model?"

"I used her for my mermaids—never mind, it doesn't matter. The thing was, I couldn't work at all anymore."

"That's what grief does," said Marnie, taking Dana's hand. Dana knew she knew: Marnie's father had died when she was only fourteen.

"Yes, it is," Dana said quietly. "I told myself Jonathan's never lost anyone close to him. He's lucky—how would he know? He's too young; he's never been that hurt or disappointed by life. . . ."

"Yet," Marnie said.

Dana nodded. She had made excuses to herself for the way Jonathan had acted. He had held her for the first twelve hours after she'd gotten the news, held her while she'd cried and keened and tried to absorb the news of Lily's death. He had driven her to the airport to go to the funeral, and he had picked her up when she came back.

"We weren't really serious," she said. "I thought we were, but we weren't. I was wrong, falling in love with someone so young."

"Do you think that's because of his age? Or because of his character?"

Dana was quiet, and she surprised herself by thinking of Sam.

Something made her think he would have been more patient with her, not try to rush her through her feelings. She had realized soon after her return from Lily's funeral that Jon expected her to be back to normal right away.

He'd pack picnics and load the car with their paints and easels, then stand silently in the doorway of their bedroom, watching Dana lie in their bed. He'd accept invitations to dinner, get upset when Dana said she wasn't going.

"You've got to get past this, over this," he'd say. "Let me help you. . . ."

"How do I get 'past'—'over'—losing Lily?" she had cried to him one day when he'd wanted to take her to Paris to paint in the Bagatelle.

"This is your life, Dana," he had yelled back. "Not Lily's, not anyone else's. She died two months ago, and you're still in bed. Hiding under the covers isn't going to bring her back."

Dana hadn't even had a response for that.

"Your niece called," he had said, sounding frustrated, knowing that the only thing to jump-start Dana was a call from one of the girls. He knew that she'd drag herself out of bed, go to the phone, and call home. Quinn and Allie could get her moving when all else, even he, had failed.

Dana had found herself living in a life that didn't work. What was she doing, yelling back and forth about her sister's death? She was learning all about walls and armor, all the defenses a person put up when fear and loss crowded in. The bedsheets were her castle walls; nothing could get in and hurt her while she lay there, warm and hidden, away from the world.

She learned other things too. She couldn't make someone—Jonathan—understand what she was going through if he wasn't ready to understand. They'd been calling what they felt for each other love. Such a beautiful word, but too big for what they had.

She pictured him now. He was so strong, so intense and talented, her beautiful lover. Tall and broad, with wide dark eyes in his tan, olive-colored skin, long black hair knotted behind his head, he took after his Greek mother. Dana had met him her first week in Honfleur. Both American artists drawn to Normandy's clear light, they had set up their easels by the port, wanting to paint the quai.

They had circled each other's work. He was good, very good. He told her that he had been watching her all along, that he was in awe of her canvas: Staring at the narrow houses squeezed together along the port, she had somehow seen the sea instead. Her canvas was a wash of blue and green, the tall port houses seen through water, shimmering beneath the waves.

"It's magical," he said, staring at her painting. "Brand new. You actually see it that way or make it up as you go along?"

"I see it that way."

"Nothing's brand new anymore. Art school's full of people trying to make their own style, find their own vision, but it's all just one big rehash. You know? It's after Wyeth or Welliver or Picasso or Renoir or Pollock or Metcalf, you do your best to make it your own, but it's always after someone. Not you, though. I've never seen anything like this before. What's your name, so I can say I knew you when we were both painting in Honfleur?"

"Dana Underhill," she said, smiling.

"I'm Jon Hull," he said, shaking her hand without bothering to wipe the paint off his first. Grinning down at their clasped fists, he'd held on tighter. "Maybe originality's catching. I'll get some of yours through the oils if I shake hard enough."

"You're very good," she said, admiring his canvas. Their ages were very much in play; she was the older, more experienced artist. She had lived all over the world, taught at RISD and Parsons, exhibited often. But she admired his technical skill, his palette, his dreamy use of light. While she examined his painting, she realized that he had not let go of her hand.

Looking into his deep-set eyes, she felt shocked by the lust she saw in his gaze, the slow smile lifting his lips. He had to be ten years younger. This was dangerous, unknown territory. Gorgeous movie stars dated younger men. Women who spent time on their appearance, who took pride in the way they looked. Dana hardly noticed. So busy painting, some days she forgot to brush her hair.

"Come have a drink with me," he said.

"No, I have to—"

"Listen," he said. "We're two American painters standing on the quai in Honfleur. See that café over there? That's where Claude Monet and Eugène Boudin set the standard for color and light. Let's do our part for Impressionism, okay?"

"Well, if you put it that way," she replied, so entranced by the idea of two Americans in France discussing art that she forgot to be uncomfortable.

They had gone to Au Vieux Honfleur, taken a table on the terrace. Jon ordered a plateau des fruits de mer, piled high with langoustines, spider crabs, the fat and meaty crabs called torteaux, clams, periwinkles, and four kinds of oysters. After one bottle of gewürztraminer they ordered another. Dana sketched the bowl of halved lemons. Jon drew the oysters on ice. She started to sketch him sketching the oysters, and suddenly he came around the table and kissed her.

They went back to her studio. She showed him her paintings and he helped her out of her clothes. They lay on the little daybed in the corner, where she often took naps during long days of work—calling up the mermaids, those muses deep in her subconscious, to help her find the inspiration needed to finish her work—and they made love.

Her studio became his studio. He told her he wanted to study under her—in bed as well as in art. He moved in the next week, lugging his belongings from the hostel he'd been staying at. They were madly in love. Jon unlocked passions Dana hadn't known she had. The mermaids became obsolete. With Jonathan Hull in her life, who needed muses? Love with a younger man was totally underrated. What man her own age had the energy, creativity, and romance to fill Dana with this lust for life?

"What are you thinking about?" Marnie asked now.

"How being with a young man isn't worth it. It's the biggest mistake I've ever made," Dana replied.

She remembered that morning when Jon told her Quinn had called. Dana had phoned back, dressed in her nightgown, helplessly holding the receiver and listening to Quinn cry and cry.

Jon had watched her from the doorway. He had held her, trying to comfort her. But when she couldn't let go, he backed off and told her he thought he needed a break. It would be good for them both, he said—he knew he was driving her crazy, telling her to smile, to get over it. Packing his easel into the car, he drove off to Étretat to paint.

Dana had known it was going to be over soon. The truth of their differences was too great to ignore. The end came with a true identity crisis. Dana had spent most of her life being independent, avoiding relationships for her art. Now she needed someone to help her deal with Lily's death and love her through the worst, but that person was never going to be Jon.

He must have begun seeing Monique soon after that day. She caught them on the daybed three weeks later, both naked and young and beautiful, and although she thought her heart would break again, it was nothing compared to the loss of Lily.

"So what you're saying is, you're going to hold him against Sam?"

"It's not like that," Dana said, "between Sam and me."

"For an artist, you're pretty blind. Even I could see—"

"Marnie, I see what I need to see," she said in a rush, disturbed by the idea. "Don't worry about me, okay?"

"Looks like you're watching the beach right now," Marnie said, noticing Dana's position by the window as she sat on the adjacent sofa, deciding to drop the subject of Sam.

"Quinn's sitting on that rock," Dana said, pointing at the tiny dark spot atop the biggest granite boulder across the cove at Little Beach.

"Keeping vigil."

Dana didn't reply.

"For her parents," Marnie said. "Martha told my mother she did it all year—even through the winter. Watched the spot where they went down as if she hoped they'd somehow appear."

Quinn, Dana thought, silently staring at that black dot on the big rock. And she thought: How couldn't he understand what happened, how death could make one person take to bed and another person sit on a rock for an entire year?

Sitting on a rock in the rain, praying for a vision of Lily, made much more sense to her than the idea of picking up a paintbrush, going back to work, pretending to get back to someone else's idea of normal. To Dana, watching the small, dark, unyielding shape that was her niece, Quinn's actions seemed the most natural things in the world.

SAM HADN'T THOUGHT about loneliness in a long time.

As a child, he had known it well. His brother was gone, his parents were distracted, and Sam had been pretty much left on his own. Now, sitting in the cabin of his Cape Dory while rain lashed the deck above, he tried to concentrate on his papers and wondered why he suddenly felt so lonely again—with a vengeance.

Life was going his way. Who could think otherwise? He was a college professor—at Yale, no less. All those years of study and research had added up to a decent teaching post. To make matters even better, when Joe finished his latest treasure hunts off the coasts of Greece and Sicily, he was accepting a yearlong fellowship at Yale. The brothers would be colleagues, but more important, they would be in the same spot for more than just a few weeks.

What else? Sitting at his desk, feeling the sea rock him back and forth, Sam made a list of reasons he should be happy.

Women liked him. Strange but true. After years in the shadow of his bigger, handsomer brother, Sam had suddenly come into his own. Maybe it was the weights. Perhaps it was the miles he ran. Probably it was the fact that he had quit trying so hard. He'd just given in to being himself, forgotten about how he wasn't now and wouldn't ever be Joe.

He liked—no, loved—his work. Being a professor was only half of it. The rest was collecting and analyzing data, being ahead of the curve on knowledge regarding marine mammals. He was writing a book on the emotional lives of dolphins, the ways they connected and communicated with each other and—bizarrely enough—the humans who studied them.

While Joe used his oceanographic background on annual trips to distant seas in search of sunken ships and buried treasure, Sam had recently—the last two winters—begun visiting the sea off

Bimini. There, in clear Bahamian waters, he had made the acquaintance of a family of spotted dolphins. Della, Minnie, and Sugar, they had welcomed him directly into their midst, leading him over the sand flats into the reef. He tracked them via transmitter and the observation of local scientists and fishermen, and the tapes of their songs and calls kept him company on long northern nights.

So why was this summer storm making him feel so lonely?

He felt like that little kid, abandoned by his brother and worried about his mother, who had wandered down to the Ida Lewis docks in search of new friends. Rain pelted the portholes, drowning out Della on the tape player. Lightning flashed, making him jump. Storms had scared him as a kid. His mother, working long hours, had never been there to comfort him. But from that first morning on the dock, the day she had asked him to join the sailing school, there had been Dana.

She had made a difference. She had plucked him off the dock, made him believe he mattered. Some days Sam had felt like a throwaway kid. His parents had gotten married without any apparent real love. His mother, a widow, had needed a father for Joe. His father, a truck driver for the lobster co-op, had thought maybe he was ready to settle down. As things turned out, he was wrong.

Sam had been the kid in the middle. By the time Dana came along, his father had died and his mother was a widow again. Dana made him feel wanted. She had acted as if he were special, as if her class wouldn't be the same without him.

He had never forgotten, after all this time. Though he couldn't, at eight, have called what he felt for her love, he knew that some kind of seed had been planted. Now, moving from his desk to his bunk, he lay still and listened to the rain. The boat rocked beneath him.

His boat—his home as well as his companion—had never felt so lonely. Reaching up to the shelf above his head, he pulled out an old notebook. This tome dated back—way back. Among other things, it held the drafts of four letters, never sent, written when he was seventeen and eighteen. More important, it contained two pictures—taken when he was nineteen, at the edge of the sea on an island—that told the story of why he'd never gotten around to mailing the letters that had seemed so important to write.

The wind and rain outside were nothing.

Seeing Dana again had started the real storm brewing. Sam read and reread the letters. He stared at the photos, wondering how it was possible that she had physically changed so little over the years. In other ways, deep-down ways, she had changed a great deal. Dana was living a life of sorrow now. Sam could feel it in his own bones, as if this gale carried that truth on the wind.

Closing his eyes, he thought back beyond the letters and pictures to the day she and Lily had pulled him from Newport Harbour. In his childish gratitude, he had promised she would never have to worry, that he'd protect her forever. She had laughed and called him her hero.

People were expected to forget things like that. Dana was young, and Sam was just a kid. But he had never forgotten. No matter what she might think, no matter whether she had never taken his promise to heart, Sam had been deadly serious.

And he knew the time had come to make good.

Dana Underhill needed him now.

He knew by the emptiness in her eyes, by the way she could no longer paint, by the desperation of her niece. Helping Quinn would be a start, but Sam knew he was really doing it for Dana.

He had a tank in his chest, mowing down everything in its path: sense, manners, the old Sam. He had connected with her long ago. Perhaps he hadn't realized until that moment on his bunk, in the cabin of his sailboat, just how much he needed to do this for her. Every girl, every relationship he had had, had been judged with her as the standard. She had been his older woman, as far out of his league as a goddess.

Those days were over. Goddesses didn't cry. Their worlds didn't fall apart when their sisters drowned. They could paint with sea and sky, and their palettes never dried up. Dana might not know it, but she was in his sights. She needed him as much as he had ever needed her, and as soon as this storm ended, he was going to save her.

CHAPTER 11

FINALLY, HOT DOG DAY ARRIVED. ALLIE WAS SO EX-
cited, you'd have thought it was Christmas morning. Quinn
watched her change her clothes twice, trying to decide on the perfect thing. When she dragged their mother's "kiss the chef" apron
out of the pantry, it took everything Quinn had to keep from reading her the riot act, telling her to pull herself together.

"It's just a hot dog stand," Quinn said calmly. "And you're not
even cooking."

"I know, but it's my first job," Allie said. "I want to look right."

"You look great," Aunt Dana said. "Just like a real entrepre-
neur."

Quinn didn't know what that meant, but she didn't let on.
Silently, she piled the hot dogs, buns, mustard, ketchup, and relish
into the big wicker picnic basket. The night before, when the rain
had stopped, Aunt Dana and she had ridden their bikes around the
beach, putting up new signs.

HOT DOG ROAST TOMORROW!
FOLLOW YOUR HUNCH, TIME FOR LUNCH,

BRING A BUNCH, COME TO MUNCH!
99 Cresthill Road, noon till one (or until we run out)

Looking at the clear, starry sky, Quinn sent a silent message to Sam. Although she was pretty sure he'd figure it out on his own, she picked up the phone and called him—just in case. She got his voice mail, so she left a message: "Hey, Sam. It's Quinn. I'm getting the money to pay you, having the hot dog stand. Come have one, okay? I'll only charge you half price. Nah, since you're driving so far, I'll give it to you free. See you tomorrow."

Now, as Aunt Dana set up the grill down by the road, Quinn settled the soda cans into the ice-filled cooler. Charcoal rattled into the kettle. The sound of a match, the smell of smoke: Quinn felt her chest tighten. Would everything always remind her of her parents? Her father had always been the one to start the grill for family cookouts. Trying to put that out of her mind, Quinn concentrated on her work.

"What if no one comes?" Allie asked, sounding anxious.

"They will," Aunt Dana promised.

"How do you know?" Quinn asked. In spite of her older-sister status, she was just as nervous as Allie. She'd never done anything like this before. Her mind filled with images of sad lemonade stands on the sides of roads traveled by practically no one, lonely children desperately waving after stray cars that would never stop.

"Because I did this myself once, remember?" Aunt Dana said confidently. She wore shorts and a white shirt, and her hair was still damp from her morning swim.

Quinn stared at her without saying anything. If her mother were here, she'd be wearing a flowing sundress and straw hat. She'd have decorated the folding table with roses from her garden, and she'd have baked corn bread flavored with rosemary and thyme. Aunt Dana turned from the grill as if waiting for Quinn to speak, but Quinn just resumed burying cans of soda in the ice. There weren't really any words for what she was thinking.

Their first customer was Quinn and Allie's grandmother. She pulled up in her little Ford wagon and did one of her classic parking jobs: with the rear end sticking straight out in the street.

"Good thing we live on a dead end," Quinn muttered.

"Quinn . . ." Aunt Dana said warningly.

"If we have any real customers, they won't be able to get by!" Quinn protested, but Aunt Dana was too busy popping the first frankfurter onto the grill to comment.

While Grandma took four—Quinn couldn't help timing her—entire minutes to doctor her hot dog with mustard and relish, the McCray clan came across the street. Marnie McCray Campbell and her daughters, Cameron and June, and her mother, Annabelle McCray, walked over and placed their orders.

"Well, Martha," Old Annabelle called out, "doesn't this just bring back memories!"

"Mmmm . . . I . . . gwuas . . . tinking . . . ame . . . ting," Grandma said with her mouth full.

"Girls, this is like one big old déjà vu," Annabelle said. "How many years ago was it now? Twenty? My God, it has to be thirty! That's right, more like thirty! Well, anyway. There were Dana and Lily, proud as punch, selling hot dogs just like you girls are now."

"Proud as punch?" Allie asked, playing right into her hands.

"Yep," Annabelle said. "With nice homemade signs just like you girls hung up, all dressed up in Martha's aprons—Lily pretty as a picture—serving up frankfurters to anyone with fifty cents to spend. Lunch for fifty cents! I fed Marnie, Charlotte, and Lizzie for less than two dollars. Those were the days. . . ."

"Yeah, the *olden* days," Quinn said.

Annabelle laughed. She was from the South, and she was polite and good-humored about everything. If she heard the tone in Quinn's voice, indicating that she didn't really feel like standing around talking about her mother, she didn't let on. Aunt Dana just stuck more hot dogs on the grill, and when they were done, Quinn slid them into the rolls.

"What are you saving up for, if I might ask?" Annabelle asked.

"It's a big secret," Grandma announced. "She won't tell anyone."

"I'll get Cameron to get it out of her," Annabelle laughed. "Right, Cam?"

Quinn shot Cameron a look of daggers. She didn't want her

getting any ideas. Quinn would go to the grave with her plan, and she didn't need any interference from the McCrays.

"Sure, Grammy," Cameron said, rolling her eyes.

Allie straightened her apron. To keep it from dragging on the ground, Aunt Dana had rolled it up around her waist. It now said just "kiss the," with "cook" bunched up in the folds. "My money's for white flowers," she said.

"White flowers?" Annabelle asked, dimpling as if Allie had just said the most enchanting thing possible.

"Why white flowers?" Aunt Dana asked.

"For Mommy," Allie said. "If we had a grave, I'd put white flowers on it. You know, Grandma, when we visit Granddad at the cemetery, how you always put geraniums there?"

No one was talking and no one was eating. Quinn felt her stomach start to churn. Grandma nodded yes to Allie's question, but she didn't say a word.

"Mommy loved white flowers," Allie said. "Daddy wouldn't care. He didn't like the garden much. But Mommy did—"

"I've always said," Annabelle began in that low-voiced southern way of hers, "that not having a grave is a mistake. The children need someplace to visit. Now, cremated or not, there's no reason why the remains can't be buried, a headstone set in place."

"Quinn tried to take her parents' ashes on the plane," Cameron volunteered.

"Well, naturally," Annabelle said kindly. "She needs to know where they are!"

Something yowled like a cat. The sound was fierce and guttural, and it seemed to come from a cave beneath the earth. Suddenly, to her shock and horror, Quinn realized it had come from her.

"They're not going to be buried . . ." Quinn said through gritted teeth.

"Darling, I didn't mean to say anything hurtful," Annabelle said.

People had started to arrive for the hot dog stand. One family parked its car behind Grandma's. Three children rode up on their bikes.

"They're not going to be underground," Quinn moaned.

"Quinny," Aunt Dana said, holding out her hand.

Quinn clenched her eyes shut. She tried to see her parents' faces. She wanted them so badly right now, her blood felt like ice water in her body. People were talking, and she tried to block it out. Her parents were safe, as safe as she could make them, on the mantel. She had to keep them there until she found out what had really happened, whether they had left her on purpose.

Suddenly, she heard a familiar vehicle: Sam's van came rumbling down the street. He had barely parked, stepped out of the driver's seat, when Quinn ran over to him. Tears were rolling down her face, and she couldn't stop them.

"Take me out there now," she said in a hot whisper.

"Now?" he asked, his eyes wide behind his gold-rimmed glasses. "I don't have my boat here."

"We have the *Mermaid*," she said, pointing at the old sailboat— its paint newly dry—sitting on a trailer in front of the garage. Quinn, who hadn't wanted to sail since last summer, now couldn't wait to go aboard.

"I know we have her," Sam said, touching the gunwale but staring at Quinn, "and I think it's time to launch her. But we have to do something else first."

"What?" Quinn asked.

"Have lunch," Sam said.

"How can you think of eating at a time like this?" Quinn asked, feeling a black hole where her heart used to be.

"You invited me, and I drove all the way from New Haven. Besides, you're going to owe me big-time. My services don't come cheap."

Quinn peered at him through her tears. Slashing angrily at her eyes, she gave him a long, hard stare, letting him know that if he wanted it to be all business, that's what he'd get. She knew plenty about give-and-take, about getting what you paid for.

She had listened to her father on the phone more than once. He had been a businessman, a real estate developer, and Quinn knew about tough negotiations. She understood about people demanding to be paid—including her father. *Ideals are nice, sweetheart,* her father had once told her, *but money is how the world works.*

"Quinn?" Sam asked, smiling as if he'd thought she would be laughing at his joke by then. Aunt Dana had walked over to stand silently beside her. Quinn felt them watching her, as if she were an egg about to break.

"I have to get back to work," she said harshly. "People came to my hot dog stand, and I'd better earn my money."

DANA HADN'T EXPECTED to get the boat launched this way, on the same day as the girls' hot dog stand. As soon as the supplies had run out and the money was divided between Quinn and Allie, Quinn began dragging the trailer toward the hitch on the back of Sam's van.

"Whoa," Sam said, going over to help her. He asked Dana; she said it would be okay to launch the boat. So they all took a ride down to the end of the beach, lifted the old Blue Jay over the sea-wall, stepped the mast, and prepared to sail.

Standing in the shallow water, hooking on the jib, Dana felt the small waves licking her ankles. Memory tugged her back to her own childhood, days of sailing with Lily, but she was brought straight into the present by the determination on Quinn's face.

"I didn't think you liked to sail anymore," Dana said quietly while Sam and Allie worked on sliding the rudder into place. Her heart was still pounding from the ruckus on Cresthill Road, Quinn's outburst and subsequent stony silence.

"That's beside the point," Quinn said.

"You don't have to snap at me, Quinn. Just because Annabelle had an opinion you didn't like, it's not my fault."

"I know. I'm sorry. And thank you for cooking the hot dogs. We made a lot of money."

"You're welcome." Dana smiled, feeling happy to be thanked and apologized to at the same time.

When Sam had checked the rudder and centerboard and Dana was satisfied with the sails, the two girls slipped into orange life jackets and climbed into the bow. Dana went next, and Sam—with his pants rolled up above his knees—pushed the boat into deeper water before hopping over the stern. He looked strong and capable, and she felt quietly touched that he had come back.

The girls, once proficient sailors, huddled together in the bow while Sam held the tiller and Dana worked the jib. Two quick tacks were necessary to sail through the narrow channel between the swimming area and the rocks at Little Beach, and Allie cried out as the boat heeled.

"We're fine," Dana said, holding one girl in each arm. "Don't worry."

"I don't like tipping!" Allie said.

"The boat knows what it's doing," Sam said. "She goes over just far enough, then rights herself."

"Aaaah!" Allie cried, clutching Dana.

"Shut up," Quinn called.

"This is Quinn's fault," Allie choked out, terror in her eyes. "I didn't want to come, but she said I *had* to, that I owe it to Mommy and Daddy. Take me back, I don't like sailing, please take me back to the beach. . . ."

"Okay," Dana said, holding the girls tighter. The sun was bright overhead, and the Sound was flat calm. Still early in the season, there wasn't much boat traffic. A light breeze blew offshore, and the hull sliced the water with a gentle whooshing sound. It was a perfect sailing day, and both girls were excellent sailors, but Dana knew they feared the same fate that had befallen their parents would take them down too. "Sam?"

"We could go back," Sam said, holding the sailboat on a broad reach, the boom swung out wide and the hull nearly flat on the surface as Dana tried to imagine Jonathan in this same situation. "But . . ."

"No buts," Allie gasped. "Please, oh, please!"

"Let him talk," Quinn said through clenched teeth.

"You're good at this, Quinn."

"I used to be."

"Sailing's like riding a bicycle. You don't forget."

"I don't want to . . ."

"He's right, Quinn," Dana said, reaching out. "You can do it.

Your mom said you're the best sailor she ever saw. Including her or me . . ."

"And that's saying a lot," Sam agreed.

Dana laughed, and Quinn almost smiled. Dana could see her smelling the wind, feeling the tiller in her hand. "Go ahead, honey."

Very slowly, with total ease, Sam loosened the main sheet and let go of the tiller. He stopped sailing. The boat drifted slowly, nose into the wind, and sat still one hundred yards off the beach. Both girls relaxed; Dana could feel the tension leave their bodies—and hers.

"Do it, Quinn."

"We're not tipping," Allie said in wonder, craning her neck like a bird peeking out of its nest.

"Look, you've got the world's best sailing teacher onboard right now," Sam said. "I know, because she taught me."

"Me too," Quinn said. "She and Mommy taught me."

"And me," Allie said.

Catching Dana's eye, Sam smiled. He had such a kind and handsome face, she thought. His eyes were so bright behind his glasses, blue-green from reflecting the sea. But she shook her head to let him know it wasn't going to work—Allie was gripping her wrist so tight, Dana thought she'd never get her to let go.

"Quinn, take over," Sam said.

"Right now?"

"Sure. Why not? Allie, you can have a turn too."

"What good will that do?" Allie asked, nails digging into Dana's skin.

"I'm not so scared when I know how to do something," Sam said. "When I feel a little more in control."

"Today might not be the day," Dana said, looking down at Allie's fingers around her wrist.

"I'd like to try," Quinn said slowly. "You want to, Al?"

"I don't know. . . ."

"Sure," Sam said. "Your aunt is the best, and I mean the best. If she could teach me to sail, she can teach anyone."

"We were on the big boat, Daddy's boat," Allie said. "But that was too huge for us to sail. And it tipped a lot."

"Heeled, Allie," Quinn said. "You're saying the wrong thing."

"We won't heel much today," Sam said. "Unless you want to."

Dana felt herself settling down. Being on the water had always calmed her, touched her deep, deep inside. Sam's voice was so quiet, as if it were part of the breeze, and she admired him for coming up with this way to help her nieces, encouraging them to sail where she'd been unable to. She felt Sam—just a little—chipping away one of the high walls she'd built.

"I'll try," Allie said in a tiny voice.

"Me too," Quinn said, and Dana saw that she was staring out into the Sound, in the direction her parents had sailed that last night.

Without anyone changing places, Dana began to refresh their memories. Sam watched her steadily, offering an invisible lifeline she never had to let go of. She showed the girls the sails, told them the difference between the jib and the main. She talked about running and standing rigging, let them touch the halyards and hold the sheets. Allie practiced sliding the jib sheet in and out of its block, while Quinn sat beside Sam and pushed the tiller back and forth.

When the time came, they rearranged themselves. Sam made room for Dana at the helm. Their hands brushed as they passed, and Sam caught Dana's eye.

"All yours, skipper," he said.

"Thanks, Sam," she whispered, and she didn't just mean his deference. Her heart swelled to be sailing again. It was the first time all summer, the first time since Lily's death. It filled her with peace to be sailing in her sister's beloved boat with her sister's two daughters, and she knew she had him to thank for it.

Sunlight glittered on the blue Sound as the girls settled into place. With Allie beside Sam in the bow and Quinn next to Dana at the tiller, very slowly they began to sail.

Allie cried out once as the boat caught the wind. Sam put her hands on the jib sheet, pointing up the mast as he taught her to trim the sail. Dana held her hand over Quinn's, letting her get a feel for the tiller, the boat pointing into the wind and over the calm sea. Then Dana slid away, and Quinn took over.

"We're sailing!" Allie called.

"We're doing it!" Quinn yelled.

Catching Dana's eyes, his face shielded against the sun, Sam nodded. Dana saw him grinning, and she knew she was doing the same thing. She tried to conjure that small boy she had taught to sail in Newport, Rhode Island, so many years before, but all she could see was a wonderful man.

His glasses might have been the same, and she thought she recognized a few freckles and a cowlick. But the wind was blowing her own hair, clearing the cobwebs out of her head and heart, making her nieces sing out loud.

"Lily," Dana said under her breath. "They're born sailors, just like us. We're doing it, Lily. Doing it for you."

CHAPTER 12

BACK AT THE HOUSE, QUINN PRACTICED TYING KNOTS and Allie drew pictures of their sailing adventure. Sam and Dana drank iced tea under the white umbrella. The sun had started to set, turning everything golden. Sam looked over at Dana. Stretched out on the teak bench, her legs seemed to go on forever. Her eyes crinkled, staring over the Sound, and he felt incredibly content to see her looking so happy.

"Thank you, Sam," she said.

"I didn't do anything," he said. "It was you. They're naturals, aren't they? Once they had hold of the tiller, they forgot to be afraid."

"That's how it always is," Dana said, staring over the water as if she were lost in a dream. Maybe she was remembering every kid she'd ever taught. Was that all Sam would ever be to her? Leaning forward, he tried to see into her eyes.

"What are you thinking?" he asked. He knew it could be anything: her nieces, Lily, some man she loved.

"About the ocean," she said.

"That's a big subject," he laughed.

"I've wanted to see them all," she said. "Every one. I've rented houses on the Pacific—in Oregon and in Mexico. A short time in Japan. I spent one winter in the Indian Ocean, in the Seychelles. Someone offered me a chance to teach painting aboard a cruise ship, and I traveled through ice in the Antarctic. Most recently, I saw the Atlantic from the other side, from France."

"A lot of ocean," Sam said.

"But right now," Dana said, shielding her eyes as the sun sank lower, turning her fair skin and white shirt rose, bathing her in light, "I'm wondering why I ever left New England. I love it here so much."

"New England," Sam said, his heart kicking over. "You're not just talking about Connecticut, are you?"

"No," she said. "I loved those summers Lily and I spent in Newport."

"Good students," Sam said, deadpan.

Dana laughed. "That's true. And I loved the Vineyard. . . ."

"The Vineyard?" Now Sam's heart did more than kick. It somersaulted and landed in his stomach. He could practically feel himself reading the ferry schedule. Driving off the *Islander* in Vineyard Haven, asking directions for Gay Head, heading up the North Road.

"You told me you saw me there."

"Yeah, I did."

"I've been thinking about that," Dana said. "Wondering about how."

"What if I tell you after you tell me why you loved it?"

"Well, it was my first house," Dana said. "Lily called it 'my sea away from home.' She thought I was a little crazy to go looking for other water to paint when I had all this." She gestured at the view of Long Island Sound, its waves purple and gold in the sunset. "But then she came to visit and understood. I stayed for just a year, then she took over. For one thing, by then she'd met her husband there."

"At the Vineyard?" Sam asked.

"Yes. I'd found a little cottage up-island, just around the bend from the cliffs at Gay Head." She closed her eyes, and Sam knew she must be picturing the great clay cliffs, the earth painted gold and brown and red as they sloped down into the Atlantic Ocean. "It's just east of Newport, barely over the horizon, but it was the most exotic place I'd ever been. I started painting the minute I arrived, and I don't think I stopped for an entire year."

"You painted the cliffs?"

"I painted the sea," she said. "It's where I began studying the water column. I thought the rocks and the seaweed and the fish and the sediment glittering in the sunlight made the most beautiful picture I could ever paint."

"Big fish off Gay Head," Sam said.

"I know. Once I was swimming at Zacks, and a surfcaster pulled in a blue shark right past me. A big blue shark."

Sam nodded. He felt the blood rush to his face, and he hoped she'd think it was just the sunset. He had seen her swimming at Zacks Cliffs. Gay Head was a small town. That day, searching for her, he had parked his car by the lighthouse and ambled down the path to the beach. He had found her, playing in the waves.

Zacks was a nude beach.

Sam was nineteen. Eleven years after his sailing lessons, after dating girls and wishing they looked like Dana, were as kind as she'd been, made him laugh like she had, Sam had decided to go searching for her.

What did he have to lose?

He'd been tops in his class at Rogers High School, on a scholarship at Dartmouth, taking the fast lane to life as a maverick oceanographer just like his brother. Falling in love wasn't happening for him, and he had a pretty good idea why. None of the girls he knew was Dana. Inspired by Joe's dauntless searching for treasure, Sam had set off on a treasure hunt of his own.

It had started with Lily. Bumping into her in Woods Hole, where he was doing a fellowship for the summer and she was waiting for the ferry, he had casually asked about her sister. The Vineyard, Lily had said. Gay Head, to be precise. And so Sam had gone, found her, swimming nude in the surf at Zacks Cliffs.

"So, how did you end up there?" Dana asked him now.

"The Vineyard?" he asked, blushing harder. "I did graduate work at Woods Hole, just across Vineyard Sound. Couldn't very well have avoided it."

"No, I suppose not," Dana said, smiling.

"We were in Gay Head," Dana said. "The whole Vineyard is great, but Gay Head is . . . magical. Lily loved it too. That little house looking over the moors to the sea. The beam of the lighthouse would sweep the walls, coming straight through our windows. After I decided to move on, Lily kept the place for a year herself. She and Mark fell in love there. In fact, that's where Quinn was conceived. She's named after the place."

Sam waited, watching emotion cross Dana's face.

"Aquinnah," she said. "That's the Indian name for Gay Head. Lily wanted to name her after the place we all loved so much."

"Did you ever go back?"

Dana shrugged, lowering her head. "A few times to visit Lily. Not enough."

"No?"

"Quinn was born there. Lily and Mark tried to make a life for themselves. Painting, Lily could work anywhere. But Mark was a businessman. He bought and sold property—but not on the Vineyard."

"The real estate was too expensive?" Sam asked.

Dana laughed. "No, Lily wouldn't let him. He wanted to develop the land he bought, and she couldn't stand to see the island spoiled. So they—"

"Are you talking about my island?" Quinn asked, coming onto the terrace with a nylon line knotted into a bowline.

"We are," Dana said, sliding her arm around her. Sam gazed at them, aunt and niece. Their faces were alike, high cheekbones and beautiful wide eyes. Their hair, as differently styled as it was, was a similar chestnut brown. Salt from the day's sail glistened in Dana's elegant waves and Quinn's myriad crooked braids.

"Martha's Vineyard," Quinn said, settling onto the blue stone terrace. "I was born there, you know. And I learned how to walk and talk there. I'm named for the most magical part—Aquinnah."

"I know," Sam said, remembering how Dana had used the same word, "magical."

"Someday I'll go back," Quinn said, and suddenly, she seemed to be speaking to the Sound, to that distant spot where her parents had gone down. "I'll see the place where I began."

"Someday," Dana said, pushing herself out of the chair. She faced west, at the stripe of dark red just above the trees of Little Beach. A crescent moon hung there, cradling Venus in its violet embrace. Sam swallowed, remembering how he had watched her one other sunset, when the Gay Head cliffs had glowed like jewels in the dying light. He wanted to tell her, but with Quinn there, he wouldn't.

"Is everyone hungry?" Dana asked. "Should I make dinner?"

"Anything but hot dogs," Quinn moaned.

"Okay," Dana laughed, heading inside to see what she could find.

Sam wanted to follow her, but Quinn stopped him. She took a folded paper from her pocket and spread it on his lap. Sam peered closely, saw that it was a chart. She had drawn a compass rose, the contours of land, a bell buoy, and a green can.

"That's where it happened," she said.

"I see," Sam said.

"It's the Hunting Ground—that's what it's called. Right out there," Quinn said, pointing at the Sound. "Just past the Wickland Shoals. Fishermen say it's the best place to fish between here and Orient Point. It's where my parents' boat sank."

"Where's the boat now?" Sam asked, staring down at the spiky braids on her head.

"Still down there. Their bodies were recovered," Quinn said with no feeling in her voice whatsoever. "They came ashore after three days. I would have found them myself if they didn't. But the boat's another story."

"Tell me," Sam said.

Quinn spun her head to look up at him. "Divers found it. They had to, for the insurance. They were going to bring it up to the surface last summer, but then we had two big storms in a row. A gale, and then that sort-of hurricane."

"Desdemona."

"Yes, Hurricane Desdemona. She moved the boat away from where it had been, just far enough so the divers couldn't find it."

"How do you know? Did they see it again?"

"No, but I know. I feel it." Quinn stood up, staring toward the Hunting Ground. Sam felt a chill, as if she were putting out radar. "It's there. Somewhere close to where they first found it. If we don't get to it first, those divers will go down again. I want to know before anyone else."

Inside, Dana began running water and clattering pans. She had turned on music; Carly Simon sang out the window, making Sam think about the Vineyard again.

"What do you want to know, Quinn?"

"I know what I hope," she whispered, "and I know what I think."

"What do you hope?"

"That it was an accident," she said in a voice thinner than the crescent moon in the western sky.

"And what do you think?"

"That they did it on purpose."

They hadn't noticed Dana. She had stepped onto the terrace, the salad bowl in her arms. Her blue eyes were clear, wide open. Sam knew she had heard, but for some reason she made up her mind not to let on. Holding the big wooden bowl toward Quinn, she held the door open behind her.

"Can you mix the salad, Quinn?" she asked.

"Okay, Aunt Dana."

"What can I do?" Sam asked, carefully folding Quinn's map, putting it into his wallet.

"I don't know," Dana said steadily, never looking away from his eyes. "What can you do?"

THEY ATE DINNER at the table. This time Quinn didn't fight anyone for their seats. Dana made sure to leave Lily's and Mark's chairs unoccupied, and that seemed to satisfy both girls. A soft breeze blew through the open windows, sending thick ropes of wax down the white candles.

It was a family tradition to eat by candlelight every summer night. Candles filled the room. Tall white ones in brass and etched glass holders on the oak table, votives in squat crystal balls on the bookshelves, bright colored candles in pressed-tin angel holders from Mexico, and glazed painted mermaid holders from Greece— gifts sent by Dana from wherever she was. Mozart played on the stereo, Dana's favorite violin concerto.

The telephone rang, and Dana went to answer. It was Victoria DeGraff, the gallery owner who represented Dana in New York. She said she'd sold several large paintings recently, and that a magazine wanted to do a story called "The Artist Who Paints Like a Mermaid."

"Will you come down for lunch soon?" Victoria asked. "And let me set up an interview?"

"I don't know," Dana said, listening to the children laugh with Sam.

"Let me put it this way. You have to. I insist! I've been selling your work for fifteen years now, the least you can do is let me take you to lunch."

"Okay," Dana said, smiling because she realized what a relief it would be to have a little of her old life back, to escape her family for a little while. They decided on the first Thursday in August, said affectionate good-byes, and hung up.

Returning to the table, Dana had to answer Quinn's third degree: Where was she going and for how long?

"New York, in a month," Dana replied. "Just for a day and maybe a night. Grandma will baby-sit."

Satisfied, Quinn sat back. Allie chattered on and on about her sailing prowess. She wanted to quit swimming and tennis, take up sailing. She'd race anyone who came along. When winter swept in, she'd be heading the Frostbite Fleet in Hawthorne Harbour.

"Captain Allie," Quinn giggled.

"What's so funny about that?" Allie asked. "Aunt Dana, were you or Mommy the captain of the *Mermaid*?"

"We took turns," Dana said, sounding stern for Sam's sake.

"Your aunt was the captain in Newport," Sam said.

"Where she taught you?" Allie asked.

"Well, she must've taught you well," Quinn said, yawning from her day in the sun, selling hot dogs and sailing, "because you did okay on board the *Mermaid* today. May I be excused?"

"Yes," Dana said.

"I'm going for a walk," Quinn said, running into the kitchen to get her flashlight. Dana knew she was headed for Little Beach; she wouldn't even try to stop her.

"I'm going to my room," Allie said.

"Don't lose that map," Quinn said to Sam, handing him what appeared to be a wad of money as she hurried out the door.

When Dana and Sam were alone, she felt that familiar sinking feeling come over her. She had to confront someone she wanted to trust, faced with blatant evidence that she shouldn't.

"Did she just pay you?" Dana asked.

"Um," Sam said, distinctly uncomfortable. "Can I tell you it's between her and me and let it go at that?"

"No," Dana said sharply.

The candlelight surrounded them, making the room glow like the inside of a lamp. Outside, the waves splashed the sandy beach. With July Fourth less than a week off, the whistle of a bottle rocket sounded in the distance. Sam craned his neck as if to watch the fireworks, but when he turned back, Dana was still watching him. The Mozart was reaching its crescendo. More than anything in life, she hated being tricked, kept in the dark.

"Tell me," she said.

"I made a promise."

"She's my charge, Sam! If I can't trust you, why should she? Jesus!" Dana burst out, thinking about how easy it was to make promises, how easy it was to break them.

"Okay, Dana," he said as if he'd been trapped. "She wants to hire me to dive on her parents' boat."

"What did she mean out on the terrace, 'they did it on purpose'?"

"That's what she thinks. That the sinking wasn't accidental."

"Oh, God," Dana said. Suddenly, her feelings of betrayal evaporated. Thinking of Quinn's pain, Dana's eyes filled with tears.

"She wants me to come up the Sound with a research vessel—I can borrow one from Yale, no problem. We have a depth sounder that can locate the boat. She thinks if I dive down and look for evidence of an accident—a hole in the bow, for example—everything'll be okay."

"And if there's no hole in the bow?"

"I'll look to see whether the seacocks are open or closed. She mentioned an insurance investigator."

"There was one," Dana said, remembering Fred Connelly—his friendly, round face, his bald head. "Suicide was never a possibility. Or if it was, he never mentioned it."

"What did he find?"

"Nothing like you're suggesting!" Dana exclaimed. "They were sailing across the shipping lane, that's all. There's a lot of traffic out there—tankers, freighters. The night was clear, but Mark might have misjudged his distance . . . it happens."

Sam nodded, but Dana could see he wasn't convinced. What had Quinn told him? What had gone wrong in this house? Unhappiness hid in the walls. Her mother hinted at it, Quinn had blurted it out. The candlelight tried to chase it away, but Dana could feel the emotion. She thought back to her conversations with Lily. Everything had always been "great," "wonderful," "perfect." Why hadn't Dana been tipped off to dig deeper?

"It happens," Dana said out loud again.

"Quinn thinks her parents went down on purpose."

"You're encouraging her in this?"

"How can you think that?"

"Taking her money," Dana said, the anger building. "Hanging around here so much."

"It's not because of Quinn," Sam said.

"She's vulnerable," Dana said, ignoring him. Her body tensed up, and she went to the window. There, across the cove, she saw the gleam of Quinn's flashlight. Playing out over the water, it seemed to point straight at the Hunting Ground.

"Yes, she is, and she has you to help her."

"I'm trying, but it's not easy. I don't understand her. I don't know what's going on in her head. I'm her aunt, not her mother, and I'm worn out just trying to keep up."

"I know, Dana."

"You don't know!" she said, a shiver going through her. "You remember me from the old days. You picture me sailing in any weather, always ready to race. Well, that's not how I am anymore," she cried, shuddering as the words flew out.

"You're strong, Dana. So strong."

"That's just what people want to think," Dana said.

"Quinn asked for my help," Sam said. He wore the same shirt he'd worn sailing, and his muscles gleamed in the candlelight. Salt crystals sparkled on his hair and eyebrows. "And I'm not backing down."

"I'm her guardian," Dana said. "If I ask you to back down, I expect you will."

"Why would you ask?"

"Encouraging her to think her parents sank their own boat?" Dana burst out. "You think that's helping her?"

Staring across the cove, they saw Quinn's flashlight holding steady. "It would be a focus for her," Sam said as he watched. "Something for her to do. Searching for evidence is real, solid, better than living with her fears."

"It's a terrible idea."

"Are you afraid it will turn out to be true?" Sam asked. "Are you using your own fear to keep her from finding out the truth?"

Dana didn't reply. She thought of Mark's locked tackle box in the garage and shivered. Why hadn't she gone back and opened it before now? What was she so afraid of learning about her sister's life?

"She's keeping vigil on that rock," Dana said. "She'd do it all night if I let her."

"Maybe you should let her," Sam said.

Dana looked over at him. "Why do you say that?" she asked.

"I'll tell you someday," Sam said.

"You know about keeping vigil?" Dana asked.

"For my father," Sam said.

Dana wanted to ask him why, but just then she noticed that Quinn's flashlight had begun to bob through the woods, across the rocks on her way home. Sam had seen it too, and he turned back to Dana.

"We're together on this?" he asked.

The word "together" was too strong. It made Dana think of being part of a couple, or a team. She shook her head, but Sam pressed on.

"You'll let me take her out to the site?"

Dana hesitated, but she nodded yes.

"I'm coming back tomorrow."

"To go out there?" Dana gestured at the window.

"No, not yet. I can't use the boat till the marine biology summer session's done with it."

"Then why?"

"Dana, what do you think?" he asked, stepping closer.

"Stop it, Sam," she said, her heart beginning to pound.

"You know, don't you? How I feel—"

She shook her head hard, pushing him away. She felt a sob press against her throat. "Stop talking like that. I'm trying to fill a role here. It's hard enough. My own life's turned inside out—"

"I know, Dana. I want to help."

"Help Quinn, then. Not me."

"What did I do to hurt you?" he asked, his forehead lined with emotion and worry.

"Nothing!"

"Someone did, then. Tell me, Dana. I'd take it away if I could."

"You don't know how," she said, shocked by the bitterness in her own voice. She had heard the saying *Hell hath no fury like a woman scorned,* but she had never before been the woman scorned.

"What happened, Dana?" he asked softly.

She pictured Monique's pretty face pressed into the pillow to avoid seeing Dana. In the same memory frame, she saw Jonathan trying to scramble off the daybed, his naked body taut and straining to grab the blanket to pull around himself. Dana cringed, remembering how they had looked: like two kids trying to hide after being caught by their parents.

Had Dana unconsciously been trying to buy a little sister? Paying Monique to model—as a mermaid, no less!—keeping her around while she tried to paint, explored the landscape of Monet and Boudin, listened to her talk about her family, the humid green fields and beaches of a homeland she'd barely known. Two expatriate women, one older and one younger, far away from the people they loved.

In the end, Dana had been hurt by the two young people she had taken under her wing.

"Whatever it is," Sam said when he saw Dana wasn't going to speak, "I can tell you don't trust me. I wish you did, but you don't."

Dana stared across the cove at Quinn's light, moving closer and closer. Sam stood right beside her, his breath warm on her cheek. He held Quinn's money, bunched up in his fist. Handing it to Dana, their fingers brushed and she looked into his eyes.

She blinked. His gaze was steady, unwavering. His eyes were bright green, and they glowed like boreal fire. She stared at him, ignoring the feeling in her hand where his fingers had touched her, and with the strings of Mozart filling the room, she made her heart as hard as possible.

"You're trying to help Quinn," she said. "It has nothing to do with me."

"That's what you think," Sam said under his breath, turning to walk away as Quinn's light came across the big beach.

IT BOTHERED QUINN that Sam hadn't stuck around to say good-bye. She also hated the idea of Aunt Dana going to New York next month, even for a day. Anything that disturbed the pattern reminded her of change, of things drifting away, of people going out for a few hours and disappearing forever. She thought of their neighbor, Rumer Larkin. How she looked after the wild things of the Point: the birds and rabbits. Quinn wanted to be like that, but with the sea. Keeping track of the sea . . .

Lying in bed, she wished she had her diary with her. She had written a good, long entry about the hot dog stand, earning the money to pay Sam, today's sail that had taken them close to the Hunting Ground. Sailing was in Quinn's blood . . . she had a mission, and she was actually making some headway.

Stars shined through the window. Allie snored from across the hall, slobbering all over Kimba in her sleep. The stairway creaked, and Quinn's heart panged. That was the exact sound her mother used to make coming up to kiss them good night.

The door opened, and Aunt Dana walked in. She sat on the edge of Quinn's bed, and they stared at each other in the dark.

"Aquinnah Jane," Aunt Dana whispered.

"Aquinnah means 'high ground,' " Quinn whispered back. "I'm named for high ground."

"The most beautiful part of the island," Aunt Dana said.

"When can we go there?" Quinn asked.

"Someday."

"It's always someday," Quinn said. "Mommy used to say the same thing. Why can't it ever be Saturday, or tomorrow, or even now?"

"Someday's better. It's always in the future, and it's always possible."

"Never thought of it that way."

"Tell me something, Quinn. My high-ground girl . . ."

"What?" Quinn asked, laughing to hear her aunt being so playful.

"Why do you want to go diving?"

"What are you talking about?" she asked, the question a punch in the stomach.

"You have to assume I know everything. I'm your aunt."

"He told you?" she asked, bypassing her aunt's joking tone.

"I overheard you. And I saw you pay him."

Quinn balled up her fists and tried to slide under the covers. She was so close: The answers were as close as *that*. Sam would dive down, tell her what he saw, and Quinn would *know*.

"I'm not mad at you," Aunt Dana said.

"But you're mad at Sam?"

"Maybe so. That's between me and him though, not for you to worry about. I just wish you'd come to me first."

"You wouldn't understand," Quinn whispered, her blood pumping like a freight train.

"Try me."

"They did it on purpose," Quinn tried to say. She didn't think the words had made it out, but they must have, because Aunt Dana flinched.

"How can you say that? Quinn, in a million years Lily wouldn't have wanted to leave you and Allie. I know that. I'm her sister. . . ."

"I'm her daughter," Quinn gasped.

Outside, the waves hit the beach. Usually, they lulled Quinn to sleep, but tonight they sounded like hammer strikes. She hated the sound of the water just then, but at the same time she wished she were sailing over it.

"Tell me why you—how you think they could have done something like that."

"Because the nightmare came true," Quinn said, clutching her hands. "Because I heard my mom tell my dad he'd thrown it all away."

"Thrown what away, Quinn?"

"Their life. That's what she said: their life."

"You heard your mother say those words?"

Quinn closed her eyes, her face hot and wet with tears. She had been in this very bed, and she had heard the words through these very walls. She could hear her mother's voice now, over the waves Quinn hated so much tonight, crying to her father the night before they died.

"Quinn? You heard Lily say those words?"

"Yes."

"What did she mean?" Aunt Dana asked into the darkness.

"I don't know," Quinn moaned. The night felt like a wind tunnel: long and dark and roaring with endless sound. Quinn wanted to disappear, but her aunt wrapped her in her arms and tried to pull her back.

"We'll find out, okay, Quinn? I have to know too. We're in it together," Aunt Dana said, huddled with her niece.

CHAPTER *13*

DANA WAS NEVER SURE WHAT TO MAKE OF COINCI-
dences. Sometimes she took a practical view, such as when two
people had the same thought or decided to do the same thing at
the same time, thinking it unlikely but possible. Other times, she
thought the stars had to be in line. That morning, nearly a week after their last meeting, when Sam just happened to drive up
Cresthill Road the very minute Dana was setting out on her mission, she wasn't sure.

"What are you doing here?" she asked, going around to the
driver's side of his van. He leaned on the wheel, nicely dressed,
grinning into her eyes in a way that made her shiver. She tried to
look away, but she couldn't.

"Came to help," he said. "I told you I was going to."

"Even though you think I don't trust you," she said, still trying
to look away. His shirtsleeves were rolled back. His bare forearms
looked very sexy, holding on to the steering wheel.

"Even so . . ."

"Why today?"

"Well," he said, rubbing his chin. "That's a good question.

Couldn't yesterday—I had a meeting with two scientists from Scotland. And the day before, forget it—had to cover for the staff oceanographer who runs the harbour study. The two days before that, I wanted to give you a break. You seemed a little tired of me, to put it mildly."

"I was," she said.

"So, my instincts were good."

"Then why are you here now?" she asked.

"Something told me to get in my van and drive here as fast as I could. That you need my help."

"I don't, Sam."

"I don't believe you, Dana. Where are the girls?"

"Crabbing."

"Kids after my own heart." He grinned. "Have you taken them sailing again?"

"Every day. But it's more like they're taking me. Quinn fights me for the tiller, and she's a total natural."

"Quinn and a boat, watch out. She'll be soloing in that round-the-world race before you know it."

Dana held in a laugh because he was so right. Meanwhile, she was quite distracted by his smile, the friendly look in his eyes, and the incredibly defined muscles in his forearms.

"Where are you going?"

"What makes you think I'm going somewhere?"

"You're holding your car keys, heading for your car. You've got a plan."

"I'm not a detective," Dana said. "I'm supposed to be an artist—I don't know what I'm doing."

"Then let me help you." The bantering tone was gone from his voice, the playfulness had left his eyes. His expression was solemn but strong as he watched her now. "Come on," he said. "Get in, I'll drive."

Her stomach lurched as she thought of the plan she had set out for herself. She wanted to send him on his way, do her work in secret. Even more, she didn't want to admit to herself how glad she was to see him. He would never learn because she would never admit that she had wondered where he'd been. Nearly seven days had gone by without a Sam sighting. Consoling Quinn, Dana had felt slightly abandoned herself.

But she refused to let on. When Sam reached across the seat to open the passenger door, Dana stood up taller and walked around the van.

"I don't know what I'm doing," she said. "But I made a promise to Quinn."

"That's good."

"I've put it off for almost a week. I keep thinking we'll sort it out ourselves. I pick up a pencil and try to draw, and nothing comes out. She *lives* on that rock. She's blocked and I'm blocked, so . . ."

"So you decided to do something about it. Just tell me where we're going, and I'll get you there," Sam said. "Whatever you're holding against me will keep till much later."

Feeling bad for her anger the last time she saw him, Dana gave him directions, and ten minutes later they were driving down the shady street past the Congregational Church and the Black Hall Gallery.

Mark's office had been located on the second floor of an old Victorian in the center of Black Hall. Pale yellow with white trim, built in the 1800s, it seemed an unusual spot for a real estate developer. Although he had owned this house, it had been sold after the deaths.

"Pretty place," Sam said, looking through the van window.

"Leave it to Lily," Dana said. "She chose the location. I've never been inside Mark's office, but I remembered the house as soon as she wrote me about it. Miss Alice's store used to be on the first floor—Lily and I would buy penny candy, and one summer I got her a silver locket."

"Maybe that's why her husband bought the house for his office," Sam said. "Because it meant something to Lily."

"I think that's true." Then, turning to Sam, "That's right, you met him once."

"I did, at the theater in New Haven. He loved his wife—that was pretty obvious," Sam said. Sitting behind the wheel of his van, he stared at the house. Everything about it said Lily. The delicate color, white gingerbread, the graceful details, the ivy growing up the chimney, the border of orange and yellow daylilies. The first floor was now occupied by an interior design firm and retail shop.

Dana gazed at the front door, shivering as she remembered the look in Quinn's eyes the other night. Her niece believed something terrible had happened, had been having nightmares about it.

Staring at the front steps, she remembered herself and Lily as children. They had loved Miss Alice's shop. It had smelled of licorice and ginger, and its glass cases held treasures beyond their wildest dreams: moonstone earrings, silver necklaces, enameled pillboxes, velvet pincushions. By saving their allowances, they managed to buy certain things of their own. The memory was piercing and true, as if the ten-year-old Lily might come running up the walk, and Dana had to look away.

"You say you're not a detective, but here we are," Sam said.

"I have no idea what we're looking for."

"So, we'll just look."

"We'll know it when we see it," Dana said.

"That's the spirit. You'd make a good oceanographer—sifting through tons of data in search of that one thing that'll tell the story."

Dana barely heard. She wanted to get this over with. She had asked Marnie if the girls could spend the morning crabbing on her rocks, and she had said yes. Glancing out the window, she couldn't stop remembering Lily as a little girl. Being here was too painful; Monique and Jon couldn't even compare. Dana would leave for France tomorrow if she could.

"Okay," Dana said after a few minutes.

"Are you ready to go inside?"

Dana nodded. They got out of the van, and for the first time since she was twelve, she climbed the wide steps. When she opened the front door, she missed the bell that used to ring there, and instead of Miss Alice's magical clutter, the design shop was filled with sleek sofas and low ebony tables.

"May I help you?" a young saleswoman asked.

"I'm looking for information about Grayson, Inc.—the real estate office that used to be upstairs."

"Oh, Mark," she said, making a sad face. "Didn't you hear what happened to him?"

Just then, a woman appeared from an inside doorway. Slender, with silver-blond hair, she wore a smart black knit suit with pearls at her throat. "I'm Patricia Wentworth. You're Mark's sister-in-law, aren't you?"

"Yes, I'm Dana Underhill," Dana said, shaking her hand, surprised that she would know. "This is Sam Trevor."

"I recognize you from your exhibit—I was there, buying a painting for a client. She's very happy with it."

"I'm glad to hear that," Dana said.

Patricia stood very still, her hands folded. The air-conditioned shop was cool; she looked completely unaffected by the summer heat. Not a blond hair was out of place. Her pearls matched the pallor of her skin tone. If Dana had wanted her house decorated, she would hire this woman for her personal taste alone. On the other hand, she found herself wondering what she was doing here and, at the same time, wishing she had worn something more presentable than khaki shorts and an old green shirt.

"Is there something I can help you with?" Patricia asked.

"We wanted to see where Mark worked," Sam said.

"His office is vacant," Patricia said. "I've been using it to store wallpaper and fabric books. But if you'd like to see it . . ."

"We would," Dana said.

Nodding, Patricia got the keys. Dana followed her up the long flight of stairs, watched as she unlocked the door. Light came through the fanlight over the front door and reflected in the crystal doorknobs. Inside the office, sample books were piled on the floor and one old bench. Furniture had been moved out; the ghostly impressions of chair and table feet made round prints in the dust.

Glancing around, Dana saw nothing at all of her brother-in-law, no left-behind desk or box or paper that might give Quinn the reassurance she was after. The walls were painted creamy yellow, the pine floors were scuffed with use. Four tall windows running the length of the house overlooked the maple trees lining Main Street. Dana saw no evidence that anyone from her family had ever occupied this empty room.

And then she did.

Above each window, in brushstrokes as delicate as anything found in nature, Lily had painted flowers. Tendrils of English ivy climbed the walls, mingling with white flowers of every kind: freesias, daisies, orange blossoms, lilies, roses, camellias, peonies, honeysuckle, and white violets.

"What's that?" Sam asked, following Dana's gaze.

"Lily did those," Patricia said.

"I know," Dana said. She walked closer to the windows, her heart beating harder. Lily's painting style was so distinctive: the way her brush formed each leaf, every petal, the way it traced the stems and vines.

Dana had seen that style in paintings, on birthday cards, on the walls of the Vineyard cottage. The shades of white ranged from nearly pale yellow to nearly pale blue, blending so subtly into the color of the walls, they almost couldn't be seen at all. Her sister's presence filled the room.

"Lily spent a lot of time here," Patricia said. "Obviously a very talented, artistic woman. I tried to hire her to paint walls for me and some of my clients, but she said no, she was too busy with the girls. She seemed to especially love the garden—we all appreciated the beauty she brought here. She and Mark seemed very close. I'm so sorry about what happened."

"Thank you." Dana was a very private person. She used her work to express everything: joy, anger, curiosity, mystery, grief. Asking a complete stranger for answers about her family seemed as alien as dancing down Main Street. But she knew she had come here to help Quinn. Glancing at Sam, their eyes met. He was sending her strength; she knew by the way he drew himself up, held her gaze. She felt a surprising surge of force coming from him, and she took a deep breath.

"Was anything wrong?" she asked.

"Wrong?"

"In his business," she said. "Do you know if there were any problems . . ." She trailed off, feeling embarrassed and exposed even to be asking.

Patricia frowned, shaking her head. "Not that I knew of. I know he developed a project in the Midwest that he had to travel to to check on now and then. Lily would stop by to pick up his mail and say how much she missed him."

"Did he go often?"

"More and more, it seemed. I attributed it to his growing success."

"He was successful," Dana said, not a question. Lily had told her how secure she and Mark had started to feel. Financially, they were in good shape. They had investments and savings, stocks and bonds.

"Yes, he was. After the Sun Center project sold so well, I started teasing him about buying Lily a Mercedes and a mink coat. They weren't like that though. The flashiest thing he bought was that boat," Patricia said, shaking her head. "I wish he hadn't."

"*Sundance,*" Dana said, making a connection. "That was the name of the boat."

"What was the Sun Center?" Sam asked, thinking along the same lines.

"Oh, some sort of assisted living center near Cincinnati. I don't know that much about it, but Lily was proud of his involvement. The place had a very positive aspect—New Age, or something. She said old age homes could look bright but feel gloomy—a place where old people went to die. And that the Sun Center was the opposite—a place where old people go to live."

"Lily *was* proud. She told me a little about it," Dana said, trying to remember the details. When their mother had moved to Marshlands Condominiums, Lily had told Dana about Mark's project. "I wish Mom could go to a place like that," Lily had said. "They have yoga classes, an indoor pool and sauna, a meditation room, movement therapists on staff."

"Sounds almost like a spa," Dana had said, laughing.

"Yes, better than visiting Canyon Ranch," Lily had replied.

"Do they take dogs? She couldn't leave Maggie. . . ."

"Is there some problem?" Patricia asked, discreet but obviously curious about Dana and Sam's visit.

"No," Dana said. "I'm just trying to piece things together. . . ."

"He was away so much that last year," Patricia said, shaking her head. "I'd like to think it was a blessing that he and Lily were together at the end, but those children . . ."

"I know," Dana said.

"Lily used to bring them with her. Sometimes they'd come into my shop and Lily would tell them about the old lady who used to sell penny candy there."

"Miss Alice," Dana said.

"Yes, that's the name. I don't come from Black Hall, but Lily used to tell me she was legendary, that all the children in town thought her shop was a mecca. She showed me the locket she was wearing, a silver locket that came from there."

"I gave it to her," Dana said, feeling a shiver go down her back.

"She had your picture in one side," Patricia said, "and her daughters' in the other. I'd watch those beautiful girls helping her with the garden and think what a wonderful, lucky family they were. How are they?"

Dana opened her mouth, but the question was too big for her to answer. Sam stepped forward, his arm brushing hers, and he spoke in a low, calm tone. "They're doing well," he said. "They're with their aunt, and that's making all the difference."

"I'm glad to hear that," Patricia said. Then, as if sensing Dana and Sam wanted time alone, she backed toward the door. "Just pull the door shut when you're finished," she said. "Take as long as you want, okay?"

"Okay, thanks," Sam said.

Dana had wandered over to the window to stare at Lily's painting of white flowers. The blossoms rose toward the high ceiling, blooming on the pale green vine.

"It's so subtle," Sam said, "you can hardly see it."

"It blends into the yellow walls," Dana agreed.

"Why did she do it that way?" Sam asked.

Dana was silent, picturing Lily's small watercolors in the upstairs hall at home, then thinking of her own huge, bold canvases. She thought of Lily's life as a wife and mother and her own life as a vagabond artist. "That's how she was," Dana said quietly. "She blended in. She put others first, and she never felt the need to shine."

"But she did shine," Sam said. "People loved her."

"That was her secret," Dana said, picturing her sister's smile. "She shined from within."

"She did," Sam said, nodding. "From the first time I ever met her."

Dana turned to look at him. He was so tall and handsome, yet thoughtful and eager to please. The sight of him—his strong arms and sharp gaze—made her heart jump, but his sensitivity soothed and calmed it down again. "How could you tell?" she asked. "You were just a kid."

Sam took a step toward her. Their toes were almost touching, and she tilted her head back to look into his eyes. "I thought you'd know, Dana," he said. "Kids can see inside a person better than anyone."

She blinked, feeling him brush the hair out of her eyes. With her shorts and scruffy sneakers, she felt almost like a little kid beside him. He looked like a man who taught at Yale: pressed chinos, blue oxford shirt, brown loafers. His hand was so tender; she leaned into his touch, closing her eyes.

"You knew Lily," she whispered. They were connected by that fact, and something more. Standing so close, she felt herself tingling. She hadn't felt this way since Jon, and although warning bells were going off, she couldn't stop.

"And I know you. I'm here for you, Dana."

Dana's hands tightened into loose fists. She wanted to believe Sam was steady and reliable, someone who wouldn't throw a person away just because her sister had died. But what if he weren't? What if he hurt her the way Jonathan had? Dana didn't think she could go through that again. While she stood there, stunned by the loss and confusion she felt, she saw him lift his eyes and look more carefully at Lily's painting.

"What is it?" she asked.

"Up there," he said, pointing at the vines and flowers above the window frame. "It looks like she painted some words."

He moved the wallpaper books off the old bench and carried it over to the window, holding Dana's hand as she climbed up. She had to stand on tiptoe to see what he had seen. Moving even closer, holding tightly to Sam's hand as she balanced on her toes, Dana could see that Lily had woven words into the petals and leaves: "I love Mark Grayson," she read. "Aquinnah and Alexandra are the best girls in the world." "Sisters forever—Dana, come home!" "Penny candy and silver lockets: thank you, Miss Alice." "The mermaids of Little Beach." A tiny bunch of grapes and "Martha's Vineyard." Wreaths of honeysuckle and "Honeysuckle Hill."

"What is it, Dana?" Sam asked, feeling the shiver go through her, from her body to his.

"She was happy," Dana said as her voice broke.

"How do you know?"

"She says so, right here." Her eyes filling, Dana read the words over and over. It was as if Lily had written a little biography on the wall above the oak window frame. Her life was her family; her heart was full of love and spirit.

"It seems she had everything," Sam said, reading the wall.

"She did!" Dana couldn't see anymore. She reached for Sam, and he helped her down from the bench. They stood together. His arms came around her shoulders, but she pulled back hard. She knew she was standing at the edge of a pit, the one that had swallowed Lily, and suddenly she turned and pressed herself into Sam's body as if he could save her life.

"Oh, Dana," he said.

She shivered and shook, ice cold inside, feeling Sam's arms around her back. He really knew Lily, she thought. He talked to her, sailed with her, saw her at Long Wharf with Mark. Holding Sam somehow let Dana know that Lily was real, that she existed somewhere besides in Dana's mind, and she was suddenly so overwhelmingly glad that he was with her.

"Oh, Sam," she cried.

"You loved her," Sam said.

"Quinn's wrong," Dana said.

"What?"

"They were happy. They didn't sink their boat on purpose. She has to see what her mother wrote."

Sam didn't reply. He didn't let go either. Dana felt his arms tighten, as if he thought her words had made her more vulnerable than before. Her heart was beating fast. It told her she and Sam were on the same side, part of the same mission. The thought made her feel safe, and the warmth and strength of his body did something to her heart that she wasn't ready to analyze.

"Don't you think she should see?" Dana asked, leaning back within the circle of his embrace. Glancing up, she read "Honeysuckle Hill"—the place where Mark had proposed to her. "She'll know she's wrong, and she'll forget that crazy stuff about the boat. . . ."

"She can't forget what she heard," Sam said.

Dana stepped away. "She heard her parents fighting. That's all."

"I know."

"All adults fight. Lily might have been gentle and wonderful, but she had a temper. I promise—I've been on the receiving end more than once. Quinn misunderstood, Sam. It was a fight, that's all."

"I know," he said, worry and something like regret in his eyes. "But she heard it right before she saw them for the last time. It's taken on greater meaning. She'll still want to find the boat."

"How do you know?"

Sam hesitated. He took his glasses off and frowned at them. Then he cleaned them with his shirtsleeve. "I know, that's all. I'll tell you some—" Putting his glasses on again, his attention was drawn back to the wall above the window frame. Dana thought he was reading Lily's writing, but instead he seemed focused on the wood frame above the panes.

Seven feet off the ground, Dana saw the glint of metal. So intent had she been on reading Lily's writing before, she hadn't noticed it. Now Sam reached up, the tails of his shirt untucking and showing his bare stomach, touching the metal with his fingers, edging it forward till it fell into his hand.

It was a key.

A small gold key, the kind that might unlock a child's diary. Sam held it for a moment, then handed it to Dana. She felt it, heavy in her palm, and she remembered similar keys from other times. Lily had been a great one for locking up her secrets.

Dana had always found her keys, her hiding places. It was wrong, she knew, but she had felt it her older sister's prerogative—

no, duty!—to search out and discover Lily's secret things. She would pride herself on never—well, almost never—reading the entries, examining the contents. Getting into her sister's head, rooting out the hiding places, had been satisfaction enough.

"What do you think it's for?" Sam asked.

"I'm not sure," she said slowly.

Dana thought of Lily's cloth- and leather-bound diaries, her lacquered jewelry box, the miniature cedar hope chest she'd received for her high school graduation. The gold key she held in her hand could have fit any of those containers, but Dana was thinking of something else: an old tackle box with rusty hinges and a relatively new brass padlock in the back of the garage. It wasn't pretty, and it wasn't delicate, but when Dana thought of it, her pulse quickened just as it had when she'd found Lily's hiding places of long ago.

AUNT DANA was grocery shopping or doing errands or something, and Quinn and Allie were supposed to be crabbing with Cameron and June, but that was for suckers. Let Allie follow the rules: Quinn had things to do.

First, a sweep of the house. It was rare these days to have the place all to herself. Either Aunt Dana was eagle-eyeing everything she did, or she got Grandma to do the job for her. Allie was practically Quinn's shadow. If Quinn went into the kitchen, so did Allie. If she decided to watch TV, guess what Allie wanted to do? Quinn hardly ever had time to herself.

Sunlight poured through the windows. On nice days, their house was the sunniest place in the world. Her mother hadn't liked curtains. She had loved light and air and the view so much, she had kept nearly all the windows bare. As Quinn walked through the house, checking out paintings and photos, books and the box of ashes, rays of sunlight lit her way.

Up the stairs, into her parents' room. No one ever went in there. Quinn sat on the bed—first on her father's side, then on her mother's side. The coverlet was old and frayed, a quilt made by her mother's grandmother. Placing her head on the pillow, Quinn closed her eyes and took a deep breath. Her mother's smell—lemon shampoo, sunscreen, mint toothpaste—had worn off. Quinn partially rectified the situation by running to the bathroom, dabbing a dot of shampoo onto one finger, toothpaste on the other, and rubbing them onto the pillowcase. There—much better!

She catalogued the bedside table: the stack of books her mother always read, a few magazines, lots of letters from Aunt Dana, an address book, a little crystal ball that happened to be one of Quinn's favorite things in the world. Similar to a snow globe, it contained a mermaid with long red hair and a green tail, and when Quinn shook it, instead of snowflakes, tiny fish swirled around.

Quinn laughed just as she had when she was a baby and her mother would shake the globe and say the magic words: "Mermaid come, tell me true, what's a girl supposed to do?"

Comforted, Quinn continued her prowl. She opened the closet, pawed through her parents' clothes. Her father's suits and blazers on one side, her mother's skirts and pants on the other. Quinn didn't like the closet much; Grandma had strewn the place with mothballs before Quinn had been able to stop her.

Now her father's bedside table—neater than her mother's—with one half-read John le Carré book, a framed photo of "his girls," and the best part—the glass of water he'd been drinking the night before he'd died. Quinn kept the level filled to the exact spot, about an inch above the bottom of the glass, to compensate for evaporation.

The bureau—a gold mine of contact. All their clothes, a few papers here and there, a junk drawer filled with memories and treasures. Quinn bypassed the bureau for now. She had other things to do before Aunt Dana came home, so she had to move fast. She barely even had time to look at the photos, the painting Mom had done of Honeysuckle Hill. The jewelry box came last.

Quinn stared at the lid. Lacquered black with a gold-leaf depiction of a plum tree on the banks of a gentle river, it had a lock that no longer worked. Why she even bothered to look inside, Quinn really didn't know. Her heart sank just as she opened the top.

Diamonds and pearls, big deal.

The pearls her mother had received for her sixteenth birthday, the diamond earrings Quinn's father had given her for their tenth wedding anniversary. A few pairs of earrings, a class ring, some pieces made by her mother's friends in the jewelry department at RISD, the mother's pin—with Quinn's and Allie's birthstones— given by their father one Mother's Day.

Quinn stared into the jewelry box, at all the beautiful things. She felt her happiness draining away, and she wondered why she always thought about what wasn't there instead of what was. Running her thumb over the smooth stones of her mother's pin, she thought of how much she had loved to see her mother wear it.

"Hell-shit!"

The voice was hers, and so was the thumping sound of her feet flying down the stairs. Out the door, across the yard, around the granite ledge, down the stone steps, and over the footbridge. Now she was on the big beach, zooming past all the happy families enjoying the sunny day.

"Hell-crap!" she yelled just to vary her vocabulary. Mothers, knee-deep in the surf, stared in horror. Little children building sand castles trembled in dread. "Fuck-nuts! Damn the beach balls!"

Her head was pounding even harder than her feet on the sand. She disappeared like a witch up the path and into the woods, over the path to Little Beach. Her heart was pumping so fast, she half expected to bleed from the ears. She reached her rock and dove for the hiding place, digging like a dog.

There: the plastic bag. She pulled out the diary and a half-smoked cigarette. Lighting up, she sneered at the sky. Her braids felt too tight today, and she imagined all her evil thoughts shooting at the clouds. Fingers burning to write, she grabbed the pen and let it rip.

It's still gone. Why do I think that by saying the mermaid poem and opening the jewelry box I'll find it? We know where it is, don't we, Quinn? Sherlock Holmes could have used you on his side. Your powers of deductive reasoning could blow the minds of even the greatest detectives. Dad's John le Carré guy couldn't even keep up with you.

Let's see. She loved it. She never took it off. Aunt Dana

gave it to her. That must mean (drumroll) she was (suspenseful music) wearing it (aha!) when the boat sank.

Sarcasm is very overrated. Even when I'm the one writing it and I'll be the only one reading it, it makes me feel worse. I know Mom was wearing the silver locket. Being sarcastic about it won't make it magically appear in her jewelry box. I wonder if it's true, the old story Mommy and Aunt Dana used to tell us: that the mermaids gather all the jewelry people lose in the sea and on the beach, wear it the last full moon of the year for the Mermaid's Ball.

I wonder whether they'll be wearing Mommy's locket this year.

Mermaids throwing their nets on the waves, catching boats and fish, wearing other people's jewelry. Those things don't sound very nice. Why do I love them anyway?

Because they belong to Mom, me, and Allie. Because we've heard them singing late at night. Because when I look at the waves—right now, sitting by this big rock—I hope I'll see a mermaid popping up to say hello. I hope she'll be someone I know.

I hope she'll be Mommy.

With that, Quinn stopped writing to scan the sea. She looked across the trail of rocks that formed the outermost point of Little Beach. The water beyond was quite calm, with small waves breaking on the sandbar. Past the bar, past the shoals and buoys, Quinn watched the blue water all the way to the Hunting Ground.

Aunt Dana would be home soon. Sam was with her. Even though no one had bothered to tell Quinn, she knew. Watcher of the house, keeper of the flame, she knew all—even more than Aunt Dana, who knew a lot. No one was more vigilant than Aquinnah Grayson. Sticking her hand in the pocket of her shorts, she came out with the present she had brought.

It was always the same, or as close as she could make it.

Never once taking her eyes off the waves, she placed the gift on the wet sand between the big rocks and the tide line, and she returned her diary to the plastic bag. She wished she had time to sail.

Now that Aunt Dana was reteaching her every day, she had her confidence back. She wanted to get in the boat and head east— maybe she'd go to Gay Head. The mermaids there were probably pretty cool. They might remember her from when she was born.

But that was just slightly unrealistic. She had more practicing to do before she could go solo all the way to Martha's Vineyard. Back to a more realistic plan: If she moved fast, she could bury her diary and get home in time to watch her favorite movie, see her parents and their amazing first baby in action—and in private. Casting one last glance at the Sound and then at the present she had left, Quinn turned around to run quickly, quickly home.

CHAPTER 14

SAM DROVE AND DANA STARED OUT THE WINDOW. When they pulled under the railroad bridge, past the small guard shack into Hubbard's Point, he sensed her tensing like a spring. They wound up Cresthill Road, past the cottages on their wooded lots, and stopped at the stone wall at the foot of her hill. Down the street, someone was warbling scales in a soprano voice. Dana catapulted out of the van.

By the time Sam caught up to her, she had opened the garage door. The space seemed empty with the boat launched, but she went straight for the back wall and crouched down. Standing beside her, Sam watched her take the tiny gold key from her pocket.

"What are you doing?" he asked as she inserted it into the padlock.

"Seeing if it fits."

Her hands seemed to be shaking so much, she couldn't get the key in right. Sam fought the urge to take over. Her brown hair fell in her face. She talked nonstop: "I thought this tackle box had to be Mark's, but then I found the key, and I know it's Lily's, and I thought, 'bingo.' "

"Bingo?"

"Mark wouldn't bother locking a tackle box. He wasn't like that. I don't know why I didn't think of Lily in the first place. Of course it's hers. Only she would buy a cute little lock with a tiny key, take the trouble of hiding it above a window. In her husband's office, no less!"

"She liked to hide things?"

Dana glanced over her shoulder to give him a dirty look—as if he'd just committed blasphemy. In spite of the disapproval she was trying to convey, she looked gorgeous and sexy. Crouched on the damp garage floor, fumbling with the lock, she had a wild look in her blue eyes. Sam really wanted to pull her to her feet, put his arms around her the way he had at Mark's office.

"She liked to hide things, yes," Dana said defensively. "But in a good way."

"A good way?"

"A playful way. A scavenger-hunt, treasure-hunt sort of way. Your brother would understand, wouldn't he? God, I can't get this key to turn."

"My brother?"

"Didn't you tell me he sails the seven seas in search of ship-wrecks? A guy after Lily's own heart. Well, he'd understand."

"And you think I don't?" Sam asked, frowning.

"I think you do," Dana said, looking up and tugging the lock. "I guess I wanted to bring your brother into this. You and I are here, doing this for Lily. Joe's the only one left out. . . ."

Sam immediately crouched down, moved by Dana's wish to include Joe. Something had changed back in Mark's office. After Sam had pointed out the words on the wall, Dana had started to trust him. She really did value family connection almost as much as Sam did himself. Right then he wanted to hold her, but she was so intent on the tackle box. He felt distracted by the shape of Dana's body under her big T-shirt, the way her cheekbones looked in this mysterious, shadowy light.

"This can't be anything, can it?" Dana asked, sounding scared as she tried to get the key into the lock.

"You know what Joe would say?"

"What?"

"That treasures sometimes come in strange packages, even old tackle boxes. Keep trying."

Suddenly, she stopped working and stared at the key. "It doesn't fit."

"Are you sure?" Sam asked, giving it a try. She was right: The key was all wrong for the lock. But it felt so good to be this close to her, their bare arms touching, her tan legs crossed as she sat on the floor, he kept at it.

"Damn," Dana said. "It must go to something else. But what's in the tackle box?"

"You think it's Mark's?" Sam asked.

"Probably. Lily didn't fish, but on the other hand, Mark didn't lock things up. Unless he had secrets we didn't know about. It's crazy—Quinn has me thinking like a Shakespeare tragedy. Whispers and threats—evil doings at the goddamn Sun Center. Let's break the lock."

"Break it now?" Sam asked, holding the tackle box in both hands.

"What would Joe do?" Dana said, and Sam loved the way she made a connection with his touchstone.

"Whatever it takes," Sam said. He hugged her, and she hugged him back. Then the challenge was on. Sam shook the box, hearing the contents shuffle around: They sounded more like papers than metal lures and sinkers. Glancing around for a place to bang the hasp, he felt Dana's hand on his cheek.

"You're a good sport," she said as his heart pumped harder. "And as good a treasure hunter as your brother."

"He'd be surprised to hear you say that." Sam grinned, noticing she didn't take her hand down. It felt soft, and he wished he had shaved that morning. Their eyes were locked. Their siblings were in the air, but in that moment, staring into Dana's eyes, Sam felt all alone with her. He reached for her hand to hold it for a minute.

The amazing thing was, she let him. They were sitting on the cool, damp floor of her family's garage, about to break into a locked tackle box while the summer day went on outside.

"You don't have to do it," she said. "It's my sister. I will."

"I'd do anything for you, Dana."

She held his hand lightly in hers, and then she turned it over. Staring into the palm, as if she were a fortune-teller and she wanted to read his future, she didn't speak at first. She tapped the back of his hand, just keeping it there in her loose grasp. He wondered whether she was thinking of what they'd been through this summer: her art show, the drive to JFK, painting the boat, sailing, finding the key. Sam was; he couldn't help it.

"You know what, Sam?" she asked, still looking at his palm.

"You're about to tell me I'm going to live long," he said.

"I'm about to tell you thank you," she said, raising her eyes to meet his. Her expression was solemn and grateful, and he wanted to see her smile almost as much as he didn't want her to let go of his hand. But she did, pointing at the box. "Do it," she ordered.

And Sam was about to. He really was. While breaking into other people's property wasn't his thing—in that way she was right, this job was more up Joe's alley—he had meant what he said: He'd do anything for her. So he pulled his hand away, got to his feet.

Finding a rusty old pry bar on a shelf, he set the box on the floor and prepared to break it open.

"Oh, Lily, don't let it be bad," Dana said as Sam inserted the bar.

Just then they heard laughter, the voices of children. People were coming down the street. Dana had barely enough time to return the box to its shelf while Sam hid the pry bar. They were standing together, trying to look innocent in the dark, empty garage, when the open door filled with the faces of Quinn, Allie, two of their friends, and a pretty, dark-haired woman in a dripping bathing suit.

"We didn't catch any crabs, but we got lots of mussels," Allie called.

"I hate mussels," Quinn said. "Don't expect me to eat any."

"Don't worry," Dana said, bending over to admire the catch.

"Hello, I'm Marnie Campbell," the woman said, coming over

with her hand out, barely looking at Dana, homing in on Sam as if she were a seagull and he was a clam. "I'm Dana and Lily's oldest friend; my kids are best friends with Quinn and Allie. You must be Sam."

"That's right," Sam said, shaking her hand. "I am."

THAT NIGHT, for reasons unconfirmed but suspected by Dana, Marnie insisted the girls accompany her, Cameron, June, and Annabelle for an evening of pizza and miniature golf. As eager as she had been to open the box before, now with the coast clear and the luxury of time to think, Dana felt reluctant.

Sam stayed for dinner. Dana filled a large kettle with butter, garlic, shallots, herbs, and the mussels. She fixed a plate of cheese and crackers, and she and Sam went to sit on the terrace.

The sun was going down, spreading lavender light across the Sound, edging the waves with gold.

"You make it seem so easy," Sam said.

"What?"

"Cooking mussels. The way you just threw everything into a pot. And you made the girls feel so good—did you see their faces when they realized we were actually going to eat their catch?"

Dana laughed. "They were just happy they're having pizza instead. The truth is, I can't cook anything I have to measure or time." Watching Sam eat, she felt happy she'd made something he liked. They ate the mussels, and as the wind picked up, she hoped the girls would remember to put on their sweaters.

"When you look at that," Sam said, pointing at the beach and the waves, "doesn't it make you want to paint?"

Dana looked down at her bowl.

"I don't know," she said.

"Seeing Lily's painting today—the white flowers and vines—I started thinking about your talent. How awful it is you don't use it anymore."

"I'll use it someday."

"If you were painting that scene, what would you use?"

"That scene, right there?" Dana asked, watching the sun behind the horizon, the rays of gold shooting into dark clouds. As always, her attention was pulled by the water, by the movement and mystery of the sea, and she began to imagine the water column just past sunset. "I'd use Winsor and Newton's royal purple mixed with dark blue; for the gold, I might use actual gold leaf," she heard herself say.

"Why don't you?"

"I can't, Sam. Don't ask me anymore."

"I won't ask you—I'll tell you. I think you should. I saw your paintings at the gallery. They're great, amazing! I'm an oceanographer, and you made me feel that I was right there, under the surface in the euphotic zone."

"The what?"

"The euphotic zone—down to two hundred feet, the depth to which light penetrates."

"That's what I paint," she said. "I never knew the name before."

Sam nodded, letting it alone. She felt the silence between them and thought about Jonathan. He had nagged her to paint till she couldn't take any more, and then he'd get quiet, poisonously silent, as if he were thinking she was the biggest jerk alive. Sam's silence didn't feel like that.

"You ready to crack the safe?" he asked after they'd finished all the mussels.

"Almost. Not quite."

"Want to go sailing?" he asked. "The moon'll be up soon."

Dana smiled.

"We could sail over that royal purple with a little dark blue sea, edged with gold leaf," Sam said enticingly. He pretended one of the empty mussel shells was their boat, and he sailed it from his hand onto hers.

Holding the empty shell, looking at its mother-of-pearl interior, Dana lifted her eyes to his. "I want you to tell me what you meant the other night—when you said I should let Quinn keep vigil on her rock."

"Just that—you should let her."

"Why do you say that? What if it's bad for her—encouraging her to watch for who knows what, hope for people who are never coming home? What do you know about it?"

"I know a lot, Dana."

"Tell me, Sam. Because I feel as if I'm in the dark on too much already."

"My father died when I was eight," Sam said. "The winter before you taught me how to sail."

Dana sailed the small shell boat across her knee. It made her uncomfortable, remembering how young Sam had been, how young he still was. Sometimes he seemed like her friend, her equal, and other times being with him brought up the hard knot of all her feelings about Jonathan.

"I know he did," she said. "Your mother told me when she signed your permission slip."

"Bet she wasn't too sad when she told you," Sam said. "I don't think she was very sorry to lose him. See, she married him fast, without knowing him very well. She was a widow with a kid—my brother, Joe—to raise. My dad delivered lobsters for the co-op, he asked her to marry him, and she thought she was going to live happily ever after."

"But she didn't?"

Sam shook his head. "She'd been in love with someone else— an artist who pretty much led her on and left her. I think you know the name—Hugh Renwick."

"Of course I know him—from Firefly Beach," Dana said, shocked. His family had been at her opening. He had been married to Augusta, and it sounded as if Sam's mother had been married as well.

"It's a long, sad story," Sam said, taking the mussel shell as she sailed it back into his hand. "But she ended up married to my dad, Liam Trevor. Joe used to call their marriage World War Three."

"I'm sorry, Sam."

He looked out to the Sound. Rangy and lean, he slouched at his end of the teak bench. His blue shirt was open at the neck, his skin smooth and tan. The look in his eyes, behind his gold-rimmed glasses, made him look weary and older. But the memory that tugged Dana's heart was him as an eight-year-old boy grasping on to sailing lessons as a way of forgetting his father had died the winter before.

"He did yell at her and Joe," Sam said quietly. "He'd explode at them, but he never yelled at me."

The waves splashed the shore as Dana waited for him to go on.

"I felt guilty sometimes. Why did they get it and not me? Sometimes I listened, like Quinn did, trying to figure it out. I heard the whole thing about Joe's father and Hugh Renwick. I'd hear Joe defending his mother, my father slamming his fist down, throwing things around. After a while, he'd come in to find me."

"Joe?"

"No, my father."

"What would he say?" Dana asked.

"He'd tell me stories," Sam said, sitting on the cool terrace. "He'd sing me songs. He was just the dad, and I was just the kid. It was exactly the way it was supposed to be—if I could block out the other stuff."

"What kind of stories?" Dana asked.

"About the lobsters he drove to market. About the places he saw, about his own childhood growing up in Ireland—the rocky bays and huge tidal pools. Joe says it isn't true, but to this day I think one of the reasons he became an oceanographer was because of things he overheard my father talking about."

"What happened to him, Sam?"

"He drove his truck off a bridge."

"Sam—"

"Christmas Eve. On his way back from New York, his truck empty after delivering a full load of lobsters to the Fulton Market, he hit an ice storm and went off the Jamestown Bridge."

Dana pictured the span over the west passage of Narragansett Bay—high and narrow, its iron towers a landmark from miles away. She had been afraid to go across the Jamestown Bridge as a child—it had always seemed so tall and menacing.

"I'm so sorry," she said, wanting to reach for Sam's hand. She had taught him to sail in Newport, in the harbour and the east passage of Narragansett Bay, just a few miles away.

"I was eight," Sam said. "Old enough to wonder why no one else in my house was as upset as I was. I walked out the door into the storm, and I walked over the Newport Bridge and Conanicut Island to get to the Jamestown Bridge."

"Why did you want to go there?"

"For the same reason Quinn wants to go to the Hunting Ground and locate her father's boat—to make sure he didn't do it on purpose."

"Why would you think he'd do that?"

"Because Joe's father shot himself," Sam said. "My mother had broken his heart with Hugh Renwick. In some ways, she broke my father's heart with Hugh Renwick's ghost. I started thinking, maybe he drove off the bridge on purpose."

"But he didn't, did he?" Dana asked, taking his hand now. She wanted to comfort him, and she wanted to be reassured that such terrible things didn't really happen. Accidents were bad enough—real tragedies. But for a parent to know what he was doing, leave his child in such an awful way . . . Dana's hand was shaking as she waited for Sam to look at her.

"No, he didn't," Sam said.

Dana shivered with relief, but she held his hand tighter.

"That's why I want to help Quinn. She has something in her mind, and she won't rest easy until we prove it's otherwise."

"That's what happened for you?"

Sam nodded. "I stood by the rail of the Jamestown Bridge while the divers went down, and I was still there when the crane pulled my father's truck up. It was an accident; we knew that for sure."

"Because he didn't leave a note?"

"Because he had my Christmas presents with him. He'd gone shopping in New York. They were all waterlogged, soaked through, but he'd bought me some toy trucks and a model train. I kept them for years."

"You did," Dana said, seeing the glow in his eyes, thinking of how very like Quinn he was: She kept everything her parents had ever given her, wouldn't even let people sit in their chairs.

"It helped when I knew for sure he didn't do it on purpose. Didn't kill himself," Sam said, turning his head to look into Dana's eyes.

She nodded, still holding his hand.

"See, Dana. That's what we have to do for Quinn."

"I know we do," she said.

When he stood, he handed her the mussel shell. As if it were Lily's boat, and she could keep it safe, she held it tight. Now he pulled her up from the teak bench, took both her hands in his. The fine shell edges dug into her palm. "Are you ready?" he asked.

"I am," she said.

She was too. After his story, she wasn't afraid anymore. Whatever was hidden in the tackle box had nothing to do with Mark and Lily's deaths. It would be drawings or family pictures, the equivalent to Sam's Christmas presents found in the cab of his father's truck. She ducked into the kitchen for a flashlight, and together they headed down the hill toward the garage.

It was pitch black inside. Located at the foot of the hill's eastern side, no light whatsoever came in. Switching on the flashlight, they closed the door behind them. Now, moving through the dark space, they stayed close together.

"I feel like a burglar," Dana said.

"It's your family's property," Sam reminded her. "And you're doing this for Quinn."

"Thank you for telling me that story," Dana said. "It makes this easier."

"You're welcome," Sam said. Dana pictured Quinn on her rock, and she pictured young Sam standing at the foot of the Jamestown Bridge. They were huddled over the tackle box now.

Outside, headlights came slowly down Cresthill Road and Dana doused the flashlight. Sam's eyes blazed, looking her way. She wondered how much he could see in the dark. She suddenly felt so tender toward him. She wanted to reach over, put her arms around his shoulders, comfort him for what had happened. Instead, she reached into her pocket and felt for the key to a lock she hadn't yet found.

Rumer Larkin drove past in her truck. Although she had been one of Dana's best childhood friends, Dana hid from her now. When she turned the flashlight back on, Sam moved forward with the pry bar.

"What could we possibly find?" she asked. "Solid-gold Kast-masters?"

"Sterling silver sinkers?"

"Treasure for the girls."

"Here goes," he said, inserting the tip, giving one sharp push.

The hasp cracked open. Dana leaned closer with the flashlight. She saw money inside, a thick stack of hundred-dollar bills held together with a rubber band. Beneath it were several documents, all officially printed on heavy stock, each bearing the heading "Sun Center, Inc."

"Oh, no," Dana said.

"Mark's project."

Dana closed the box. She couldn't look anymore. She didn't understand what it meant, but she somehow knew what she had just found was the opposite of Christmas presents in Sam's father's truck. Outside the garage, she heard Marnie's car pull into the gravel-strewn driveway across the street.

"They're home," Sam said.

"Quinn . . ." Dana said, closing her eyes.

"Be strong for her and Allie," Sam said, sliding his arm around her. She couldn't resist; she felt his support, and she was glad to have it. "That's what they need."

"You know, don't you?"

"I'm sorry, but I do," Sam said.

Dana had a pit in her stomach. It got worse as they opened the garage and walked across the street. Quinn and Allie were racing around, eating vanilla cones. The story of Quinn's miniature golf victory came flowing out, with Allie pumping her fists in sisterly support.

Dana laughed and nodded. She appeared to listen, to hear every word. Overhead, the summer breeze rustled the oak leaves. Stars shined in the dark blue sky. The children laughed and shouted. Marnie accepted Dana's thanks. No one knew what was going on in Dana's head, no one but Sam.

He touched her shoulder, and when she dropped her hand behind her back, he held it tight. No one saw. Even Quinn, distracted by the joys of a July night, forgot to be vigilant. It was just Dana and Sam, waiting at the foot of the Jamestown Bridge or four fathoms above the *Sundance,* knowing there were more answers to seek, more questions than anyone had ever thought to ask.

CHAPTER 15

THAT NIGHT, DANA COULDN'T SLEEP. THE TACKLE BOX full of money loomed in the dark. She tossed in her sheets, just above and below the level of dreams. Stars hung outside her window. She watched the constellations tell their stories, and she made them her own. The Two Sisters danced in the sky. The Betrayed Lover hid in her cave. The night was full of secrets.

She thought—or dreamed—of Sam. He was in her mind, trying to pull her back to earth. Out of the cave, down from the dance. He was such a grounded person, trying to help her find her way here on earth. For as long as she could remember, Dana had been drawn to archetypes. She had lived like a constellation, wheeling through the sky, a collection of stars that never really found a home. Artists, sculptors, nomads, seekers.

Sam was . . . well, he was Sam. She lay awake, picturing how comfortable he seemed. He seemed to like who and where he was. The French had a phrase for him: *bien dans sa peau.* "Comfortable in his own skin." And lying in bed, the heavy gray dawn light coming through the windows, she pictured his body, his skin.

That glowing tan, from days spent in the sun on his boat. He seemed to radiate contentment. She saw the smile just behind his golden-green eyes, telling her he had learned how to be happy, that it was a secret he'd like to share. She had known his life hadn't always been easy, but now that he'd told her about his father, she understood that he, too, had been on the other side of sadness. For the first time in weeks, she felt like painting, and she knew he had something to do with it.

She finally got out of bed. Taking a bike ride to the post office, she found a letter from Isabel: *We miss you! How is your life among your nieces, your return to your childhood home? Plenty to paint when you return, and everyone hopes it is soon. Even Monsieur Hull. Yes, Monique seems to have fled the scene, gone back to Paris or Vietnam or wherever she came from, and Jonathan moons around the harbour, painting terrible flat pictures for the tourists and smoking too many cigarettes.*

Dana already knew. Jonathan himself had written to her already, saying essentially the same thing. Seeing his name, hearing about life in Honfleur, flooded Dana with a strange and perverse longing—strictly from habit. She had once hoped for a life with Jon Hull, and Dana was a person who took her own dreams straight to heart.

To chase them away, and to keep from obsessing about the tackle box, she took Allie sailing. And when they got home from a long, beautiful broad reach past Firefly Beach and back, she found a package by the kitchen door. Tied up in brown paper and twine, it had an envelope attached. While Allie went inside for her snack and lemonade, Dana opened the package.

Her heart jumped. Inside were tubes of Winsor and Newton's dark blue and royal purple, along with a full range of other colors. Included was a bag of brushes and a small cellophane square filled with twenty sheets of James's Gold Leaf. The note read: *Dana, you don't have to be a detective. You're an artist. Please let me make the calls, okay? Meanwhile, the rest of what you need is in the garage. Love, Sam.*

Beginning to smile, Dana walked down the hill and opened the garage's heavy door. Inside, across the space from the tackle box, she found several five- and six-foot lengths of two-inch pine, a roll of canvas, a can of gesso, and a small bag of nails. Beside it all, wrapped in a huge red bow, was a brand-new hammer. Dana got the message: Sam wanted her to build a canvas.

The thing was, after her night of lying awake, she wanted to build one. She found herself spreading out the stretchers, nailing them together with all her might. The tackle box was right where she had left it, sitting in the corner of her vision as she pounded nails and tried to decide what to paint.

Only once did she check the box: The five thousand dollars were still inside. She kept working, pulling the canvas tight, brushing the gesso onto the cloth. A storm of emotions swirled through her chest. Everything she hadn't painted in the last year wanted to come out. All her doubts and fears, her anger and grief, her love for Lily, her hurt for Jonathan, swirled inside like a tornado trapped in a box.

While the gesso dried, she went to check on the girls. Allie was reading, and Quinn had disappeared on one of her jaunts. Checking with the binoculars, Dana found her sitting on the big rock, staring out to sea. Wanting to do her part to help Sam, Dana called Marnie to talk some more about the Sun Center.

"The Emerald City," Marnie laughed. "That's what Lily and I called it—a nice place for old mothers so daughters wouldn't have to worry. We were going to send Martha and Annabelle there. Lily thought daughters everywhere would thank Mark for building it. Health and wellness for the elderly: what a revolutionary idea!"

"Did she ever say anything bad about it?"

"Only that it was too far away, that it kept Mark away from home too much. You know Lily, Dana. Joined at the hip with everyone she loved: She felt the same way about you and France. If it was possible for someone to be mad at a whole country, well, that's how Lily felt about France. It had you in its clutches."

"It did," Dana said.

"The anniversaries are coming up next week," Marnie said. "One year—I can hardly believe it."

"Neither can I."

"Do you have any plans for a service? Maybe it will be the right time for Quinn and Allie to let you scatter the ashes."

"I hope so," Dana said. But when she hung up, her thoughts

were more on the Sun Center, on what Sam might find when he made his calls. She wondered where he was, why he hadn't given her the packages in person. She wondered what he was doing, when she would hear from him again.

But Jonathan had once treated her wonderfully too.

AS MUCH AS Dana wasn't a detective, Sam wasn't really one either. But he did have his brother's blood, which gave him certain investigatory advantages. To make sure he was proceeding correctly, he dialed Joe's cell phone from the deck of his boat and wondered where it was going to ring.

"Connor," Joe said gruffly, answering the phone.

"That's nice," Sam said. "Someone calls to say hello, and you practically bark into their ear."

"You know what time it is here?"

"I would if I knew where you were, if you ever got around to letting me know."

"Didn't Caroline send you a postcard?"

"Don't blame it on your wife—she sends me plenty of postcards. The problem is, they arrive a week after you've moved on to the next place. Where are you?"

"Onboard the *Meteor,* off Madagascar."

"Doing what, or shouldn't I ask?"

"Diving on a wreck. What else?"

"You're a long way from Firefly Beach."

"No kidding. Caroline's mother calls twice a day, asking when we're coming home."

"When are you coming home?"

"In October. Is that why you called? Ya miss your big brother that much?"

"Don't flatter yourself," Sam snorted. "I'm calling because I need to pick your sneaky mind."

" 'Sneaky'?"

"Yeah. All that red tape you have to cut through, getting to the wreck. You know, local officials, national officials, rival dive teams, permits, archaeological considerations, crap like that. How do you get to what you want?"

"I treat it like a research problem. Treasure, empirical data, it's all the same thing. You make notes, set goals, look at the hypotheticals. Shit, it's late here. What's your situation?"

"What do you make of a tackle box filled with cash?"

"Bigger fish than fish." Joe chuckled.

"No kidding." Sam stared at the deck at his feet. Par for the course: him on one boat, Joe on another, several oceans apart.

"Tell me the particulars, kid," Joe said. "I'll give you my sneaky mind for free."

Sam let him have it. He told his brother about the Graysons' boat going down, their daughter thinking it wasn't an accident, the box of money. Joe listened, seeming to take in every detail.

"Sounds like someone found some trouble," Joe said after Sam was finished filling him in.

"That's what I think."

"Cash in a box makes me think kickback, bribe, graft. Maybe Mark got paid off for something."

"For what though?"

"He's a developer, right? Maybe some guy with a field paid Mark to put the old-age home there."

"They do that?"

"God, you're naive. You wouldn't believe the number of palms I've crossed with silver over the years. It's the way of the world. Haven't you ever slipped a maître d' twenty bucks for a better table?"

"This wasn't twenty bucks. It was a few thousand."

"Yeah? Well, sounds like you're on it. You'll find out, I'm sure. But I've got a question for you. You've given me the rundown, told me the players. What I want to know is, who is she?"

"What?"

"The aunt. Who is she?"

"What the hell does that have to do with anything?"

"Plenty," Joe said, whistling. "You have research grants this summer. Getting you out of your lab is nothing short of a freaking miracle, so she must be something special. Sam, the detective—way to go!"

"Shut up, asshole."

"Hey, don't talk to me that way. I'll get Caroline after you. Seriously, Sam—what's the deal?"

"I know her from way back. We're old friends. I'm just doing her a favor."

"Holy shit," Joe bellowed all the way from the Indian Ocean. "It's not her, is it? The mystery woman?"

"Shut up."

"The girl you followed to the Vineyard? It is, isn't it? The none-of-your-fucking-business lady?"

"The what?"

"That's what you said to me every time I asked you about her. I'd come back from Belize, and there you were, stupid in love, and no matter what I asked, you'd tell me 'none of your fucking business.' That's how I knew you were in deep. You'd never talked that way before. It's her, isn't it?"

Sam ignored him. He stared down at the piece of paper before him. He already had called information, gotten the number for the Sun Center in Cincinnati. What the hell he was going to ask, he didn't know. Joe was whistling on the phone from Madagascar, and Sam wasn't one bit closer to knowing what to do next.

"You still there?" Joe asked.

"Yeah."

"Okay. You asked me what I do to get past red tape."

"I did."

"I do what I do best. Ask nice, sign on the dotted line, and get diving. That's your plan, isn't it?"

"What are you talking about?"

"The boat—*Sundance,* didn't you say? The kid thinks her parents scuttled the boat? Find out for her. Go down there."

Sam closed his eyes, rocking on the water. The sun baked down on his bare shoulders. It felt hot and dry, and he wanted to dive into the bay and wash everything off. He knew Joe remembered Sam's old vigil—waiting for the divers to pull his father's truck up.

"What should I look for?"

"You know, Sam. Open seacocks. A lack of structural damage. When can you get down there?"

"Next week. After the summer session's over and I can use the research vessel. It has the echo sounder I need—unless, of course, you and Caroline are planning to come back sooner. I could really use the *Meteor.*"

"If I weren't so greedy, maybe I would. This is a big one, Sam. More treasure than I've ever gone after before. A caïque filled with South African diamonds, straight from the mines and headed for India. Fit for a sultan."

"A sultan, that's you," Sam said. "Well, thanks for the advice."

"One last thing. The aunt—what's her name?"

"None of your fucking business," Sam said, hanging up the phone.

A WEEK WENT BY and everything seemed different. Quinn didn't know what was going on. Sam kept calling. He'd ask for Aunt Dana, and they'd have long conversations, with her keeping her voice down low. Or he'd leave strange messages on the answering machine like: "I called our friend in Ohio, he's getting back to me this afternoon. So far, I'm not getting any red flags, but I'll keep trying."

Quinn tried to keep from going mad with curiosity. Perhaps the oddest thing of all was that Aunt Dana had set up a studio in the garage—the grossest, darkest place there was. Spiderwebs were everywhere, and not a bit of light came in unless the door was open.

Running down the hill with Sam's latest message, Quinn found her aunt standing before the empty canvas.

"What's a red flag?" Quinn asked.

"Gale warnings," Dana said, "if you're talking about sailing. Why?"

"Sam said so far he's not getting any red flags. What's that mean?"

"I guess it means everything is going well. That it's smooth sailing," her aunt said, staring intently at her canvas as if she were seeing something that wasn't there.

"What's he doing? Why haven't we seen him lately?"

"I guess he's busy, honey," her aunt said, still staring at the same spot.

Quinn exhaled noisily. She had thought she wanted her aunt to start painting, as extra insurance that they weren't going to move to France. But this wasn't so great. Aunt Dana had barely left the garage in days. She had set up her easel, arranged her paints and brushes on a table, opened a fresh can of turpentine, gotten messy mixing paints. But although she hadn't actually started painting yet, she was standing there as if waiting to get struck by a bolt of inspiration, straight from the blue.

When Quinn's mother had painted, she had done it on the dining room table, and she hadn't gotten so involved: She could start and stop with no problem, and when Quinn talked to her, she put down her brush and listened.

"Will he come see us soon?" Quinn asked. "He's supposed to do that job for me. . . ."

"I'm sure he'll do it." Peering at the canvas, Aunt Dana took a step forward. She touched her finger to the canvas, made a gentle line, stood back. Even though she didn't like being ignored, Quinn's heart felt a sort of peace, watching her aunt get ready to work. She came around the easel to look.

It was blank. Her aunt's brush was dry. It was like seeing a pilot in his uniform, ready to fly, waiting for his plane. Or a writer, holding a pen, waiting for ideas. Quinn felt sad, looking at her aunt's empty canvas, and she put her arms around her.

"Thank you, honey," Aunt Dana said.

"What's wrong?"

"Nothing."

"It's this garage, isn't it? I wish you had more light. Is your studio in France this dark?"

"No. In Honfleur I have a big window that lets in the north light."

Quinn put her hands on her hips and walked around the garage. She felt like her father, the way she had seen him march around building sites over the years. "You should have one here," she said. "We could saw a window right there—that's north, isn't it?"

"Yes, it is," her aunt said. "How do you know that, Miss Aquinnah Jane?"

"I have a good sense of direction," Quinn said, feeling proud.

"That's all I can say. Mom said it's from the fact I come from high ground, that I was born seeing everything all around."

"That's a wonderful quality to have."

"She made me promise to protect what I saw. She said I could be steward of the land—especially on the Vineyard."

And then, by the way her aunt took a deep breath and laid her paintbrush on the old table beside her, Quinn knew she was in for a serious talk.

"Uh-oh," Quinn said.

"Come outside," her aunt said. "Into the light."

Walking out of the garage, they both blinked in the sunshine. It was a hot summer day, and light sparkled off the Sound on both sides of the Point. They leaned against the stone wall, facing the McCrays' house. Aunt Dana's chest rose and fell with every breath, and Quinn felt her aunt's desire to take care of her. Quinn closed her eyes and wished she were a very little, much younger girl.

"What is it?" Quinn asked.

"The day after tomorrow," Aunt Dana said.

Quinn blocked her ears. "Don't say it. I know!"

"Quinn . . ."

"It's the anniversary. July thirtieth, I know!"

"I was thinking we should do something, honey. To commemorate your parents' lives."

"I do that every day," Quinn said through clenched teeth. She felt the pressure building inside. Aunt Dana meant well, no doubt about that, but if she didn't stop talking about this, Quinn was going to blow up. They went sailing all the time now—nearly every day. Aunt Dana was going to say they should scatter the ashes in the Sound . . . she was, Quinn could just tell.

"I mean in a special way. After my father died, we always used to visit his grave on the date of his death. Grandma would pick flowers from the garden. Lily would pick out a poem, and I would paint him a picture. We'd go to the cemetery and read him the poem, leave the flowers and painting beside the stone. . . ."

"My parents don't have a stone."

"I know," her aunt said quietly. "That's part of the problem. I've been thinking. . . ."

Quinn shook her head so hard, an elastic flew off one of her braids. "Don't say it! I don't want them to have a stone!"

"Quinn, their ashes can't stay on the mantelpiece forever!"

"Yes they can," Quinn snarled.

"I'm talking like this to you because you're the oldest. But it's not fair to Allie. Remember when she said she wanted to leave white flowers for her mother? I think it's time to give her a place to do that."

"No," Quinn said, refusing to hear. She glared at her aunt, and suddenly, she felt furious about everything. What was her aunt even trying to paint for, when there were so many questions to be answered?

"They loved the sea," Aunt Dana said. "We could scatter their ashes there, Quinn. Out in the Sound here, or anywhere you want. We could get a stone for them, put it in the herb garden. . . . You could visit them there, not have to go all the way over to Little Beach."

"You said you'd help me," Quinn said, the words flying out. "That night, when I told you what I thought. But you're not helping, not at all. You're just trying to get me to forget!"

And she ran off, leaving Aunt Dana with her clothes and hands streaked ten different shades of blue, to run down the path and beach to the only stone, the only place where Quinn ever felt safe anymore. The gifts she left were always gone, as if someone had picked them up, and that had to mean something.

CHAPTER 16

ON THE ACTUAL DATE, THEY DID GO SAILING. THE three of them dragged the *Mermaid* off the beach and into the water. Dana stood by, watching Quinn rig the boat. She was expert and precise, just like her mother. Allie took charge of the jib, just as she'd been taught. While Dana usually took the helm, today she gave it to Quinn, and they sailed easterly in silence—except for the quiet rush of water against the hull—pointing toward Martha's Vineyard.

Later, Dana and Allie picked a bouquet of white daisies and put them in a vase on the old oak table. They lit a candle and told each other stories about Lily and Mark. Across the bay, Quinn sat by her rock. She sat there all afternoon, until the sun went down. When it started getting dark out, Allie got tired and started to yawn.

"Can we go upstairs, so you can read to me?" she asked.

"You bet," Dana said, holding her hand.

Allie crawled under her covers, arm slung around Kimba. His threadbare face gazed up at Dana, and she remembered the day she and Lily had bought him at the toy store. She read from *Winnie the Pooh* while Allie snuggled against her leg.

"Do you think Mommy knows about the white flowers?" Allie asked, stopping her in the middle of a sentence.

"That we picked them for her?" Dana asked. "Yes, I do."

"Because she can see down from heaven?"

"Yes," Dana said slowly and simply.

"Where is heaven?" Allie asked. "Is it in the sky?"

"Some people think that," Dana said.

"I don't know where to think of them," Allie said. "Mommy and Daddy. I wish I did. Quinn thinks they're in that old can on the mantelpiece, but I don't. That's not them, is it?"

"No, it's not, Allie."

"Quinn goes to Little Beach and sits on her rock . . . I don't have a place to go to like that. And neither do you."

"I know."

"I loved them just as much as Quinn," Allie said. "Just because I don't go to Little Beach and sit on a rock all day doesn't mean I didn't."

"Allie, they were your parents and you'll love them forever," Dana said, giving her a huge hug. "I know that, and so do they. So does your sister."

"I just hope she does," Allie said, and she let Dana hold her for a long time, until she fell asleep and Dana heard a knock at the door.

It was Sam. He stood outside, his hair and glasses glinting in the porch light. Through the screen, Dana could see that he was holding a bouquet of white flowers. Opening the door, she let him in.

"I thought of you all day today," he said, handing her the bouquet.

"These are beautiful," she said, smelling the honeysuckle trailing down the side.

"I tried to remember all the flowers in Lily's wall painting."

"You did a good job. These were all there," Dana whispered, her heart aching as she looked at the roses, lilies, freesia, and camellias. "I wish Allie weren't asleep. I'd love to show her. We picked Lily a bunch of daisies."

"Where's Quinn?"

Dana pointed at the window. The sun was down now, but in

the darkness they saw Quinn's flashlight playing across the waves. It beamed from the top of the big rock into the Sound, like a miniature lighthouse showing her parents' spirits the way. Through the open window a breeze blew, making Dana shiver. Sam stood right beside her, and she felt her breath coming faster and lighter.

"They died a year ago today," Dana said, her chest aching.

"I know," he said, brushing her shoulder.

"I don't know what to think. I look out into the Sound, and I don't want to believe what Quinn says. . . ."

"Dana," Sam interrupted her gently. "I want to talk to you. Okay?"

Dana felt her stomach lurch. She nodded, leading him into the living room. The candle she and Allie had lit still glowed on the table, sending shadows flickering across the glowing wood ceiling. Her shoulder burned where Sam's fingers had touched her. But she watched him straighten up, and she knew they were going to discuss Quinn's business.

She saw Sam watching her, a protective, tentative look in his eyes.

"It's okay," she said. "I'm ready."

"Are you sure?"

She nodded, feeling his concern.

"Nothing makes sense," Sam said quietly. "I called the Sun Center, and they're nothing but pleased with Mark and the job he did. I talked to the director and the head of expansion. Seems they've got plans to add on more rooms."

"But the money—what's it from? I took the tackle box upstairs to hide it from the girls, and I counted the money—it's five thousand dollars."

"It's a lot," Sam said. "My brother said money sometimes changes hands during construction projects, but I haven't found anything like that yet."

"I was thinking it's not enough for a bribe—it must be something else," she said, not wanting to disagree with him after he'd done so much work.

"I hope you're right, I really do," he said.

"What else could it be though?"

"Well, what about the key? Have you figured out what it goes to yet?"

Dana shook her head. "No, but I haven't really had time to look. I called Fred Connelly, the insurance guy. He gave me rough coordinates for the boat's former location, but he said she'd shifted so much during last year's storm, he wasn't able to find her again." She handed Sam the insurance report with the finding typed "accidental death," on one line, "vessel foundered," on the other.

"We'll find her," Sam said, holding her hand as he took the report. "That's one thing I wanted to tell you—the research vessel's available on Monday. Is it okay if I tell Quinn?"

"Yes. I want you to," Dana said, staring at their fingers, his on top of hers, interlacing as they held the horrible document.

"As long as we're still together on it. I didn't want to tell her if you'd changed your mind," he said, now gently sliding his hand away.

"I haven't," she whispered, her eyes hot. "It's all I think about instead of painting."

"I know."

"How?" Staring at his hand, she wished he'd take hers again. What did it mean, the fact that she wanted to hold Sam Trevor's hand so badly that she thought of him when she couldn't sleep at night?

"I looked through the garage window, and I saw that you'd built the canvas. That's good, Dana."

"It's blank, though. You must have seen that too."

"You'll paint soon. I have confidence in you."

"I'm trying," she said, her throat aching with old sorrow.

They were standing so close, almost touching. Across the cove, Quinn's light played across the waves. Dana thought of that last evening Sam had been over, when she'd told him the colors she would use: dark blue, royal purple, and gold. They were almost the same tonight.

"When I was in grad school at Woods Hole," Sam said, "Joe gave me a small sailboat. He knew I couldn't be that near the water and not sail—thanks to you."

Dana couldn't speak. Sam's voice was soft and low, and he held her gaze with his gold-green eyes.

"Well, I used to hang around the docks. There was an old guy who used to be a sailor, and he asked me something. What does an old seaman do when he tires of the sea?"

Dana looked up. For some reason, the question chilled her heart, and as if he could read her mind, Sam moved closer. She shivered, thinking of that old seaman, thinking of herself.

"See, he'd lost the feeling of enchantment with life," Sam said quietly. "He'd tired of feeling the waves beneath his feet, of shipping out and seeing new ports. That was his life, but he couldn't do it anymore."

"So what did he do?"

"Became an old drunk on the dock."

"That's sad," Dana said, her eyes filling. If Sam saw, he didn't say anything. He didn't move at all, just sat very still and waited for her to go on. "I don't drink," she said. "And I don't sit on a dock. But I know how he feels—about the enchantment with life."

"I know you do," Sam whispered, taking her hand and making every bone in her body feel liquid.

"I built a canvas," she said. "I set out the paints you bought me. Mixed them, and everything. I stare at them, wanting to paint, but I can't."

"Dana . . ."

"I can't paint. I'm wrecked," she cried, staring out the window to the dark purple water of the Hunting Ground.

Sam moved toward her. He wore a T-shirt, and his muscles glowed in the candle flame. Dana covered her eyes with her hands. She thought of Mark's boat, wrecked at the bottom of the Sound, hole in the bow or the seacocks open, and she realized she felt the same way. One day she'd been sailing along, loving her life, and the next she had filled with water and sunk to the bottom. She had lost her sister, her lover, and her belief in sharing.

"You're not wrecked," Sam said, wrapping her in his arms. "You're not, Dana. You're incredible."

"I don't feel it."

Dana leaned into his chest, unable to stop the tears. Her mouth was open against his shirt, and she tasted the salt of his sweat and the sea. His arms were gentle around her shoulders, and his hands stroked her back with the same rhythm of waves hitting the shore. He led her over to a chair; without knowing, he had chosen Lily's. She looked up through tears, realizing he was holding her hands.

"Listen to me," he said. "I'm here to help you."

"You can't," she said.

"I made a promise to you twenty-one years ago. It's taken all this time for me to be able to keep it."

"What was it?" she whispered.

"To protect you. To save you the way you saved me."

"This is different," Dana said, touching her own heart. It hurt, deep inside, with an ache she had never before imagined. Lily's death had left her with a broken heart, and Jonathan's betrayal had torn it apart. "All I did was pull you out of the water."

"That's what I'm going to do for you," Sam said, looking into her eyes. "Pull you out." There was nothing remotely like Jonathan in Sam's eyes. No asking, no demanding or bargaining or impatience. They were filled with longing, and Dana knew: It was a passion to give, not take.

That was one of the scariest things she could have seen at that moment. She felt so depleted. With two little girls to love and raise, trying to do it on her own, she would have loved to reach out to someone. But how could Sam really help? He was young, and she was afraid he would expect quick results.

What if she trusted him and he turned impatient, like Jonathan? She couldn't handle someone expecting things of her, making demands, measuring her against a timetable. Not for a long time, if ever. Outside the window, something flashed by. It was a shooting star, sea fire sliding down the tail of a mermaid, Quinn's flashlight, or one of the fireflies from Firefly Beach: Whatever it was, it gave Dana the will to ask.

"How?" she whispered. "How are you going to pull me out?"

"Like this," he said, holding out his hand. He clasped hers and pulled her out of her chair. They stood face-to-face, and he stared into her eyes for a long time, as if he didn't know what to do next.

And then he did. Tenderly, so softly she almost thought she was dreaming, he kissed her lips. She felt a shiver from the top of her head down her spine, and her knees went almost weak. His mouth was hot, and she stood on tiptoe to get closer. The candle sputtered in a burst of wind. Sam drew her even closer, and she realized she was standing on her toes on top of his bare feet, kissing him as if he were doing what he'd promised to do, save her life.

Dana had to grip his forearms, lower her head. This was Sam. Sam Trevor, the little boy she had taught to sail. Her mind was racing, telling her she was crazy, that this was wrong. She was driving straight into another crash.

"What are you thinking?" Sam asked.

"About how young you are."

"Souls don't have ages, Dana," he said, pulling her into his arms and kissing her again. She held on tight, feeling their hearts beat through their T-shirts, electricity making her skin tingle all the way down to her toes.

"Sam, I can't do this . . ." she began, stepping back.

"Because of our ages?"

"No, not just that," she said. "It's everything. Lily, the girls . . . it's all a jumble for me." She thought, trying to sort it out enough to explain. "Because I'm not ready. I was hurt by someone in France. I know you're different, you're not him, but he was younger than I am too. He wanted to rush me into painting before I could even think about it."

"Do you think I'm doing that?"

Dana shook her head, taking his hand. "No, it's very different. But I'm confused. I don't know what to think."

"I do," he said, smiling.

Dana wanted to say more, but just then she noticed that Quinn's flashlight had begun to bob through the woods, across the rocks on the way home. Sam had seen it too, and he turned back to Dana.

"She's coming," Dana said.

Sam took her hands. He held them very lightly in his, looking into her eyes the whole time. "Find what you need," he said.

"What I need," she said, thoughts flooding in, "are the answers,

I guess. Why my sister died. And her locket—she always wore it, you know. I wish her daughters could have it." She looked at Sam. "You're talking about when we dive on the *Sundance*. . . ."

"No. I mean in your life," Sam said. "I don't want to see you hurting like this, Dana. Just like that old seaman, I want you to find your enchantment with life again."

Dana's eyes filled with tears because she wanted that so much too. She thought of the paints in the garage, and for one moment her fingers tingled with the desire to pick up a brush.

"There's something else I have to ask you before she gets back."

"What?"

"About New York. You're going next Thursday, right?"

"Yes. To meet someone for lunch," Dana said, remembering that he had been to dinner the day she'd made the date.

"Will you save that night for me?"

"Oh, Sam," Dana said. "I don't know. . . ."

"Look. Monday we're diving on the *Sundance*. Depending on what we find, if everything works out the way I think it will, I want you to meet me at the fountain at Lincoln Center," Sam said.

"Why?"

"I'll tell you when I see you," he said. "Will you?"

"Maybe," she said. "That's the best I can do."

"That's the best I can ask for," Sam said. And, kissing her one more time, he left her standing in the middle of the living room, wondering why she suddenly had such a burning desire to paint, when Quinn walked through the front door.

SHE DIDN'T WASTE TIME asking herself or anyone else. After midnight, when both girls were in bed and asleep, Dana slipped outside. She walked down the hill to the garage, and she stood in front of her canvas. Inspiration washed over and through her, and wherever it came from, it made her feel grateful to Sam. She mixed her oils, and for the first time in many months, Dana began to paint.

QUINN GOT THE message: Monday was the day. Sam was coming over with a big-ass oceanography boat, and they were going to get all the answers they needed. But this time, when she went down to the garage to tell Aunt Dana the news, she got the shock of her life.

Aunt Dana had been painting. She must have been at it all night.

The painting was only partly finished, and the garage was as dark as ever, but even so, Quinn could see how beautiful it was. The blues and purples blended together, and flashes of gold hit the wave tops. Down below the surface, the water was still and calm. Blackfish and cunners swam amid the kelp. Quinn must have gasped, because her aunt smiled and asked, "What?"

"You're really painting," Quinn whispered.

"I am."

"I didn't think you ever would. Not here."

"I didn't either."

"What made you start?"

Her aunt was silent. She wiped her hands on the sides of her jeans, where she had already left many streaks of paint. "It was just time, Quinn," Aunt Dana said. "Someone helped me see that. No matter what mysteries we're facing, we still have to live our lives."

"Who was the someone? Me?" Quinn asked.

"You were one someone." Her aunt laughed.

"Sam's the other, right?"

"Maybe."

"Do you like him?"

"I think I do," her aunt said. Quinn wanted her to say more, but instead, she blushed, as if the heat had just shot up. Staring at her aunt, Quinn noticed how happy she looked. The happiness was in her eyes and skin, not in anything as obvious as a smile. She was glowing, as if starting to paint had made her feel right again, like the old Aunt Dana, the Aunt Dana Quinn hadn't seen since before her mother had died.

"Aunt Dana?" Quinn asked.

"What, honey?" Aunt Dana asked, touching her brush to the blue paint, lightly stroking it onto the canvas.

"Why is every day so different?"

"What do you mean?"

"Why can you paint today and not yesterday? Why was Mom here two August fourths ago but not today?"

"Those are the mysteries I was just talking about, Aquinnah Jane."

"What do you think we'll find on Monday?"

Aunt Dana laid down her brush, came around the easel to hold Quinn and stop her heart from beating out of her body. Sometimes all Quinn could do was run as fast as she could, but right now she let her aunt put her arms around her and stroke her head.

"Whatever we find, I'll be right there with you," Aunt Dana whispered.

"Promise?"

"I do."

"What if it's bad, Aunt Dana?"

"We'll be together. We'll deal with it then."

Quinn closed her eyes. She felt glad her aunt wasn't telling her to look on the bright side, that they'd find only good things. Her mother had done that sometimes, told white lies to cover up her own worries and fears. She had done that about the business trips, and when Quinn had written angry things in her diary, her mother had read it.

"I wish we had never left Martha's Vineyard," Quinn said. "Stayed there from the time I was a baby."

"Why?"

"It was our special island, the place I was born. We were so happy there. I wish we could all go back, turn back time to those days. . . ."

CHAPTER 17

THEY RODE ACROSS THE WAVES ABOARD THE *WESTERLY*, the research vessel Sam had brought. Looking east, holding Allie on her lap, Dana glanced at Sam. He smiled at her, and she smiled back, shivering in the breeze that blew through her hair. From the deck, they could practically see the Vineyard beyond the horizon.

Dana thought of the carefree happy days she and Lily had had on that island, before men and children and responsibilities had come to take them away from each other. The ship rode across the Sound, the engine thrumming.

Because the ship belonged to Yale, Sam had brought two graduate students as crew—one of them a lovely twenty-two-year-old woman. The vessel was a sixty-five-foot trawler, bequested to the marine studies department by a wealthy alumnus, and it was furnished with more equipment than anyone could imagine.

Sam was captain. He steered with Dana, Allie, and Quinn beside him in the wheelhouse. Quinn made sure he had her hand-drawn map spread out before him, but Dana noticed he relied more on the chart and GPS coordinates—the Global Positioning System, bouncing air waves up to a satellite as a way of determining position—glancing from the instruments to the chart table and back. When he looked at Dana, she felt a shiver run down her spine.

She felt so torn. She wanted to trust him completely. He was sacrificing so much time to help her and the girls. Buying her the paints had been such a loving gesture, one she'd never forget. But as the boat pounded across the waves, she remembered how hurt she had been before. She found herself comparing everything he did to Jonathan: Would Jon have helped her this way? Would he have been this kind to the girls? Wasn't it possible to have good intentions and still give in to passion for someone younger, prettier, wilder?

She found herself watching the female grad student. Her name was Terry Blackstone. Tall and tan, blond hair streaming behind her in the wind, she looked ready to play volleyball. Her white shorts rode low on her hips, her tight blue T-shirt revealed a bikini top underneath.

"We're far from shore," Allie said nervously. "Farther than when we sail."

"Not a lot," Dana said, dragging her eyes away from Terry, pointing out their regular sailing route along the shore.

"You didn't have to come," Quinn reminded her. "You could have stayed with Mrs. Campbell."

"I wanted to come for Mommy and Daddy, but I don't want anything bad to happen, like the thing that took them. . . ."

"Don't be scared, Al," Quinn said, reaching into Dana's beach bag for Kimba, pressing him into her sister's hands.

"You either." Allie smiled.

Dana was silent, letting the sisters take care of each other, just as she and Lily had once done. Sun sparkled on the Sound. Pleasure boats crisscrossed their path, sailboats heeling over, motorboats pulling water-skiers, Jet Skis jumping the wakes. Terry and Matt—the other grad student—talked quietly at the rail.

They passed the green can buoy that served to mark one end of the Wickland Shoals and the red bell buoy that marked the other. Beyond that was open water. Turning to look over her shoulder,

Dana saw the Connecticut shoreline behind them, shimmering in a sea of haze. Looking forward, she saw the North Shore of Long Island a bit farther away.

"Are we at the midpoint?" she asked.

"Not yet," Sam said. "But almost."

"How can you tell?" Quinn asked. "Just by looking?"

"No, your aunt's the artist, the one with the excellent eye," Sam said. "Me, I have to rely on electronics."

"Sam is an excellent navigator," Terry called. "Get him to tell you how we all made it back from Montauk in a gale!"

"You all went to Montauk?" Dana asked, unable to block the jealousy.

"To chase a pod of dolphins," Sam said, oblivious. Dana nodded. She couldn't stop looking at Terry's long legs. Monique had been twenty-five, just three years older. The day before she'd found her with Jon, Dana would have said she wasn't the jealous type. She had never considered other women to be rivals before. Now she gazed at Terry and wished her heart would stop hurting.

Sam showed Quinn and Allie how to work the GPS. Dana watched as Sam pushed the buttons and Quinn marked the chart. "But there's another way to tell where we are," he said after a minute.

"What?"

"See that?" Sam asked, pointing forward.

Dana and her nieces looked through the windshield down the bow. Terry and Matt were watching too. There, straight ahead, the water seemed to rise and fall in ocean waves. It was wake left, not by the pleasure craft of a few minutes ago, but by a passing oil tanker.

"The shipping lane," Sam said as Dana picked up the binoculars to look. The ship was longer than a football field. It was black and red with stripes of rust running down its hull. Because it rode low in the water, traveling from east to west, Dana figured it was full of oil, heading to New York from the port of Providence.

"We're going in there?" Allie asked, shrinking into Dana's lap.

"Not quite," Sam said. "Just close enough."

"The Hunting Ground," Quinn breathed, and Dana shivered.

Now a barge came along, piled high with containers. The tow rope was long and hard to see, but the tug pulling it carried markers on a mast. Sam pointed them out, telling Quinn each marker represented twenty feet of tow line. Dana watched as Quinn, trying to listen, seemed mesmerized by the huge wake and wash generated by such enormous vessels.

Sam switched on the depth sounder. His crew—Terry and Matt—stood beside him, watching the chart for marked elevations and comparing it with the sonar. Dana forgot to be jealous. She sat still, one arm around Allie. Quinn took a step backward, melting into her side as she had years before, when she was a very little girl. The feeling they were close to where Lily and Mark had died came upon them like fog, and they knew to get through it they were going to have to stay together.

QUINN SWORE SHE heard the bing that marked the spot.

Every damn bing sounded the same as the sonar swept down from the *Westerly's* hull, sending sound waves straight to the bottom of the Sound. But suddenly, there was one sound like a bell—a short, sweet hello from the sea bottom that told Quinn they had found her parents' boat.

"It's here," she said to Aunt Dana and then to Sam. "We've found it."

Sam looked at her as if she were crazy, or perhaps the youthful savant that she was.

"I think you might be right," he said.

"I have powers," she said, trying to sound calm. Her heart was making that damn near impossible though. It was as if she had a puppy in her chest, trying to get out. Squirming, thrashing, bumping all over the place.

"You're the captain today," he said.

"Excuse me?"

"This is your charter," he said. "We're here because of you."

"I know," she said. This was her cue. Digging into her pocket, she came up with the cash. "I gave you that big payment before, and here's six more dollars. You know the hot dog stand came up a little short. I'll get you the other two bucks as soon as I can."

"You look like a person who's good for your debts," Sam said.

"I am," she said. Then, turning for confirmation, "Right, Aunt Dana?"

"Absolutely," Dana said, looking pretty in white shorts and a white shirt and a paint-stained blue cap. Her brown hair was messy in the wind, and she looked like a little kid trying to be a grown-up.

Quinn, her sister, and her aunt watched Sam getting into his wet suit. He looked cute and thin. His ribs were defined, his stomach tan, and Quinn found it very interesting the way Aunt Dana stared while pretending to watch a freighter going down the shipping lane.

Clearing her throat, Quinn said she had to go to the head. Aunt Dana said, no problem. Climbing down below, from the wheelhouse to the cabin, Quinn reached into the waistband of her shorts. An exception had been made.

Usually she never dared bring her diary home. After the reading incident, she had vowed to leave it buried at Little Beach. But today she needed it with her. She absolutely wanted to record, for posterity and sanity, this day's events as they happened.

Curled up on a settee down below, she began to write.

> *We are onboard the RV* Westerly. *Sam is about to dive down to the bottom and find out the truth. It's a sunny day. For some reason, I thought the sky would be gray and the water black. I know the answers won't be good ones. Sam thinks they will—I can tell. He wouldn't dive if he thought they wouldn't.*
>
> *I remember the day Mommy read my diary. She was so mad. Her face looked like one of those cartoon monsters with her eyes big and her lipstick too dark, making her mouth look mean. She was holding the diary, shaking it in my face.*
>
> *"You spy on your father, you listen to his phone calls," she said. "That is not what a good daughter does. It isn't*

trusting, and it isn't right. Doesn't he put food on our table? Doesn't he travel all over the country to find the right projects? There are grown-up things you can't understand."

Well, Mommy, tell me, then. Tell me the grown-up things I can't understand. She never did. She never did tell me. All I had were the phone calls and the fights. If she didn't want me to eavesdrop, why did she yell so loud? Did she think I couldn't hear? How Allie managed to sleep through all that, I'll never know.

"Parents fight," she'd say, trying to stop me from crying. "I love your father so much. Sometimes I react too strongly to what he does—he builds houses in beautiful places. People need places to live, not just birds and animals!" Cuddling me, promising me they still loved each other, saying that fathers did what they had to do to support their families. That Daddy built homes for families, made old people good places to live in. The ghosts of their fights still keep me awake.

Now Sam is getting ready to dive down. What will he find? There's a whole story in that boat down there, if only the right person tries to read it. Just like there's a whole story in our house, in the yard, in the garage, in the other diary. Aunt Dana could find it, I suppose—I wish she would.

She's my good aunt. I love her so much, almost as much as I love them. She's looking after me and Allie, helping us find the way to live without them. It's not easy. Most kids my age still think their parents are perfect. I know mine weren't, but I just wish they hadn't decided to leave.

While Sam pulled on his wet suit, his mind raced with many memories. He thought of a day two summers ago, diving on the *Cambria* with his brother, Joe. The old barquentine had wrecked on the Wickland Shoals over a hundred years ago, and Joe and his crew had salvaged the ship and treasure. Sam's gaze drifted across the Sound to the spot. He still had the scar from where he'd been cut with a cable, and he still remembered the shark that had swum into his blood.

It had been a mako. A man-eater—as dangerous a shark as was found in these waters. Joe had claimed it was a harmless blacktip, but what did he know? He was just a geologist. Unable to help himself now, Sam looked for fins.

Another memory surfaced. He saw himself as a boy, waiting at the foot of the Jamestown Bridge. It was Christmas morning, and his father was dead. He could see the ice and snow, feel the cold in his bones. Thinking of Quinn down below, he knew this was her bleak Christmas morning. It didn't matter that the August sun was beating down, that the thermometer registered eighty-five. The girl was ice cold inside, and she would be until Sam came up with the truth.

Dana was watching him. He felt her gaze on his bare chest, and he sensed her coming as he pulled on the black neoprene jacket. She placed her hand on his back.

"Thank you," she said.

"I haven't done anything yet," he said.

"You've done so much. Getting the boat, letting Quinn feel like it's because of her. She's down below, writing in her diary."

"A diary?" Sam looked up. "Have you tried the key we found?"

Dana shook her head. "I'd never read her diary, no matter what. That's sacrosanct."

Sam held her face between his hands. He remembered kissing her in her house, holding her in his arms and feeling her warm body. Right now her niece and the crew were watching, and he didn't care. He kissed her forehead, the tip of her nose. He thought of her teaching sailing—not to him, but to her frightened nieces, helping them lose their fear of the water. "You're a good aunt, Dana," he said.

"You've said that before," she smiled.

"That's because it's so true."

Dana seemed about to say something, but then Quinn came bounding up from the cabin and asked when the dive was going to get under way. She was paying the freight, after all. She wanted a return on her investment. Watching Dana take a deep breath, prepare to set her straight, Sam nodded. He was thinking of Christmas morning on the bridge, remembering how hard it had been to wait.

"We're going in," he told his crew, and he and Terry dove overboard.

THE SOUND WAS CALM, but the shipping traffic created big waves in their wakes. Big white waves tossing the *Westerly* like a duck in the bathtub. Matt and Terry had set out tubes with dive flags on them, indicating that divers were down below.

Good, Quinn thought. She didn't want anyone getting hurt on account of her. Aunt Dana kept watching her, as if she thought Quinn might lose her mind, go mad right there on deck. To reassure her, Quinn tried to smile.

"It's hard to wait," Aunt Dana said.

"Not really," Quinn said, acting cool.

"She's lying," Allie said, fingering Kimba's ear. "She's sweating it."

"You don't even know what he's doing down there," Quinn said.

"Sure I do," Allie said. "Finding Daddy's boat."

"Yeah? Why?"

"Because it doesn't belong on the bottom," Allie said as if Quinn were an idiot. "It's supposed to be *floating*."

Quinn smacked her head. "If you were any more of a genius, I'd be in trouble."

"Thanks for noticing," Allie said, clutching Kimba.

"How could I miss it?" Quinn asked. At the stern of the boat, Matt was lighting up a cigarette. Quinn would watch him, and if he didn't throw the butt overboard, she'd grab it for her own.

"That's enough, Aquinnah," Aunt Dana warned.

At the sound of her voice, Quinn forgot all about smoking. In fact, she stopped being twelve and went straight back to three. Curling up against her aunt's side, Quinn felt like a tiny girl. Her aunt's arm came around her. Quinn closed her eyes tight and tried not to see. She just wanted to feel: the sea rocking her, her aunt holding her, the sun on her face.

But even with her eyes closed, she saw: The boat was untouched, unharmed. Sam was going to come up and tell her her father had opened the seacocks. She just leaned against Aunt Dana and settled down to wait.

SAM HAD ENOUGH air to last an hour, and that was good, because what he had thought was the *Sundance* was actually an old container. Forty feet long and twelve feet wide, it was about the same size as the sailboat. The echo sounder had picked it up, and Sam had assumed the rest. Marked in German, it must have fallen off a freighter coming from Hamburg or Bremen.

He and Terry swam slowly south into the shipping lane. She came from San Diego, and she was a good diver. The insurance company's information had *Sundance* just north, but that big storm last summer, Desdemona, had shifted the bottom. Sam used his knowledge of tides and currents—along with models he had worked out on the Yale computer—to project drift.

"Has to be around here," he said into the murky water. Bubbles left his mouth, and he imagined them going straight up to Dana. She was on deck, watching out for him. He'd never brought anyone out with him before. He thought of the *Cambria* dive, with Caroline waiting on deck for Joe, and as he thought of Dana, he was beginning to realize what it felt like to have someone.

Beds of kelp and colonies of mussels drifted in the current. A huge vessel passed overhead, creating a blast of stormy surface swells. Sam kept his focus on the bottom, straight ahead. He saw a shadowy shape the size of a sailboat lying on its side.

Sam swam closer. He circled the hull. The stern stuck slightly up, as if the bow had taken a dive straight from the surface to the sand. Stenciled in dark blue, made almost black by algae, was the name and port:

SUNDANCE
BLACK HALL, CONNECTICUT

A chill went through Sam's body, and he couldn't help thinking of the divers who had found his father's truck. The stainless steel rails and rigging were coated with green seaweed. The white paint was dark green with plant growth. Terry pulled out her camera and began snapping pictures.

Trying to breathe steadily, Sam swam toward the stern in search of the seacocks. The insurance company had stated that they had been closed, indicating an accident; although that first sighting had been sufficient, *Sundance* had shifted before final photos had been taken. Wanting to be sure, Sam swam down. There they were, both seacocks shut tight, just the way the investigator had found them.

Sam knew a trick the insurance diver might have missed. It took all his courage to make him proceed where he had to go. He was doing this for Quinn and Dana, but even more, he was doing it for Lily.

He knew that now. She had been his friend, Dana's sister, and one year ago she had died here. She had been young. Her daughters were the spitting image of her and her sister, and she had been raising them with everything she had. God, it was sad that it had come to this, the end of a beautiful life in the cold water at the bottom of Long Island Sound.

Sam edged his way through the seaweed, across the deck, into the cabin. It was dark as pitch in there, darker than Dana's garage at night and twice as cold. Sam could hear his own breath in his ears. The current swirled around him, a frigid salt river. It tugged him away, making it hard for him to maneuver into the hold.

Secrets of death, secrets of the deep. Sam felt the spirits of Lily and Mark, and he felt the spirit of his father. He had come close, twice, to dying like them at the bottom of the sea. Once Dana and Lily, the other time Joe, had saved his life. Grasping on to the companion ladder, hauling himself deeper into the cabin, he knew those were the people he loved.

You needed love to get yourself through a thing like this, Sam thought. There was no other way. Two people had died in there. Their kids were waiting up above. Sam's hands were shaking as he switched on his light, pointed it into the dark. The beam picked up tables and settees, now on their sides, their cushions chewed up by fish and crabs. It illuminated pots and pans, lanterns, nestled on the bottom, on what had once been the vessel's starboard side.

Sam went straight for the floorboards. He took a quick, thorough look. Except for buckling that must have resulted from the sinking, from one year of lying on the sea bottom, everything looked normal. He lifted the trapdoor, shined his light into the engine compartment.

What did Sam know? He was an oceanographer, not an engineer. But everything looked okay to him. He paid special attention to the Lion shaft, a section of the engine that flowed directly into the sea. The skipper of his grad school research ship had once shown him how to reverse the switch and let seawater in instead of cooling water out—"the surest way to scuttle a boat and fool the insurance companies," the captain had said.

But the *Sundance*'s Lion shaft was in full-forward position, showing no bad intent on the part of the Graysons. Exhaling with relief, Sam turned to leave the cabin. Halfway out the door, he turned for one last look. He remembered Lily's locket. If only he could find it for Dana, he would give her something to hold on to.

His beam swept the cabin. It picked up dull glints of brass and steel. Several pictures, bolted to the wall, had disintegrated into shreds. Sam held his light steady, wanting to find that final gift. Eventually, he had to give up.

Swimming out of the boat, he found Terry waiting to return to the surface. Sam nodded, circling his hand to indicate he wanted one last swim around the boat. Nodding, Terry followed. They held tough against the current, pushing forward toward the bow. When they got there, Sam held on to the rail. Tendrils of green seaweed blew backward like hair in the wind. It coated the stanchions and lifelines, the broken halyards and forestay. Short strands of hair mixed in, thin and brown.

Sam frowned behind his mask. He reached out, very carefully freeing several bits of hair. It felt rough and scratchy. He knew what it was, a better gift than the locket. He had Quinn's answer, and taking care to stay below his own bubbles, Sam swam for the surface.

CHAPTER 18

"THEY HIT A TOW ROPE," SAM SAID, WATER STREAMING from his wet suit.

Dana held out her hand, and he placed the crimped, twisted bits of hemp in her palm. The girls huddled over, as if she were holding something beyond value, as if she possessed the golden fleece. Allie had Kimba in a fierce headlock, trying to get a closer look.

"Are you sure?" Dana asked.

"A tow rope?" Quinn asked.

"I'm positive," Sam said. "One of the things about being a marine biologist is knowing every variety of seaweed known to man. I did my thesis on Chondrus crispus—that Irish moss stuff you see in tidal pools. Believe me, I know seaweed. And this ain't it."

"So what if it's a tow rope?" Quinn asked. "What does that prove? What about the seacocks?"

"They were closed," Sam said, smiling over the girls' heads at Dana. He had been right all along. He had encouraged Quinn, and in spite of Dana's reservations, he had been absolutely right.

"Thank you," Dana said. Her heart felt so free, she couldn't believe it.

"Will you please tell me about the tow rope?" Quinn asked, stamping her feet.

Dana watched Sam sink down to Quinn's eye level. Dana placed her hand on Quinn's shoulder as Allie scrambled into the circle of her other arm. She wanted to defend her nieces against what they were about to hear. Because even though the news was good, there was no evidence of sabotage, their parents were still dead, and they had died a terrible death.

Terry was at the helm, steering the ship back toward Black Hall. Matt lay on the foredeck, sleeping in the sun. Moving across the Sound, away from the site, Dana held tight to her nieces and waited for Sam to speak.

"They were in the shipping lane," he said.

"I know," Quinn said.

"Why were they there?" Allie asked.

"To get from one side of the Sound to the other, it's necessary to go through it."

"Your parents were out for a moonlight sail," Dana said. "It was a gorgeous, clear night. They must have caught the wind, taken off on a broad reach toward Orient Point. . . ."

"Mommy said that's what sailing was," Allie said. "Flying on wings that weren't your own, anywhere you wanted to go."

"That sounds like your mommy," Dana whispered.

"But the tow rope," Quinn said sternly. "Tell us what happened."

"They must have sailed between a tug and a barge," Sam said. "And hit the rope."

"But their boat was big," Quinn said. "A lot bigger than the *Mermaid*. They could have snapped any dumb rope."

"Not a tow rope," Sam said gently. "It's thick, Quinn. The diameter of a tree trunk. You saw the one that went by before."

"They would have seen it," Quinn said, talking fast, gesturing with her hands. "If it was that big, Daddy would have headed off the wind, waited for the barge to pass. And what about those markers you told us about—showing the length of line?"

"Tugs carry warning lights," Dana said, agreeing with Quinn. "They would have seen the lights. . . ."

"We weren't there," Sam said. "Anything could have happened."

"But I want to know," Quinn said, her eyes glittering with angry tears.

Dana tried to pull her closer, but she snapped her arm away. She stared at Sam, waiting for him to speak.

"My brother is an expert on shipwrecks," Sam said with compassion in his eyes and voice. "He's an oceanographer, just like me, but he's made his living diving on wrecks all around the world. He told me one thing, Quinn, when I was feeling just like you, when I wanted more answers than the wreck was able to give me."

"What did he tell you?"

"That some things we're not supposed to know. We have to look as hard as we can, then know when it's time to give up. That's the time we have to lay the whole thing to rest."

Dana watched Quinn, feeling her throat tighten. She knew Sam was talking about a grave, about laying Lily and Mark to rest for good. Quinn's eyes closed, and two tears squeezed out.

"You've done so much, sweetheart," Dana said. "You hired Sam to investigate the sinking, and he's told you it was accidental. He'll report what he found to the Coast Guard and the insurance people. Right, Sam?"

"I will," he said.

"You don't have to worry anymore—your parents wouldn't have left you on purpose."

"They wouldn't," Allie said, tugging Quinn's hand.

"It's like my brother says," Sam said. "Some things we're not supposed to know. We've looked as hard as we can, Quinn, and now it's time to give up."

Quinn stood in the middle of the deck, her braids shooting out like angry lightning bolts. Her fists were clenched; if she felt her sister's touch, she gave no sign. Clear tears streamed down her tan, freckled face. She refused to open her eyes, and she spoke so softly, it was almost impossible to hear her voice.

"I'm not ready to give up," she said. "Mommy, Daddy, I'm not ready."

THAT AFTERNOON, after Sam had dropped them off at the Moonstone Dock, Dana put the girls into the car and went back to talk to him on deck. Matt and Terry were in the wheelhouse, ready to go. Sam held the spring line, ready to cast off.

The vessel nudged the weathered old dock. Other boats moved slowly by, mindful of the no-wake rule. In the golden-blue light, Sam's eyes were soft green, the color of rushes in the marsh behind them. He looked at Dana and through her, as if he could somehow see what the day had meant to her.

"Sam, I wanted to thank you for what you did," she said.

"It's okay, Dana," he said. "I wanted to."

"I was with Quinn and Allie on deck while you dove down below. We never took our eyes off the surface; it was as if you were their guardian . . ."

" 'Their'? You mean the girls'?"

"I mean Lily's and Mark's. We felt so grateful to you. And that you found those rope fibers . . ."

"You knew all along how it would turn out," Sam said.

"I did."

"Quinn will figure it all out. Her head's spinning right now—I know mine was when I was in her shoes, when they came up from my father's truck. . . ."

"Thank you, Sam. You really will report what you found? I want the tugboat found. I want them to know what they did."

"I will, Dana. There's one more thing. . . ."

"What?"

"I looked for her locket."

Dana's heart sped up. "Her locket?"

"The one you bought for her at Miss Alice's. If she always wore it, and no one has found it, I thought it might be down there. But I couldn't see it anywhere."

"You looked . . ." she said, too moved to speak.

"I did."

"Oh, Sam."

"You know why."

"So the girls could have it?"

He shook his head. "Because of the way I feel about you, Dana."

Terry cleared her throat, and Dana looked up to see the younger woman pointing at her watch. She was lithe and blond, with southern California ease and elegance. At that instant Sam saw the look on Dana's face, and he took her hand.

"She's not even here," he said, staring straight into Dana's eyes.

"She wants to go."

"I want to stay."

"Sam . . ."

"I have to get back, and you probably want to be alone with the girls. You have a lot to talk about."

"She's your age," Dana said, her throat raw as she looked at the beautiful girl, as light as Monique was dark, waiting for Sam to take the boat down Long Island Sound. "She's lovely."

"She's my crew, that's all," Sam said. "I didn't dive on her sister's boat, look for her sister's locket. I don't care about her sister's kids. I don't love her. . . ."

"Love?" Dana asked, her heart racing.

"She doesn't fill my mind, take up all the room in my heart," Sam said. "But you . . ."

"Don't, Sam!" Dana said, feeling panicked.

"Let him go," Sam said. "Whoever he is, whatever he did to you. I'm not like that, Dana."

"I know you're not," she whispered. But did she really know that?

The girls couldn't see from the car, and the crew had their backs turned, so he kissed her hand. Dana felt a light shock go through her skin and bones, all the way through her body. She had seen Sam in his wet suit, his shoulders straining the tight black. She had kissed him in the dark, felt his arms around her body. Now his eyes were burning into hers, telling her the fear she felt was a lie, that the truth was as plain as the moon rising in the sky.

Suddenly, looking into his golden-green eyes, she believed that something between them was ready to shift for good—if she would let it. He squinted into the sun, a starburst of lines around his eyes. She found herself wondering whether he remembered New York, their plan to meet there on Thursday, and she wondered also what she dared to hope would happen.

As if he could read her mind, he asked: "The fountain, right?"

"Lincoln Center, Thursday night?"

"I'll see you at seven," he said. "Okay?"

"Okay," she said with one last glance at Terry.

She had hung the gold key she'd found in Mark's office from a length of silk twine around her neck, too long for the girls to see, in the place where she wished she could wear Lily's locket. Leaning forward to kiss her, Sam held the cord between his fingers. She didn't want him to let go; his mouth felt hot against hers, and it tasted salty like the sea. When she pulled back, he glanced down at the key.

"Is that Lily's?" he asked.

"Yes," she said, touching it. "It doesn't seem as important now. None of it does—I wish we'd never found it. Or opened the box."

"The box of money," Sam said. He kissed her again, as if he could take back what he'd just said. Terry called again, and when she said impatiently that she had a date that night, she wanted to get home to get ready, Dana had to smile.

But even as she backed away to return to her nieces waiting in the car, his words hung in the air. The hidden cash, the secret key: two things that didn't add up to the happy ending she wanted to write to her sister's mystery.

AT GRANDMA'S CONDO, all was peaceful. There was a crazy, somber tone that reminded Quinn of a nightmare or the day of her parents' funeral: bizarre and unreal, as if all you wanted to do was wake up.

The condo looked across the marsh. Hello! That's why they call it Marshlands Condos! Quinn banged her head against the wall to remind herself not to be stupid. Her little braids formed handy shock absorbers that kept her brain from banging around.

God knows her brain was getting a workout. Trying to analyze those kinky little rope fibers, see what Sam and Aunt Dana were jumping up and down about. Quinn got the part about her parents hitting the tow rope, but she didn't get the part about her mother crying that night before, saying he'd thrown their life away. Brain bruise deluxe-arama.

The meal sucked. Poor Grandma didn't realize how much everyone hated cube steaks. As a supposed treat, she had marinated them in Wishbone salad dressing. She served them with Tater Tots and green ketchup. For dessert, what else: pudding pops.

Quinn chowed down just so they could hurry up and get back to the beach. Allie refused to touch the steak, so Aunt Dana went into the kitchen to make her a toasted cheese sandwich. For at least the tenth time that day, Quinn's eyes filled with tears.

How had her mother become such a good cook? With Grandma frying steak and Aunt Dana burning the bread, where had her mother gotten her cooking talent? Quinn missed her all the time, but she honestly didn't believe she had ever missed her mother so much as she did at that moment.

Tenderloin, swordfish, soufflé, chicken cordon bleu, veal stew, Caesar salad . . . her mother cooked like a dream. She had fed her family the same way she had loved them: with passion and fervor and constant creativity. Tonight Quinn didn't want to remember that her mother had yelled at her father, that she had read Quinn's diary. She wanted only to recall the love in the hugs and kisses and food on the table.

"May I be excused?" Quinn asked the minute she had hidden her last bite in her napkin.

"Sure," Grandma said. "I was watching old movies before, honey. If you want, there's one still in the VCR."

Quinn ran into the living room. One thing she had in common with Grandma: They both loved home movies. While Allie colored pictures on the low table and the adults talked in near whispers, Quinn hit the button and watched the tape begin to play.

It was their last vacation at Gay Head, many summers ago. The weathered cottage, its field of salt hay. There was Mommy, beautiful in one of her bright sundresses. Daddy stood behind her, coming toward the camera with Quinn standing on one of his shoes and Allie on the other. They were happy together the year before the yelling started. The sun was out, glaring into the camera lens.

"Grandma, you always shoot into the sun!" Quinn shouted now.

"I know, I know. I'm too old to learn," her grandmother called back.

Now she and Aunt Dana started talking in a low voice. Quinn got the gist: Aunt Dana was explaining about how Mark had run into a tow rope, how it was a horrible tragedy that shouldn't have happened. Grandma was clucking at first, but soon she started sniffling, saying, "My baby, my baby," under her breath as the sobs came and Aunt Dana had to comfort her.

Quinn watched the home movie. There was her mother—Grandma's baby—smiling into the camera, dancing with her family. It was a Vineyard reel—their family name for the dance they had created—swinging each other to the sound of the waves and wind.

"My baby," Quinn whispered out loud, watching herself be passed from her father to her mother. Now she was in her mother's arms, feeling the sunlight come from above, feeling her mother's locket and the little key bump the top of her head.

There they were, right in the movie, catching the light: the silver locket Aunt Dana had given her mother and the tiny key her mother had worn on the same chain around her neck. Silver and gold: They didn't match, but they went together. *Besides my daughters, my two most prized possessions,* her mother had said of the locket and key.

Her mother had always kept a diary: like mother, like daughter. She had taught Quinn the pleasures of writing everything down, the necessity of it. And after a while, when it became as natural as breathing, the way it helped to figure everything out.

Her mother had taught her that diaries should be hidden. Quinn didn't know her mother's secret hiding place, but even if she did, she would never have breached it. Never in a million years. No matter how bad things got, how curious Quinn felt, she would never read her mother's diary. And she would have expected her mother, knowing how precious a diary was, to treat Quinn's with greater respect herself.

But this wasn't the time for blame, for anger. What was done was done.

"Grandma, Aunt Dana," Quinn called as her mother danced for the camera, that wonderful Vineyard light shining on the key and locket. "Come watch the movie."

"Soon, honey," Grandma said.

"In a minute, Quinn," Aunt Dana said, then lowered her voice again, telling Grandma about the dive, asking her questions about Daddy's projects, saying maybe it was time to stop looking, time to set all the questions to rest.

Staring at the key around her mother's neck, Quinn knew that was out of her control. Questions couldn't be set to rest until they were good and ready. The waves charged in beneath the Gay Head cliffs like mermaids' horses, fast and white. Blinking at the screen, Quinn could almost see the mermaids now, right behind her mother's head, dancing in circles with Quinn on her toes.

"I want to go back there," Quinn whispered.

"Where?" Allie asked, looking up.

"Martha's Vineyard."

"What do we need all that water for? We have the Sound."

"You weren't born there," Quinn said, her voice nearly as dreamy as the feeling in her heart. She wanted to see the place again before it was all built up, ruined by development. She looked at her mother's and father's faces and brought them into her mind. "You didn't live with them there."

THAT NIGHT, when the girls were in bed and the moon had fully risen to flood the eastern sea, Dana threw on her robe and went out into the yard. Once again, she couldn't sleep. More than anything else, she wished it were Thursday.

She wanted Sam.

She wanted to talk to him, to sit up with him in the thin, silver moonlight and talk about another night like this. How could Mark not have seen the tow rope? Dana gazed over the Sound, at the white light spread over the waves, and wondered how it would feel to be sailing along, to feel your boat be pulled into the sea beneath you.

She wanted to ask Lily, and she wanted to talk to Sam. Instead, the only thing she could think of doing was to go down into the garage and try to make sense with her brush and paints. This was her language, the way she had always solved her mysteries before. Turning to her canvas, she let herself work.

The dark, purple water topped with fine gold-edged waves. Staring at the painting, Dana touched her brush here and there. She worked on the seaweed and eelgrass below. Weaving the mermaid into the work, she wondered why she had ever thought she'd needed Monique for a model. She found herself painting Lily's face.

There in the dark garage, her sister came alive. Her features flowed from Dana's brush, and her bright eyes met Dana's and smiled. Her hair fell loosely around her beautiful face, the same face Dana saw every day when she looked at Quinn and Allie.

"Tell me what I need to know," Dana said, painting furiously now.

Outside, leaves rustled above the garage roof.

"What do I need to know to help Quinn? Allie's all right," Dana whispered. Her brush flew across the canvas. Blue-black water, clear as glass. A silver locket tangled in the weed. "But I'm worried about Quinn. She won't let go of you."

An owl flew into the garage, roosting in the rafters. It might have frightened Dana, but she barely noticed.

"She keeps your ashes on the mantel. Yours and Mark's. She's convinced there's more to your story, that we have to find out before she's ready. Oh, Lily. I am too," Dana said. Her hand brushed the key around her neck, and with absolute urgency she painted a tiny gold key lying in the sand. "What happened? What did you and Mark do?"

CHAPTER 19

As THURSDAY APPROACHED, THE GIRLS FOLLOWED DANA as if they were baby chicks and she were the mother hen. The plan was for Martha to come to Hubbard's Point and stay overnight, with Marnie available for backup. Quinn objected every inch of the way.

"It's not fair to Grandma," she said while Dana got dressed. "You know how the salt air bothers her arthritics."

"Arthritis," Dana corrected her. "But it's kind of you to be so concerned."

"Well, I am. And I'm worried about Mrs. Campbell too. She's always looking after us, and I think it's too much. Mommy took turns with her—we'd take care of her girls once in a while."

"That's a good point. We'll have Cameron and June over when I get back tomorrow."

"Tomorrow," Quinn said, rolling her eyes in disbelief and despair. "I can't believe you're just leaving us here. What if something happens? New York is too far for you to go without us. You should take us, Aunt Dana. That way, if you need us, we'll be right there—we'll keep you safe."

Dana smiled at Quinn, touched because her niece was thinking of something happening to her—not to them. In Quinn's world, bad things happened to the adults, the parents. Dana, dressed in her all-purpose art-world black Catata suit, took Quinn's hand and pulled her to the edge of the bed.

"I'm going for only one day," Dana said.

"A day and a night and at least part of tomorrow," Quinn scowled. Allie, who had been silent until then, rolled out from under the bed and grasped Dana's ankle.

"Don't go," Allie said.

"It's the little girl who lives under the bed," Dana said, lifting her up and setting her on the pillows.

"What about your painting?" Quinn asked. "Your gallery lady will understand—in fact, she'll want you to stay here and work. Give me the phone—I'll call and tell her how beautiful it is, how it's your best one yet."

"New York is too far," Allie said.

"Unless you take us," Quinn jumped in. "That's alternative number two. Number one is that I call the gallery lady, number two is that we go with you."

"Okay, you two—listen to me," Dana said. She took a deep breath. "I have to go, and that's that. I'm very careful—always. I've spent lots of time in lots of cities, and New York is one of them. And I plan to come home with presents."

"We're not material," Quinn said. "We don't care about that."

"Presents, Quinn," Allie whispered, tugging her sister's shirt.

"Come here and hug me," Dana said, wrapping them in her arms as tightly as she could. Her heart hurt with how much she loved them. Outside the window, pine trees swayed in the August breeze, and joyful seagulls wheeled and cried. It was almost enough to make her change her mind and stay home.

Almost, but not quite. Dana needed a day away. She didn't want to think about her sister's problems anymore. She needed a break from these children she loved so much. She craved a business lunch with other grown-ups, an afternoon of wandering the galleries of SoHo with no one wanting anything from her—a taste of her old life, when all she had had to do was paint the pictures and let others sell her work. And she needed to see Sam. That night, seven o'clock at Lincoln Center . . .

"What's that?"

At the sound of Quinn's voice, Dana pulled back. The jacket of her suit had fallen open to reveal the small gold key on the silk cord around her neck. The girls stared, mesmerized, at the key.

"Is it Mommy's?" Allie asked.

"Why do you say that, Allie?"

"She had one like it."

"Do you know what it went to?" Dana asked, her stomach flipping.

"Her diary, I think," Allie said. She giggled nervously, but her eyes looked upset as they swung to Quinn. "She tried her key on Quinn's diary to see if it fit before she broke it open. Mommy's key didn't fit."

"Shut up, Allie."

"What happened, Quinn?" Dana asked, shocked.

Quinn shook her head, her face growing red. Allie moved closer on the bed, as if to comfort her sister. The younger girl looked up at Dana. "Mommy read her diary."

"Is that true?" Dana asked.

Quinn nodded, ashamed.

"Why did she do that?"

"She said she was worried about Quinn," Allie said. "That she didn't want to, but she read it for Quinn's own good. It made Quinn really mad."

Quinn was shaking. Scowling, beet red, she looked ready to bolt. Dana took both her hands and shook them gently. "I don't blame you," she said. "Your mother was wrong to do it."

"Even though it was 'for my own good'?"

Dana shook her head, remembering back thirty years. "Quinn, I'm sorry to tell you we come from a long line of diary readers. When I was your age, or a little younger, my mother got it into her head that I was taking your mother and Marnie—Mrs. Campbell—on dangerous expeditions."

"Like where?"

"Well, on rowboat picnics out to Gull Island. And across the railroad tracks to look for Indian caves. And trying to swim across the Sound."

"Were you?"

"Umm, of course not." She coughed. "I would never do such dangerous things. What do you take me for? The fact is, I wouldn't have written about it if I had. But my mother thought I might have, so for my own good she rooted out my diary and read the whole thing."

"Were there boys in there?" Allie asked.

Dana nodded gravely. "It was loaded with boys."

"Mine's not," Quinn said. "I haven't had time for boys."

"Well, anyway, my mother read my diary, and I felt as if she had read my soul."

"I felt like that," Quinn said.

"It took a long time for us to build our trust back."

"It would have," Quinn whispered, "but my mother died first."

Dana hugged her. "Now I almost wish I weren't going to New York," she said. "I'm really glad we talked about this. I'm coming back tomorrow, and I promise not to read your diary. I promise, Quinn. No matter what happens."

"Really?"

"Really and truly. And, Quinn—I know your mother wishes she hadn't read it either."

"How?"

"Because I know your mother. She let her maternal instincts get in the way of remembering what it was like to be a girl. Don't be mad at her for that. It only means she loved you so much, she couldn't help herself."

"I wish she was here so I could hear it from her," Quinn whispered.

"So do I," Dana said into her braids.

ONCE SHE CLIMBED onto the train, Dana felt like a different person. Her mother and the girls stood on the platform outside the small blue station, seeing her off. They might have been waving white lace handkerchiefs and she might have been a boy departing for war, so great was the pathos in their faces.

But as the train picked up steam and headed west, Dana felt the responsibilities of aunthood flying off her shoulders. She was a single, world-traveling artist once again, leaving behind the pressures of small-town child-rearing, of suburban life. The train was air-conditioned. Outside, steam rose from the Connecticut marshes. The tide was out, and crab tracks scuttled through the mud. Herons hid in the shadows. New Haven and Bridgeport were hotbeds of traffic and trackside drama. Whizzing by, Dana saw it all. It was a child-free feast for her eyes.

She got off at Penn Station. Instead of getting a cab, she took the subway: the three train, down to Fourteenth Street. She meandered past the brick town houses along Twelfth Street, into the West Village. With time to kill, she stopped at a café on the corner of West Fourth and West Eleventh. The pictures on the wall were of Brittany, and drinking her espresso, she felt homesick for France.

Making her way through the Village, she window-shopped and people-watched. It wasn't at all hard to get used to. This was how she had lived for so long: losing herself in the world, using the details of everyday life to inspire her art and spark her muse.

When she came upon a small boutique that sold nothing but mobiles, she saw one with mermaids: five smiling mermaids swimming through the air, their hair streaming out behind them. Dana actually bolted away from the window. She didn't want to think about Hubbard's Point, the ocean, or any of her personal mermaids today.

Crossing Houston Street, she entered SoHo. This part of town was late to get going. The cafés were just starting to fill up. Dana felt a twinge—although she had always been an early riser, Jonathan had loved to have his coffee and croissant at their local *boîte* just before noon. She hurried along.

Shops and restaurants abounded. SoHo had changed over the years. When she'd first graduated from RISD, this had been the domain of artists living in lofts in the beautiful old cast-iron buildings. She and Lily had considered applying for AIR—artist-in-residence certification—and trying their luck in the big city.

They had gone to the Vineyard instead. Even now, Dana felt the pull of downtown New York. It was wildly energetic, filled with artists like herself, but she knew the sea always won out. Victoria DeGraff, her friend and gallery representative, knew that. She had planned their luncheon at Luna Mer: Moon on the Sea.

First, Dana went to the DeGraff Gallery itself. Located on the corner of West Broadway and Spring Street, its large windows were filled with two of Dana's underseascapes. Her name had been stenciled in classic white: dana underhill, new work.

When Dana opened the door, Vickie's young assistant called her from the back. Vickie herself swept down the long space—no one in SoHo called their rooms "rooms"—in her flowing gold Tibetan robe, her dark hair cut as close as a bathing cap, and kissed Dana on the cheeks three times—Belgian style—before folding her in a huge American hug.

"Darling, darling, darling. I have missed you!"

"And I you," Dana replied.

"Here you are! In person, and on canvas. What do you think?"

"It's hardly new work," Dana said, looking around. "I did these five years ago."

"I know. Thank God for the backlog. Who can predict when the blocks will come?" Saying "block," she shivered at the word.

Dana nearly told her the block was over, but she didn't want to curse herself. Art was a strange thing—a gift beyond measure, and she knew better than to take it for granted. Guiding her by the arm, Vickie led Dana around the gallery. Dana saw her old paintings, greeting them as if they were old friends: the scene done in Corsica, the one from Positano, two done on the Isle of Wight, the rest in Honfleur.

"Underhill Undersea," Vickie said. "That's what I'm seeing right now."

Dana nodded. She wondered how she had managed to make each undersea environment so specifically its own. The marine life was different, of course, but it was the color of the water that identified each place. *Royal purple and dark blue . . .* she thought of the paints Sam had given her, and she looked at her watch and thought about that night.

Moving along, she saw that Vickie had put out one actually ancient painting: It dated back to the Vineyard days. Dana recognized the clams, the bluefish, the spent shell from the old army bombing range at No-man's Land—the deserted island just east of Gay Head—the gloriously nude mermaid, one of the only obvious ones she had ever painted.

"Where did you get this? I don't remember you having it," Dana said.

"One of your first collectors died," Vickie said. "His wife put his entire collection on the market, and I had to break the bank to buy you back. You are a valuable commodity, my dear. But it was worth it—early Underhill. Thank God for death—it gets you back into circulation."

Dana nearly jumped.

As if realizing what she'd said, remembering Lily as the source of Dana's block, Vickie grabbed her arm. "Dana, I'm sorry."

"It's okay, Vickie," Dana said, staring at the mermaid who was, in fact, Lily.

"Come on, before I have to consume my other foot as well. We have a lunch date with Sterling Forsythe, an absolutely charming journalist from *Art Times*. Don't tell him I told you, but he's madly in love with you. He's heard the ridiculous rumor that you and Jon are done for good, and he hopes to do this fabulous article on you and get you to capitulate. Don't you dare, Dana."

She laughed, still gazing at the Vineyard painting. She had done it that first summer in Gay Head, fresh out of art school. She thought of Sam, and for the first time in a while, it clicked that he had mentioned the Vineyard to her several weeks earlier, something about seeing her there. . . .

"What is it?" Vickie said.

Dana laughed, shaking her head. "Nothing. Just that I've been so busy lately, I haven't had time to think."

"About Jonathan."

Dana stopped smiling. "Not about him."

Vickie pointed at a small canvas on the brick rear wall. Dana hadn't seen it before, but together they walked the length of the gallery. It was a portrait of her done almost a year earlier, not long after Lily's death. Jon had caught the sorrow in her gaze, the intensity of her stare. She was nude. They had just made love, and her arms were flung wide on the bed in helpless abandon. The picture was emotional, erotic, and to Dana, incredibly disturbing. Their lovemaking had been only half there during those months. Dana would try, but her heart wasn't in it.

"He wants me to represent him," Vickie said. "He told me you two should be together in all aspects of art."

"Victoria," Dana said, turning her back and feeling the searing pain of that terrible memory. "He is full of shit. I'm hungry—can we go to lunch now?"

"Yes, we can. Off we go to Luna Mer with the woman who paints like a mermaid!"

QUINN HAD THE RUN of the house. Let's face it: Grandma was no Aunt Dana. She stationed herself by the window and watched everyone on the beach, sighing to herself just about every minute on the minute. Quinn went upstairs. She went into her parents' bedroom and lay on the bed. She smelled their pillows and checked their bedside tables. She shook the mermaid globe and watched the minuscule fish swim around.

"Mermaid, mermaid, tell me true, what's a girl supposed to do?" she asked.

And the answer came!

Quinn was going to build a window so Aunt Dana could have the north light. She tore downstairs, past Grandma sighing at the sunny day. She had to keep Aunt Dana here, painting happily, so she wouldn't go back to France. Hoisting the heavy garage door, she slid inside.

Her father's tools hung on the back wall. Dragging over the stepladder, she pulled down a saw. With a worn wood handle and a rusty pointed tip, it had long been used to trim shrubs, cut the lower branches off Christmas trees. Using her superior sense of direction, Quinn once again located north and went to work.

Standing on the ladder's top rung, she examined the wall. It was old and uninsulated; light came shining between the boards.

She slid the saw's point between two slats and began to move her arm back and forth.

Aunt Dana, Aunt Dana, the saw seemed to say. What if Aunt Dana decided not to come back? What if she liked New York more? Quinn's mother had always said Aunt Dana was a vagabond, that nothing could make her settle down.

"Settle down here," Quinn said, sawing as hard as she could. The noise seemed very loud in her ears, but who was around to hear? Grandma was going deaf, and she was too busy watching the beach. If Allie came along, Quinn would threaten her with the death of Kimba. And Mrs. McCray and Mrs. Campbell spent most of their time on the rocks and pier, listening to the waves, too busy having a good time to worry about. Sam, on the other hand, might hear.

At that thought, Quinn began to saw faster. Sam wouldn't mind—in fact, he might even help her. Quinn knew he was her ally. Something deep inside told her he wanted Aunt Dana to stay around almost as much as she did.

The thought of Aunt Dana with that gold key was strong in her mind. If Sam stopped by, Quinn just might share with him the location of certain things. His brother was a treasure hunter; Quinn would see whether that trait ran in him as well.

She sawed with all her might, thinking of her artist aunt, in search of the north light.

CHAPTER 20

SAM COULD FEEL DANA'S PRESENCE IN THE CITY, AS clean and clear as the Atlantic wind, cutting through the hot smog of the New York streets. First, he took care of business. He had a meeting at Columbia University, way uptown, with a colleague who specialized in dolphin psychology. Then he took the nine train down to Ninety-sixth Street, switched to the number three express, and rode two more stops to Times Square.

He made straight for the offices of the Sun Corporation—the parent of the Sun Center complex in Cincinnati, Ohio. Late nights without Dana, he'd found himself hitting the Internet, searching for clues about Lily. He'd surfed around, hitting sites on, of all things, retirement villages. There he had found the Sun Center with its home office located on Broadway and Forty-sixth Street.

Times Square was jam-packed with kids. They crowded the island in the center of the street, screaming up at the studios of MTV. Some were college-age, most much younger. Sam scanned the girls in their bathing-suit dresses. Some were Quinn's age. He stopped short, face-to-face with one of his Plankton 101 lab students.

"Juliana," he said, surprised.

"Professor Trevor! I didn't know you liked Pink Frog."

"Pink what?"

"The group. I know—you probably think Yale students don't listen to pop, but what can I say? It's summer vacation. I thought you were going to be in Bimini." She took a step closer. She was very pretty, and her body was barely covered by the nylon fabric with nearly nonexistent straps, and she smelled like flowers.

"Nope. I changed my mind."

"So you decided to come hang out in the city?"

"I'm meeting someone."

"Are you sure?" she asked, giggling as she tripped slightly, steadying herself on his arm. "Because I don't really have to hear Pink Frog. I'm just bored. I live in the city—Upper West Side. I thought maybe I'd try to get on Urban Blanket Bingo, hope to get discovered so I never have to do a thesis, but oh, well . . . would you like to get a cup of coffee?"

"Thanks anyway," Sam said, backing away. He could still smell her perfume, and he looked down at her cleavage, at her skin damp with sweat. She was a junior, nineteen or twenty years old, closer to his age than Dana. But he didn't care about her any more than he did about Terry or any of the others. No matter what Dana thought, there was only one woman for him. He smiled and waved good-bye.

"Even Yalies should walk on the wild side. You're missing a good time," she called after him.

"No, I'm not," he said under his breath, heading north toward the offices of the Sun Corporation. The midday sun was straight up, beating down. Crowds jostled him on their way to lunch. He walked between the tall glass towers of midtown Manhattan and thought about what he was doing, helping Dana.

This was what partners did for each other, he thought. He hadn't had good role models at home, but during the last two years, he'd gotten to watch Joe and Caroline. They had the kind of marriage he wanted someday. They respected each other's differences, and they worked hard to be each other's mate.

Caroline helped Joe cut through the red tape necessary for international dives, and he let her know he wanted her along, that his life was better with her there. They spent one month a year at her hotel, the Renwick Inn, connecting with its spirit and helping it to run smoothly the other eleven months, and they made time for her family and for Sam.

What Sam saw himself doing today was helping Dana cut through the red tape of her sister's story. He walked into the marble lobby and told the guard he wanted to visit the Sun Corporation. A phone call was made. Sam was told he could stop by the public relations office on the twenty-fifth floor. They issued him a badge, and he walked to the second bank of elevators.

The Sun Corporation lobby was yellow. Graphics of the rising sun covered the walls. The receptionist buzzed him in, and he walked down a brighter yellow corridor to the PR office. Framed photos of the sun shined down from all sides. Sam was greeted by a tall, balding man wearing a blue suit and red tie.

"May I help you?" he asked, smiling in a way that made Sam think he believed Sam had elderly parents to consider.

"I'm interested in the Sun Center in Cincinnati, Ohio."

"Ah, the Buckeye State! I'm a Midwesterner myself. Got family out there?"

"Well, not quite," Sam said.

The smile became less radiant. Still, the man seemed friendly. His name was Francis Corwith. Shaking hands, Sam introduced himself. They sat in Francis's office, a small yellow cubicle with no windows but several photos of the sun. Francis slid a glossy brochure across the desk and began talking about the company philosophy, about wellness and optimism going hand in hand. "A sunny day is a healthy day," he said. "That's our motto."

"Sounds good to me," Sam said, rolling the brochure into a tube, wondering how to start.

"What brings you to us today?"

"Well, something sad," Sam said, deciding to be straightforward. "A friend of mine had a brother-in-law who died last year. Mark Grayson?" He paused, watching for any reaction.

Francis Corwith looked startled, but then he just shrugged and reapplied his smile.

"And someone's in need of a place to live? Would it be his mother? I didn't know Mark, but when someone young dies, the word spreads. Terrible thing. Well, if we can be of help. Normally, I'd suggest you go straight to the facility—Cincinnati, did you say?"

"Yes, but—"

"Here's some literature on that particular property. We're very proud of it—it's one of our newest. Built on beautiful parkland, with a natural pond and old maples, a waterfall that many people say is the prettiest they've ever seen."

"Mr. Grayson developed that property?" Sam said, watching for a reaction. The only ones he perceived were regret and sympathy.

"Mark Grayson, yes, I believe he did. Well, it's a testament to our operation that the families of many people who have worked with and for us make the choice to join us when the time is right."

"I'm sure it is," Sam said. Francis Corwith shook his hand, just as friendly as he'd been before. So Sam tucked the brochures into his bag and wondered what he'd do until seven o'clock that night, when it was time to meet Dana.

DANA LOVED the experience of lunch that day—at a restaurant with starched white linen napkins, not the kitchen table with paper towels torn off a roll.

The northern Italian food was delicious, but even better was the fact that she didn't have to think. She didn't have to worry about Quinn sitting on her rock, about getting Allie to swimming lessons on time, about what to have for dinner. She didn't have to stand in a dark, damp garage with no north light, painting the first canvas she'd touched in over a year. She didn't even have to let herself be haunted by images of Jon and Monique, lying on her studio couch.

All she had to do was eat good food, be flattered by Vickie and Sterling Forsythe, talk about her work, and wonder what would happen when she saw Sam. They sat outside, on a narrow wrap-around porch painted blue and white, with beautiful tiles hand painted with scenes of Italian beaches. Sterling's tape recorder whirred along, reminding her that this was an interview.

"Underwater," Sterling said. He was a big man with wavy dark hair and glowering eyes. He had the habit of saying words, single words, just dropping them in the middle of the table like little bombs set to go off and make Dana start talking.

She twirled a strand of black cuttlefish pasta.

"Undersea," he said, trying again.

"Dana, darling," Vickie laughed. "Don't be obtuse."

"I'm not," she said. "I'm just wondering what to say about it."

"You paint it," he said. "You have lived it—all over the world. Coastlines from here to Japan, am I right?"

"One year in Japan, yes."

"Which, among them all, would you say was your favorite?"

"Well, New England," she said.

"Yet you haven't lived there in over a decade. You reside in Normandy. What keeps you so far away from a place you claim to love?"

Dana ate quietly. She had been asking herself the same thing. Was it because she loved it so much that she had wanted to stay away? Loving a place, loving people, always led to heartache. It was easier to choose beautiful places she wasn't quite so tied to, places whose landscape didn't make her feel like crying, whose hills and sands weren't inhabited with the ghosts of those she loved. But all she said was "I've wanted to see the world. I thought it would make me a better painter."

"And I daresay it has," Sterling said. "Something else for your consideration: blue."

"Blue?"

"Yes. You know it's your signature color. With all your undersea Impressionism, having explored each ocean's shades and hues, how many shades of blue do you think you've used over the years?"

"One hundred and four thousand, six hundred and eighty-one," she said deadpan.

"Seriously?"

"Absolutely."

Vickie looked unsure whether to laugh or get mad. Dana smiled at her. She hated being interviewed. What did she have to say that was worth reading? She was just a person profoundly unsuited for nine-to-five work. She had found a way to support herself, make a good living, that let her use her God-given talent. But she couldn't exactly say that.

She had to play the game. Art critics liked her to be mysterious and cool. They loved the fact that she was an expatriate, that she had never married, that her paintings contained so few human elements. Although very few people, even journalists, actually saw the mermaids she disguised as weed and currents and fish in her work, this man was saying she painted like a mermaid, down in the deep.

"Love," he said, bringing his hand down on the white tablecloth.

Dana stared at his knuckles, at the back of his hand. The word brought three faces to her mind, and they were there right now, surprising her by their particular presences.

"Tell me about love," he said.

"Dana doesn't talk about her personal life," Vickie said, leaning forward to chide him; he was her friend, and he was supposed to know what was off limits.

"The art world was fascinated with your mentorship of Jonathan Hull," he said as if Vickie hadn't spoken. "Although personally, I thought him beneath you all along. An opportunist."

"I didn't see him that way," Dana said, staring at the bottle of olive oil. Golden as sunlight, filled with sprigs of rosemary and thyme, it smelled as sweet and fragrant as France, but to Dana it suddenly went sour.

"He wasn't an opportunist," Vickie said. "He's incredibly talented. Dana saw it first, but the rest of us see it now."

"Vickie, I love you," Sterling laughed, "but you seem to forget: I'm interviewing Dana, not you. Dana, would you like to have dinner tonight? I promise you, going out with a man my age will be much more fun. I'll like the same music you do—we'll have the same frame of reference."

"Thank you," Dana said, trying not to show her anger. "I can't. I'm meeting a friend later."

"Not Jonathan Hull?"

Dana shook her head, her shoulders tightening.

"Personally, I'm glad. Although it would make a great end to my story—you two getting back together."

"It won't happen."

"Never say never," Vickie chided.

"Never," Dana said.

"There's never an end to Dana's story," Vickie laughed. "Don't try to pin her down—she'll just move to a different continent. Make herself a brand-new home."

Dana laughed then. Jonathan and Monique faded, replaced by three different faces in her mind. Usually the thought of a new continent would send a jolt of electricity through her: a dream, if not a plan, to move on. She had never lived in Australia, for example. Or Antarctica. Plenty of ocean in both those places.

Instead, listening to Vickie and Sterling talk, she knew she didn't want to go anywhere new. She felt just as happy as she had that morning, to be on her own in New York for a day. But right now, the thought of home meant Hubbard's Point. It meant the gray shingled cottage, Lily's overgrown gardens, the dark garage, the stone steps down to the beach. It meant Quinn and Allie, and to Dana's amazement, it seemed also to mean Sam.

She couldn't wait for this luncheon to finish so she could go to her hotel for a shower and a nap, to change for the night ahead. After coffee, when Sterling asked and was denied a third time for dinner that night, Vickie made Dana promise she'd stop by the next day.

"For your check," Vickie said. "And a little something extra. You haven't forgotten about money, have you?"

Dana shook her head, shivering as she kissed Vickie's cheeks three times and remembered the money in the box. They promised they'd see each other tomorrow, before she left, and then Dana grabbed her bag and started walking uptown.

THE WINDOW was a piece of cake. Quinn couldn't believe it. She sawed ten inches down, ten inches across, ten inches up, and ten inches across the top. Her father would have been proud. It took her all day, and she now had a muscle in her right arm the size of a grapefruit, but no one could accuse her of lack of determination.

Now Aunt Dana had the north light.

If Quinn could have wrapped it up in a bow and handed it to her, she would have. The window was pretty much square. Not perfectly square though, more like a leaning trapezoid. The leaning window of Hubbard's Point.

Just as she was getting ready to clean up the old boards and head over to her rock, she heard voices outside. Moving closer, she saw it was Grandma and Old Annabelle. They stood in the road, talking to each other, just the way Quinn's mom and Marnie had done, the way Quinn and Cameron sometimes did now.

Seeing them there in their flowered dresses and sun hats was enough to get Quinn all choked up. This was all wrong. The old mothers were supposed to die first. Quinn's mother was supposed to be alive. She felt a kick in her stomach, as if the wrongness of it all might just kill her.

Chest tight, she turned toward her window. It was really good, the best window any artist could hope for. Quinn prayed Aunt Dana would like it enough to stay. As much as she loved her grandmother, she didn't think she'd be able to bear living with her the rest of her life. Grandma had so many aches and pains, and she just didn't get it. She didn't get Quinn's hair or her writing or the way she had to spend hours every day at Little Beach.

She didn't get it, but Aunt Dana—and Sam—did.

Aunt Dana and Sam; now, that was an idea. Staring at the window, mulling over the future, Quinn was absolutely shocked to see the two old ladies staring back at her, framed by the opening.

"Ohmygod," Grandma cried, clutching her throat.

"I told you, Martha," Annabelle said, frowning so hard, the tip of her nose touched the tip of her chin. "I heard sawing."

"Quinn, what have you done?"

"Sawing," Annabelle said, shaking her head from side to side. "Sawing, sawing, sawing. Marnie kept telling me it was a crow. T'ain't a crow, I told her. I know a crow when I hear it, and that sound t'ain't a crow. It wasn't, was it now?"

"Quinn?" Grandma asked, her blue eyes watery and sad, the way they always got when one of her granddaughters—usually Quinn—had let her down.

"This is a north window for Aunt Dana," Quinn said.

"Now, Quinn," Old Annabelle said, her southern accent getting thicker by the moment. "You know your daddy knew a thing or two about building."

"I know."

"Now, don't you think if your daddy wanted a window there, he'd have put one there?"

"You should have asked me before you did that," Grandma said gently.

"I was just trying to help," Quinn said defiantly.

"That's a good way to help the garage collapse, that's what you're going to help," Annabelle said.

"She's right, Quinn," Grandma said. "What if you cut through a support beam? Your aunt's painting could be crushed before she's even half finished."

"People could die, dear heart. Never mind the painting," Annabelle said.

"I didn't cut into a support," Quinn growled through her teeth. Her father had taught her that much. She knew all about support beams and carrying walls, she knew that was the whole source of the trouble, the bad thing, the terrible fight, her mother's awful words. The whole truth came crashing in on her.

People could have died in the building her father had taken money for. They didn't, but they could have.

"Well, get out of there before the garage falls on you," Grandma said.

"Call Paul Nichols," Annabelle instructed. "He'll buttress up the wall, and you won't have to worry. Though he does charge an arm and a leg."

"We'll have to have a few more hot dog stands to pay for him," Grandma said, starting to laugh, but Quinn didn't stick around to join in. She had to get out of there as fast as she could, as far as she could. She knew where she was going and what she was taking with her.

CHAPTER *21*

THE SUMMER NIGHT BY THE FOUNTAIN AT LINCOLN Center felt festive and alive. People strolled through the plaza arm in arm. A light wind blew the water, and a fine spray cooled Dana's face and arms. Lights were coming on in the surrounding apartment buildings; beyond them, the first bright stars had appeared in a lilac sky.

She had called her mother to check on the girls. "They're fine," her mother had said. "A little brouhaha with Quinn, but nothing too severe. She's over at Little Beach now."

"What kind of brouhaha?"

"Oh, sweetheart. Don't worry. I'll tell you when you get back. Just have fun, and we'll see you tomorrow."

Dana had hung up, relieved. A brouhaha with Quinn was absolutely par for the course; if there wasn't one, she might worry. Set free for the night, she was ready for anything.

She saw Sam coming from a long way away. As she sat on the edge of the fountain, her heart beat faster. He was so tall and good-looking, and even from there she could see the light in his gold-green eyes. Perhaps for the first time that summer it hit Dana: Sam had sacrificed most of his vacation to help her and the girls. The thought struck her, joined by excitement.

"You remembered," he said, walking over to her.

"Did you think I wouldn't?" She smiled. They stood facing each other and for a moment felt awkward. But then Dana remembered Vickie's three kisses, and she did it to Sam: one cheek, the other, the first one again. On the third kiss, he caught her and kissed her on the lips. The kiss was fast, but he held her with his arms and made her shiver all the way from her head to her toes.

"You look beautiful," he said into her ear.

"Thank you. You look great too."

"I wanted to meet you somewhere where we wouldn't get our feet sandy."

"This is the place," Dana laughed, looking around. The fountain's rush filled her ears, and she thought of London, of Rome. "It's like being in Europe. I feel as if I'm at one of the great music festivals."

"That's good," he said, pulling two tickets from the pocket of his jacket. "We're going to a concert. Mozart."

"My favorite," she said.

Sam nodded. "I thought so. You play it at Hubbard's Point so often, I couldn't resist when I read about this in the paper."

"Sam . . ." Dana said, touched that he would be so thoughtful. He didn't give her the chance to thank him again. Taking her hand, he led her slowly across the plaza, past the great concert hall with its magical, soaring Chagalls, to the small amphitheater behind.

Under the stars, in the middle of New York City, they listened to "Eine kleine Nachtmusik." Sam held Dana's hand, and she found she didn't want him to let it go. She was moved by the music, by his thoughtfulness—the fact he would notice something like her love of Mozart and arrange this surprise.

The strings touched her heart. They made her rise and fall, like a mermaid swimming in a calm sea. She held Sam's hand the whole time. This was strange, different for her. Holding hands had never been easy for Dana. Her hands were her expression; she painted with them, mixed her colors, brushed the canvas.

Sitting with other men, she would always move about. If they tried to hold her hand, she would pull it back. She would touch the air, direct the music, paint imaginary scenes of the feelings the music brought up in her.

Not tonight. She sat perfectly still, holding Sam's hand. The music was playful, joyful, yet underneath she heard tones of past loss. Something about it made her think of Quinn and Allie, and she knew—just by looking at his face—that Sam was thinking of them too.

His eyes were soft green, the color of summer grass, and she thought about how long she had known him. She remembered those eyes—filled with joy his first day of sailing, wild with terror the day she'd hauled him out of Newport Harbour. Right then, sitting at the concert, she felt a rush of affection for the boy she had known back then that swelled into passion for the man he had become, the man who had cared about her enough to bring her here.

When the concert finished, still holding hands, they walked past the fountain. She didn't know where they were going, and she didn't care. They started to walk east, talking about the music.

She told him she'd fallen in love with Mozart during art school, when her favorite teacher told the class he kept it playing while he worked, that he loved to fill his studio with music.

"Do you do that?" Sam asked.

"I do," she said. "Not in the garage at Hubbard's Point, but at home."

"France?"

"Yes, Normandy."

He asked, and she told him about her studio there: the ancient house, the barn out back, the huge arched window facing north.

"Must be brighter than the garage," he said.

"Yes," she said, picturing its view across meadows and the English Channel.

"Do you miss it?"

"In some ways, I've missed it all summer . . ." she said, trailing off.

"And now?"

For the first time in hours, she pulled her hand away. They had strolled along Central Park South, turned right onto Fifth Avenue.

Even at ten o'clock, the city was bustling. Tourists thronged the streets, gazing up at the Beaux Arts buildings, walking past Tiffany's and Bergdorf Goodman.

"And now . . ." Dana said in a low voice. "I don't know."

As if that were all the answer Sam needed, he nodded in silence. They walked a little farther, and then he hailed a cab. After holding the door for her, he climbed in and gave the driver an address on Bleecker Street.

It was a jazz club. "We had Mozart for you, and now I want to give you the music I love," he said.

Dana smiled, delighted by the idea of "giving" someone music. They went inside, down a long stairway. Completely dark except for votive candles burning in blue glass holders on each table, the place felt like a cozy den. Dana and Sam sat side by side on a tight banquette in back, listening to the musicians—a trio of piano, bass, and horn.

If Mozart had been summer, this music felt like winter. Warm—no, hot—and sexy, the jazz melted Dana inside. She forgot about the August sky, about the sea. She was deep in the mud. Sam had taken her hand again, and that was just fine with her. She painted in her mind: a clam, buried deep in the velvety silt, the whole water column extending above her for miles upward. When the music stopped, Sam turned to her.

"Do you like it?"

"I love it."

"I remember the first time I ever heard live jazz," he said. "My brother had been telling me about it for years, saying he'd take me to a little club in New Orleans. . . ."

"Your brother lived in New Orleans?"

Sam laughed. "Joe lived everywhere. He was like you—so many places to see, I think he was afraid he'd run out of world. That he'd be bored. New Orleans was one of his favorites. He befriended an old pirate in a jazz club on Bourbon Street, bought a presumably useless treasure map from him, and wound up getting rich on the gold he found two hundred yards off Key West."

"And did he wind up taking you to hear jazz?"

"No." Sam shook his head. "I did that on my own."

"In New Orleans?"

"Martha's Vineyard."

Dana was silent, staring at the blue candle on their table. Without looking up, she heard Sam go on.

"Circuit Avenue, Oak Bluffs. It was my first night there. I didn't know my way around the island, and I ended up in a bar—the Star Thrower. Three guys were playing, just like tonight. It was the greatest music I'd ever heard."

"How long ago?"

"Ten years."

Dana pictured the Gay Head cottage, the painting tent she'd erected in the backyard.

"What were you doing there? On the Vineyard?"

"Looking for you."

Once again, Dana fell silent. She didn't know what to say, but her heart was racing. She thought of someone throwing a star—white fire hurled through the sky, landing in her heart.

"I knew you were on the island," he said. "I'd never really lost track of you."

"We knew each other only that one summer. And you were eight."

"Maybe you had to know what it was like at home to understand. I'm not sure myself. You taught me sailing. It was the best thing that had ever happened to me. My mother was there, but . . . not there."

"I know. I'm sorry, Sam."

"You were amazing. You cared about me, Dana. That meant more to me than you can imagine. Then summer ended, and you were gone. I was back to feeling like I didn't matter. I couldn't wait till the next summer. . . ."

"And I didn't go back to Newport," Dana said.

"No. I went down to the Ida Lewis Yacht Club, and they chased me away. The new teacher wouldn't even talk to me. The kids laughed, thought it was hilarious."

Dana's throat ached, thinking of her young friend Sam, and she just kept staring at the candle flame darkened by blue glass.

"So I got busy. Got a summer job at the lobster company and

kept it till high school. I thought of you a lot. You'd changed my life that one summer, and that's not something I could forget. But you were out of my mind—or on the edge of it—until ten years ago, when I was in college myself."

The waitress passed by, taking orders. People at the next table laughed loudly, and Sam waited for everything to settle down.

"I was nineteen, about the age you had been when I met you. Maybe a little younger, but I knew you'd been in college. I started thinking about you then, wondering where you were, what you had done with your life. I was on the way to becoming an ocean-ographer. I wondered whether you had stayed an artist."

"I had," she said.

"I know. I called RISD—told them I wanted to buy one of your paintings. They looked you up and said you were represented by Victoria DeGraff, here in New York."

"I still am."

Sam nodded. "She was very nice, friendly. Said she'd send me a catalogue of your recent work, that you'd recently been acquired by the Whitney and the Farnsworth museums. I took that to mean your work was out of my price range, but I didn't let it stop me. I asked where you were painting. . . ."

"The Vineyard," Dana whispered.

"Yes. She said you had gone back to live on an island you vis-ited periodically, off the coast of Massachusetts, on painted cliffs overlooking the sea."

"Gay Head."

Sam nodded. "I didn't know the island, but Joe told me. He gave me grief for chasing you."

"Because I was too old for you?"

"No." Sam smiled. "I didn't give him the details. Back then, he was just constitutionally opposed to chasing anyone. That was be-fore he set his sights on Caroline, but that's another story."

"I'd love to hear it."

"See, I'd never thought you were too old for me. Too cool for me, maybe. You were an artist getting famous. I was just a student. He didn't want me getting hurt."

Now Dana looked at him. The trio was back, getting ready to play. The bass player lifted his instrument, holding it against his chest as if it were a woman. She gazed at Sam, saw those warm green eyes.

"Did I hurt you?" she asked, and although a touch of sadness entered, none of the warmth left.

"No. You didn't. Not intentionally."

"What happened?"

"I went to find you. Gay Head's small—back then, there were just a few houses. I found the lighthouse. . . ."

Dana could see it now, the dark redbrick lighthouse on the sand hill, surrounded by salt hay, its white and red beam shining out. Aquinnah: high ground. She could see the cliffs themselves, brilliantly pigmented clay, rising out of the blue sea. She and Lily had played with Quinn on the beach below, looking up at the red and orange clay stripes, one hundred million years old, imagining they saw fossils of prehistoric whales, dolphins, island deer, wild horses.

"And then I found your house. I knew it had to be yours because there were sails drying on the bushes. . . ."

"Lily and I had brought the *Mermaid* to the island with us."

". . . and because you had made a tent to paint in. It was canvas, stretched over cords draped from the tree branches, and inside was a painting. One of your undersea canvases, the first I'd ever seen."

"I just saw that painting today," Dana whispered, thinking of her visit to Vickie's gallery.

"A girl who paints in a tent—that's what I thought. It's what I still think," Sam said. "A tent, a garage. What an artist—you have it inside you."

"Why didn't you stop to see me?" Dana asked. "After you'd come all that way?"

"I did see you," Sam said, looking down and away, then back into her eyes. "On the beach."

"The beach?"

"Zacks Cliffs."

Dana smiled and wanted to laugh. "The nude beach," she said.

"Exactly."

Dana laughed. "Not that any beach Lily and I found ourselves on couldn't be nude."

"I know. You're artists, free spirits. All those life-drawing classes."

"If our teachers couldn't find a model, we'd volunteer. We used to laugh and say we weren't very good New Englanders. We'd lost the puritan gene somewhere along the way. I guess that's one reason I took to Europe so fast . . . Lily always loved to visit me there. We'd go to the beach and skinny-dip, and—"

"You weren't with Lily," Sam said.

"No?"

"When I saw you at the Vineyard, you were with a guy."

Dana thought back. It was long ago, and she had had many boyfriends since then. Ten years ago, at Gay Head, she had been seeing Christopher Laster. A sculptor from Brooklyn, spending the summer in Menemsha, he had been wildly talented and very romantic—two qualities Dana had been completely drawn to. But they hadn't lasted; she hadn't even wanted them to. As she recalled, they hadn't even made it through the summer.

"He wasn't important," she said.

"I didn't know that."

"None of them were. It sounds callous, I know, but back then all I cared about was painting."

"You were nude, playing in the surf. You were the most beautiful thing I'd ever seen. I stayed there for a minute, just watching you. He was there, but I hardly saw him. It was just you. . . ."

"Sam . . ."

The musicians started to play, and the audience settled down. Dana couldn't look away from Sam. His eyes were troubled, and she tried to imagine what she would have said or done if he had come down the beach and called her out of the waves.

"I never forgot," he said now, over the music.

"I wish," she began.

"Come on," he said, putting his arm around her. "Let's go. It's not right to talk while they're playing, and there's still more to say."

But once they got outside, they couldn't seem to think of what it was. Sam put his arm around her, and Dana leaned into his body. They walked east through the Village, past brick town houses rosy in the lamplight. Cafés were lively, but neither of them made a move to stop. Once they got to Sixth Avenue and crossed it, Dana knew she was taking him to her hotel.

The small hotel was located midway down Eleventh Street, between Fifth and Sixth avenues. It reminded Dana of a place she might find on the Left Bank in Paris or Bloomsbury in London. Yellow with stone steps and a glossy black door, the Lancaster welcomed them with bright, brass lights.

Dana asked at the front desk for her key. Sam didn't ask any questions, and he didn't seem nervous. She led him into the tiny elevator, and when they got to the fourth floor, he took the key from her hand and unlocked the door.

Inside, he put his arms around her. They held each other for a long time, and Dana felt his skin hot through his shirt. Tilting her head back, she let him kiss her mouth. He was hungry, insistent, but she was even more so. She heard a sound, and it came from her.

They undressed each other. She unbuttoned his shirt, unzipped his pants. Her heart was going so fast, she thought she might faint. Every inch of her skin tingled as he took off her black jacket, unzipped her black skirt, trailing his fingers across her hips, her belly.

At first, she thought of Jonathan. For two years they had painted and played together, traveled around Europe, sailed in the Aegean. Dana had imagined marrying him, having his baby.

But he hadn't been kind. He hadn't been patient, and he hadn't understood about losing Lily. While Dana's chance, and her desire, to ever have a child of her own ticked away, Jonathan turned away from her for something easier. He had cheated on her with a friend. She tensed, remembering how easily he had betrayed her, how quickly she had kicked him out. In spite of that, she was the one who felt discarded.

Sam touched the cord around her neck. His fingers followed the silken strand down her chest to the gold key that hung there. He kissed her throat and collarbones, and when he got to the key, he held it against his lips.

"I want you, Dana," he said, embracing her.

And she knew then, by the way her legs went weak, by the way she leaned back to kiss him, that she wanted Sam too.

They led each other to the bed, and they lay down. Dana made love to Sam, kissing him all the way down his body. He was so hard and beautiful, and she licked his skin, tasting the salt that made her think of every ocean she had ever painted.

He rolled her onto her back, holding her hands in his, climbing on top and looking straight into her eyes. His expression was full of fire, and as their eyes met, something in her chest began to let go.

The dammed-up feelings of last year came pouring out. She clutched his shoulders, feeling his muscles and firm skin, reaching around to hold his back, hold him closer. He gripped her hands, staring into her, his eyes gold-green and hot and steady, warmth pouring from them into her soul.

She felt him deep inside her, and she wanted to close her eyes to preserve the feeling, to freeze it forever. But she was afraid to, she didn't want to let him out of her sight.

"Dana, we're together," he said now, moving like the ocean over her.

"Together," she said, the word feeling different than it ever had before.

"Forget everything we know," he said. "We're starting now."

"Forget . . ."

"All of it," he whispered.

"I can't. . . ."

"Anyone who ever hurt you. Any loss, Dana. Forget it. I'll never leave you, never let you down."

"Sam," she said, feeling the waves surround her. She was in a gentle sea, enveloped by love, by Sam. She was a mermaid flying through the ocean. Now she did close her eyes, and she let the feeling overtake her.

"What is this?" she asked.

"Love, Dana," he said.

And Dana said it too. She never said "love" to men. She had taught herself so long ago that love was for sisters, nieces, mothers, paintings. She had been with men, liked them, maybe even felt love deep inside, but saying it was something else.

She said it now: "I love you, Sam."

"I love you, Dana."

Looking into his eyes, she held the key around her neck. "I can't believe this. There's one person who would be so happy if she knew. . . ."

"Lily," he said, looking into her eyes.

"I know," Dana said. She held his hands tight, feeling her chest fill with emotion. Sam knew everything: He had been with her this amazing, terrible, wonderful summer, and he understood that it began and ended with Lily.

"She loved you, Dana," he said.

"She did. . . ."

"I could tell that first summer. I watched the way you were together, and I knew that's how it should be done. You both showed me love."

"That's how Lily was," Dana said. "Full of love. For everything—people, animals, the land . . ."

"You were too. You're the one who first took me in—saw what I needed. Just like you're doing for Quinn and Allie. You could be back in France now, but you wouldn't leave. You couldn't."

"Thank you for seeing me that way," Dana said, clasping his hands. When she was with Sam, she felt like her best self. He saw her in a way she wanted to see herself, and she knew she was being transformed from the inside out.

He proved it to her then with his body, and she took it in and gave it back. Outside and far above the city, the stars shined. Down here the rivers flowed, and the traffic moved, and somewhere not far off were ocean waves calling them back, sparked with sea fire and filled with past and future secrets.

But for then, right there, Sam and Dana held each other and knew they weren't going anywhere.

CHAPTER 22

THE NEXT MORNING DAWNED HOT AND CALM. THE eastern sky glowed rose-red, and Martha thought of the old saying: Red sky at morning, sailors take warning. She fed Allie her Cheerios and took Quinn's granola from the cupboard. Puttering around the garden, she wondered why Quinn hadn't gotten up yet. It wasn't like her to sleep late.

"What time's Aunt Dana coming home?" Allie asked.

"On the five o'clock train," Martha said, pulling a few weeds. She looked up; although the sky was clear and blue overhead, that stripe of red across the horizon made her think they were in for a blow later.

"Is Quinn still in trouble?"

"I wouldn't say she's in trouble," Martha said. "But I think she could have used better judgment."

"You're mad about the garage."

"Well, it worries me that she would take it upon herself to saw a huge square out of the north wall without even consulting an adult. If she'd cut up the garage, what will she do next?"

"She did it for Aunt Dana," Allie said. "So she could have the north light and want to stay."

"Want to stay?"

"Here, with us. Quinn's afraid she'll go back to France."

Lips thinned, Martha picked weeds from between the thyme and sage plants. The poor children, thinking they were going to be abandoned. She had been so lucky; her parents had both been so healthy, had lived into their nineties. She couldn't imagine the thoughts that went through her granddaughters' heads, losing their parents, thinking their aunt would leave them.

"She did it to be nice," Allie said, holding her bowl of Cheerios. "And she got you mad at her."

"I'm not mad anymore. Mr. Nichols will be over soon to check on the structure and make sure it won't collapse. I know Quinn meant well. If she hadn't run off to Little Beach last night, I could have told her that."

"That's where she goes," Allie said as if she were stating a simple fact of life.

"Well, be a good girl, will you, Allie? Go wake your sister up and tell her I want to see her. *Before* she goes to Little Beach for the day."

SAM AND DANA woke up in each other's arms. Dana's eyes were closed, but her heart began to beat faster the minute she realized where she was. Sam's body felt strong but so relaxed—as if he knew he was exactly where he was supposed to be. Dana felt the same way, and she loved the way Sam kissed her, stroked her hair, made love to her slowly. He let her fall back to sleep while he ran downstairs to get coffee and the paper.

She woke up a second time, and he propped pillows behind her back so she could have breakfast in bed.

"What's the weather out?" she asked.

"I'm tempted to say it doesn't matter," he said, sitting beside her. "But actually, it feels like it's going to storm. The air's heavy, and the barometer's falling."

"Oh, I left the boat on the beach," she said. She knew that

meant they should hurry home, but she couldn't imagine reentering the real world yet.

"The weather's probably fine there, and will be longer—storms come from the west."

"I don't want to leave," she said, holding his hand.

"What if we didn't?" he asked, leaning down to kiss her neck, her lips.

"Quinn would terrorize my mother."

"And the boat would wash away. . . ."

"Ahhh," she said, leaning into his body, curved around her as he kissed her shoulder.

"You're riding home with me," he said. "I know you took the train in, but I'm not letting you take it home. My van's in a garage near Lincoln Center. . . ."

"That's a much better idea than taking the train back. I have to stop at the gallery first though. Vickie has a check for me."

"Sounds good. And I'll get you home in plenty of time to pull the boat up to the seawall," he said. "And to see the girls."

Dana nodded. She reached for his hand and held it. He made her feel so safe, partly because he understood her connection to home, to Hubbard's Point. He wasn't trying to convince her to fly off to Marrakesh, he didn't love her because other people thought her brilliant.

Sam was a family man with a shortage of family, and Dana was a single aunt with more than enough family to go around. Very slowly, he peeled the sheet down from her naked shoulder, starting to kiss her all over again. Closing her eyes, she pulled him closer, right into the bed with her, never wanting this morning to end.

SAM WAS LIVING in a new zone. This was beyond-his-wildest-dreams territory. He had Dana in his arms. The amazing thing was, she had been there all night and half the morning. She showed no signs of wanting to pull back, leave, or otherwise escape. In fact, she hadn't even taken her hand out of his.

Sam had been awake since six. He always woke up early, being on the boat and feeling the swells as the launch went by. But today he wakened just so he could look at Dana. Hiked up on one elbow, looking into her face, he'd tried to tell himself this wasn't a dream.

What had changed? He didn't know, couldn't say. At the summer's start she had seemed pretty much indifferent to him—maybe a little fond of the young boy she used to know. She had turned angry when she'd felt he was going behind her back with Quinn. He remembered her furious eyes, her scalding tone.

But somewhere along the line, their connection began to shift. Caring for the girls, looking into Lily's death, they had started acting like partners. He felt like that for her, that he knew. When she said she had a boat on the beach, he knew he wanted to help her move it. And that was the least of it—Sam knew he'd do anything for Dana.

That's why now, when she'd taken her hand out of his long enough to get dressed, he watched her slip on her black jacket and then reached for her hand again.

"I stopped by the Sun Corporation offices yesterday," Sam said, pulling the brochures out of his bag.

"You did?"

He nodded. "The man I talked to knew of Mark."

"He said that?"

"Yes, he did. They'd never met, but he had heard about what happened."

"Did he say anything? React in any way—"

"No," Sam said, reassuring her. "He didn't. Not at all. There wasn't anything negative."

Dana stared at the brochure. It was slick and glossy, about as far from her life and the life of her family as anything Sam could imagine. He watched her pick it up, look at the pictures of old people in the pool, practicing yoga, doing the sun salutation by the waterfall. The brochure looked packaged and fake, and everything about Dana and the people she loved was as real as could be. Sam took it out of her hands.

"Dana . . ."

"He really said nothing negative?"

"Really."

She glanced at the brochure again. "Mark knew the promotion material was necessary to sell his properties, but I think he was kind of embarrassed by it."

"Because Lily was such a nature girl?"

"I guess so. I know she worked at his office sometimes, but I think she was happier not knowing everything." Dana looked up, her eyes bruised. "I don't want to think about it anymore," she said. "I just want to go home to the girls and have everything be okay."

"I know," Sam said. "But Lily left that key on the sill. You loved her too much not to find out what it's for. I think I know you well enough for that."

"It's about this place," Dana said, looking at the brochure

"I'd like to think the truth doesn't matter—Mark is dead, and whatever he did, it's over with now," Sam said.

"It matters to me," Dana said, "and it does to Quinn."

"Then we'll find out what it is," Sam said, and he held Dana until it was time for them to go to the gallery.

"GRANDMA," ALLIE SAID, talking and running at the same time. "She's not in her room or in her bed or anywhere!"

"Slow down, Alexandra. What are you talking about?"

"Quinn didn't sleep in her bed! There's a big lump there, just like a person, but it's just her dirty clothes. Pants and shorts and shirts and the grossest socks you can imagine and her underpants and T-shirts with ice cream on the front and—"

"She didn't sleep in her bed?"

Allie shook her head, her eyes filled with terror. Martha went back thirty years to the day Dana had run away. There had been a big fight over watching the fireworks somewhere her father hadn't thought she should be, and Dana had disappeared. The resolution— exactly where she had gone and when she had returned—was less clear in Martha's mind than the terrified, grief-stricken look in Lily's eyes when she had found out her sister was gone.

"Now, let's think," Martha said. "Where could she be?"

"Little Beach!" Allie and Martha said at the exact same time.

And pulling on her sun hat and beach shoes, Martha and her younger granddaughter set out to bring Quinn home.

THE GALLERY WAS QUIET. It officially opened at eleven, but Vickie must have gotten there early. Her assistant sat at the front desk, cataloguing slides. Dana opened the front door, and the little bell rang out.

Sam wanted to look at every painting. Dana showed him around the floor, telling him stories about each canvas. "I did that one in my studio at Honfleur," she said, pointing at the murky brown harbourscape, "and that one in a hotel room in the Azores." Some were near-shore and others were deep-sea, and Sam kept his arm around her and made her laugh by finding every mermaid within seconds of looking at the canvas.

When they got to the back wall, he stopped short in front of the nude. Dana had forgotten it was there. She tried to pull him away, but he wouldn't move. His feet were planted firm on the shiny wood floor, and he stared at the painting with surprise that turned into an almost-smile.

"Come on, Sam," she said.

"That's not a self-portrait," he said as if he wanted her to contradict him.

"No."

"I probably shouldn't ask who painted it," he said. "I sounded jealous enough when I told you about seeing you at Zacks Cliffs ten years ago."

"Jealousy never works very well," Dana said, tugging his hand to move him away, thinking she wanted to keep him from anything connected to Jonathan. They might be the same age, but otherwise they were completely different. "What does that matter? I told you yesterday—I've posed plenty of times. It never matters. I'm an artist, so when someone else needs a model—"

"This is so beautiful. Whoever painted it wasn't just 'someone else,' " Sam said, examining the painting. "He knew you."

"What even makes you think it was a he?" Dana asked, trying to laugh.

"Are you saying I'm not?"

At the sound of Jonathan's voice, she turned around and gasped. The sound came out as a cry, and Sam quickly took her hand. Looking sheepish, Vickie came out of her office with one arm linked in Jonathan's. "This is your surprise," Vickie said. "I know I said I have a check for you, and I do, but I also asked Jonathan to meet us here."

"What . . . ? No!" Dana said, all her instincts kicking in.

"Surprise," Jonathan said, stepping forward to kiss her.

Dana felt rather than saw Sam move away. Jonathan enveloped her in his arms, and she had to push hard to free herself. She looked up into his face. He was as attractive as ever, very thin and languorous. His black hair was cut quite short now, and his tan was deep and dark. It looked great beneath the soft cotton shirt.

"How do you do?" he said to Sam. "I'm Jonathan Hull."

"Sam Trevor." He shook hands with both Jon and Vickie.

"I caught her, didn't I?" Jon asked, gazing at his portrait of Dana. "Her eyes, her feelings. That wild hair . . ."

"You absolutely did," Vickie said, obviously nervous. "You captured a moment in time—the months after she lost Lily. I mean, look at her face. I remember talking to her during that period, and—"

"I'm standing right here," Dana said dangerously.

"Oh, honey. I know. Certainly you are. That time was so dark—that's how I see it. You lying there in bed, thinking about Lily. You couldn't even paint. . . ."

"No, I couldn't," she said softly.

"So I had to paint for both of us." Jon sounded as tender as she had ever heard him. He stood between her and Sam, looking into her eyes.

"Forget what happened," Jon said, holding her upper arms.

"Forget?" she asked as if he were speaking a foreign language.

"I made a mistake, Dana. You were so different, everything had changed, and I didn't know how to act."

"That's true," she said, picturing him on the daybed, making love to Monique.

"She meant nothing to me. You know that."

"Oh, dear," Vickie said, finally catching the drift of the conversation. She turned to Sam, smiling. "Maybe we should make ourselves scarce."

"Dana?" Sam asked.

"I'm coming with you," Dana said, trying to pull away from Jonathan. Her heart was beating fast; she didn't like confrontations anyway, but especially not with someone she had once loved.

"Forgive me," Jonathan said quietly. "We were artists, you know? I made a mistake—you don't know how much I regret it."

Dana took a deep breath, looking into his eyes. Even now, in spite of his apology, she saw the anger in them; she saw frustration there as if he were trying to rush her through this. Although Sam stood back, he stayed just behind Dana; she sensed him there, in case she needed him.

"There's nothing more to say," she said quietly.

"You were in bad shape," he said again. "I was in the studio—I'm sorry about the rest, but I had to paint for both of us. One thing led to another. . . ."

"You didn't have to paint for both of us," she said. "You didn't have to do anything. You just had to let me be."

"Let you be—"

"Let me be with Lily. That's what I was doing."

"You mean *without* her!"

"She's my sister," Dana said sharply. "I'm never without her."

"Joe would like that," Sam said, quietly supporting her.

"She was gone," Jon said, ignoring Sam. "And I was trying to pull you back to reality. You were lost, Dana. Say what you want, but she was gone and I was losing you too. That's why I—"

"She was with me," Dana glared, interrupting him.

"However you want to put it," he said, laughing awkwardly. "It's over now. Let's talk it all out, Dana. Vickie was nice enough to get us together—have lunch with me. I'll listen all day. Please—just calm down."

"I am calm, Jon," she said.

"I want you to come home. Honfleur misses you."

She shook her head. "My boat's on the beach and the weather's changing. I have to go."

"A change, great!" Jonathan said. "A storm. We love storms, Dana. The higher the waves the better, right? You can take me up on the roof—I'll supply the wine. We can watch the tide rise and the wind blow. We'll end this fight and get on with things."

"She says she has to get her boat off the beach," Sam said.

Jonathan looked at him, angry, dismissive, amused. Jon had perfected that hip, edgy look Dana knew well from cities in Europe and even in New York. Sam, in his spectacles and rumpled shirt, looked like he'd been up all night, studying for an exam.

"Then I'll help her do that."

"Jon," Dana said, moving between them. She held his wrist and looked into his face. She had thought she loved him once. He was young and bright and full of promise. They had had a wonderful, wild, creative time together. She didn't want to hurt him to get back at him, but she knew she could never be with him again either.

"What?" he asked, for the first time looking afraid. "I want to help you. Show me your family place, Dana. Show me what made you, what you love. I thought you'd be bringing your nieces home by now."

"I am home," she said, so definite that she shocked herself.

"What?" Vickie asked.

Sam didn't speak, but Dana could feel him at her side, almost as if they were connected by an invisible thread.

"You're home?" Jonathan asked.

"Yes."

"There? In Connecticut?"

"It's best for the girls."

"And what about for you? You're an artist, Dana. Just look around the gallery—you think you can produce this level of work with two brats to take care of? Give me a break—"

Dana didn't wait to hear the rest. She really couldn't blame Jonathan for what he didn't have in the first place.

"Good-bye, Jonathan," she said to his face.

"We'll talk later," he said. "When you're alone, and not under the influence of whoever—"

"His name's Sam, and I'm not under his or anyone's influence. It's good-bye, Jonathan. All on my own—just good-bye." As he stood there with his mouth open, Dana turned away.

"Good-bye, Vickie," she said, kissing her friend three times as Vickie handed her her check.

Then Sam reached out to take her hand and pull her to the curb, into a cab, just as the first raindrops started to fall. Dana turned to look at him, and although she thought he was grinning, she didn't get to see because he pulled her into his arms to kiss her as the cab bolted into the traffic.

QUINN SAT ON HER ROCK, staring hard into the distance. The weather was brilliant. The sky was bright blue, with no trace of the red line they had seen that morning. She could see the Hunting Ground, for the moment as calm as glass. Boats sped past, both sail and motor, on their way somewhere.

Beside her, on the big rock, were the *Mermaid's* sail bag, Quinn's diary, a duffel bag filled with supplies, the tackle box, and the gift she always brought with her. She wouldn't stop bringing her presents, but after today she wouldn't be leaving them in the waters of Little Beach.

Quinn was leaving. Her heart was too filled with pain to stay. Finally, she understood what Aunt Dana had meant, wanting everyone to go to France instead of living here.

Hubbard's Point was full of memories. Everywhere Quinn looked, she thought of her mother and father. The good memories, like planting the herb garden and filling the picnic basket, and the bad memories, like standing in the upstairs hall, listening to the yelling, like waking up in the morning and realizing her parents weren't in their bed, like the look on Grandma's face when she told Quinn and Allie their parents weren't coming home at all, like finding the tackle box filled with money under Aunt Dana's bed.

This was what Quinn's mother had been talking about: the

bribe. Quinn had put together the rest. She hoped Aunt Dana wouldn't hate her for taking it, but Quinn had something she had to set right—and she needed the money to do it with.

Quinn sat ramrod straight, immovable on her rock. She thought about the window she had cut for Aunt Dana. It was a good deed, done out of love and just the smallest amount of selfishness. Yes, it was true: She thought if she gave Aunt Dana some north light, she might feel more inclined to stay forever. But more than that was the true desire to make her aunt happy.

Grandma and Annabelle had come along, accused her of making the garage unsafe. What if it collapsed and someone died? That's exactly what Annabelle had said, and it had reminded Quinn of those terrible words her parents had said to each other that last night.

"What if someone finds out?" Lily cried. *"Have you been doing this all along? You've ruined us, killed our family! Taking bribes—is this how we afford our life, the boat?"*

"Lily. You know it isn't, and you know that isn't even what's bothering you. The kids will hear, you'll wake up all the neighbors."

"That beautiful land . . . our sacred ground."

"Someone would have developed it, Lily. The owner died, what did you think was going to happen? The heirs approached me because they know I love the island, that I'd respect the land."

"Honeysuckle Hill . . ."

"We have kids to send through college. We have bills to pay."

Lily wept silently. She didn't speak, but Mark did. *"You know I don't take bribes. Jack Conway gave me jobs when I was a kid. He's old now, and he didn't think I'd hire him if he didn't"—Mark chuckled, as if he thought the whole thing was hilarious—"pay me a kickback."*

"It's not funny!"

"No kidding. What am I supposed to do with a goddamn tackle box filled with five thousand dollars? 'Five large,' he said to me in that smoker's voice of his, from about a million Camels. You'd have thought we were two gangsters making a deal."

"He hasn't built anything to code in twenty years," Lily said. "He'll probably do it wrong, and the houses will collapse."

"That should make you happy." Mark's voice was full of affection and amusement.

"Don't patronize me, Mark Grayson."

"Come on, Lily. Cheer up. Jack just wanted to be involved—he's not the primary builder." He cracked up again. "Five large! You'd have thought I was Marky the Mobman. I guess he thinks that's how we do it in the big leagues."

"I don't really care about the money—I know you'll give it back to him. But Honeysuckle Hill . . ."

"I know. I'd preserve it if I could. But that would cost millions of dollars. We can't afford to buy it, so wouldn't it be better if I developed it than someone else?"

"No," she whispered stubbornly.

"Come on, Lily. Me and Jack—we're islanders. We'll take care of the place."

Lily sniffled.

"Sweetheart. Jesus Christ. The girls are asleep. Let's go for a sail and talk it over. I love you. I didn't do anything wrong, or at least nothing very wrong. People make mistakes, and if I did that, I'm sorry. I was just trying to save an old man's pride."

"I know."

"Come on, honey. It's a beautiful moonlit night. We'll take the boat out for a sail, get rid of the cobwebs and talk it over. What do you say?"

"I don't know. What if they wake up?"

"They'll be fine. We'll just be gone a couple of hours. Look, if it'll save our marriage, don't you think it's worth it?"

"I guess so. . . ."

Quinn shivered with the anguish of remembering. Not having slept at home last night, she felt exhausted. After Grandma had finished yelling at her, she grabbed her flashlight and came over here to write in her diary. Then, instead of going home, she curled up in the *Mermaid* and fell asleep. With the stars above and the sound of the waves on the beach, it was the closest she felt to her mother in over a year.

And when she woke up, she had her plan; it came to her in her dreams. She would sail away. She would sneak up to the house, get the sails, and take *Mermaid* somewhere far from here, to an island just over the eastern horizon.

Her diary was with her now. Double-wrapped in plastic to survive any waves that might come into the boat, it was ready to go. All Quinn had to do now was leave the gift. . . .

"Don't trip, Grandma," came Allie's voice down the path through the woods. "Watch out for that root."

"Run ahead, Allie," Grandma called. "See if she's there, will you? My hip isn't doing so well." Maggie barked with the joy of being loose on a forest trail. Even a shar-pei probably heard the call of the wild.

At the sound of Allie's footsteps, Quinn slid down from her rock as fast as quicksilver. She pulled her things after her, shoved them into a dry tidal pool. Huddled at the rock's base, she heard her sister approach just so far, take a quick look, and then go running back. Maggie came running over, but Allie grabbed the dog into her arms. "Don't, Mag," Allie said. "You'll get wet and dirty in the seaweed." Hearing Allie's breathless little voice filled Quinn's eyes with tears.

"She's not there, Grandma," Allie said. "We'd better go back home and wait for her on the hill."

"Oh, I'm worried. I hope she's there."

Quinn cried. She knew she'd miss her grandmother, but even more, she'd miss her sister. She'd miss her blond hair and curious eyes, the way she sucked her thumb and twirled her curls, the funny faces she made to crack Quinn up. Quinn would even miss the total devotion she gave to that dumb feline scrap, Kimba.

But she wouldn't miss the way Allie thought she was the only one who knew her mother liked white flowers. Once she was positive, one hundred percent sure she was alone, Quinn reached into the sail bag and pulled out the gift.

She always left it, every day, for the mermaids that swam in the Sound and spun their nets from the moonlight above Hubbard's

Point. Even more, she left the gift—one every day, whatever was in bloom—for her mother. A white flower.

"For you, Mommy," Quinn whispered now, laying the white lily in the calm water, watching it float on the surface, beneath the clear blue sky, toward the Hunting Ground. Quinn would be there soon. She would follow the white flower, follow her mother, sail the *Mermaid* to where she knew she had to go.

CHAPTER 23

THE STORM SEEMED TO FOLLOW SAM'S VAN FROM THE
Henry Hudson Parkway to the Connecticut Turnpike. The road
ahead of them was dry, the miles behind them drenched with
rain. It was one of those summer gales that came out of nowhere. The radio reported airport delays and flash flooding; tor-
nadoes had been reported in Lincroft, New Jersey, and Windsor
Locks, Connecticut.

"Are you okay?" Sam asked.

"Jonathan, you mean?"

"Yes. It couldn't have been easy to see him."

"It was the best thing that could have happened. It was good-
bye, and we both knew it." She paused, thinking back. "A real
face-to-face good-bye, I mean. Not just anger or hurt feelings. The
last time I saw him was a frenzy of drama—a lot of dust had to settle. I've realized it was over for months now—"

"Since me," Sam said, grinning.

Dana grinned back. "That's possible, though I was the last to
know."

"You're a fast sailor but slow in certain other areas, Underhill."

"Like what?"

"Like finding a good guy to love you."

"That'd be you?"

He laughed. "Yes. Better late than never though. Solitude is one thing, but just wait till you see what togetherness does for your painting. . . ."

"That's what Lily used to say," Dana said. Thunder sounded, and she glanced out the window.

"We'll beat the storm," Sam said, leaning forward to look up at the sky. It was dark behind them, in New York, sunny ahead, in Connecticut.

"I hope so," Dana said. "My little boat . . ."

"We can't let the *Mermaid* wash away," Sam said. "She's a Blue Jay, the boat that first brought us together."

Dana smiled. Sam was a sentimental man. He kept track of things in a way that reminded Dana of herself and Lily—and Quinn and Allie. Leaning forward, she saw what he did: a line in the sky. The front was traveling slowly, obliterating the blue sky with black clouds. She felt as if they were racing it, trying to reach Hubbard's Point before the front did.

The goal was to save the boat, she thought, holding Sam's hand as he drove the van. But why was her mouth dry, her stomach flipping? She had a feeling the stakes were higher, much higher, than a small sailboat sitting at the end of the beach. She had the feeling she was trying to get to her sister's home—her home—before something terrible happened.

THE SAILS were heavy and huge. Quinn tried to remember which was the head and which was the clew. She rigged the jib first, threading the sheets through the blocks, letting the sail flap in the breeze. Next, she stowed all her stuff—her canteen, a blanket, and the tackle box full of money—up front. She had a long sail ahead of her, and although the day was sunny, waves could get pretty big and she wanted to keep everything as dry as possible. To be extra safe, she secured her double-wrapped diary around her ankle with a bungee cord.

Last of all, she rigged the mainsail. Once she hoisted the sail up the mast, she might as well announce her intentions to the world. Grandma would be sitting in her chair by the window with Maggie, and this would really give her something to sigh about. If she happened to be watching the beach, the white sail would be as obvious as a red flag. She might just call Hubbard's Point security to stop Quinn from sailing.

Now, trying to push the boat down the beach into the water, Quinn threw her back and legs into the mighty effort. She moved the boat a foot, and then another foot. This would be much easier with another person. Sam, Aunt Dana, her mother, her father. Thinking of those faces gave Quinn the strength she needed to keep pushing. "Two are better than one," her mother always used to say, grinning when Quinn would help her in the herb garden.

"Quinn, wait a minute!"

"Oh, shit," Quinn said, looking up. She had asked, and she had received: Here came Allie, running down the beach in a cloud of knees, elbows, and Kimba.

"You think I didn't see you at Little Beach?" Allie asked. "Well, I did! And I didn't tell!"

"You'd better not tell about this either," Quinn warned. She made her face and voice mean to scare Allie away. Dammit, now she was going to get choked up. She had wanted to avoid saying good-bye.

"Who would I tell?"

"Grandma, Aunt Dana . . . but you'd better not."

"I won't, how can I?"

"What do you mean?"

"I'm going with you."

Quinn couldn't believe her ears. Allie would be no good on this mission whatsoever. She would be right in the way.

"No way," Quinn said.

Allie just nodded, her blond curls bouncing with fervor. "Yes."

"You don't like sailing. You're afraid of heeling, and we're going to heel—a lot." When Allie's determination seemed only to increase, Quinn widened her stance and knew she had to get tough. "You'll cry. You're a baby—look, you couldn't even leave Kimba for one minute. There he is, stuck to you like glue. That dumb feline scrap . . ."

That did it. Allie's eyes filled with tears. They ran down her cheeks, and her lip trembled, making Quinn feel awful. But she had to stay focused: She was on her way, and she wanted to leave before Grandma saw the sail and called to stop her. Glancing at Allie, her heart ached. But she started pushing the boat into the water.

"I'll leave Kimba behind," Allie cried, pulling on Quinn's shorts, "if you'll take me with you."

"I can't, Al," Quinn said, starting to cry herself.

"Where are you going?"

"Far away, Allie. Really far away. I'll call you when I get there, okay? You can take the ferry out."

Standing in the shallow water, her feet buried in sand, Allie held Kimba to her eyes and sobbed. The waves splashed her ankles and the boat. Quinn held the side, keeping the boat steady. She watched her sister, and her heart did somersaults. There was no one in the world Quinn loved more than Allie. She wasn't perfect, and she cried a lot—but even Quinn was crying now. The trip *was* long, and it *would* be lonely. . . .

"Okay, Allie. Jump in."

"You mean . . . ?"

"Yes, you can come."

"Should I run up to the house and take Kimba back?"

Quinn shook her head—partly with impatience at the idea her sister actually thought Quinn would wait while she went up the hill and back and partly because Quinn herself kind of wanted Kimba along. He was a tie to their babyhood, to their parents. "You can bring him," she said. "Put on your life jacket."

"Thank you, Quinn," Allie said, scrambling over the side into the *Mermaid*.

Quinn followed. She adjusted the tiller, lowered the centerboard. She checked her diary, made sure it was secure to her ankle. Pulling on her orange life vest, she told Allie to do the same. Trying to remember everything Aunt Dana had taught her, she sat on the leeward side and trimmed the sails.

"Where are we going anyway?" Allie asked as the boat caught

the wind and wobbled around the rocky promontory of Hubbard's Point. By way of answering, Quinn reached into her pocket and handed her the compass.

"Martha's Vineyard," Quinn said.

"That's far!"

"Yes," Quinn said, looking up at the blue sky, the puffy white clouds along the western horizon, "but it's a beautiful sunny day, and that's where we're going."

"Why?"

"To pay someone back for Mommy and Daddy."

"Who?"

"I'll tell you when we get there." Then, drawing on her amazing sense of direction, Quinn said, "It's easy, Al. All we have to do is sail east, exactly east, over the horizon. Watch the compass and make sure it stays on ninety the whole way."

"Ninety," Allie said, clutching Kimba and the compass.

"And don't worry—we'll stay out of the shipping lane."

"Good," Allie said, sounding only a little frightened.

"Here we go," Quinn called out over the whistling rigging to the soft white clouds quickly encroaching from the west.

MARTHA HELD MAGGIE and paced the yard. Now they were both gone: Quinn hadn't been home all night, and Allie had run off to find her. They were so young, such little girls, and the storm was coming. Then Maggie nestled in Martha's arms, licking her cheek. Needless to say, Maggie would rather be off chasing raccoons, but she sensed Martha's deep worry. Oh, the uncomplicated, gentle love between humans and pets: if only family relationships were this simple.

Annabelle and Marnie had gone off in their car, searching all the beach roads. Martha could almost see them inching past the recreation area, the tennis courts, the old cemetery, the small beach by the railroad tracks, the tracks themselves—especially the bridge over the channel, where kids loved to fish and jump into the water. Cameron and June had scoured the rocks, sweeping their binoculars over the sea as well, all the way out to Gull Island.

Now, walking down the yard, Martha saw an old van pull next to the wall at the foot of the hill. Dana and Sam got out, wreathed in smiles. Waving, they started up, but then Dana's attention was pulled toward the garage.

Paul Nichols had left the door open. Walking down, Martha saw Dana and Sam inside, gazing around at the new window, at the metal supports Paul had brought over from the boatyard to stand under the beams. Dana's easel had been pushed to the side, the painting covered with a drop cloth.

"What's going on?" Dana asked.

"Your niece decided you should have some north light," Martha said gravely, pointing at the crooked square cutout.

"Quinn did that?" Dana asked, sounding delighted.

"Yes, she did. Failing to notice, poor child, that that is a carrying wall, that it wouldn't take much to make this old garage collapse. I asked Paul to do what he could, especially with the storm coming."

"Is Quinn okay?" Dana asked.

"Well . . ." Martha began, Maggie nuzzling her for support.

"She means so well," Sam said. "I was like her when I was her age. Ready, fire, aim."

Dana laughed, pulling up the drop cloth to check on her painting. Martha hated to say what she had to say—she knew how hard it had been for Dana to start working again. Healing was taking time for all of them, and this was nothing more than a slight setback. "Quinn seems to have gotten it into her head . . ." Martha began.

"Did she move the boat?" Dana asked.

"The boat?"

"The *Mermaid*," Dana said. "She—or someone—must have moved it to higher ground. Sam and I drove by the beach on our way up here, and it was gone. I figured with the storm coming, you must have told Quinn to get someone to help her move it."

"She's not here," Martha said. "I thought she must be at Little Beach, but we couldn't find her. Annabelle and Marnie are out looking right now. I called Rumer, so she's on the lookout too."

"The boat's not on the beach," Dana said, turning pale.

"This is Hubbard's Point. It's so safe, she wouldn't leave. Running away to Little Beach didn't seem like a very bad thing, Quinn does it all the time," Martha said. "Should we call the police?"

"We should call the Coast Guard," Sam said.

DANA COULDN'T SIT STILL. She walked all through the house, in and out of the rooms. The storm had hit full blast, and waves were pounding the beach. White foam topped the Sound's surface. The wind blew leaves off the trees. A branch fell from the tall pine nearest the road.

Sam was out with the Coast Guard. Boats had been dispatched from New London and Groton. Small-craft warnings had been replaced by full gale warnings. A shiver ran down Dana's spine. If her sister and Mark had died on a calm, moonlit night, what could happen to Quinn and Allie in a storm like this?

Her mother sat by the window, keeping vigil. Sheets of rain pelted the glass, but her mother just stared through them, looking for a white sail. When Dana came downstairs, she held back for a moment. She thought of all the loss her mother had suffered, and her heart aching, she went to stand beside her.

"Hi, Mom," she said.

Maggie looked up and barked. "It's the Mags," Dana said, glad to see the dog keeping her mother company, glued to her mistress's side.

Her mother couldn't look away from the window. She stared at the Sound, from the beach where the boat had been, all the way out to the red and green buoys of the Hunting Ground.

"Where are they?" her mother asked.

"I don't know," Dana said.

"I want to blame someone. When Sam told us about that tow rope, I felt so grateful. Someday soon we'll know what company owned that tug, which one owned the barge, and we'll know who to blame for Mark's and Lily's deaths. But when I think of the girls, all I can blame is myself."

"No, Mom. It's not your fault."

"I should have watched them more. The minute I knew Quinn hadn't slept in her bed, I should have called the police. But I kept telling myself *It's Quinn—she's a free spirit, just like her aunt. She's just on one of her adventures. . . .*"

"You think she's like me?" Dana asked, filled with emotion.

"Exactly like you. Lily thought so too."

"What do you mean?"

"The way she's always seeking," Martha said without taking her eyes off the sea. "Looking for more, the most life has to offer. Lily loved that about her. *She'll be a nomad, just like Dana, I'll be visiting them both in Timbuktu,* Lily used to say."

"I didn't think Lily liked that about me. She always wanted me to come home."

"She loved it about you, but yes—she wanted you to come home. You were her sister, and she missed you."

"I miss her," Dana said, her eyes burning with tears.

"Oh, I know you do, honey."

They sat together, thinking of Lily, keeping watch for her daughters. Dana could hardly bear the anxiety, the not-knowing and waiting to hear. She wanted to paint, to go down into the garage Quinn had tried to transform, use the north light to paint a magical talisman, something that would bring the girls home. That made her touch the key around her neck, think of the locket Lily had always worn.

"Remember Miss Alice's store?" Dana asked her mother.

"Of course I do. The place where you and Lily spent every cent of your allowance. Until you started saving up for the boat . . ."

Dana shuddered, wishing she and Lily had never bought the *Mermaid*. "When I went to Mark's office," Dana said, "I started thinking how cool it was, right upstairs from Miss Alice's shop. Do you think that was Lily's doing?"

Her mother smiled. "Definitely. Lily loved connection. Mark having his office there was a connection to you, to your childhood, to so many things."

"Miss Alice's shop," Dana said, picturing the shelves crowded with penny candy, books, china tea sets, and glass bowls.

"It's where Lily bought her hope chest."

"Her what?"

"Her hope chest." Her mother shook her head. "That's what she used to call it anyway. It wasn't very big—about the size of a schoolbook. You must have seen it in her room."

"She had so many boxes over the years."

"Well, this one was special. It was inlaid with moonstones, supposedly found on Little Beach. It's where she used to keep her diary. Back when I committed the cardinal sin of reading it . . ."

The moonstone box. Dana hadn't thought of it in years, but she could see it now: polished mahogany with a row of small glowing stones all around the edge.

"The things I'd do over if I could," her mother said. "Never invade your rooms, never read your diaries, trust that you'd turn into the wonderful women you both became."

"Thanks, Mom," Dana said.

"It bothered me so much, seeing that box on her bureau," her mother said, wiping her eyes. "I stuck it up in the linen closet so I wouldn't have to look at it. Made me feel ashamed of myself every time—"

"The linen closet?"

"Upstairs," her mother said. "On the top shelf."

Dana kissed her mother's head. Maggie jumped off her lap and headed up the stairs, as if something had suddenly become more important than staying with her mistress. Dana didn't know what she was hoping to find, but her heart was racing as if Lily had just walked into the room.

SAM STOOD on the deck of the Coast Guard boat, scanning the water all around. The driving rain stung his eyes and rolled off the yellow slicker. The boat was beating back and forth through the Hunting Ground, the destination Sam and Dana had predicted the girls would head for. A hundred yards away, in the shipping lane, a tanker and barge passed each other.

"Why here?" Coast Guard officer Tom Hanley asked. "There's nothing out here."

"It's where their parents' boat went down."

"I know—the *Sundance*. I got called out on that one. But what would two little girls be doing, coming to the place their parents drowned?"

"You don't know them," Sam said, picturing Quinn.

"Terrible thing, that sinking," Hanley said. "Could not make heads nor tails of it. Calm night, solid boat, good sailors."

"They hit a tow rope," Sam said, watching a tug approach from the west.

"Really? How do you know?"

"I dove on the boat. Found rope fibers and sent them to a captain in your squad. The chances of locating the tug aren't great, but he's checking the shipping records from that night."

"Well, makes sense," Hanley said. "Think about it—this is Long Island Sound. All these pleasure boats skipping around, and this here's the superhighway of commercial boat traffic between Boston and New York City. It all comes through here—people try to cross the highway, they might get hit. It's amazing it doesn't happen more often."

"I hope it doesn't happen today," Sam said, watching for the *Mermaid*.

"Shit, if the weather doesn't get them first," Hanley said, shaking his head. "As storms go, this one isn't very bad. But they're so young, and that's a very small sailboat they're in."

"I know."

The boat moved slowly west, away from Hubbard's Point and toward the green can that marked the start of the Hunting Ground. The Sound was rising, four- to five-foot waves forming peaks and troughs, but if it had flattened out and Sam had turned around to look behind him, due east, he would have seen a small blue sailboat, one of its white sails ready to tear, beating eastward away from the Hunting Ground toward the island of Martha's Vineyard.

CHAPTER 24

THE WEATHER CHANGED VERY FAST. THE DAY HAD been so bright and calm, and now the sky was gray and the waves were big. Not huge, like in hurricanes or even nor'easters, but pretty tall. Higher than any waves Quinn had ever sailed through in this boat. She held the tiller with all her might, pulling it in against her chest, surfing into the trough just to keep the boat from flipping over. Allie stared at the compass as if it were a crystal ball. Kimba was drenched in the crook of her arm. Everyone was drenched.

"Ninety, Quinn!" Allie called out, reading the compass.

"Good going, Al."

"Are we almost there?"

Quinn exhaled. Jeez, what did she think this was, a car ride? It was just like Allie to get bored on a trip, have to ask every two minutes whether they were almost there. Their mother used to think up games to keep her occupied: count the license plates from all fifty states, watch for white horses in the fields, ask who will be the first to see the Welcome to Rhode Island sign?

"Are we, Quinn?" Allie asked as the waves got bigger. "Almost there?"

"Allie, do you see any signs? How about a mileage marker?"

"Don't yell at me."

"I'm only yelling so you'll hear me over the wind," Quinn said. The wind howled in her ears. It had torn the jib just slightly, about halfway up, and that one rip made the sail now sound like a wildly snapping flag. She would never have set out if she had known the weather was going to do this.

She glanced from right to left, trying to get her bearings. They had left Orient Point far behind an hour earlier—the land on her right. To the left, they had passed Silver Bay and New London, and now she thought maybe they were passing Noank. That big land mass almost dead ahead had to be Fishers Island.

"Is that the Vineyard?" Allie screamed, taking her eyes off the compass for ten seconds.

"Nope. It's Fishers."

"Let's stop there, Quinn!" Allie shrieked. "We can wait for the storm to be over and start up again later."

Quinn narrowed her eyes, holding the tiller so hard, she was getting blisters. The rain pelted her face and braids. Allie's idea had merit, but it was flawed. If they did stop, grown-ups might find them and send them home. They'd be grounded for life, never get this chance again. The tackle box filled with money was nestled in the bow, as safely stowed as Quinn had been able to secure it.

The other problem was herself. She had to admit something: She was scared. Not just for herself but for her sister. This storm was more than a little rain. Once they got past Fishers Island, they'd be out of the Sound, into the ocean. Quinn had never sailed in the ocean before.

"What about our mission?" Quinn asked, wiping her eyes to look at Allie.

"Paying the man back?"

"Yes."

"Can't we do it later?"

"We might not get the chance."

"It's for Mommy and Daddy?"

"Yes, it is."

Allie gave it some thought, then nodded hard. "Okay," she said. "I want to keep going."

"You sure?"

"Ninety, Quinn," Allie yelled over the wind as she started staring at the compass again. "Keep going!"

Why did you do it, take it. . . . You've ruined us. . . . Quinn heard her mother's voice crying over the sound of the wind. She caught her breath on a sob.

"No one can ruin us, Mommy," she said out loud, and she didn't even care if Allie heard. They were in this together, all of them, the Grayson sisters and their parents, even Aunt Dana and Grandma; Quinn knew it was up to her to make things right for her family, no matter what.

So, pointing into the storm, Quinn kept sailing.

THE LINEN CLOSET was just a simple cupboard of two old doors, one over the other, cut out of the same dark wainscoting as the rest of the walls. The bottom level was filled with extra blankets, quilts, and mattress pads. The upper door opened to reveal four shelves, the lower two filled with towels, the top two stacked with sheets. Standing on tiptoe, reaching as high as she could, Dana found the moonstone box.

She took it down and held it in her hands. It felt heavy, and when she moved it, things slid around inside. The tiny lock was half an inch in diameter, and when almost by instinct Dana inserted the key hanging around her neck, the box opened.

A sound escaped her, and Maggie danced at her feet. As she lifted the lid, her heart pounding as she thought of what might be inside, her eyes filled with tears. There was Lily's locket.

Dana's fingers closed around it. She felt the size and weight: a sterling silver oval, hand-tooled and etched, quite heavy, the approximate size of a misshapen, somewhat oblong silver dollar. The hall light, an overhead globe, was too dim. Dana carried the box and locket into her sister's bedroom for better light.

Sitting on the edge of the double bed, she opened her hand.

There it was, right in her palm. The locket her sister had worn against her skin for twenty-eight years. Dana had bought it for her when they were thirteen and eleven, and over the years it had held pictures of just about everyone Lily held dear. No wonder Sam hadn't found it on the sea bottom; Lily would never have worn her precious locket out sailing.

Hands shaking, Dana opened the locket now. She undid the clasp with her thumbnail, feeling the small click of release. The two silver ovals, hinged on one side, fell open like a book, and a second, even tinier key dropped onto her lap. Dana closed her eyes, almost afraid to look. When she finally did, her pulse began to race.

On the right side, Dana stared at a small shot of Lily and the girls in the herb garden. Mark must have taken it from far off, but it was a portrait done in love by someone who had known the subjects very well. Lily wore her sun hat, and she was circling both her daughters with her arms.

All three smiled at the camera. The picture showed Quinn before her rasta phase, her brown hair beautiful and flowing in the sunlight. Allie's bright curls gleamed, nearly as brightly as her smile. Each girl playfully wore one of Lily's garden gloves, holding her trowel and rake like scepters. Lily held a small book in the hand she rested on Quinn's shoulder, a pen in the one on Allie's.

The other side of the locket held a picture of Dana and Lily. The same era as the garden photo, it must have been taken about three years ago. Dana stared at it, seeing the love in her sister's eyes. Her heart ached, realizing how much she missed that love. As she drifted to the window, looking for boats, she knew she'd never feel such deep, abiding, forever, knowing love the same way again. Yet, wishing for it, missing it terribly, made her thoughts turn to Sam.

Sam was out there, looking for the girls. Dana trusted him so deeply. He had inserted himself into their family just when they all, but Dana especially, needed him most. She wanted him to bring home Lily's daughters; more than anything, she wanted to care for those girls the way her sister would want her to.

Right there, in their own house, the home Lily had loved so much. Dana thought about blame, her mother trying to blame herself for the girls' sailing away. Maybe it was actually Dana's fault, she thought, holding the locket. She shouldn't have gone to New York, left Quinn alone when she was so vulnerable and volatile.

"I'm sorry, Lily." Her voice broke as she spoke to her sister's picture. "I didn't mean to cause them harm. Tell me what to do—please, Lily. Help me know what to do!"

Now, when she looked at the picture of herself and Lily, she noticed the chain around Lily's neck. It held this locket, and just behind it—glinting gold—the tiny key. Dana saw it with a start, and she touched the same key on the cord around her own neck.

Looking right at the picture of Lily, Quinn, and Allie, Dana saw the book.

It was a reddish volume, almost brown in color. Quite small, it was the size of a child's diary. Peering more closely, Dana saw by the strap and lock that it *was* a diary. Rain lashed the windows, and strengthening wind snapped the awnings. What could it matter? They'd found the sunken boat, learned about the accident. The tackle box of money was a source of shame, something concerning the Sun Center, but what did it have to do with their family today?

The locket burned in her hand. She stared at the pictures, and something made her glance at the little globe beside Lily's bed. The mermaid seemed to beckon, and Dana lifted the glass and shook it. The water swirled with tiny red, yellow, and blue fish. The globe had come from Miss Alice's shop, around the same time Dana had bought the locket.

She's magic, girls, the old lady had told them, her fingers gnarled around the precious crystal ball. White hair pulled back in a bun, face as wrinkled as an old witch's, Miss Alice had stared into the mermaid's globe with love and joy, and somehow Dana and Lily had known that any magic that came from her hands was of the best, kindest sort. *Mermaids exist, you know. They live right here in New England. They spin nets out of moonbeams, and they pull stars down from the sky. Whenever you need their help, all you need to do is ask. Say Mermaid, mermaid, tell me true . . .*

"What's a girl supposed to do?" Dana asked out loud now, by-passing her sister Lily for the surest help of all. She shook the globe, and the fish swam madly around. Something made Dana look back at the pictures in Lily's locket, at the diary in her hand.

Dana spun back in time. Where had Lily hidden her diaries?

Under her mattress, behind the books in the bookcase, over the window, in the attic: Dana had found all of those places, and Lily had known. But there was one place Dana had found that she had kept secret. Lily's last spot, the one she'd used before they'd both started art school, that Dana hadn't let on about.

Since finding the gold key—the wrong one, as it had turned out—she had wondered where the adult Lily would hide a diary. But why would Lily try to improve on perfection? Why hadn't Dana thought of it before now?

Because she hadn't asked the mermaid, she thought, tearing down the stairs, out the kitchen door, into the rain, the second key held tightly in her hand.

THE COAST GUARD boat beat north and south across the Sound, with Sam standing on deck with binoculars. He trained them on the Hunting Ground, from the red bell to the green can, into the shipping lane, all the way to Orient Point.

"No sign of them?" Hanley asked.

"No."

The rain hadn't let up, and the wind had slightly increased. Sam leaned against the rail to keep from losing his balance. Thinking of two small girls in a small sailboat filled him with fear, and he kept the glasses fixed to his eyes.

"No pleasure boats out here at all," Tom Hanley said. "For once, people had their eyes on the sky. Most people, that is. Sorry."

"It's okay," Sam said.

Sam could have sworn Quinn would come out here. Where else would she go? A novice sailor, she definitely had Underhill blood. Sam had no doubt her mother and aunt would try sailing in this, feeling the ultimate in wind and sea. He remembered from that summer in Newport, when Dana had let the class sail and race in the midst of small-craft warnings.

The captain slowed down, and Sam's gut lurched—for a minute he thought some debris had been spotted. If they didn't find the boat, they might still find bits of wreckage. They might come upon the girls clinging to the mast.

"What's he doing?" Sam asked, turning to look up at the bridge.

"Going back," Hanley said.

"But they have to be here somewhere!"

"We'd see them if they were. Maybe they've ducked into a cove or beach somewhere. We'll ride along shore, look for them there."

Sam put the glasses back to his eyes. He began to scan the Connecticut shoreline, still looking for signs of the *Mermaid,* for Dana's nieces waving for help. Knowing what she'd been through with Lily, he wasn't going back to her without them.

"THIS IS IT, Allie," Quinn said as they flew along the north shore of Fishers Island.

"This is what?"

"*It.* Our last chance to stop."

"Our last chance before what?"

"The open ocean."

"Is it scary there? Worse than this?" Allie called.

How could Quinn answer that question? She hung on to the tiller with white knuckles, the waves starting to splash over the bow. The boat was moving so fast, the water washed through the hull like mercury, running out the drain holes in back. If she had a speedometer, she'd bet it would show they were going a hundred miles an hour. But she didn't, so all she could do was guess.

"Worse than this!" she yelled. "Bigger waves and more wind."

"Will we tip?"

"I won't let us."

"Are there shipping lanes?"

"Don't think so! The ocean's too big!"

"What if we sail right past the Vineyard? What if we miss it?"

"Then we'll wind up in France, and Aunt Dana can come to

get us!" The boat rose and crashed on a wave, knocking the laugh right out of Quinn's mouth. "But we won't miss it, Al. Just keep us on course. That's your job. Mine's sailing the boat, yours is reading the compass."

"Ninety, Quinn!"

"Ninety, Al," Quinn yelled over the wind as they rounded the island's northeastern point and sailed straight into the Atlantic Ocean.

DANA DIDN'T HAVE a coat or hat on, and she didn't have a shovel. She held the second key in her teeth and knelt in the herb garden, digging with her bare hands. The rain fell in sheets, blowing in off the Sound, flooding the small garden.

Built in a circle, surrounded by a stone wall, the garden was twelve feet in diameter. Lily had planned it herself, laid out every inch back when she and Dana were still in school. Even then her love of flowers and herbs was great; her specialty as an artist had always been to paint landscapes and botanical specimens, and their mother had given her this spot to plant any kind of garden she liked.

Flat blue stones had been placed at intervals to make weeding and planting easier. The herbs were arranged in perfect Lily-order: sage plants to the north for wisdom; thyme to the west for long life; lavender to the south in memory of their father and others who were gone; rosemary and mint to the east for love.

The spicy, mysterious scents rose around Dana, mingling with the richness of soaking-wet earth. She dug around the rosemary, Lily's favorite herb, and around the thyme, Dana's own. Racking her brain, she tried to remember. Years before, she had seen Lily sneak out to the herb garden at night, her diary in hand. It had clicked instantly: She's going to bury it there, to hide it from us.

Dana still didn't want to read her sister's diary. She thought of how it had always been her big-sister challenge to find it, know its location. That was all: Knowledge had been power or, perhaps, love. Actually reading it was different.

She couldn't explain why, but just then she felt it was her last hope, the only chance she might have to save her nieces' lives. Lily, or the mermaid, or both, had sent her out there in the pouring rain to find Lily's diary and find the truth.

But it wasn't there.

The garden was pocked with holes, as if a dog had forgotten where it had buried its bones. Leaning back on her heels, Dana let the rain pour down her face, soaking her mud-stained hands and knees. She wished Sam were there to help her dig, tell her what to do next.

Her eyes traveled around the small garden and suddenly came to rest on the sundial. She hadn't seen it at first. The old brass dial, green with verdigris, nestled beneath the herbs. Verbena and blue moon lobelia grew around it, and tendrils of white honeysuckle had covered it over. Cemented into its base since the house had been built in 1938, the sundial had been placed there by their grandfather.

Touching the brass pointer, rusted greenish-blue, Dana was amazed to feel it wobble. She leaned forward in the mud, rain in her eyes, and pulled the entire sundial out of its cracked cement base. There, hidden in the well beneath, was Lily's diary.

Wrapped in thick plastic, it had sat in its waterproof tomb all this time. Dana pulled it out, held it to her chest with the key in one hand, and let the rain wash her tears away. Lily had knelt here every day, weeding her garden, hiding her diary—first from her mother and sister, then from her husband and children.

Now, rather than having a sense of betrayal, Dana had the definite feeling of collaboration. Lily had led her here for a reason, and Dana believed it was to save her girls.

"I found it, Lily," she said, her right hand tightly holding the key she had just taken from the moonstone box, "and I'll find them too."

Then quickly, but being careful not to slip or drop the precious book in the mud, Dana walked into the house. She bypassed her mother, staring silently out the living room window with Maggie once again lying on her lap. It was as if the dog had done her job and could rest again.

Dana walked straight upstairs, water streaming onto the polished fir floor. Into Lily's bedroom, where she pulled the door closed behind her, she wrapped a towel around herself and sat down on the bed.

Fingers shaking, she held the tiny key. She inserted its tip into the small round lock and turned. Nothing happened. Withdrawing it, she used her towel to clean any rust that might have formed on the lock and tried again. The key fit.

This time the key turned. The lock released, and Dana pulled the strap. She began to read:

Hello, new diary. You're just the latest in a long line, but I love you already. Get ready to hear it all, the good and the bad. I tend to be an emotional kind of girl, and it helps me to pour my heart out on paper. This saves my loved ones from bearing the brunt of my feelings.

I don't like to yell at my husband, and I really don't like to yell at my kids. But no one's perfect—life happens. Mark is my mirror—I look at him and see what I could do better. When he's abrupt with Quinn or impatient with Allie, I get so mad at him. Not that he's that way often. He's a great father. I'm really lucky.

What an interesting start to my new diary! It's all about Mark. Well, it's always easier to look at his behavior than my own. So let me gripe a little, tell you what he's been up to.

His company is doing great. Grayson, Inc., is developing two major new projects, one in Cincinnati, Ohio, one right here in Connecticut. Both are retirement communities: the wave of the future. Of course we both know this: Mom's getting so old, and Mark's parents both died in that gloomy place near Providence. So developing old-age homes is good—Mark's a kind, good-hearted man, and he's very conscientious about the properties he's doing.

The bad news is that Cincinnati's so far away. He travels there a lot—and I mean a lot. The way he oversees the project is unbelievable! He practically has to check every hammer and nail to make sure it's up to code. The contractor calls with one tiny question, and Mark hops a plane to the site.

I think I liked it better when he wasn't so successful. We didn't have as much money, but we had enough. Who cares about new cars, a bigger boat? I like the Mermaid just fine. It's only January, and he's already talking about buying a big sailboat for the summer.

February second—Groundhog Day. I hope the little critter doesn't see his shadow. I don't want six more weeks of winter! Both girls have colds. Allie is a little dream. All I have to do is give her crayons and paper, and she's happy. But Quinn. My God, she's the stuff-up beast of the Western World. She's driving me crazy, wanting to go outside and play. When she can't breathe and has a fever of 101!

She wants to visit her aunt for spring vacation. Excellent idea, my beautiful beast! I could use a dose of Dana. France wouldn't be so bad either. But I'd probably take one look at her life—nonstop painting, that romantic studio she has, that handsome young lover—and want to trade places.

Dana could come home here, take over motherhood and Mark, let me have painting and France. I am mad at Mark today, in case you can't tell. He's in Ohio again. Something went wrong with the yoga room. The flooring wasn't padded enough, or something. He was concerned about the old people's knees.

What about my knees? I asked him on the phone. They haven't been wrapped around your hips nearly enough lately. I'll be home tomorrow, he said—hold that thought. Yeah, well, if he's not careful, I'll fly off to France and trade places with my sister. I'll have my knees wrapped around some young stranger before he can say Abracadabra.

Dana smiled at her sister's words, skimming through the pages. She went through all of February and March, stopped in April.

First shoots up in the garden. Branches pink on the trees.
Allie doing ballet and soccer at school, Quinn confounding
everyone as usual. She loves to hike, climb trees, listen at
keyholes. Schoolwork needs attention. Mark never here
to help with homework—Cincinnati done with, but
something new in Massachusetts. Got to run, pick up
Allie at ballet—

New boat came yesterday. Okay, I was wrong: She's
gorgeous. I love her, and so do the girls. Our first major sail is
going to be to the Vineyard, but right now we're just
going to sail around the Sound. We're naming her Sundance,
in honor of the project that paid for her: the Sun Center in
Cincinnati. It's such a fine place, and Mark is so proud of it.
If only there were another one like it here in Connecticut,
it would be perfect for Mom and Maggie, even fussy Old
Annabelle. The place he developed in Hawthorne didn't
turn out to be half as wonderful. Let's hope the one in
Massachusetts is more like it. For some reason, he doesn't
want to talk about it though! Massachusetts is a big state—is
the place in Boston or Springfield, I asked. Neither, he said.
Well okay . . . twenty questions, anyone? Then he smiled,
said "southeastern Massachusetts." Ah, your home territory,
said I. The Cape and Islands? Close enough, he said. Fine,
my darling. In the category of well-enough-alone, I'll let it
be. He has ancient aunts living in Hyannis, Chatham, and
Edgartown. Perhaps it's getting too close to the bone.
Building old-age facilities in Ohio is one thing; building
them for your aunts might be quite another. I'm just glad
Mark's the one doing this—he really cares.

The boat is great. She's so seaworthy, last night we were
lying on the deck, imagining what it would be like to take
the girls out of school next year, sail across the Atlantic to
France. Surprise, Dana! We're going to live together again,
one way or another!

*Unfortunately, I don't think it's really likely. Mark's
business is absolutely exploding. Since the Sun Center, lots
of communities are interested in his work. He was always
good, but this has brought him a new level of attention.*

*He says we'll have no financial worries after this year.
The girls' education will be nearly paid for, the mortgage
almost paid off. I know this is the accumulation of years of
hard work, of being true to a vision.*

*Mark is so kind. He hires good people, the ones he can
trust. He is true-blue, and he's absolutely scrupulous.
When he found out that plumbing supplier was using
shoddy materials, he made sure the contractor fired him
on the spot.*

*I love our life. We sail, we garden, we take care of our
family, we're good to each other. I get to paint, and I have a
beautiful house to do it in. Plenty of scenery around here.
Mark loves my sister, and she loves him too. If only she lived
closer—then everything would really be perfect.*

*The June Full Moon—mating season for horseshoe crabs
everywhere. Maybe Mark and I should try to make a new
baby tonight. When he gets home from Massachusetts,
maybe I'll take him down to the boat and show him my new
moves. Do I have any? Maybe it's time to find out.*

*Is it possible that just last week I was saying our lives were
perfect? What a lie. Or should I say, what a liar.
Mark's been lying to me. He says he hasn't, but that's a lie
too. He says when he said "southeastern Massachusetts" it
wasn't just a way to squirm out of saying "the Vineyard."
That's right—his new development isn't a retirement
community at all. He claims he never said it was, I just
assumed—based on the fact that that's what he's been
developing the last three years!*

*Mark's new development is a tract of four big, huge,
ugly houses on Martha's Vineyard. My beloved island—the*

place where Dana and I first lived and worked as artists, Mark's and my first home, the place where Quinn was conceived and born. But worst of all: the land is Honeysuckle Hill.

Our sacred ground . . . he proposed to me there. We've camped out so many June sixteenths, the anniversary of his proposal. I can't believe it.

He says he grew up on the island. It's more his than mine, he says. Off-islanders never understand, if he wants to make money off the rich summer people, that's his prerogative. He says I was always too romantic about the place, too unrealistic. His excuse for not telling me!!! I wanted the sandy roads to stay unpaved, the moors to stay wild: well, islanders have to eat, he said. His brother needs the work, and old-timers—the heirs—need to sell their land.

I hate this. I think he's making the mistake of his life.

Dear diary, I think you're my only friend. At least for today . . . I had another fight with Mark. He showed me plans for the development—it's on the west side of Honeysuckle Hill, thank God, not the east, the part where he proposed. But still, the houses are so huge and gross. They look like McMansions: point and click your way to yet another bay window, another fanlight, a widow's walk on the roof. They're the stuff I hate to see on the islands, everywhere on the New England shore. Even here in Black Hall . . . they're springing up everywhere.

Do I sound like a supportive wife of a real estate developer? No, I don't. Have I had my head in the sand, just because most of his work has been out of sight, in areas not dear to my heart? I want to call Dana, but I'm ashamed to tell her what Mark's doing.

Dana held the diary and cringed. How could Lily have been afraid to call her? But on the other hand, what would Dana's reaction have been? She would certainly have taken Lily's side, wished Mark could keep Honeysuckle Hill unspoiled. She read on, one page after another now, without skipping anything.

Today I bundled up my paints and brushes and took the girls out to Gull Island for a painting expedition. En plein air . . . It was wonderful. We borrowed the Campbells' rowboat, and all I could think about was the Mermaid. Why haven't I launched her in so long? I've been so busy with Mark's dreams, I'd forgotten about some of my own. What about painting, sailing the Blue Jay? Dana would have been proud of me.

Quinn's been worried lately. She's heard Mark and me fighting a lot lately. Yesterday she asked me if we were getting divorced. No, I told her. Sounds like it, she said.

So today I was a good mom, true to myself at the same time. Mark and I love each other. We'll get through this. We're both strong-willed people with definite opinions. Mine is that he should leave the Vineyard alone! I think about all the birds that live there, the migratory hawks and ospreys, the owls . . . he says four families will love the houses he's building. I'm jealous of those families.

Oh, God. Help me stay calm, not show the girls how upset I am. Tonight Mark came home, said he had something to show me. He was laughing in that great way he has, appreciating everything and everyone. I was ready to laugh too—we've been so angry at each other.

He showed me an old tackle box. Heavy-duty plastic, dark gray, scarred from lots of old fishhooks. On it, attached to the hasp, was a small brass padlock. I asked him what it was, and he opened it up.

Five thousand dollars was inside. Old bills, mostly fifties and hundreds, looking like someone's life savings. That's pretty much what it was, he said. Jack Conway, the old handyman who lived behind the fish market in Quissit, wanted to work on the development. He wasn't slick

enough to be hired straight out by the contractor, so he
came to Mark and asked for a job.

Mark told him he couldn't take his money, but Jack
insisted. It was a matter of pride, Mark said. Jack has a bad
leg and a bad back, and he used to have a drinking problem.
No one will hire him, but Mark felt sorry for him—so he
said he'd find him a place in the project. Jack refused to take
no for an answer. He gave Mark the tackle box and said he'd
go to his grave with the secret.

So now Mark has an old crippled drunk working for
him. He's not in charge, but what if something goes wrong?
What if he makes a mistake that gets someone hurt? Not
only that, but my husband took a bribe. Mark thinks the
whole thing's hilarious. He says the project will take Jack all
through the year, that it will give him a good income—
$30,000 or so. And once Jack's worked for a while, he'll give
him back the tackle box.

Of course, none of that is the problem. The problem
is that Mark's putting up new houses on the island, the hill
I want to stay the same forever. I want Quinn's Aquinnah—
High Ground—to be the same for her children as it was
for her.

I am furious.

Quinn really tried my patience today, but I did something
I'm not proud of. She pushed and pushed, asking why Mark
and I aren't getting along. She heard me crying and him
yelling, and she said if it kept on, she might as well kill
herself.

Oh, my God.

She actually said that. Maybe I'm making excuses, but I
didn't feel I had any choice. I went straight into her room
while she was at swimming lessons and read her diary. Allie
was home with a sore throat, and she saw me. Not knowing
where Quinn kept her key, I tried my own. Naturally it didn't
work, so I cut the strap.

I deserved what I got. My daughter wrote about crying

*herself to sleep, being so worried about us getting divorced,
not understanding what was going on. I am really reacting
badly to Mark's project—it runs so deep! The Vineyard is
my spiritual home, where I fell in love with Mark and had
Quinny. It's where I last lived with Dana. . . .*

*I have to let this go. Hearing my daughter—she's only
eleven!—say she felt like killing herself worries me crazy.
I'm so mad at Mark for taking Jack's money. I told him the
sight of the tackle box makes me sick—he retorted with
some wise remark about taking the good with the bad. He
stuffed some old Sun Center papers inside and said I might
not like everything, but I had to look at the whole picture.*

*I threw the tackle box in the back of the garage. I hope
he takes it to the dump.*

Dana read the last entry, dated July 30 of last summer, the day
of Lily's death.

*Okay. Truce. The moon is out, shining on the calm, dark
sea. My children are fast asleep in their beds. Moments ago I
was the mad twin, screaming like a banshee at their father,
the love of my life. Call it full-moon fever, call it PMS, I
was really a big fat jerk. Said things I wish I could take back.
I accused Mark of ruining us, killing our family—a really
cruel reference to what Quinn said three days ago, which I'd
already told him about.*

We're going for a sail.

*The girls will be fine. They will, won't they, dear diary?
I've never left them alone in the middle of the night before,
but on the other hand, I've never screamed at my husband
like that either. He wants to make it up to me. I want to
make it up to him. Maybe we'll make love on the waves.
Maybe we won't.*

It doesn't matter. I love him.

*And I love them. It scares me to say this, but I love them
even more than him, more than Dana, more than my own*

*life. I hate that I've hurt Quinn so much, fighting with her
father. I never heard my parents yell that way, and I'm upset
with myself for doing it. She knows I'm ashamed of Mark
for taking that money—she heard me call it a bribe. She
knows the man who paid it was old and crippled . . . ouch.*

*It's a crystal-clear night, and the breeze is blowing a
steady seven. My daughters are world-class sleepers. I can't
remember the last time either of them woke up before
morning. No nightmares, no sleepwalking, nothing but
sweet dreams. They'll snooze the night away, and I'll be
home in an hour. Maybe forty-five minutes.*

*Oh, the moon is so beautiful. As I sit here on the herb
garden wall, I see the moonlight spread all across the sea:
from here to the Vineyard to France. The mermaids have
cast their net; Miss Alice would say they're watching over us.*

*All of us, all of the mermaid girls: Mom and Dana and me
and Quinn and Allie. We are so, so lucky to have each other.*

When Dana finished reading, she had tears running down her
cheeks. She had just spent an hour listening to Lily's voice, and she
missed her more than ever. Moving quickly, she went into her
room and checked under the bed. The tackle box was gone, but
even before that, she'd known where Quinn and Allie had gone.
She picked up the receiver and dialed Sam on his cell phone.

"Hello?" he said.

"It's Dana—"

"Any sign of them?" he asked. "Have they come home yet?"

"No," she said. By his questions she knew he hadn't found
them either, but she hadn't expected that he would; he was searching in the wrong place. "They're sailing to the Vineyard."

"Martha's Vineyard—in this?" Sam asked, his voice loud with
disbelief.

"I'm positive," Dana shouted so he'd be sure to hear above the
wind. She knew her nieces' vision of family had come from Lily,
and she knew what that was. "They have a debt they think they
owe. Their parents'—they're going to pay it back."

Sam called out to the captain, and Dana heard something about radioing ahead to boats closer to the area.

"They're dropping me off—I'll be right there to get you," Sam said, hanging up.

And Dana went to get ready, to grab her rain slicker, and be waiting at the wall when he came to pick her up for the drive to the ferry.

CHAPTER 25

THE COAST GUARD HAD BEEN ALERTED IN NEWPORT, Woods Hole, and Menemsha, and Dana told herself the girls would be safe now, that if Lily and the mermaids had brought them all this far, they'd keep watch just a little bit longer. While Sam used his cell phone to call the Steamship Authority, Dana said good-bye to her mother.

"I'm so worried," Martha said. She hadn't left her post by the front window, sitting in the chair with Maggie at her feet. "The storm isn't letting up at all."

"I know, Mom."

"What can they be thinking? Are you sure they've sailed to the Vineyard?"

"That's where they're heading. I'm almost positive."

"And you and Sam are going to drive to the *ferry*? Is it even running?"

"Yes."

Martha shook her head as if it were the craziest thing she'd ever heard. Probably it was. But Dana felt as if she were operating under orders from her sister, that she didn't have much choice in the matter. Kissing her mother, placing Maggie into her arms for comfort, she ran outside.

Sam had the van started, the windows defrosted. The rain made visibility difficult, but he drove fast and carefully.

"How do you know?" he asked as they sped down I-95.

"That they've gone to the Vineyard?"

"Yes. You know. It's not a guess, is it?"

Dana shook her head. She felt the emotions fill her chest, sting her eyes. Having kept everything inside for the last hour, she wanted to pour the whole thing out. But wouldn't it sound ridiculous, like wishful thinking?

"Lily told me," she said, not able to judge how it might sound.

"Lily?"

Dana nodded. She rubbed her eyes. "She really did, Sam. I know it sounds nuts, but she showed me where to look for the answer, and when I did, she told me where they are."

"I believe you."

"How can you? I'm not sure I even believe myself."

"I know all about unusual communication, Dana."

Her head snapped to look at him. Sitting in the driver's seat, Sam Trevor looked like a reasonable man. Tall and secure, fit and lean, his glasses on his straight, handsome nose, he looked like who he was: a man who taught at an Ivy League college. Yet here he was, agreeing with the impossible.

"Tell me," Sam went on, "what she said."

And Dana did: She told about being led to the locket, to the pictures—the story they told, sending her to look in the herb garden, eventually to Lily's diary. "The whole time," Dana said, looking with wonder out the window at nothing in particular, "I heard her voice. She was speaking so gently, leading me along. . . ."

"She needs you to save her daughters."

"But how, Sam?" Dana asked. "How can she be talking to me?"

"I study dolphins. You know about them, right? That they communicate with each other in very sophisticated ways that we humans haven't quite figured out. They swim together, and with a few clicks or the lash of a tail, they tell each other where the food is, that danger is present, even that they love each other. They speak to each other across long distances even when they are out of sight."

"How do they do that?"

"No one really knows." Sam reached into the glove compartment for a cassette tape, and he placed it into the player. Pushing start, he waited for the music to start.

It was the sound of dolphins. The tape was mostly silence—to the human ear, Sam explained—with a few clicks and trills, some low moans and grunts. "What we can't hear might be a whole love story to the dolphins," Sam said. "They're adapted to listening to each other, to voices too soft for humans to pick up."

"Too soft?"

"Like Lily's," Sam said. And he reached across the seat to hold Dana's hand, because without even looking he knew she had started to cry. "Lily's been talking to you all along, Dana."

"How do you know, Sam?"

"Because I sometimes hear my father. He tells me I'm a good guy, that I'm on the right track. He has an Irish accent, and I hear him most at night, when I'm alone on my boat. Malachy Condon helped me understand."

"Who's he?"

"He's an old Irish guy who lives in Nova Scotia, probably the world's most gifted listener. An oceanographer like me, but a class all to himself. He lost his son Gabriel, and the dolphins taught him how to get him back: to listen to the right things."

"What are the right things?"

"Oh, they're different for every person," Sam said, holding Dana's hand a little tighter. "Gabriel was a poet, so Malachy learned to hear the poetry in everyday life. My dad was an Irish truck driver, so a lot of what I hear is kind of rough and salty. But with Lily . . ."

"It's beautiful," Dana said, hearing her sister's voice. "And it's sharp and it's funny."

"I used to listen for you," Sam said. Glancing across the front

316 · Luanne Rice

seat, he caught Dana's eye for just a second. There in his gaze she saw intense longing, and she had the feeling it went back decades, to the time they first met.

"What did you hear?"

"I heard waves," Sam said. "That might sound strange, but that's what it was. I'd lie in my bed and think of you, and I'd hear breaking waves, rolling over the shallows. . . ."

"You live on a boat."

He shook his head. "On a boat, the waves are different. You're in them, on them. The waves I heard were onshore. They were rolling in after being at sea, after years at sea—one last stretch across the sandbars, cresting white and breaking hard before washing up on the beach."

"Waves . . ." Dana said, closing her eyes, knowing that Sam was right—she had always lived within hearing distance of the waves breaking onshore.

"They brought me to you," Sam said. "After all this time."

Dana said, her eyes flying wide open and gazing across the seat at this man who was taking her to find her nieces, "However it happened, whether it was the waves or Lily or both, I'm so glad they did."

Sam nodded, but he didn't speak. Maybe he didn't have to. The dolphins sang on the tape, but the van was filled with other voices as well: Lily's, Sam's father, Sam and Dana themselves. Listening, Sam kept driving and Dana kept praying. They still had miles to go.

THE STORM WAS BAD. Allie kept them heading east, and Quinn did her best to hold the tiller straight. Her arms were getting tired, and she wished her eyes had windshield wipers. The visibility was terrible. The waves were huge. The life jackets were chapping their skin. Quinn didn't get seasick, but if she did, now would be the time.

"Where are we?" Allie yelled.

"We're almost there!"

"Really?" Allie cried with a sob of relief.

"I think so," Quinn called back.

The truth was, she had no idea. The rain was falling too hard to see anything. The wind hooted around them, and the jib had finally bought the dust. It flew in tatters, like a torn white bedsheet hanging to the forestay. Quinn's heart was in her throat. She sensed her sister's panic. Allie was doing her best to stay brave, but it wasn't working. Even Quinn was terrified.

"Oh, Quinn!" Allie screamed as the boat hit a big wave and nearly went over.

"Hang on, Allie."

"I'm trying."

Quinn's hands hurt from grasping the tiller. Her skin had blistered, and now the blisters were breaking. The wooden handle was slippery with blood and rain; she wanted to let go, to push the water out of her eyes, but she didn't dare. She knew she might not be able to grab on again.

The next wave came out of nowhere. Quinn had been pointing straight, taking most of the waves head-on, but this one smacked them broadside. Allie shrieked as the *Mermaid* shuddered with its force, heeled almost over, and righted herself.

"Kimba!" Allie screamed, lurching to the side.

"Hold on, Al," Quinn demanded, too worried about her sister to care about the stuffed toy.

"He's overboard," Allie cried, holding the gunwale as she hung over the waves. "Oh, no. Quinn, Kimba fell in!"

"Jeez, Al. Get back in the boat," Quinn yelled.

"Save him, please save him, Quinn."

"Jesus Christ."

"Don't swear!"

"Goddammit, crap-shit!"

"It's not his fault!"

Quinn knew they should keep going. Their only chance was to ride out the storm. If she stopped sailing now, they might capsize or start drifting. They were right on course—her father had taught her about dead reckoning, and the only thing she knew was that they'd been pointing ninety ever since leaving Hubbard's Point. But Allie was leaning overboard in her bright life vest, sobbing her heart out.

"Okay," Quinn said, gritting her teeth. "Coming about."

"Thank you, thank you," Allie wept.

"Hard alee . . ."

The boom cracked overhead, the sail filling from the other side. The boat rocked on the big waves. Forward and back, sideways. Quinn scanned the waves for Kimba. She started swearing under her breath, then out loud. The sea was gray and black, and there was no way that dingy, threadbare, laundry-faded feline scrap was ever going to show up.

"Kimba, Kimba!" Allie called as if he could actually hear her.

"We can't keep looking. We'll get off course, we have to—"

"There he is!"

Quinn focused her gaze to where Allie was pointing, and damned if she wasn't right! There, bobbing in the waves as if he belonged there, smiling up with his cute little lion face, was Kimba.

"I'll get him," Quinn said. She maneuvered over the best she could. Coming closer, ten feet, nine, eight . . . Reaching out, letting go of the tiller with one hand, leaning over the waves, she caught the soggy, sorry, soaked scrap of lint from the bounding sea.

"You're the greatest," Allie sobbed, reaching for him. "You're my hero!"

And those were the last words Quinn heard before another wave caught the bow and flipped the boat upside down.

THE YACHT *ENDURANCE*, a forty-foot yawl out of Stonington, Connecticut, was sailing through the storm toward Newport, Rhode Island, when the owner, Crawford Jones, thought he saw a small sailboat go over just south of Point Judith.

"What's that?" he asked his friend, Paul Farragut.

"What's what?"

"Did you just see a sail over there?"

"All I can see is the future," Paul said. "It's warm clothes, a big steak, and a dry martini at the Black Pearl."

"I'm serious. I think I saw a boat capsize."

"Where?"

"Right there," Crawford said, pointing southeast.

"Maybe it was an idiot windsurfer trying to catch the storm swells. Let's see if he gets up again. . . ."

The two men were silent, sitting in the cockpit and trying to see something that probably wasn't even there. The rain drove into their eyes, and the waves rose and fell, making visibility poor.

The *Endurance* had sailed to Bermuda and Halifax, had crossed the Atlantic in weather much worse than this. The men were best friends, expert sailors who had sailed together since childhood; they didn't feel any danger for themselves. They were both hungry, and although they were dedicated blue-water sailors, they were eager to reach Newport.

"It was nothing," Crawford said. "I'm ninety percent sure."

"Ninety percent?"

"Shit."

"Yeah," Paul agreed. "We'd better check."

Turning the wheel, the men brought the *Endurance* about and sailed southeast to investigate.

"HANG ON, ALLIE," Quinn said as another wave broke over them.

The force smashed her head, filled her mouth with salt water, tried to pull her off the overturned boat. Allie was right beside her, clinging on to Kimba and the boat with the same tenacity. As long as they could see and hear each other, they were okay. But when the waves knocked them underwater, Quinn couldn't see and she felt panic.

"Quinn, are you still there?"

"I'm here."

The sisters talked to each other constantly. The boat had flipped at least twenty minutes before. Although the sea was summer warm, the waves were too big to withstand much longer. Quinn was nearly blind with terror.

She held the tackle box under her left arm. The waves tried to rip it from her, but she wouldn't let go. Although she knew money didn't matter, she was on a mission for her parents. This whole disaster had begun with her wanting to repay their debt, and she couldn't bear the thought of failing.

"Drop that box," Allie ordered.

"When you drop Kimba."

That made Allie cry, and instantly Quinn was sorry. She was too sarcastic. It was a bad trait, and she was really seeing all her bad traits just then. Her impatience, her freshness, her meanness. Her little sister was awash in sea waves, and now she was choking on tears too.

"I didn't mean that," Quinn said.

"You saved him for me," Allie gulped. "I know you didn't."

"Then why are you crying?"

"Because I'm scared we're going to die."

Another big wave came, knocking them off the boat. Quinn held on to the box, grabbing for Allie. Dragging her sobbing sister back to the boat, she practically threw her against the side. She knew they had to hang on. That had been rule number one whenever their mother had taken them sailing: *If you ever capsize, girls, stay with the boat no matter what,* she had said.

"Don't let go, Al," she commanded.

"I'm getting tired, Quinn."

The waves hit them, made Quinn see stars, and this time when she went under, her mother's voice just kept going. *Keep holding on, my love. Whatever you do, Quinn, don't let go of the boat.*

Mommy, is that you?

It is, Quinny. Hold on. Let go of that box. Drop it now. Tell Allie to let go of Kimba. She'll be fine, you both will, but you need all your strength.

Was it possible? Quinn shivered with joy. She had just heard her mother's voice, felt her presence in her heart. "Hold tight, Allie. Someone will come along and rescue us. Remember the mermaids? They're coming, Allie."

"There aren't any mermaids," Allie said. Quinn looked at her face. She was pure white, and her lips were blue. The tips of her fingers, clinging to Kimba and the boat, looked almost transparent, like little fins. Her mother's voice continued: *Give her hope, honey. Tell her to drop Kimba, use both hands. You too—both hands right now!*

"There are, Al. They're going to save us. There's one here now, and I think it's Mommy. Hang on."

"Mommy!"

Allie's hand slipped. She fell into the waves, and slapping the surface in an exhausted attempt to swim, pulled herself back. Quinn had a pit in her stomach, and her head was getting light. Were the words real? She had to do something.

Now, Quinn.

The tackle box was weighing her down. It contained five thousand dollars, and all she wanted to do was repay that old man, Jack Conway. This was for her parents, maybe the last thing she would ever do for them. The desire had driven her this far, through the storm, and she hated to give it up. But she knew, looking at her sister's face, hearing her mother's voice, that she had to.

"Oh, Mommy," Allie cried.

"Allie," Quinn said as a wave hit them both. "Listen to me."

"I thought you said Mommy was here. But where, Quinn? Where is she?"

"Holding us up, Al. She's with us now."

"Why can't I see or hear her?"

"I don't know—listen to me. She says you have to drop Kimba."

"I can't, Quinn," she said, hysterical.

"Allie—I'll drop the money first, okay? Then you can let go of him. Mommy says so. . . ."

That's it, my brave girl. Keep going. . . .

"I can't . . ." she cried.

"He won't drown," Quinn said. "He knows you love him. He'll go down to the bottom of the sea, to be with Mommy and Daddy."

Yes, honey. With me. My baby's toy . . .

Allie seemed to hear that. She kissed Kimba, still unable to let go. Quinn looked at the gray plastic box.

You too, Aquinnah. Let go now.

The box had caused her parents so much unhappiness, and she had believed the only way to give them peace would be to return it to its owner. But she heard her mother's voice, and she had to save her sister, so she dropped the tackle box into the deep gray sea.

Wonderful, honey. That's it. Now hang on. Watch your sister. . . .

Seeing Quinn drop the box, with a huge sob Allie kissed Kimba and let him go. She wept, holding on to the side of the boat with both hands. Quinn pressed up beside her. Their legs moved in the same rhythm underwater, trying to stay afloat. Her chest ached. From swallowing so much salt water, her throat stung.

"Oh, Mommy," Allie cried, her head on the boat's blue bottom.

Touching her head to her sister's, Quinn rested there too. She imagined Kimba drifting far into the deep, and for some reason that made her cry almost as much as Allie. She felt so tired. The sea was pulling them down, and she almost couldn't fight anymore. "Mommy," Quinn said. "Mommy."

Suddenly, she wasn't tired anymore. She looked over at Allie, and she seemed to be holding herself up more easily. Quinn's legs felt like sand; she stopped moving them, and now she knew for sure that someone was holding her up. The same was true for Allie. Resting against the boat's bottom, her sister seemed to float easily.

My darlings, the voice came. *I love you so much.*

"Is it . . ." Allie began.

"Mommy?" Quinn asked.

Aquinnah and Alexandra.

"Where are you? We have to see you," Quinn demanded.

"She's here," Allie cried, her face glowing. "I hear her!"

I'm always here. Whether you can see me or not, whether you can hear my voice or not.

"You saved us!"

Your love saved each other. Remember that always, children. The love of sisters is even more powerful than the love of mermaids.

"But what about mothers?" Quinn asked, holding her sister's hand.

Oh, that's the most powerful love of all. It lasts forever. Remember that, Quinn and Allie. Whenever you feel alone, remember: I'm your mother. For ever and ever.

"I tried to make everything right," Quinn said. "To pay the man back. I wanted to do it for you and Daddy."

Thank you, sweetheart. My good, loyal child.

And suddenly, they heard the sound of wind, but it was actually a big sailboat coming at them. Quinn knew she should yell and wave to attract its attention, but she didn't want her mother to leave. Neither did Allie; her sister had her face in the cloudy water, looking into the waves for the source of that voice they both loved so much.

"Don't go," Allie called.

"Mommy!" Quinn yelled.

The big sailboat bore off the wind. Quinn could see that the mainsail was reefed, but now it came down entirely. The motor started. Driving closer, the captain peered over the side.

"Are you both okay?"

"Yes," Quinn said, her teeth chattering.

"It's just the two of you? Was there anyone else aboard?"

"Not *aboard*," Quinn said, answering as honestly as she could. The man wore a white slicker, and as he leaned over, Quinn pushed her sister up into his arms.

She wanted to stay in the water as long as she could. The waves pushed her legs. She felt the force against her ankles, her knees—or was it something else? When she was very little, she had loved to play in the bathtub. Her mother would hold her feet, teaching her how to kick.

I want you to be a strong swimmer, Quinn. We live by the sea, and I know you're going to grow up to be a beach girl just like me and your aunt. When the tides are strong, or you find yourself far from shore, just kick your legs and get yourself back to safety. Kick, kick, kick. That's my girl.

"Kick, kick, kick," Quinn said out loud now, just as she had then.

Sisters, her mother said. *Love your sister, Quinn, the way I love mine.*

"Aunt Dana," Quinn said.

The water surged with more force than ever before.

"I love her too, Mommy. And so does Sam. You don't know him. He's kind of young, but he's wonderful. . . ."

I do know him, sweetheart.

"Sam helped me know that you didn't leave on purpose."

Never, Quinn. Never would I leave you on purpose.

Quinn's voice caught in her throat. She could hardly speak for joy, and for all the love she felt for her mother.

"Okay, now you," the man said. Reaching down his arm, he waited for her to grab hold. She hesitated, looking around.

Just to the west, a wave rose. The water spread thin in a long green curl, as if it were about to break. Transparent, the crest was filled with fish. Quinn saw them all—blue, red, orange, looking like a school from the tropics, like the tiny fish in the mermaid's globe.

On deck, Allie was waiting. She was wrapped in a blanket, and she opened it up to let her sister inside. Quinn huddled against her, and together they stared over the rail into the sea.

The men were on the radio. Quinn heard them calling the Coast Guard, the airwaves crackling with static, to say they had pulled two young girls out of the water, right at the mouth of Narragansett Bay.

"Not the Vineyard?" Allie asked.

"Not quite," the captain said. "That's where you were going?"

"Yes," Quinn said. "We had an errand."

"In this storm?"

"It was important," Allie said sadly.

"Well, we're taking you into Newport," the other man, tall and blond with a Navy haircut, said. "If that's okay with you. Your aunt will be waiting for you there."

Quinn remembered what her mother had said about sisters. She had a lot to tell Aunt Dana. Nodding, saying it was okay, she held Allie's hand. The men turned the boat around, and the two sisters stared off the stern.

"Are you looking for Kimba?" Quinn asked.

Allie shook her head, her eyes shining. "Mommy has him," she said.

Quinn nodded. She didn't have to say anything because she knew Allie's words were true. But she couldn't stop scanning the sea, watching for another clear wave, as if it were the mermaid's globe.

The girls stood together, holding hands, not saying one word about what had just happened.

And neither girl said one thing as they took their last look at their sailboat, the Blue Jay their mother and aunt had bought with the proceeds of their hot dog stand so many years ago. Watching with a lump in her throat, Quinn saw the name done in proud gold letters:

MERMAID

Aquinnah Jane Grayson held her sister's hand, watching as that painting on the boat's transom, done by two other sisters of one mermaid with two gilded tails, was covered by one great wave. The sailboat hovered just beneath the surface. Quinn held her breath, watching. And then it sank into the sea.

EPILOGUE

THE FERRY RIDE WAS BRISK, EXCITING. THE SEA AND sky met in a line of vibrant blue, and the air held the first true chill of autumn. Dana stood on deck with Sam. She kept a close eye on Quinn and Allie, thinking the ride might make them nervous, but it didn't at all. They leaned into the wind, never taking their eyes off the waves.

It was Columbus Day weekend, the first long weekend since school had started. Dana had reenrolled the girls in Black Hall. She couldn't pinpoint any single moment when she knew she wasn't taking them back to France; the change had come gradually, over the summer. If there was any one instant, she might have said it was that moment, driving the girls back to Hubbard's Point after they had nearly drowned in the surf off Newport, that they had pulled up to the house and Sam had said, "We're home."

Sam stood beside her now. He had his arm around her shoulders, as if the jacket she wore weren't enough to keep her warm. She shivered in the October chill, and as if it went straight through him, he held her closer. They had caught the ferry in Woods Hole;

he had shown the girls where he'd gone to grad school, the stone library on Eel Pond, where he'd spent so many hours dreaming of their aunt.

"Are you okay?" he asked.

She smiled, looking up into his green-gold eyes. They were bright today, reflecting the golden sky and the autumn colors on-shore. She had never felt so known by any person but Lily. Sam could tell with a glance what she was feeling. Her mission in life—whatever it was—seemed to suit him just fine, and he always seemed happy to be along for the ride.

"I'm fine, Sam. How about you?"

"I'm great. A long weekend with you—what could be better?"

"We're doing Quinn's mission."

"An excellent reason to come to Martha's Vineyard."

Dana laughed, snuggling into his arms. But deep down, she still wished she could change life, wished there were a different reason for coming.

Now the announcement came, that it was time to return to the cars. Downstairs everyone went, climbing into their vehicles and feeling the sense of anticipation that comes from getting to the is-land.

With the girls sitting in back, Dana reflected how they had all come full circle. This was the island where Quinn was conceived and born. The girls had been rescued just a few miles south of Newport, where Dana and Lily had first met—and rescued—Sam. The summer had ended, but life was just beginning. They had money to repay, ashes to scatter; the girls were finally ready. It was Dana who wasn't sure she wanted to say good-bye.

The *Islander* bumped the dock. As if Sam could read her mind, he reached over to take her hand. He drove the van onto the dock, and the minute the tires hit solid ground, Quinn breathed: "My is-land. I've come back at last."

THE FIRST STOP, even before getting to Gay Head, was an old garage in Quissit. Quinn had the address all written out. Down Main Street, past all the restaurants and inns and ice cream shops, was a narrow lane. The houses there were small and old. Across from the fish market stood Conway's, an old filling station, the pumps no longer working, with an apartment out back.

Aunt Dana had looked up the address. She offered to walk in with Quinn, and so did Allie. But Quinn said no. This was really between her parents and Jack. Quinn was just their emissary.

"Looks like this is the place," Sam said, staring at the white-washed building.

"Yep," Quinn said, holding the new tackle box on her lap.

"You don't have to do it, Quinn," Allie said.

"Yes, I do," Quinn said, taking a deep breath. She looked at Aunt Dana and Sam in the front seat. She tried to smile, but she felt too nervous. "I'll pay you back. I promise."

"Don't worry about that," Aunt Dana said.

"We trust you." Sam grinned.

"We'll have to have a lot of hot dog stands," Allie groaned. And with that, Quinn got out of the car.

She walked up the short sidewalk. Yellow leaves covered the trees. A picket fence surrounded the white building, and pink roses were still in bloom. She thought it funny that a garage would have roses. The garage and fence looked freshly painted, and there was a new truck in the driveway. Quinn's stomach flipped, but she knocked on the apartment door anyway.

An old man answered.

"May I help you?" he asked.

"I'm here to see Jack Conway," she said as businesslike as possible.

"That'd be me. Come in."

Right inside, Quinn saw the walker. She glanced around. The place was bright, with the sun streaming through the square windows. Crocheted doilies covered every surface. Photos of the old man with an old woman hung on the walls. Facing him, Quinn handed him the tackle box.

"I believe this belongs to you," she said.

Looking confused, he opened it. The bills were different. The old ones had sunk to the bottom of the Atlantic Ocean. But Quinn had borrowed five thousand dollars from Aunt Dana, and together they had gone to the bank, to convert the check into cash. On the way they had stopped at Bayside Bait to get a new tackle box, as close as possible to the old one.

"What's this?" he asked.

"It's the money you gave my father," Quinn said. "I'm Aquinnah Grayson."

"Ah," the old man said, and his watery blue eyes turned sad. "Mark. I heard about what happened to him and your mother. I'm sorry."

"You paid him—" Quinn had to hold back from saying "off."

"Yes, I did."

"You didn't have to. My sister and I want you to have this back." She looked around the small, modest room. Obviously, he could use it. Anyone could—five thousand dollars was a lot of money—but maybe Mr. Conway in particular. Quinn saw bottles of medicine on a table across the room; through an open door, she saw someone lying in bed, covered with a blanket. She tried not to stare.

"Your father helped us out," he said.

"Who is it?"

"Emma, my wife."

"How did he do that?"

"He gave me a job. It's not easy, at my age, getting hired for work like that. I'm a carpenter by trade. My father taught me everything he knew, and I've carried on my whole life. We're is-landers, see? This filling station belonged to Emma's family, and I took it over when I married her. We had a ground leak with the pumps about ten years ago, and we couldn't afford the cleanup. Had to close."

"Oh," Quinn said.

"I got work where I could, but it was scarce. Lot of young guys coming over on the boat, taking the best jobs. I've known your dad a long time—he used to pump gas here for a summer job. And he worked with me, banging nails."

"Really?" Quinn asked, looking outside as if she might see her father standing at the pumps, building things.

"Yes. He was always a good boy. When we heard he was

developing those tracts down the way, Emma told me to see him. She's got diabetes now, poor circulation in her legs. We need the money for her care and everything else. She told me to take a chunk of our savings, give it to Mark as a sign of goodwill—to slip my name at the head of the list for carpenters. Damned if it didn't do the trick."

"He never spent it," Quinn said, pushing the box closer. "He never would."

"Well, I didn't want to take the chance. Mark's a good man, but he had business to think of. Would've been easy for him to give the job—building the foundations—to someone half my age. But he gave it to me. Did a damn fine job too. Best new construction on the island."

"My parents would want you to have this back."

"Please keep it. I gave the money to Mark, and it's only right his children should have it."

Quinn shook her head. Her braids were much longer now, and they brushed her face. She wouldn't be deterred, and she had other aspects of her mission to accomplish. "It's a different tackle box," she said. "What happened to the other one is a long story, but the money's all there."

"Well, thank you, young lady. You're just like your father— very generous."

"I hope your wife gets better," Quinn said, glancing at the bed in the other room.

"I'll tell her you said so," Jack Conway said, shaking Quinn's hand as he led her to the door. Walking down the path, smelling the October roses as she passed the white fence, she saw her aunt, sister, and Sam watching her from inside the van, and she gave them two thumbs-up and started to run as Allie opened the door.

THE ISLAND had changed in some ways. Many big, new houses, like the ones Mark had built, dotted the landscape. But mainly, looking across the rolling hills and long salt marshes, Dana thought it was the same as she remembered. They drove up-island, past fenced-in pastures and golden meadows, the old stone walls covered with briars and vines. They passed Alley's Store and the old graveyard, with the Atlantic Ocean shimmering on the left and the inner harbour of Menemsha a bright blue jewel on the right. They passed Honeysuckle Hill, four new rooftops nestled into the tall trees; Dana found herself unable to really look.

When they got to what should have been Gay Head, the sign read aquinnah.

"Oh, my God," Quinn said, seeing it.

"They changed the name because of you?" Allie asked.

"Probably," Sam said. "Makes sense to me."

But, in fact, that was the real name of the town. It had always been the Indian name, and by a narrow margin the town council had voted it in again—they were told by Elizabeth Raymond, the woman from whom they picked up the key to their cottage.

It was the same place Dana and Lily had rented so many years before. While the girls jumped on the bikes they had carried on car racks, Sam and Dana walked around the place. They found the spot in the yard where Dana had staked her tent, her outdoor studio where she had painted her first sea-columns.

They sat on the porch, gazing across the long, amber meadow that led to the bright blue ocean. Dana knew the path that led past the brick lighthouse to the beach, but for now she was content to sit beside Sam and feel the memories of that long-ago time sweep through her with the ocean breeze.

At night the full moon rose out of the sea, turning the island silver. They cooked bluefish on the grill, and both girls were yawning before they had even finished eating. The sea air and the full moon and the new-old island had gotten them, along, perhaps, with the knowledge of what they were going to do the next day. They shared a double bed, the brass box of their parents' ashes on the table beside them, and they were fast asleep by the time Dana walked in to kiss them good night.

"How are they?" Sam asked, sitting on the porch. His face looked ruddy in the light of the gas hurricane lamp, his eyes bright green. Moonlight spread across the field, turning it gold.

"They're asleep."

"Good," Sam said, pulling her close. He was very respectful, not wanting them to see him and Dana sleeping together. But when they weren't looking, he wanted to hold her all the time. She leaned into him now, feeling her heart beat with his through their thick sweaters.

"I can't believe we're in this same house," she said.

"It's the one I drove by," he said. "And saw you painting in the yard. Do you think if I'd stopped then, we would have been together all this time?"

"I don't know," Dana said, kissing him and thinking about the mysteries of time, about how love and secrets seemed so intertwined, like the vines growing on the Vineyard walls. "But I don't want to think so. I don't want to think of all that wasted time. . . ."

"Wasted time?" he asked, holding her on his lap.

Dana couldn't help it. She touched her stomach. She thought of the girls sleeping inside the house, how she had never had a baby of her own. She thought of the time she had spent in solitude, denying the possibility of love while she gave everything to her art, to paintings of the deep blue sea. She thought of Jonathan, of the mistrust and betrayal that had brewed between them. Years alone, then with the wrong man. Gazing across the space, she smiled sadly. Sam was so bright and handsome, so full of love. He would make a wonderful father.

"Thinking of life," she said. Of her nieces', just beginning, of Mark's and Lily's, all over, of herself and Sam, of the babies she had never had.

"Oh," he said, trailing off.

He kissed her face, her lips. She held on, filled with passion. But she knew life was strange. It had given her this wonderful man to love just as her body was getting ready to stop being able to have a family. She was forty-one, almost forty-two. She had spent her whole life painting and adventuring, and it had taken Lily's death to bring her home, make her want to settle down.

"What are you thinking of?" she asked, holding his face in her hands.

"You," he said. "How beautiful you looked playing in the waves . . ."

"That was so long ago," she said. "I was as young as you are now."

"You're more beautiful now," Sam said.

"No, I don't think so."

"You are, Dana. I love you."

"I love you too, Sam," she whispered. The air was spicy with the scent of salt, apples, wood fire, and grapes. They heard the salt hay blowing in the breeze, and they saw the moon shining in the sky overhead. The lighthouse stood there, a dark sentry in the moor, shining its beam across the sea.

"You say you're thinking of life," he said.

"Yes, I am."

"Am I in it?"

"Oh, Sam . . ." She didn't know what to say. Yes, he was in it. But how long would he want to stay? She had lived so much longer than he had. She knew how people changed their minds, how they could be ripped apart in an instant.

"I want to marry you, Dana."

She felt his arms around her body. He kissed her tenderly, and he felt so strong and warm, like someone who would never let her go. His lips kissed her mouth, her neck, and they whispered into her ear,

"I want to be your husband. I want to be their father."

" 'Their'?"

"The girls'. We can adopt them, Dana."

"Quinn and Allie," she said.

"I want us to do it for Mark and Lily," Sam said. "Do the best we can, give the girls everything they would have had."

"I want that too," Dana said, her eyes flooding.

"And a year from now," he said, stroking her head, looking straight into her eyes, "I want us to come back here, to this exact house, with our baby."

"Ours?"

"Yes. If you marry me now, we can do it. It can happen—we'll be teaching our baby to swim at Hubbard's Point next summer. Marry me, Dana. Say yes."

And so she did. "Yes," Dana said to Sam, sitting on the front porch of that little Vineyard cottage with the Atlantic breeze blowing through their hair. They rocked and kissed, holding each other for hours while the stars wheeled through the sky. She thought of love, and she thought of life, she dreamed of the children she and Lily had been, and the ones sleeping inside now, and she dreamed of the ones she and Sam would have.

If it were a painting, it wouldn't be a water column.

It would be a family, playing on a wide, sandy beach at the edge of a calm sea. The sun would be setting, and a full moon, like the one in the sky now, would be rising. Mermaids would have cast their nets, and the sea would be alive with silver fish. The people, all standing together, would be a family. The love on their faces would be as true as life, more real than wishes. It would be the love Dana had in her heart.

That would be her painting, and she knew, holding Sam that moonlit Vineyard night, that it would be her life.

They stayed awake all night. Partly because they didn't want to let go of each other, partly to keep up the delight they felt about what was to come. But mostly, Dana knew, as a way of keeping vigil with Lily. As a way to prepare for saying good-bye.

THE SEA WAS FLAT CALM. The boat was small, a little lobster boat Sam had borrowed from an old retired oceanographer who lived on the island. Quinn and Allie wore their life jackets, standing on deck while Sam drove them from Edgartown Harbour all the way around the island to Gay Head.

The cliffs looked bright red and orange in the sunlight. They rose from the sea, and some of their clay had washed off, turning the near-shore water opaque. Quinn scanned the scene. She looked for the lighthouse, and from there she found their cottage, her superior sense of direction working again.

She thought about it now: how she had cut the window for Aunt Dana, how she had told Allie to keep them heading east to get to this island. Well, the window was working out fine. Mr. Nichols had shored up the old garage, building a skylight in the process. It was going to be Aunt Dana's official studio, a gift from Grandma.

And this trip to the island was working out too. Quinn held the brass can, but Allie didn't move too far away. The time had come to scatter their parents' ashes. The girls were finally ready, and what better place than the sea, just off the island where they had met?

"Tell me where," Sam called from the wheelhouse.

"I will," Quinn called back.

She and Allie glanced back at Sam and Aunt Dana. They were standing very close together, looking like a team. They kept smiling, as if they had a secret, and yawning, as if they hadn't slept all night. Quinn didn't have to read any diaries or eavesdrop at any doors to know they were getting married. She had a special sense for big things, and she could read it in their eyes.

"Where should we do it?" Allie asked.

"I don't know," Quinn said, looking around. "Where do you think?"

"Up there," Allie said, pointing at a patch of clear water where the sunlight looked like diamonds.

Quinn nodded. Just seeing the spot gave her a lump in her throat. She held the box tighter to her chest. Allie slipped her hand under Quinn's arm, touching the metal box. They stood locked together, the two sisters and their parents, just the four of them, alone for the last time.

"This is it," Allie whispered.

"I know."

"Do you have the flowers?"

Allie went to the place behind the wheelhouse where she had laid the bouquet—the last flowers from their mother's garden at Hubbard's Point, some white roses from the garden in Aquinnah.

"Right here," Quinn said just as the boat reached the spot.

Sam cut the throttle. He and Aunt Dana came up front. Very gently, Aunt Dana tried to take the box. Quinn's hands stuck to it; she couldn't seem to let go. But then she saw Allie smiling, and she did.

Aunt Dana was looking at the box. Her blue eyes looked very gentle. She had a soft smile on her face, but tears were pooling in her eyes. She held the box as if it were the most precious thing in the world. Then, very carefully, she pried the lid off the top.

Quinn and Allie dipped their hands in, taking handfuls of their parents' ashes. They threw them overboard, letting the wind scatter them across the waves. They had died in the ocean, and Quinn knew it was the place they had loved best. She pictured her father at the helm of his boat, and she saw her mother standing beside him, smiling with love.

"Mommy, Daddy," Quinn whispered so no one else, not even Allie, could hear.

She heard Allie whispering the same thing. Then Aunt Dana reached in, and when she let the ashes blow from her hand, Quinn remembered what her mother had said about sisters: *Love your sister, Quinn, the way I love mine.* So while Aunt Dana was scattering the ashes of her sister, Lily, Quinn took the hand of her sister, Allie.

"You too, Sam," Quinn said.

"Oh, that's okay," he said. "I don't belong—"

"Yes, you do," Quinn said insistently. "You're part of our family. We wouldn't have this boat if it weren't for you. Go ahead."

"Please," Allie said.

And so Sam took his turn, while Aunt Dana slipped her arm around his waist, hiding her face in his shoulder so no one would see her crying. Then Allie stepped forward with the white flowers, and she threw them in.

Allie's flowers, Quinn's gifts. They were taken every time. Every single time, Quinn thought now.

She had to turn her face away, because she was crying too. This was really good-bye. Her parents were in the sea for good. She watched the sunlight sparkle, taking their ashes and the flowers farther away. She thought of the full moon last night, and wondered whether some of its silver light was left on the waves, whether mermaids were swimming just beneath the surface to take her parents to a better place.

"Good-bye, Mommy," Quinn whispered, tears shining on her cheeks as the sunlight gleamed on the bright blue waves.

Good-bye, my love, good-bye, Aquinnah Jane. . . . I know you are safe, I know you are loved. . . .

Quinn heard the words in the wind, and when she turned to look over her sister's shoulder, she saw a clear wave breaking on the shoal, its transparent curl filled with tiny bright fish and a shining green tail. And Quinn could swear that although the sun was still up, she saw a mermaid's silver net, filled with love and sea fire and an armload of white flowers.